To DEARES … OL

Wishing you … Christmas wi… of … family

LOTS OF LOVE

Anne

Susan Rae Fox began her career as a magazine journalist before becoming a copywriter, Creative Director and finally Managing Director for a Durban-based advertising and promotions agency.

Retiring after thirty years in the industry, she now avidly and happily pursues a long-held dream of writing novels. Susan lives in St Francis Bay in the Eastern Cape, with her husband Ron and their four beloved dogs.

The St. Jude Village Chronicles II:
Going Under

Susan Rae Fox

The St. Jude Village Chronicles II:
GOING UNDER

AUSTIN & MACAULEY

A CIP catalogue record for this title is
available from the British Library.

ISBN 978 1 905609 536

www.austinmacauley.com

First Published (2009)
Austin & Macauley Publishers Ltd.
25 Canada Square
Canary Wharf
London
E14 5LB

Printed & Bound in Great Britain

For my family, most especially Ron and Peta.

My name is Rachael Wood and I am a writer of some small repute, though not widely known, not yet. I hope this book may change that.

This is the second of my chronicles in which I aim to tell, as far as I am able, the truth of what happened in the village of St Jude. Much has already been written and you will, no doubt, have read various newspaper reports and perhaps heard some of the gossip and speculation, people going on about the tragedy, putting forward their own theories, most of them far-fetched and some frankly laughable.

For those who may not have read my first chronicle, here is a brief history.

Our story takes place in the remote and lovely village of St Jude, a mere speck on the eastern coastline and named after an unfamiliar patron saint in whose ears only the desperate whisper their prayers. Alas, they may as well pray to a brick wall.

St Jude is deaf and quite possibly blind too: he hears and sees nothing even though there is the sound of loud and plaintive wailing from the village, from all those poor, lost souls crying out for absolution, kindness, reprieve, happiness, health and various miracles.

The Grants, Alec and Caron, are in crisis, their shaky marriage crumbling with Caron pregnant against her husband's will and nine-year-old James in flight: running from home, running from the sadness, the pain, the lies, the secrets and whispers behind closed doors.

Village matriarch, Edwina Hurley, prepares to die but who will inherit her legacy; who will stand watch over the diminishing coastline; who will hold back cliff-hanging seaside homes that threaten to topple into the sea and, above all, who will take care of beloved and infirm Thomas when she is no longer there?

God has turned as cold and hard as marble, abandoning Mickey, deserting her at a time when she needs Him most with Folly desperately ill, with the house tumbling around her ears, with malevolent, evil-hearted Jordan Black waiting for her in the darkness, intent upon harm.

Gay artist, Chris Lourens seeks the strength to sculpt an angel before AIDS finally ravages his body and steals his mind. His greatest fears are not for himself but for the women in his life: for Ginny, his devoted and adoring mother. How will she survive without him? Inga, who has lost her heart to him and, sensing rejection, flown home to Sweden to the sweetly consoling arms of her father and her friends. What of her? Can she endure the lasting loss?

Sensible, overburdened Grace Frey, the village doctor feels everyone's pain, not least the guilt and anguish suffered by her husband Ian who, in the grip of blackest depression, has become someone else, a total stranger: where oh where is the man she once married, will he ever return?

Strong, confident Sarah Kennedy should not trouble us as she comes to terms with life alone after David and fills the empty void with other things: with the Lourens' gallery, with the dog Lucky, with good friends like Ben Barker, surely she is happy, surely she can find love again in our peaceful, unworldly village?

And so, my pen scratching upon the page, the tale begins again.

What will happen to these people? Miracles are scarce, kindness is hard to come by. Who among them will be saved, and who will go under?

Chapter 1

Mickey and James

I am intrigued by the idea of life changing in seconds. You awake one morning to a day like any other until fate intervenes, something cataclysmic happens, and nothing is the same again. Two planes fly into the World Trade Centre and irrevocably change the entire course of history. A crazed gunman cold-bloodedly shoots students at a university and innocence is forever lost in a hail of bullets. A truck ploughs into a car paralysing a mother and killing her infant children so that all her days thereafter are dark and hopeless.

I suppose what I am trying to say is that you never know what life has in store; there you are, merrily gathering rosebuds and seconds later, you may be dead.

As a writer, I am curious about the ways in which people cope, or do not cope, with the anguish and despair that follows a life-changing experience. One thing I have learned is that only a hairline divides sanity and insanity, which is why it's so easy to slip over to the other side.

Afterwards, when it was over, Mickey would forget so much of what happened by filling her mind with blackness to obliterate the sordid, humiliating, painful details of the rape in the kitchen that night. She remembered exchanging desultory small talk with Black. She had encouraged him to tell her of his business, his clients and future prospects, pretending to listen to his slurred, boastful replies. She had drawn out the conversation in the hope that he might be lulled into thinking her interested and perhaps look more kindly, more sympathetically upon her.

Did he guess she hardly heard a word he said, her concentration fixed on saving herself and Folly from certain danger? She felt she could see into his mind, see the evil that lurked there. There was a knife in the top kitchen drawer, perhaps three giant strides away from where she sat.

A large knife with an ivory bone handle, worn smooth over time, with a sharp, narrow, pointed blade. She visualised the contents of the drawer: the clutter of knives, forks, spoons, a ball of string, the end of a pencil, some coins, a postcard. She pictured herself rising with a fluid movement, placing Folly on the seat of the chair, gliding to the counter, opening the drawer, reaching for the knife, gripping the handle, plunging the point of the blade deeply …

"You're not drinking! That's good whiskey. Christ sakes, lighten up, Chickie. Have a drink!"

She remembered bracing herself. She had sipped the whisky, the rasping, bitter medicinal taste catching in her throat. Setting down the glass, she had stood, laying Folly in his blanket, on the chair. She held her fingers to his heart for a second or two until, reassured by its rhythmic boom-de-boom, she straightened, inching towards the counter, saying, in as normal a voice as she could muster, "Do you mind? It's late and I must make Folly something to eat. He's very ill as you can see and…"

Black was suddenly at her side, standing close, too close, and with a strange expression on his face that she could not read. She remembered placing her hands flat against his muscled chest, striving to push him away and feeling powerful resistance as he pressed closer. She remembered that the part of her brain that remained in control cautioned her not to shout for fear of frightening Folly or angering Black. That part of her brain reasoned that if she were silent and pliant, everything would be over quickly and perhaps he would not hurt her.

He was talking, saying something, she could see his mouth moving, but her ears were filled with a dull buzzing and her skin prickled with heat – was she going to faint? – and so she heard nothing distinct that he said before he jerked her head forward and lunged; grinding his lips upon hers, shoving his tongue into her mouth.

She was conscious of the sensation of being violated by this hard, thrusting muscle, tasting of acrid smoke and alcohol and she gagged, gasping for breath.

He pulled back and, leering, eyes half-closed, said, "Been a long time, eh? You want it, Chickie, don't you? You want it *bad*"

She would not remember the way Black pushed her onto the table, his hands yanking up her shirt, tearing at the buttons, unzipping her denims and fondling her roughly. Nor would she remember the way she repeated, over and over again, "Oh, God, please help me! Please help me, God!" – but so softly that only the sibilance of her whispering could be heard.

Afterwards her whole body would be bruised; her cheek swollen, a bump on her forehead, a cut on the back of her head, her arms and thighs scratched, but she would not remember, in any detail, how he slammed her backwards so that she lay flat on the table, how he wrenched down her jeans, ripped off her pants and forced her legs apart before entering her with a searing, burning pain that changed the colour in her mind from black to molten red. And because she kept her eyes tightly shut, she never knew the details of how his face contorted, how his body heaved and how he panted, his breath coming in hot, fetid bursts as he cried: "C'mon Chickie say; 'give it to me!' Go on, say it. 'Give it to me'!"

And then it was over. She felt the dead weight of him lift as he moved away from her and heard the rough tearing sound as he zipped his jeans. Dragging down her shirt, she rolled off the table, reaching for her clothing to cover herself, still mechanically whispering, "Oh, God, please help me," as waves of fear, shame and pain washed over her.

She supposed he must have said something then, but she didn't remember and nor did she recall him picking up the whiskey bottle before he left. She heard the bolt slide in the door, heard the engine sputter and the skittering of gravel as he drove away.

Perhaps she sat, holding her clothes to her body until she grew chill and pulled them on. She had no memory of dressing herself again.

But she would never forget how still and quiet Folly was, and it was only when she picked up his lifeless body and saw his lolling head, his empty, vacant, sightless eyes that she began to scream.

Late that afternoon, James, still hiding beneath the darkly cool dune shrubs, paged through his favourite book, *Harry Potter and the Chamber of Secrets*, lost in a magical world of wizards, forbidden forests, enchanted castles, swivelling staircases, great halls and dungeons. A world in which anything was possible and those who were good and brave were always victorious. *Lucky, lucky Harry!* James thought about the blue car again. He would have given *anything* – even his prized telescope – to have been able to fly unseen on the next stage of his journey, high above St Jude, in a modified 1962 Ford Anglia. Failing that, a magic broomstick would do. But he had neither, and it was hard going, all this walking, especially if you didn't know exactly where you were going. James closed the book. The sun was beginning to dip in the sky and clouds were turning salmon pink. It was getting late and nobody had found him yet. As far as he could see, nobody was trying to find him, he hadn't seen a search party of any description all day and now the beach was completely deserted except for a few noisy gulls squabbling over a dead fish.

The water in the estuary was blackening, tiny birds swayed on the feathery reeds at the water's edge. He thought he might be feeling scared. His breath was coming more quickly and he had a sick feeling in his stomach, though maybe that was because he was so hungry. Worst of all, his clothes were getting dirty. There was mud on the turnups of his jeans, thickly caking the soles of his Doc Martins and something green and smelly smearing his red t-shirt! There was even sand in his pockets and a faint dusting of it on his face and in his hair. He turned his pockets inside out and batted at his hair but it didn't make him feel any cleaner. He wished he'd thought to bring another pair of jeans and an extra shirt. Tonight he would change into his favourite blue, red and yellow Superman pyjamas but just thinking about them made him feel sad because he missed his bed and his room. He *ached* for them. And it was funny but he half-wished Caron would hurry up and come and find him and take him home where he would be safe. Except he wouldn't be truly safe ever again: Caron and his dad would be angry with him for running away, they would never stop quarrelling and now there was also a baby to worry about.

The only thing to do was to be brave and keep walking until he could find a place where he could cook the sausages taken from the fridge this morning and watch the stars until it was time to go to sleep.

James crouched in the hideaway, holding his breath and listening hard, but he couldn't hear anything, and so he crept out, returned the book safely to his bag and began trudging across the sand towards the edge of the estuary, looking back now and then to make absolutely sure that he wasn't being followed.

Caron couldn't reach Alec on his mobile though she left dozens of hysterical messages, each more desperate than the last.

She wondered if this were a punishment of some kind and if he had decided not to answer her calls or listen to her messages. If this were the case, it was fair to suppose that he didn't yet know that James had run away. This behaviour was typical of Alec who was usually unforgiving after a quarrel and took days and sometimes weeks to thaw.

She had taken a recent photograph of James to the village police station to report him missing. The inspector on duty had made rumblings of sympathy while noting the details but hadn't seemed particularly concerned and said that a 'Missing Persons' file would only be opened once the boy had been missing for twenty-four hours straight. "He'll turn up," he had said, with a cheerful smile. "They usually do. Visiting a friend, most likely."

"But, James doesn't have any friends!" she had cried, terror in her voice.

The inspector had tried to soothe her, saying that he was pretty sure the boy would be home before nightfall, but Caron was inconsolable.

"I keep imagining the most terrible things!" she blurted. "I can't get the images out of my head!" She pictured James being picked up by a paedophile and hurt, even murdered! James venturing too far onto a sandbank at the estuary and drowned at the river mouth or, worse, washed out to sea! James knocked down by a hit and run driver!

"I feel as though I am going mad!" she said, her mind spinning from one horrifying possibility to the next. The inspector had calmly advised her to remain at home.

"Best place for you," he suggested. "Stay put and wait until the boy turns up. He will, you take my word for it."

But how did he know James would turn up? He knew nothing about James! Knew nothing about how stubborn James was, how determined he could be when he got an idea in his head.

"He's only nine," she wept. "He shouldn't be out there, all alone. Can't you do something, please? I'm begging you!"

"Go home," the inspector repeated. "I'll call you later. By then your son will be home, safe and sound."

She left the station feeling utterly helpless. Did the inspector have any idea how hard it was, sitting at home, doing nothing?

She ignored his advice and trawled the village roads even driving out as far as the Evans' dairy farm, although it was unlikely James would have been able to walk that distance. She kept returning, every hour or so, to the beach, convincing herself that she would find him there. She clambered down the rocks and ran up and down the shore, sobbing, pulling at her hair, tugging at her skirt. *Look at me*, she thought, *I am not myself.* She wondered if an excess of progesterone and oestrogen in her newly pregnant blood stream had made her so emotional and unbalanced that she tore at her hair and garments like a crazed, grieving, biblical figure.

At three that afternoon, Caron called Alec's office.

"He hasn't come in today." His secretary sounded vaguely surprised. Caron, feeling foolish, murmured her thanks and, replacing the receiver, knew with sudden clarity, exactly what had happened. All this time, while she had been going off her head, James had been with Alec!

Alec had returned home in the early hours of the morning, after she had fallen into a fitful doze. He'd woken James and taken him away, leaving no note, no message of any kind. Presumably he'd thought she might have guessed at James' whereabouts, but why should that be so? How like Alec to make her suffer this unnecessary agony!

Exhausted and drained, Caron slipped off her shoes and collapsed upon the king-size double bed in their cool bedroom. She lay on Alec's side, her head on his pillow, burying her face into the cotton pillowcase that smelled only faintly of him and powerfully of the floral fabric conditioner that she used to soften the wash, and fell into a deep sleep.

The party at The Two Potters gallery went on until late. Many guests drifted off to attend the Hurley function but there were others who wandered in from Edwina's 'Picnic in the Park' to satisfy their curiosity and follow Ginny, who led the way through the gallery like a seasoned tour guide, pointing out the new displays of desirable wares, describing their charms, taking guests to the book shop and finally to the café where additional hot and cold refreshments were offered on silver trays. Backwards and forward she swept with one group of guests and then another. *I can do this*, she thought, delighted with her performance. *I still have a role to play: I am not useless after all.*

It fell to Chris to take on the mantle of celebrity artist, though, truth be told, he felt ill-at-ease at being presented with so many gushing, rhapsodic compliments on his latest works: the dramatic seascape, the likeness of his mother quilting in the lamplight, and, of course, the angel.

It was the angel that critics and guests found most compelling. Many stood rooted to the spot staring transfixed at the painting for some time before moving on to examine the other canvases on display. Norman Holden, austere art critic from the *Port Victoria Times*, held court in the centre of a knot of visitors, discussing contemporary art and, with a mock bow to Chris, acknowledged the artist as one of the finest in the country.

Amused, Chris observed the way Holden advanced upon the painting of the angel, the hushed audience trailing behind, as he loudly expounded upon the treatment of the feathers in the powerful wings. "Extraordinary," he said, holding forth, "how the artist has captured such minute details; see here, the difference in texture between the sheen on the vaned feathers above and the softness of the downy feathers below."

The group turned to Chris, heads nodding, eyes filled with respect. He tensed uncomfortably; had he even been remotely conscious of the textural differences between vaned and downy feathers? Or had he painted instinctively, as he always did, referencing small details from years of watching birds rise in flight or preen their wings in the sunlight. He almost laughed at the pious expression on the critic's face – what rot the man spoke! What did he know of art? Had he ever painted *anything?*

"Oh, darling!" Ginny had exclaimed, glowing with pride. "This is your night! Holden is so impressed with your work; did you hear? He's returning in a few days, bringing a photographer from *The Times*. He intends a double-page spread on the work of Chris Lourens, that's what he said. I couldn't be happier! You deserve this, you've been *discovered* at last!"

She'd spun away, skirts swirling, bracelets jingling, to welcome Donna Banks, art critic from *The Herald* and drag her into the gallery to stand before the angel.

"This is a Chris Lourens," he heard his mother announce. "Norman Holden is most impressed. He rates Chris as one of the finest artists in the country and is planning a feature in *The Times*! Two full pages, I believe!"

Donna Banks jotted something in her notebook. "So," she invited, "do tell me about this Chris Lourens."

"Oh! I can do better than that!" Ginny beamed. "Come and meet him yourself."

Once the critics and guests had finally departed and the gallery was their own once more, Ginny, Chris and Sarah drank warm champagne, pecked at the remains of congealed cocktail sausages and hardening cubes of cheese, and smiled at one another. Ginny's smile was the brightest.

"We've done it!" she cried fiercely. "We've re-invented The Two Potters. And, in a way, we've re-invented ourselves too! All credit to you, Sarah, this is your vision, you made it happen! And Chris, the critics will write about you, you'll become famous, your work will be in demand. And as for me, well, *look at me*!"

Ginny's eyes shimmered. She dabbed with a paper serviette. "Crying with joy!"

Sarah and Ginny left Chris to lock up. He waited until their excited, chattering voices faded and then switched off the lamps, one by one, until only the flickering lights from a cluster of votive candles remained, throwing elongated shadows against the wall.

"You've been *discovered*!" his mother had said. Discovered? What did that mean?

Surely he should have felt something: a sense of achievement, of pride, some pleasure? He felt nothing, not a flicker of emotion, nothing at all. None of it mattered, not now. Norman Holden, Donna Banks – what did they know? How important was their homage? Holden, in his black velvet dinner jacket with a red rose in the lapel, so eloquent about the texture of feathers, had missed the entire point of the painting. The concept of the angel burning with love, guarding them from unforeseen danger, keeping them safe.

He could barely see the painting in the darkness, but was conscious of the presence of the angel, her eyes upon him. He saw Inga standing there holding the pose, the shining nimbus of fine hair, her lovely face filled with deliberate gravity.

Throughout the evening and into the night, Chris had caught himself glancing at the doorway, watching the arrival of guests, looking for someone. *I'm looking for her*, he thought with a jolt. *For Inga! I keep waiting for her to walk through that door.* But Inga had fled to Sweden, perhaps never to return and he would have to make do with her painted likeness. Chris blew out the candles and locked the front door to the gallery.

"I have a buyer for your painting," Holden had said. "An art collector of some distinction. Name your price!"

"It's not for sale," Chris had replied.

His response had been automatic. The painting was too precious to part with while he still lived. Once he had gone, his mother could decide what to do with the canvas.

Keep it or sell it. Once he had gone, it would make no difference either way.

Through the endless night, Mickey sat unmoving, cradling the stiffening dog in her arms. Shock and cold had rendered her unable to think or move so that the simplest of actions, like moving, required conscious thought. Her lips were cracked and dry and yet the act of moistening them with her tongue too much effort. It was as though all electrical communication between synapses and nerve cells had ceased. As though she'd turned to stone.

By morning, as dawn streaked the sky with crimson, Folly's body was so hard and lifeless Mickey felt she might have been holding a branch. She kissed him, one last time, in the soft place between his ears, and wrapped him tenderly in a clean sheet. After setting his body between the pillows on her bed, she showered away the stench of Jordan Black that still clung to her skin and hair.

As she towelled herself dry, moving as slowly as an invalid, Mickey remembered that rape victims were not supposed to bathe until they had been examined by a doctor, but by then, it was too late. She made a mug of black tea and spooned in extra sugar, for shock, and then, from habit, picked up Folly's saucer. She stared at the pale blue dish with the faded garland of pink roses in the centre for a long while, fighting tears, before setting it down again. She looked around the kitchen: so many reminders; his drinking bowl; the yellow plastic packets of pills; phials and syringes; his brush clotted with fine, golden hairs; his red leather leash hanging from a coat hook on the wall, his blanket draped over the back of the chair; an old chewed ball. She felt her knees give way and held fast to the kitchen counter thinking: *I can't break down now. Now is not the time. I have to think clearly and be strong. Later I can give way to this, but not now.*

Mickey gazed through the kitchen window and thought with wonder: *This is a day, like any other, a normal day! How astonishing that the world had not changed, that birds still sang!*

There were things she would have to do. Important things. When she could think and speak calmly she would visit the police station and lay a charge of rape against Jordan Black. She would also inform the police of the money she had paid as a deposit on the job, and demand that it be repaid immediately. Jordan Black would never, *neve*r set foot on her property again!

But her most immediate priority was Folly. She would carry Folly's body to Dr Barker and ask that he be cremated and his ashes returned to her. Her father had once presented her with a gift of silver locket to mark the occasion of her twenty-first birthday. Never worn, the locket had been kept in a rosewood box. Now she would wear the locket with a sprinkling of Folly's ashes inside the heart. She would never remove the locket and would die with it around her neck. She would place the rest of Folly's ashes in the wooden box, beside her bed.

Dr Barker would be surprised to hear she no longer wished to bury Folly in the garden at Northwind Nursery. They had talked about this. She had told him she had picked out a pretty place near a rusting metal obelisk where a tangle of agapanthus, foxgloves, daisies and miniature roses grew in wild profusion.

But now her feelings had changed. With the hand of God no longer upon the house, it felt unsafe. Could she ever be happy here? Could she live here after what had happened? And if she had to leave the house, could she abandon Folly, buried beneath the rusting obelisk?

Dr Barker would understand that only by cremating Folly could she keep him safe. The world might look the same from the kitchen window, but it was not the same. God had not listened to her prayers. He had not heard her cries for help. God had watched while Jordan Black had raped her, as Folly lay dying. Even now, God remained silent. He had deserted her as her father had done before Him. He could no longer be trusted to behave as a kindly, caring parent.

It's not true, she thought. *God doesn't have His eye on the sparrow. God doesn't see the sparrow fall.*

Alec Grant had driven his new four-door, black sedan well over the speed limit for most of the night; racing from St Jude to Port Victoria and then on to Hunter's Creek and beyond to Twin Harbours. As he drove, he was conscious of being propelled by fury; his jaw clenched tight, his brow knotted, a vein pulsing in his neck, the muscles in his right shoulder pulled so tight that he felt, at some point, they would snap with tension and fly apart.

How had this happened? How had he allowed Caron to trick him like this? How had he been so taken in by her? She'd led him to believe that the relationship had changed; that she was happier, enjoying sex and feeling positive about their marriage, their future together. She'd let him think she was growing fond of James and one day, perhaps, would love him as her own son. She'd been so different lately: easier, more spontaneous, more loving. Less tense, less anxious, less demanding. She'd smiled and laughed more, fed them delicious meals and bought James expensive gifts. And all the while she'd planned to betray him by falling pregnant after he had told her, so many times, that he did not want another baby.

From the very beginning, he'd made this a condition of their marriage; James would be their only child. He'd given Caron every opportunity to reject his proposal but she'd agreed and given her word. And now she was pregnant! And she wanted, what? Wanted him to be happy about the fact? Wanted him to change his mind about a second child?

He'd explained everything before. Told her that he was not a natural father and, even with James, the act of being a parent did not come easily, that he found it all such bloody hard work. He wasn't up to it again, not at his age, all the sacrifices, all the time that had to be invested in a baby, all the worry, the late nights.

"I don't love you!" he had shouted, teeth bared like a snarling animal. "Do you hear me, Caron? I don't love you enough to have a baby with you. It's too much to ask!"

"You don't love me?" she'd repeated, face grey, contorted with crying.

"No! I don't love you! I don't think I ever did. Sex was good. I needed a wife, a mother for James. Once we were married, I knew we were dead wrong for one another. We're chalk and fucking cheese! And now you've purposefully tricked me! What do you expect from me? What do you want me to say?"

Weeping, she'd been unable to answer. He'd clenched his fists watching her flinch as though he were going to hit her when he'd *never* touched her in anger before. He'd known then that he had to get away: away from Caron, away from the fear and fury in the room, away from a problem that could only be resolved in one way.

"You a visitor here?" asked the woman at the Twin Harbours Motel where he had stopped, haggard with weariness, after ten the next morning.

Alec had nodded, unwilling to speak, beyond asking for a room for the day.

"You might be interested in some of the tourist attractions in the area." the woman said, kindly handing him a glossy brochures and two pamphlets.

Mute, Alec handed over his credit card, signed the till-slip, and replaced the card in his wallet.

"No luggage?" asked the woman.

"Can you show me the room, please?" Alec picked up a folded newspaper from the desk and followed the woman down a passage.

"You have a nice day!" she said, cheerily, as he bolted the door.

After showering, he slept like the dead until three-thirty when he checked his mobile and listened to the messages left by Caron.

"James has gone missing! I can't find him! I think he's run away! Please come home now, Alec! Help me find James!"

The messages, one after the other, barely intelligible, were all the same: "Alec, James has run away. I've looked! I can't find him anywhere!"

Alec called Caron's mobile, called the landline at the house, and listened to the interminable ringing. 'Pick up, Caron! Pick up!' But there was no answer.

Alec put his head in his hands. "Damn you, Caron!" he said. "Damn you to hell!"

Chapter 2

Edwina and James

The distinguished Poet Laureate Dawood Hill, was one of the guests attending the glittering relaunch of The Two Potters, and on this occasion Sarah had persuaded him to sign copies of his new book of poems: 'Voices in Stone'.

Hill stood uncomfortably behind a glass-topped table upon which was balanced a tower of slim blue-bound volumes. "Rachael Wood," I said, proffering my hand, "I am a great admirer of your work!" Hill shook limply and then, accepting my newly purchased copy of his book wrote: 'From the poet; Dawood Hill', in scratchy blue biro on the inside of the dust jacket. I don't know what I expected. Something more personal, perhaps? Something clever or witty? A line of verse?

As a published author I am always flattered when someone who has bought one of my books asks me to sign it. But Mr Hill handed back my book and quickly turned away, as if to forestall any further communication. His wife, a sturdy little creature in pleated skirt and twin-set, bustled over to apologise. "He's shy," she explained. "Nobody expects a Poet Laureate to be shy, but he is. He hates crowds, hates fussing, hates people staring. He has no charm. He's not what people expect." I felt sorry for her. "It's refreshing," I lied, "to find someone who doesn't dissemble and pretend to be what he is not. Someone who lets the world see him, just as he is, warts and all." The poet's wife showed well-kept teeth in a grateful smile, "You're too kind," she said. "Imagine," I said, warming to my theory, "if all of the individuals in this room were honest enough to drop their masks and display their true colours. Wouldn't that be something to see?"

At home after the launch, Sarah, found herself too excited to sleep. Lucky was spending the night with Ben and she missed his welcoming bark, his happy, beating tail and the way he padded loyally at her side, wherever she went. This would be the first time they'd been separated and she felt the loss of him keenly.

Although it was late, Sarah brewed a pot of tea and drank it sitting in the window-seat, the curtains open to the night sky.

"Well?" she summoned David, raising the steaming cup. "I think that went off rather well, don't you?"

She listened, closing her eyes to hear more intently. The clicking of the clock on the mantle; curtains brushing against the sill; hawthorns rattling in the garden; the intermittent croak of a solitary frog.

"Am I losing you?" she wondered aloud. When last had she heard him distinctly? When last had she been able to clearly visualise the details of his face, his hands or the way his hair sprang back from his forehead, thick and flecked with grey? On those occasions when she willed herself to remember, she sometimes saw instead her father's carved features, his beaky nose and proud chin or her affable grandfather's myopic, red face, wispy white curls combed carefully over his pinkly mottled head.

She was even less sure of David's voice: the timbre, resonance and emphasis he might have placed upon certain words or phrases though often, in dreams, she heard his infectious laughter and woke yearning for him.

The memories were all as sharp and clear as ever, except for the time when David was dying: she had thrust away all those desperately sad images so that they'd become indistinct, like a photograph under water.

She no longer slept with his green sweater for comfort or delved into the box of cards he had given her to mark birthdays or anniversaries and tearfully read his devoted and loving messages. She had ceased paging through his last diary and stopped pressing her ear to the receiver to listen to the innocent cheer of his recorded voice.

"It's been a year," she said. "A year of keeping you alive, holding onto you, loving you. I love you still, but you're leaving me, David, I can feel it."

Tonight she'd hoped David might rejoice with her over the success of the evening, the rebirth of the gallery. "A milestone!" he'd have said. "I'm so proud of you!" But would he have said that, or was she putting words into his mouth?

The truth was that, alive, David might not have as been as generously supportive of her involvement in the gallery as the dead David seemed to be.

In fact, if she were completely honest, her husband had always been dismissive of those who worked in 'retail'. Once, when they were first married, she'd mentioned the possibility of co-owning a fashion boutique with a friend, and he had laughed derisively. "I can't imagine you as a *shop girl!*" he had said, scathingly. "You're better than that, Sarah. Stick with marketing. That's what you do best!"

She picked up the silver framed image of the two of them together before his illness and studied the likeness. His arms wrapped around her, she looking up at him, both of them laughing. They seemed so happy. The Sarah in the photograph seemed younger: hair cut shorter, face less lined, body fuller. Who *was* that woman?

She had changed so much since David's death. If he were still alive, would he love her now as much as before?

She shivered. She could feel David's shadowy presence in the room, but it was very faint. She could not imagine life without him, but it seemed she had no choice in the matter: David was leaving her, for the second time.

"I'm so high on morphine," Edwina whispered to Thomas, bending to his ear, "that if I weren't holding onto your hand, I would rise into the air like a helium balloon."

Thomas looked up, old man's rheumy eyes swimming and shook his head as if to clear it. "What did you say, darling?"

"I said I'm as high as a kite!" laughed Edwina, "But don't tell a soul; let them think it's the champagne!"

Thomas gave a faltering smile, looking vague and lost. Parties were not his thing. He did not enjoy the throng and press of the crowd the noise of music, laughter and talk made him completely deaf. He'd been lip-reading for most of the evening, without much success, and was trying to get by with a smile, a nod, a lift of one bushy brow. He wished sadly that he had been given a comfortable chair to sit in but Edwina had stressed the need for mobility and so he remained a prisoner in his wheelchair, banged and bumped so often by the jostling crowd, that he was getting a nasty headache.

"I feel marooned," he said. "Set adrift. Rudderless."

Edwina saw his lips moving. "Speak up!" she demanded. "Don't mumble!"

"Would it be rude," he croaked, "to be asked to be pushed to safety and left in peace, somewhere on the fringe of the party?"

Edwina's eyes flashed. "I can't hear a word! What is the matter? Aren't you enjoying yourself? Do make an effort, Thomas. This is a party, quite possibly our last fling. Be sociable. Mingle!"

Thomas lifted two fingers to his head in a mock salute. "That sounds like an order," he said, gamely pushing his wheels forward into a clutch of milling guests who parted to let him through.

Truth be told, Edwina was enjoying herself less than she would have admitted to anyone. The noise in the room seemed exceedingly loud and why on earth had she invited all these people? They washed up against her in waves: their mouths moving, voices braying, eating, drinking, laughing, talking, shouting. Where did they find the energy? The appetite? They shimmied and swooned to the strains of music from the St Jude Chamber Ensemble who, early in the evening, had abandoned Chopin, Beethoven and Bach for more popular melodies from George Gershwin, Irving Berlin and...

She listened carefully: "Oh dear," she mouthed to Grace Frey, who had shoved her way through the throng to kiss Edwina on the cheek. "We seem to have deteriorated to Barry Manilow."

"Can't smile without you!" sang Grace, off-key. "What's wrong with Barry Manilow?"

"Silly and sentimental," declared Edwina. Her eyes seemed unnaturally bright, her colour excessively high.

Grace peered. "How are you feeling?"

Edwina uttered a dramatic sigh and made fluttering movements with her hands. "Grace, dear, can we dispense with the patient-doctor routine, just for once? Or do you fully intend to *ruin* my party?"

Grace laid the back of her hand against Edwina's flushed forehead. "You look a little feverish," she said. "Are you in pain?"

"Where is your husband?" asked Edwina. "Why are you alone? I haven't seen Ian for weeks, possibly months! Why has he gone to ground?"

"He's looking after the children," Grace answered shortly, looking away.

"What's wrong with your housekeeper, that dreadful Hook woman? Can't she take care of Josh and Rosie for one night? Don't know why you put up with her!"

"Annie Hook has worked for us for years!" Grace's voice sounded unnaturally tense. "And why are you changing the subject?"

Edwina bent towards Grace. "I think we're both doing that," she smiled. "Tell me what's wrong."

"Why should there be anything wrong? I don't know what you're talking about?"

"Are you going to shock us all with a divorce?"

"Oh, Edwina! Nothing like that! Do stop poking and prying."

"I have a sixth sense. Your husband is not himself and you are unhappy. Am I wrong?"

Grace put her hands over her ears. "The music! Too loud! I'm off to find a glass of wine. See you later."

Stumbling past the dancers on the floor, Grace fled through the French doors and into the garden. There were fairy lights in the trees, floating candles in the pool, arrangements of white rose trees in pots.

She sank into a wicker chair and wondered why on earth she had come. Out of a sense of politeness, of kindness for her dying patient? And this was how Edwina repaid her!

"Has she upset you?" asked Thomas, from the shadows.

"Yes," said Grace flatly. "The thing about Edwina," she explained, "is that she always knows everything. Or thinks she does. She listens to gossip, sniffs around. She's forgotten that people in polite society don't overstep boundaries: my private life is private!"

"She means well," said Thomas mildly. "She cares about you. Thinks there may be problems at home. She worries about such things."

"She has enough on her own plate without concerning herself with me! I gather she's discussed my private life with you? Who else has she spoken to? Before you know it, the word will be out that Ian and I are getting a divorce and that's simply not true!"

Thomas lifted a finger to his lips. "Here she comes," he warned.

Edwina, leaning heavily upon the arm of one of the black-suited wine waiters, shuffled to a chair beside Grace and sank tiredly into the cushions.

"I seem to have offended you," she ventured. "Forgive me. I don't mean to pry, but, as we both know, I don't have much time left and can't afford to shillyshally. The thing is, Grace, I believe I may be able to help."

Grace snorted. "Highly unlikely!"

Edwina continued. "People who've seen him recently, believe that Ian is depressed. Frankly, I'm not surprised. I hear there's not enough work in St Jude. I imagine time hanging heavily, a possible loss of confidence as the outcome. His wife supporting the family and working all the hours God sends. It stands to reason."

Grace opened and closed her mouth.

"Hear me out! I may have something of a short-term solution to this problem. As you know, we are looking for someone to head Save the Beach project and the Environ Group. I would like to propose that Ian takes my place on both committees."

"But, what does Ian know…?"

Edwina shushed her. "I believe he has the necessary passion and drive and can learn anything else he needs to know. I am willing to play the role of mentor. Your husband is highly respected in the community and I'm convinced the current members will support my nomination. Both positions come with a small remuneration. What do you think?"

Grace leaned over and took Edwina's hand. "I think you are a witch!" she said gratefully. "A good witch, but a witch nonetheless."

"I take it you approve, then? Excellent! I shall contact Ian and set up a meeting. I anticipate reluctance on his part but, as you know, I'm most persuasive and believe I can convince him that this might prove an excellent opportunity!"

"I agree with you, my dear!" commented Thomas. "Never thought of Ian as a possible candidate, but now that you mention it…"

Edwina turned her attention to him. "Why on earth are you hiding out here, alone in the darkness, when I distinctly told you to mingle with our guests?"

As afternoon turned to dusk, a light breeze stirred and the sky darkened.

James was feeling ill. That morning, as he'd bravely stuffed his clothes into his backpack it had been light, the sun was streaming through the windows, and he'd forgotten that he was afraid of the dark. So afraid he had a lamp glowing through the night beside his bed and Caron always left the bathroom light on in case he needed to walk down the passage alone, when everyone else was asleep.

He wasn't sure which was worse: turning back admitting defeat or going on and finding a place where he might hide for the night.

The problem about going home was facing them. Caron and Dad would be furious; he would most likely be punished. There would be earnest discussions about the difference between right and wrong and, afterwards, he'd be given extra-school work and no treats allowed. It wasn't the punishment that bothered him, not really. It was the no-talking part he hated.

After the Spelling Bee, Caron had gone very quiet. She'd pinched her mouth into a tight line and made her eyes seem smaller. He'd been scared and kept out of her way until he could tell, from her voice, that things were okay again. His Dad was different. He said things like: "I'm disappointed in you, James," which made him feel ashamed.

He didn't want to disappoint anyone, especially not his father but it was so hard to do everything right and sometimes he made people cross, without meaning to.

Running away it would be another thing that Caron and Dad would fight about. His Dad would probably say it was Caron's fault and put the blame on the baby.

The baby was a really good reason not to go back home. Why did Caron need a baby? What was it his dad had said? Isn't James enough for you? Well, now everybody knew the answer to that.

Running away was still the best plan. If he stayed away for a very long time everyone would miss him and when he came home at last in a police car with a really loud siren they'd be so happy to see him and Caron would know she didn't really need a baby after all.

The thing to do, James decided, was to be brave. And the best way to be brave was not to think about being afraid of the dark but to think of something else. Something like the sausages he was going to cook. Pork sausages: his favourite. He would eat the whole packet and then go to sleep. He was very tired with all the walking and planning and thinking and he would try to fall asleep very quickly and then it would be morning. By morning he'd have been missing for a whole day and a night. That's probably when the police with their tracker dogs would come looking for him. Maybe there would be television cameras?

He would have to be very careful about choosing the perfect hiding place for the night.

It would have to be safe; out of the reach of poisonous snakes or wild animals. It would also have to be dry and clean. The estuary was a pretty good place and close enough to one or two houses, so it wasn't really too isolated. There was one big house just beyond the dunes, and, as James watched, he saw lights being switched on in one of the downstairs rooms.

He found the perfect hidey-hole quite close to the house. It was high on a flat, hard sand dune and protected by a screen of thick, scraggly bushes and one or two smooth rocks. Pieces of crumbling driftwood were littered about. "Very good, James!" he whispered, congratulating himself. His lair was magical. The sand was soft and dry, the overhanging branches smelled of something like the eucalyptus his mom used to rub on his chest when he had a cold and, if he looked through the twisted branches, he could see the big house in the distance.

To test the hiding place, James lay down upon the sand, using his backpack as a pillow and pretended to be asleep. The sand was still warm, the leaves rustled in a friendly way, the shrubs crowded thickly, keeping out the wind. "Very good, James!"

His stomach growled. The sausages! First, he'd have to collect a hefty pile of driftwood, enough to make a good-size fire. The wood was crisp and dry and he laid it carefully, as his dad had once shown him, making a neat nest of thin branches stuffed with dry grass and brittle twigs.

He cut himself tugging at the grass: a painful tear on his index finger that stung and bled. James watched ruby droplets dripping onto the sand and felt woozy. He wondered if he might bleed to death so that by the time they found him, it would be too late! His dad would have told him to suck his finger to keep it clean, but he hated the sight and taste of blood and so he removed his Superman pyjama top from his backpack and wound it tightly around the torn finger.

His breathing quickened. Everything was getting messy. Blood spattered his t-shirt and dribbled over his socks and shoes. His hands were sticky with blood and now his pyjama top was stained with it. Quite a lot of blood for such a small cut! James sat still for a while, thinking. He could feel his throat closing and tears filling his eyes. *Don't cry! Don't cry.* Too late, he felt the wetness on his cheeks. *Big boys don't cry. That's what Dad always said.* He wiped his face and unwrapped his finger. It had stopped bleeding but for a small crust of dried blood at the tip. Nothing really. Nothing to cry about!

James took his father's heavy gold lighter from his backpack and flicked it once, twice, holding the flame close to the tinder-dry twigs. It took a few tries before the wood caught and a jumping flame appeared. James blew upon the flame and, with a stick, pushed a clump of dry grass towards the lick of flickering fire. The wood burned with a satisfying hiss and crackle. Smiling, James leaned back on his haunches. "Very good, James!" In no time the wood was reduced to flaking, crumbling cinders, more twigs and branches would have to be collected to keep the fire alive. What a lot of hard work to cook a few measly sausages. James added more wood to the fire. When he took the sausages from the wet, slimy package they were warm and limp. He shuddered at the damp, squishy feel of them. The first sausage fell at his feet. James kicked sand over it so that the smell of meat didn't attract man-eating animals that might creep up and devour him while he was asleep. Caron had told him that the only animals found in the estuary were harmless otters, honey badgers and molerats but his father had once seen a bush pig boar hiding behind the rocks, not far from here.

How could you know, for sure, that big male bush pigs ate only grasses, bulbs and tubers? How could you know that they didn't really prefer *flesh?*

He'd heard that there were nocturnal porcupines living here too. Porcupines that could fire off sharp quills at you, like arrows, if you surprised them. James looked nervously over his shoulder but there was nothing to be seen but the big house, shining in the darkness.

James speared the second sausage with a slender stick and held it over the sputtering flames. The stick broke and the sausage flipped into the fire. James watched as it caught alight. Another sausage gone! Two whole sausages wasted! He gave a sorrowful sigh.

The flames grew smaller, the outer branches crumbling to ash. Billowing smoke stung his eyes, filled his mouth with a burning taste and made him cough. The fire was dying again: he would have to collect more driftwood to cook his dinner. He'd used the wood close by; the sand had been picked clean. He would have to slide down the dune to the very bottom to look for more. A flock of birds flew overhead. He jumped at the sound of their flapping and screaming, their shrill calls making the hairs stand up on his arms. Briefly he wondered if he should throw sand over the fire and forget about cooking the pallid sausages, but hunger drove him forward. He sat upon his bottom and using his feet as paddles, manoeuvred himself down the steep dune until he reached the bottom where the sand was strewn with branches and sticks, dried and bleached by the sun so that they looked like the bones of dead men. He began gathering them, making a bundle. Once he had his precious load, he craned his neck to gaze up at his eyrie. It seemed so far away. The dune loomed tall and sheer. A mountain. Everest.

"Wish I were home," he muttered. He said the words very softly so that nobody could hear him.

The last of Edwina's guests departed after one o'clock the following morning; stumbling drunkenly down the wide stone steps to the parking area, tooting hooters and flashing lights as a final farewell to the hostess.

Once they'd all gone, Edwina and Thomas made their way to the sitting room where the chandeliers still blazed. Edwina asked for black Earl Grey and nibbled the last of the salted biscuits.

"Is that all you've had to eat, all night?" enquired Thomas.

"Who thinks about food at a time like this? What a success! What a triumph! The *piece de resistance* of parties!"

"Eh?"

"Of course it's all in the planning and I take some of the credit for that. The catering, the music, that delightful woodlet of topiary rose trees, the happy combination of like-minded guests!"

Thomas took pleasure from her happiness. "A very fine evening, my dear."

"That photographer from the – oh, what's the paper called? *The Times*? *The Independent*? Did you see him? Flash popping all evening. Interviewing guests. We will be featured in all the society pages."

Edwina scanned the emptied room; balls of crumpled serviettes, empty wineglasses, and bowls of nutshells covered the surfaces of tables. The white linen tablecloth bore traces of pink wine stains, purple fig juice and cheese crumbs. Chairs had been moved, drawn closer, a forgotten fur draped the back of the damask sofa and a lost earring glittered in the pile of the Axminster rug.

Thomas felt as though his ears were stuffed with cotton wool; his head throbbed, his eyes stung. The room smelled of stale perfume, of heady hothouse flowers, spilt wine, ripe cheese and cigars. He cleared his throat.

"Bed calls, my darling," he apologised. "I can't keep my eyes open. Do forgive me. Goodnight!" He blew a kiss as his wheelchair moved slowly over the carpet towards the doorway.

"But, Thomas, you can't go yet!" Edwina's voice was as imperious as ever.

He turned his head.

"We haven't done the party post-mortem! Births, deaths, divorces, scandals. Who is sleeping with whom? Who has lost the family inheritance? Who has an unmentionable disease? Come and talk to me!"

Thomas paused, pondering his reply. She had grown more

autocratic since this illness, more demanding, less tolerant of the needs of others. Surely she knew how his body ached, how much he truly loathed these frivolous social assemblages, how he yearned for the sanctuary of his quiet bedroom?

"Please, Thomas!"

Thomas shuffled his orthopaedic footwear on the plate at the bottom of his wheelchair. He sadly dismissed the comforting thought of goose down pillows, clean pyjamas folded and waiting, the corner of the bed cover turned invitingly back.

He swivelled the wheelchair and sailed towards Edwina wearing a merry smile.

"Ah," he cried cheerfully. "Gossip! Have you heard, my dear, that the Hart-Davies are taking separate holidays this year? He is sailing off to Barcelona, while she is following in the footsteps of Shirley Valentine and hot-footing it to Greece."

Edwina chortled. "More Earl Grey, I think," she said. "And, oh, perhaps a slice or two of hot toast, what do you say, Thomas? Ring for one of the maids. Let's catch them before they slink into the night."

Dear God. She could not imagine life without him: this ancient old man, slumped like a bag of laundry in his wheelchair, his wispy hair looking like the fluff on a newborn's head, his milky blue eyes growing more vacant, day by day.

"My constant companion," she said sweetly. "The love of my life."

"What's that?" Tomas blinked, surprised.

Edwina recovered. "I swear Charlotte Wise has had a facelift," she announced with glee. "Her eyebrows touch her hairline, her hair drapes over her ears and she looks like a constantly startled penguin! Those little clues are always a dead giveaway, don't you think?"

Laden with his load of dried brushwood, James clambered clumsily up the dune. He panted as he walked, the sound of his rasping breaths whistling sharply in his ears. At last he reached the top. He stopped, eyes widening with shock and fear.

Somehow the dune grasses and shrubs behind his campfire had caught alight.

He could see the flames creeping higher and higher, ripping through branches, flattening a thicket of tall grasses. He opened and closed his mouth. He tried to shout. HELP! He thought the word, could see it clearly in his mind printed in large capital letters. PLEASE, HELP! But the words remained locked away and silent. He opened his mouth again. Help. A whisper, no more, no one would ever hear him. He stood legs frozen, completely unable to move. Fuelled by the night breeze, flames began to leap from one bush to the next, engulfing the shrubs in a spreading sheet of flame. He heard a startled mewling, birds, roosting for the night, rising in panic from the trees. Their warning cries awakened James. He turned and tumbled down the sand dune, his throat closing, chest burning. It was only as he skidded to the bottom and struggled with leaden feet across the sand that he remembered he'd left his asthma pump in his backpack, at the top of the dune where the fire now burned and smouldered.

He ran, sobbing, each breath a knife-thrust and as he plunged through waving salt grass he whimpered to himself, "Help! Please, help!"

Chapter 3

Ben and Ian

"This day will end.
Another will come.
The hands on the clock will take us past
Sorrow and fear
The dull ache in the heart.
New bells will toll and seasons turn
Constellations will drift
Tides will change
The earth will pivot
Memory will fade,
Pain diminish
Life, as we know it, will resume.
Gather up courage
Let it shine
The human spirit will prevail."

Dawood Hill. Poet Laureate. 2006.

I couldn't articulate it at the time but afterwards, looking back, how foolish I felt, how frivolous and empty-headed to be pondering such vanities as whether to wear a sweeping grey silk gown or black satin culottes to a night of partying while elsewhere in St Jude life-altering dramas were taking place.

How could we know, that as laughter rang out and the music played during a night of champagne and celebration taking place simultaneously at The Two Potters and Hurley House; the estuary had been set alight and the wind was herding the flames towards a cluster of thatched houses high upon the ridge above the darkening sea?

How could we know that, on this night, Mickey had been raped, James had run away from home and Ian was alone in the house with the children when The Oysters caught alight?

Ben, with Lucky at his heels, sprinted across the beach as the sun fell into the sea, the sky grew dark and the dune grasses cast long, waving shadows on the sand. Birds scattered, rising from the bushes, making their way towards sheltered eaves or trees where they would spend the night. As he ran, Ben's mind was on his last conversation with Sarah.

"I'd like to come," he'd said. "I'd like to be there, at the gallery re-launch. You've told me so much about it. I'd like to see it all for myself."

Sarah had given her winsome smile. "And, of course, I'd like you to be there too!" she'd said. "But, Ben, I need you to take care of Lucky. I don't know what time I'll be home, very late, probably. He'll be anxious, shut up in an empty house. Please look after him for me. I'll take you on a guided tour of the gallery next week, I promise."

He'd wondered if she were fobbing him off. If she didn't want to be seen with him and have people jumping to conclusions about their relationship, assuming that, because they were together, they were a couple.

"You don't want me there?" he'd asked, wounded.

"Don't be silly! It's nothing like that! But, Ben – a gallery launch! Not your kind of thing. Artists, sculptors, potters, book collectors; St Jude's eccentric, arty set. You'd be so bored!"

"I see." He'd tried not to show how hurt he'd felt. "Of course I'll take care of Lucky. You're right, they're not my kind of people. More at home amongst farmers. That's what you think, right?"

Distracted, she'd missed the pain in his voice. "Pick up Lucky at six, if you can," she'd replied, relieved. "I'll collect him tomorrow morning. And thanks, Ben! I'm so grateful."

He had been astonished at how lovely she looked when she opened the door that evening: a simple, slim-fitting black shift dress, pearls at her neck, her hair held back with silver combs.

"Sarah! You're beautiful!" he'd said, softly.

She had laughed, excitedly. "I'm nervous," she admitted. "Got butterflies. Fingers crossed that all goes well. There's so much at stake!"

She'd waited until the dog was seated in the old van, face pressed against the window, like a child. She'd waved as the van rumbled away. Agitated, Lucky began to whine.

"Calm down, boy. Quiet now." Ben spoke soothingly to the dog. It was always the same: Lucky was nervous without Sarah. He would quieten soon, but the first half hour was always difficult. Lucky panted, twisting his head until Peace Cottage had disappeared and he could see the house no longer. Still the dog whined.

Ben drove slowly past The Two Potters where he saw a procession of dark-suited musicians arriving and heard distant laughter from within. He sighed and swung off the road, heading for the beach.

Ian had bathed Josh and Rosie and dressed them in their pyjamas with a promise that, if they were good, they could watch the *Shrek* video for the umpteenth time after supper.

They were eating chicken with noodles and singing a nonsense song; something that Rosie had made up with Josh yelling out the chorus: "bum, bum, bum!" – his face screwed up, laughing insanely at his first 'rude' word.

"That's enough, Josh!" Ian raised his voice above the maniac shouting.

"Bum!" screamed Josh, for good measure, and stuffed his fingers up his nostrils.

It was obviously going to be a long night.

Grace had begged him to come to Edwina's party. "Let's dress up and have a night on the town," she'd pleaded. "It will do us good to get out, have a glass of wine, talk to people, dance, enjoy a laugh. It'll be like the old days."

"Sorry, darling," his voice had been genuinely contrite. "I'm not up to it. But you go, Gracie. Go and have some fun."

"It's no fun going to a party on my own, you must know that! And people will talk. They'll wonder where you are, what am I to say?"

"I'll be here, looking after the kids. Tell them that."

But he was surprised, on the night of Edwina's party, to see Grace at the looking glass, wearing a red party dress smelling faintly of mothballs and clipping on dangling earrings. "So, you *are* going then?"

She'd nodded, earrings bobbing as she swiftly applied lip-gloss and studied her reflection in the mirror.

"Life goes on!" she'd said, tiredly. "I can't keep waiting for you to pull yourself together, Ian. Edwina is expecting me and I don't want to disappoint her."

"I see."

She'd lifted her eyes to his mirrored reflection. "And I can't face another night at home with a silent husband!"

He'd heard her heels clipping the wooden floor, heard her kiss the children goodnight and then the door slam shut.

Ian walked through the house switching on lights. The windows were open to the night and a breeze stirred the curtains. Above the house, seagulls spread their wings and cried out to one another.

Dinner over, Ian settled children and dogs before the television and stood in the doorway until he could hear Rosie and Josh happily singing the opening song from *Shrek. Thank God for the grumpy green ogre and Princess Fiona.*

He glanced at his watch – half an hour in the workshop, and then he'd take the kids to bed and read them a story.

He surveyed his workbench. The tools shone brightly: sharpened and ready for use beside a heap of rough sketches on thick, white drawing paper. He picked up one of the pages and shook off a fine layer of dust. Stacked wood: maple, birch, Oregon pine lay in fragrant piles.

"I can't keep waiting for you to pull yourself together, Ian." He heard his wife's dispirited voice.

He was going to lose her if he wasn't careful. He imagined her in the red dress. Imagined the way she tossed her hair back when she laughed. He saw her drinking champagne, talking to friends, making the age-old excuses: "Ian is taking care of the children tonight. It's so difficult to find a reliable baby-sitter." He saw her being whirled out onto the dance floor, leaning into an embrace, looking up and smiling the way she did, the way that melted your heart.

"I can't face another night at home with a silent husband!"

Ian slammed his fist onto his workbench.

"For God's sake Frey!" he shouted. "Get it together, will you!"

Ben was alarmed when Lucky, sniffing the air, began to run ahead of him, galloping across the wide stretch of sand towards the estuary.

"Lucky!" he called. "Lucky! Come here, boy!"

Obediently, the dog looked back, pausing before sprinting ahead. Ben saw smoke in the distance, a plume rising beyond the trees. He ran on. As he grew closer the smoke had become a billowing cloud floating high above the dunes near the estuary. Panting heavily, Ben stopped and surveyed the scene.

It looked as though the dune vegetation had caught alight: he could see a wall of flames, just below the smoke, making for the houses on the hill. He patted his pockets. His mobile! Where was it? Left behind in the van. Shit! What to do? Turn back, run and call for help? Fire brigade? Ambulance? Police? That was, by far, the most sensible decision – but where was Lucky? He whistled for the dog, called his name over and over again, voice tight with tension. Damn dog! For some reason, Lucky had run directly ahead, right into the path of the flames. There was nothing for it but to follow and bring the dog back to safety. If anything should happen to Lucky, Sarah would never forgive him – hell, he'd never forgive himself!

Ian smelled smoke and, looking out of the window, saw a dense cloud rising from the estuary. He dashed from the workshop, bolting into the house, skidding on the wooden floor. The dogs began barking. Ian scooped wide-eyed Rosie and Josh in his arms.

"Come on, kids!" he cried, trying to sound normal. "Let's play a game! Hide and seek! OK?"

He ran through the house picking up toys, a couple of books, a blanket from the sofa. Rosie giggled nervously. Ian whistled for the dogs. Where? Where could he leave them all? Where was it safe?

His pick-up was in the driveway, keys in the ignition. He deposited the two children in the front with the toys and blanket; shouted for the dogs to jump in the back and drove behind the house, away from the trees, screened by a high stone wall. With any luck, the wall would conceal all evidence of the fire.

"Hide and seek!" he said, breathlessly. "Wait here for me, kids. Don't move! Promise? I'll come and find you soon. OK?"

The children stared at him silently, eyes huge.

"This isn't hide and seek," Rosie said. "You can't tell us where to hide, that's not how you play the game." She blinked, mouth trembling. Josh put his thumb in his mouth.

"Please, Rosie!" Ian cried. "I won't be long! I'll come and find you soon."

He switched on the light in the cab and thrust a nursery rhyme book at her. "Read to Josh – there's a good girl!"

"The pigs!" demanded Josh. "Do the story about the pigs!"

Rosie paged through the book.

"Once upon a time, there were three little pigs," she said quietly.

Ian locked the truck and ran towards the front of the house.

James tripped over a rock and fell headlong onto the beach. Sprawled, sand in his eyes and mouth, struggling to breath, he listened to his heart booming.

The sound filled all the spaces in his mind so that he could hear nothing but the boom-de-boom, boom-de-boom.

The only other sound was the thin whistling he made as he breathed in and out. He tried to remember what he was supposed to do when he had an asthma attack. Dr Frey had told him to be as quiet as a mouse and not to be scared. She told him to use his asthma pump until he could breathe normally, but the asthma pump had been burned up in the fire with his Superman pyjamas, the sausages, his favourite Harry Potter book and blue backpack. He could smell smoke and taste it: thick and black in his mouth. He wondered what Caron and his dad would say if they knew that he'd set the bush on fire?

He badly wanted to cry, but he could only make a funny squeaking noise as tears rolled silently down his cheeks.

The dog stopped running and stood alert, ears pricked, listening.

Beneath the roar of fire ripping through shrubs and trees, he picked up high-pitched, strangled sobs of fear. He turned his head this way and that, lifting his nose, sniffing deeply. He gave a short bark before running swiftly, lightly across the sand, black and white coat flying as he sped towards the dunes.

The tide was coming in; waves spilled over the sand, flooding into the estuary.

The water was rising fast, covering the reed beds, submerging the waving eelgrass. Silver shoals of fish swarmed in from the sea. Shells were turned and tossed.

Very soon the flooding plain would cut off all access to the beach.

Ian dialled the St Jude Fire Brigade and waited, swearing under his breath while the phone rang. As it was picked up, he barked into the mouthpiece: "Fire in the estuary; making its way towards The Oysters and the houses beyond. Send the fire truck! Do you hear me? Send the fire truck immediately."

He slammed down the phone and ran upstairs, taking the stairs three at a time.

In the bedroom, he wildly opened cupboards, flinging things aside, searching through their contents until he found a thick pile of winter blankets. He pulled out three and then turned and looked frantically about the room. What to save? The photographs? Where were the albums? Grace's precious jewellery? Family heirlooms? He shook his head. Impossible to think about such things at a time like this. Carrying the blankets, he flew downstairs and grabbed the fire extinguisher that was mounted on the wall in the kitchen.

Outside the kitchen door, Ian turned on the fire hose and soaked the blankets. Dry-mouthed, he watched as the fire, driven by westerly winds advanced upon the house. The speed was breathtaking. Flames shot from tree to tree; engulfing a copse of Port Jackson willows, tearing up the trunks and into the branches where oil-rich leaves exploded like rapid gunfire. With the fire extinguisher in one hand and a heavy, water-soaked blanket in the other, he marched grimly towards the flames.

Ben floundered across the sand. The tide was coming in: he could feel cold water filling his boots, swelling around his ankles, making it impossible to run. Shit! The estuary was flooding. Soon they'd be completely cut off from the beach: driven closer towards the bush fire. The air was thick with smoke and ash. Red sparks floated and danced like dust motes. Trees exploded like firecrackers. "Lucky! Lucky! Here boy!" He pitched his voice above the crackling and spitting of flames.

Where was the blasted dog? Why had he run away? What was he doing? How close was he to the fire?

Ben's instinct was to turn and run for his life. For a moment he wavered. But what would he say to Sarah? How could he face her? And what kind of man would he be to leave a helpless animal alone in a blazing bush fire with no way of escape?

He tramped on, boots heavy as lead, squelching, trousers soaked. "Lucky, Lucky, here boy! Come *here!*"

James floated in and out of consciousness. A metal point, buried deep in his chest, moved with a jagged pain every time he breathed. The sand was wet and getting wetter. His clothes were drenched. Too tired to sit up, he lay flat, lapped by advancing and retreating waves, eyes shut, listening to the fearsome sound of bullets flying past his ears as the night grew black. He dreamed, slipping into Harry Potter's world, stumbling upon the magical Ashwinder: the pale-grey serpent with blood red eyes that slithered from the embers of a magical fire. Had the Ashwinder come to consume or save him? The serpent's fiery eyes, lumps of glowing coal, bore into his. He could feel the snake's hot breath like steam upon his face. The snake's tears dripped upon his cheeks, hotter than boiling soup. He could hear its barking echoing in the air. *Barking?* James looked up into Lucky's shining brown eyes, inches from his own. He felt the dog's wet tongue, warm dog-breath in his face. Lucky stood above him; legs straddled, head turned towards the beach, uttering short, high barks.

The dog fell silent, nose quivering, ears flattening. Before he sank once more into soft blackness, James knew Lucky had come to save him!

Tossing the empty fire extinguisher aside, Ian pounded the flames with a blanket. High on adrenalin and fear he felt possessed of inexhaustible strength and power. His arms pumped up and down as he swung the blanket high above his head and then down upon the flames, beating them into submission. He was hampered every few minutes as the edges of the blanket flickered and caught alight and found himself leaping and jumping, dancing a crazy dance, stamping out the smouldering blanket before resuming his maniacal pounding once again.

Where were the fire team? How long since he'd made the call? Minutes? Hours? How long did it take for them to reach the houses above the estuary? Ian listened for the sound of the approaching siren and heard only the fury of the fire and the terrifying ricocheting volley of rat-tat-tat blasts that rang out every few minutes.

His body felt scorched, blackened and blistered by intense heat. The smoke suffocated, catching in his throat, making his eyes stream. Spluttering and choking, he turned the fire hose upon himself before dousing the blanket once more. The night was incandescent; sparks danced like fireflies. He lifted the blanket high and brought it down with all his might: he felt invincible; strong enough to hold back the unrelenting blaze, strong enough to save the world.

Ben heard barking. The barks were persistent. Short, sharp cries coming from the base of a dune near a circle of rocks. Lucky was just ahead. He struggled on in waterlogged boots until he saw the dog and beckoned frantically, "This way, boy. Come to me!" Lucky remained unmoving, head up, tail wagging. He appeared to be guarding something. What? Edging closer, Ben saw that Lucky stood over the figure of a child lying prostrate on the sand.

He lurched towards them. Ben recognised the boy – James Grant, the little kid who lived next door to Sarah. What was he doing by himself out here at this time of night? "James?" he leaned over the boy. "Are you alone? Is anyone here with you?" The boy opened his eyes, black against the blue-white of his skin. He opened his mouth. He wheezed.

"James! Did you fall? Have you hurt yourself? Are you ill?" Ben ran probing hands over the boy's soaked clothing, feeling his limbs, testing for broken bones. The child was icy-cold and stiff, water streamed from his clothes.

Lifting James in his arms, Ben turned and doggedly began to retrace his steps, Lucky at his side. He shambled along, cursing himself for not removing his boots before picking up the boy: unhampered, he would have be able to move more quickly. James trembled in his arms. Would they make it in time, before the tide rushed up to the rocks, cutting off the pathway, leaving them stranded? Would he have the strength to cover the distance carrying the sodden, shivering boy all the way? James stared up with agonised eyes. "It's Ben Barker, James," he said calmly. "Sarah's friend. Try to breathe slowly and don't be afraid." At his side, Lucky panted. "You're safe, James. Lucky is here too," said Ben. "We'll take care of you."

By the time the St Jude Fire Brigade arrived, siren shrieking, Ian's workshop had caught alight. The barn went up in minutes: the stored furniture and stacks of wood feeding the flames as they shot towards the thatched roof. Glass shattered in the windows with a noise like a whip cracking. Glittering shards flew into the darkness.

"Let it go! Let it go!" Ian shouted to the firemen. "Save the house! The workshop is nothing!"

There were only four men working that night: a skeleton staff on duty since most of the volunteer team were enjoying a night off at The

Two Potters or Hurley House. Two firemen trained their hoses on the roof of The Oysters whilst the others stood shoulder to shoulder with Ian in the path of the blaze and fought it back.

Ian laughed out loud when he saw Tubby Archer, owner of the local brickyard, arriving on a bulldozer. "You're a bloody genius!" he shouted as Tubby swiftly steered the dozer backwards and forwards, demolishing burning shrubs and trees near the house, creating a firebreak. The Wilsons arrived next: Jenny and Bruce, weighed down with sacks and extinguishers followed by the Hamilton family from the house on the ridge and then Anna Mooney pulled up in her Landrover and began pouring mugs of hot, sweet coffee from a thermos. "Keep your strength up!" she cried, face flushed with heat and excitement.

An hour later the worst was over and the fire was finally under control.

"Got off lightly!" said the fire chief afterwards. "You might have lost everything: the whole house, the contents. Your lucky night, I'd say!"

Ian surveyed the damage. The workshop had burned to the ground and the thatch roof, above the bedrooms, had been damaged. The garden was gone and the deck charred. But the children were safe and, aside from the thatch and perhaps a little smoke damage, the house stood almost untouched.

When he reached the truck, Ian found the terrified dogs cowering in the back and Rosie and Josh asleep on the front seat.

Rosie opened her eyes. "Are we still playing Hide and Seek?"

He pressed his lips into his daughter's hair.

"Our lucky night!" he murmured.

The journey, in the dark, was treacherous. The water rose to Ben's thighs forcing him to lift James higher, holding the sick boy above the blackening waves. He staggered, falling against rocks, arms scratched, clothes torn. Lucky swam strongly at his side.

By the time Ben and the dog clambered up the bank towards the waiting truck, all three were exhausted, chilled to the bone and dripping wet.

The hospital was quiet. The nurse on duty took one look at James' blue lips and rushed him to the emergency room.

Ben paced until the doctor on duty came out to talk to him.

"He's had a close call," the young intern said sternly. "Another half an hour or so and you might have lost him! How did this happen?"

Ben held up his hand. "I don't know. He's not my boy," he said. "I'll alert the parents: tell them he's here. Will he be all right?"

The doctor gave a nod. "I'd like to speak to the parents," he said firmly. "Tell them to get in touch immediately."

Arriving at the Grant's house, Ben saw a car in the driveway – with the driver's door wide open. The front door of the house was ajar, he could hear shouting inside. He made a fist and banged loudly.

Alec Grant came to the door, face ashen, jaw tightly clenched. Caron, hovering behind him, had obviously been crying.

"It's OK!" Ben said, reassuringly. "I've found him! He was on the beach, near the estuary."

"Thank God!" Alec grabbed Ben's hand and held it. "Thank God!"

Caron began to sob quietly.

"Where is he?" Alec looked over Ben's shoulder.

"Don't panic," Ben warned. "James had an asthma attack. They've got him on oxygen at the hospital."

Alec spun around and grabbed a bunch of keys from the hallstand.

"I don't know how to thank you," he said, helplessly.

Ben shook his head. "You'd better get to the hospital."

Alec sprinted to the car.

"Alec! Alec! I'd like to come!" Caron ran after her husband. Ben saw the man fling himself into the driver's seat, saw the doors being locked, heard the car starting up.

Hand covering her mouth, Caron watched as Alec drove away.

Ben shuffled his feet uncomfortably. "Do you need a lift? Want me to take you to the hospital?"

Caron turned and faced him. "I'm not wanted there," she said, pitifully.

"I'm sorry." He looked down at his sodden boots, anything to stop staring into those tragic eyes.

"Don't be," she said. "It's all my fault. Thank you for finding James. We've been so worried. He ran away. We had no idea where he was, where to look…"

"Well, he's fine now. Be right as rain in no time. By the way, I'm a friend of Sarah's. Ben Barker, the local vet. There's not a lot I can tell you, but if you need any details about what happened tonight, call me."

"Thank you!" Caron stood unmoving as he walked away.

Lucky, curled on the seat, head on his paws, waited patiently in the cab. Ben glanced back, briefly, before driving through the gates. She was still standing in the darkness, a sad silhouette against the glow from the open doorway.

Grace, returning home late after Edwina's party, was startled to find lights burning throughout the house. Pulling up outside the garage, she saw an empty, black pit where Ian's workshop once stood. She felt a wave of cold fear.

Had he burned down the workshop? Hurt himself? Had it come to this?

Flinging open the car door, Grace was overcome by the acrid smell of fire and smoke. She stumbled towards the house, calling her husband's name: "Ian! Ian! Ian!" Where was he? Was he safe? Were the children safe?

He stood waiting in the open doorway, his arms wide.

She threw herself at him, burying her head in his chest. They clung together. Finally, Grace pulled apart. "Your face is black," she said. "Your clothes are wet. You smell of smoke. What happened? Tell me!"

"A fire broke out in the estuary. A westerly wind drove it right to the edge of the house. The willows caught alight and fuelled the blaze."

"The damage?"

"Workshop's destroyed. Some of the thatch above the bedrooms will have to be replaced. The deck has been burnt. Your garden, Gracie! Your garden's gone!"

"Where are the children? The dogs?"

"All asleep."

He heated hot milk laced with brandy. They sipped it at the kitchen table, holding hands, eyes locked.

"I've just had the most terrible thought!" She shuddered violently. "Suppose you'd come with me to Edwina's party? Suppose we'd left the children alone with Annie Hook?"

He put his huge hand on hers. "Don't think of it," he said. "It didn't happen."

"I begged you to come. I was so angry because you refused. Thank God you were at home to keep them safe!"

She stood up trembling. "I must see the children!"

He took her hand and led her up the stairs to where Rosie and Josh lay sleeping.

Chapter 4

Mickey and Chris

It was all over the village next morning: a fire had broken out in the estuary and Ian Frey, together with the St Jude Fire Brigade had bravely fought and subdued a wall of flames that threatened to destroy the houses high on the ridge above the dunes.

When the damage was surveyed it was found that The Oysters was the only house touched by the fire though much of the vital dune vegetation had been razed to the ground. An emergency meeting of the Environ Group was called and Edwina invited Ian to attend. Concern was raised about the Port Jackson Willows and the Acacia Cyclops – the inflammable alien plants covering the dunes to the west of the beach. "They're a fire hazard!" pronounced Edwina. "They must be removed immediately."

Ian, who assumed he'd been asked to the meeting to give a first-hand account of the incident, was open-mouthed when Edwina suggested he take charge of the bush-clearing project. He was even more astonished when, at the close of the meeting, Edwina nominated him as her worthy successor. "All in agreement, raise hands!" she demanded boldly and all those gathered felt compelled to obey.

"Congratulations!" she said, leaning forward and pecking Ian's surprised cheek. "You've just been elected the new Chairperson of Environ!"

Ian remained behind at the end of the meeting. He was shocked at how much Edwina had changed since he'd seen her last. Her sallow skin, parched and withered, hung loosely from her bony frame: her face looked sunken, her brittle cheekbones protruding.

"What's going on?" he asked.

Edwina gave a deeply penetrating stare.

"I believe we may be able to help one another. I need a successor to take over as Chairperson of Environ and the Save the Beach Project and you need something to occupy your time and energy. Am I correct?"

"You may be. But, I'm not qualified for these positions!"

"Nonsense! Who amongst us *is* qualified? You know as much as anyone about St Jude's unique environment. You're sincere and honest and, as far as I can see, extremely hardworking. You are liked and respected. These are ideal qualifications."

"Well, I'm flattered, of course, but …"

Edwina hooted. "Bollocks!" she said, rudely. "Flattering you is the furthest thing from my mind. I have a job for you! I have held these positions for many years and now, for private reasons, I must relinquish them. I believe you are the man to take my place."

"Why me?"

"You're a good man, Ian. And I believe you share my passion for preserving our uniquely special environment for the next generation. For your Rosie and Josh. St Jude is being threatened by erosion, global-warming and over-development. I've played my part. My work is done. Now it's your turn."

Ian was speechless.

"Say something!" she demanded.

"I know so little. Can you teach me?" he asked, finally.

Edwina smiled with relief. "I hope you're a fast learner. We haven't much time."

Mickey handed the precious bundle to the vet who took it in his huge hands, face crumpling in sympathy. "I'm sorry, Mickey. I know how much you loved Folly. But he was living on borrowed time. I hope he died in his sleep?"

Mickey's eyes did not stray from the dog's shrouded body. "I want him cremated," she whispered, "and his ashes returned to me."

Ben looked closely. She looked dishevelled. Her blouse was worn inside out, the label showing on the outside and her hair needed brushing. Without Folly in her arms, she seemed not to know what to do with her limbs. They hung, uselessly, at her sides.

"How are you feeling?"

Mickey shrugged. "I don't know."

"Have you anyone to talk to? A friend? Family?"

"No."

"It might be a good idea to see a doctor. Get some tranquillisers. Something to help you through the next few days."

Mickey fumbled in her pocket. "Do you need money? For the cremation?"

"We'll sort that out later. Did you hear me, Mickey? Get some help from your doctor."

Mickey turned her watery blue gaze upon him. "Nothing can help me now," she said.

He walked her outside. They stood in the shade of the spreading trees.

"I know this seems like the end of the world," he said gently. "And I also know that nothing will replace Folly. But, when you're feeling stronger, we'll find another dog for you to love and care for. "

She seemed in a daze. She turned and held out her hand, shaking his formally.

Her hand was frozen.

"Mickey?"

"Call me when you have Folly's ashes. I'll collect them right away."

Feeling helpless, he watched her walk away.

The sun shone golden through the leaves and black moths skimmed above fragrant fynbos. The air was filled with the trilling of tree frogs and the drone of bees advancing upon mimosa blossoms. He saw and heard none of it. Christ! What was happening to the world? So much bloody sadness and misery! That poor little kid last night, that performance with the parents and now this!

She'd looked so stricken, and so awry! He wondered if she might be unhinged enough to try and harm herself?

He shook his head and walked back to the surgery. Once the body had been cremated he would take the ashes to Mickey's house and see what kind of state she was in and whether she needed some kind of medical attention.

"I want to report a rape!" Mickey said to the sergeant on duty.

"You want to report a rape?" he repeated tonelessly. "Who's been raped?"

"I have."

The sergeant called for the Detective Inspector.

"She says she's been raped."

Detective Inspector Hector Jansen narrowed his eyes, squinting coldly.

"You want to lay a charge? Want me to open a case docket?"

"Yes!"

"You sure?"

"Of course I'm sure! Why do you suppose I'm here?"

Mickey was taken through to the Detective's office. He sat heavily on the swivel chair behind his desk and motioned that she sit opposite.

Mickey noted that the Detective had a missing button on his jacket and his hair had recently been cut very short. His neck looked red and raw, his ears loomed large. He took a gulp from a cold cup of tea, without offering her anything.

"You need to make a detailed, formal statement in writing about what happened," he explained. He avoided her eyes, examining his hands, clasped, upon the desk. He had very clean, short fingernails. "We'll use this statement to investigate the rape. If we're going to charge someone with this crime, your statement will be required to take the case to court. Do you understand?"

"I think so. You want me to tell you exactly what happened?"

"In writing. And you'll need to sign your statement."

Mickey gave a nod. "I understand."

The Detective picked up a fountain pen and uncapped it slowly.

"Is there a police woman on duty?" Mickey burst out.

Detective Jansen stared coldly.

"No," he said, shortly. "There is not. Are you ready to give your statement?"

It took over an hour for Jansen to take down the details of the rape and an account of her relationship with the rapist Jordan Black.

"I also want to lay a criminal charge against Black," Mickey said.

The Detective frowned.

"He's stolen money from me and I want it back!"

"Are you accusing this man of theft? Do you want me to open another case docket for theft?"

Mickey skin prickled. "Is it too much to ask?"

The policeman shrugged. "It complicates everything," he said, sullenly. "Let me get this straight. You want to lay two charges against Jordan Black: one for rape, the other for theft?"

"That's what I said."

Detective Jansen made a point of deliberately looking at his watch before turning to a clean page in the charge book.

"Right!" he sighed. "Let's get on with it."

Afterwards, once she had read and signed both statements, the Detective picked up the phone. "You will need to be examined by a doctor for forensic evidence."

"I had a shower afterwards. It will have washed away the evidence."

The Inspector regarded her suspiciously. "Do you have the clothes that you were wearing during the rape?"

"Yes."

"Bring them in so that they can be examined."

"My clothes were removed during the rape. I wasn't wearing them. I don't know how much good they'll be."

"They will be required as evidence."

The Detective made a note on the charge sheet. "Do you want the suspect arrested?" he asked.

Mickey faltered. She hadn't thought this far ahead. "Yes, I suppose so. I want him punished. And I want my money back."

Mickey began to tremble. "He knows where I live. He's very violent."

For the first time during the interview, Mickey observed a flicker of something like sympathy.

"The suspect will be arrested. If he is granted bail, he won't be allowed to talk to you or threaten you in any way. If he does, get in touch with us."

Mickey stood to leave. Her legs had turned to water.

"You don't believe me, do you?" she cried. "All the time I've been here, giving you my statement, all the details, you haven't believed a single word I've said, have you?"

The Detective's face remained impassive. He pushed back his chair and rose to his feet. "You should see a doctor," he advised. "Get some medication to prevent HIV/AIDS. And call the Rape Crisis Centre. They'll provide counselling and advice."

Mickey turned on her heel and hurried towards the door.

"Did you hear me, Miss Graham?"

Mickey ran from the police station.

At home, she walked through the empty house. Silence filled the rooms. The roof was open to the sky. Folly's blanket lay over the back of the chair.

She had never felt so utterly alone. From habit, she began to pray:

"Oh, God, please!" and then stopped herself, the words dying on her lips.

"You don't care," she accused. "You probably don't even exist!"

Chris prepared to carve the angel. He had set up a massive log of sweet-smelling cedar in his studio. The trunk stood over two metres tall, propped up against the wall, near the window where the light was good. Chris had contemplated the carving for days. The preliminary work was done. He had photographed the finished clay maquette from every angle, carefully enlarging the black and white prints to draw up a clear footprint that lay upon the worktable. Working from this, he had marked off the exact positions of the head, torso, waist, wings and the angel's legs and feet on the trunk.

Running his hands over the wood, he breathed in the spicy, resinous scent. He had chosen this piece of cedar because, observing it in the lumber yard, he had foreseen the angel in its shape.

The wood was soft yet durable and would prove resistant to decay. Thousands of years ago, before the birth of Christ, King Solomon's temple in Jerusalem had been built from cedar. Cedar would do well enough for Edwina. The statue would stand in the gardens of Hurley House in all weathers, untouched by blistering heat, ferocious storms or buffeting winds. It would remain standing long after he and Mrs Hurley were both dead and buried.

Contemplating it now, the enormous chunk of wood filled him with terror. These last few nights he had woken after midnight, sweating in fear. His arms were weak, his legs shook, racked with pain. Was he up to the task? Would he ever find the strength to carve this sculpture or would Edwina die before she'd set her eyes upon her Guardian Angel?

"What are you doing, darling?" Ginny stood in the doorway.

"I'm going to sculpt the angel. I've put it off long enough. I must begin today."

He lifted the chain saw: a cutting chain, clamped between two steel discs.

"You're not using *that*?"

"This is what I always use. You know how it's done. I must cut away the bulk of the wood and roughly define the angel ..."

Ginny's face looked horrified. "No! Not this! Suppose it slips? Suppose you can't hold it? Don't risk it, darling. Use something else. This will do well enough." She handed him a hatchet.

"That will take far too long. This is faster, more effective." He turned away, the chainsaw in his hands.

"Chris!" He was startled at the shrillness of the cry. "Chris, don't use that thing! You can't! You'll have an accident!"

"I'm fine, Ma. I can handle it."

She held out her hands for the tool. "Give that to me."

He held it firmly. "You're being …"

"I *know,* darling! I know how you feel."

He widened his eyes in surprise.

Ginny rushed on. "Do let's stop playing these silly games! I can see the medication isn't working, how ill you really are. You should be in bed, resting, not trying to carve a great lump of wood with a *chainsaw,* of all things! Oh darling, don't be such a martyr. Who cares about this god-forsaken statue?"

"I do." He spoke firmly. "I care. You're right, Ma. I am sick and yes, the drugs aren't working, but we've been through that before. Grace is hopeful there are other remedies."

"Stop being so brave! You look dreadful…"

"Listen to me, Ma. I made a promise and I can't go back on my word. Besides, I want to do this, even if it's the last thing I do. It matters. It's important."

Their eyes met and held.

Ginny gave way, resigned. "Well, if you must do this, you need help. I've been thinking. I have an idea," she offered.

He his mouth tightened with impatience.

"One of my better ideas, darling, so take that look off your face! I'd like to find someone to do the heavy work: roughing out the shape so that you can concentrate on the detailed carving."

"You're insane! This is *my* sculpture and it must have integrity. I can't get someone else to do the work and then claim it as my own."

"Well share the credit, then! I don't care what you do Chris, but you cannot carve anything of this size without help. I'm still your mother and I'm putting my foot down." Ginny lifted her size five slipper and stamped it hard upon the floor.

A smile played at his mouth. Ginny stamped her foot again.

They both laughed.

"You're impossible!" he said.

"No more than you! We're both as stubborn as mules, it's in the genes, darling!"

She put her hand upon his arm. "You know you can trust me, don't you? You can talk to me and tell me how you're feeling. I won't fall apart. I promise. No more secrets, Chris. We must fight this together, the way as we always have."

Her expression was filled with great tenderness. "Now, give me an hour or so to make a few calls. I won't be long. Rest and conserve your energy. Will you do that for me?"

Without waiting for an answer, Ginny fled.

Chris sank into the chair and considered the cedar trunk. The angel was hidden in the wood. It would take great reserves of strength and energy and any combination of tools: angle-grinders, hatchets, knives, gouges, sanding discs, chisels and mallet to slowly, laboriously bring her to life. He flexed his hands. "Don't let me down now," he begged. "Three weeks. That's all I ask. Three weeks to carve the angel and then I'm done!"

Inga went out walking, alone, without her father, so that she could think clearly.

She wore a fine woollen coat and stout walking shoes, a knitted cap pulled low over her ears. The day was fine but cold. Six degrees. Soon temperatures would plummet further. She had been walking in these fields all her life and yet she might have been a stranger, a passing traveller, for all they meant to her.

"I want to go home, Papa," she had said, last evening. They had eaten their evening meal and had been sitting together at the table, drinking aquavit, talking about the old days and reminiscing. They had spoken of her childhood: the holiday villa with turrets and verandas; the grass sprouting white daisies; wild Chervil, croquet outdoors; Baltic herring; smoked reindeer for dinner; cherry pancakes for dessert; the cry of curlews filling the air.

"Do you remember?" Her father's eyes were dancing. "Your mother was terrified of the Peacock butterflies? Those huge coloured wings with strange markings. She ran from them, screaming!"

"Did you hear me, Papa? I want to go home."

"But you are home," he had said, brows gathering, face darkening. "This is your home, Inga. *This* is where you belong."

"No," she had replied softly. "Betty's Bay is my home now. I miss it. The Yoga Centre. My studio loft. My friends. I miss everything!"

"You are thinking of him again?" The question had been a bitter accusation.

She had decided to be honest. "All the time. Every moment. Every hour. Every day. I cannot stop thinking of him."

"Yet you know nothing can come of this relationship?"

"Yes."

"So, we agree on something?"

"Nothing will come of it – but I love him anyway."

"You will break my heart. Do you hear me, Inga? You will break your father's heart! Don't you care? Don't you care at all?"

Hands stuffed in her coat pockets, Inga walked along the shoreline of the archipelago. She stumbled over tussocks in the grass and bent to pick tansy, St John's Wort and sprigs of wild heather. She lifted the aromatic bouquet to her nose, her eyes on the sky. She saw his face in the clouds, his body in the alder and ash trees. Wherever she looked, she saw only him. "Chris Lourens!" She shouted his name but the cry was lost amidst the honking of wild geese.

There was nothing for it. She would have to break her father's heart or have her own cleft in two. Tomorrow she would book her flight home.

"Wait for me!" she whispered with a thrill of joy. "Wait for me!"

Friends were invited to a farewell meal.

"The Last Supper," her father said, making a joke of it, though his face was tortured.

After dinner, he presented her with a velvet gift box containing a necklace of fiery opals that had belonged to her mother.

Inga stared at the crescent of iridescent flaming stones. "But opals are unlucky!" The words were out before she could stop herself.

Her father looked stung. "They are not! That's a myth. Opals are well known to posses the powers of healing."

"Thank you, Papa." Inga took the gift and hung it about her neck. "It is very beautiful!"

Before bed Inga removed the necklace and replaced it in the velvet box. She searched her room for a hiding place and found one behind a pile of leather bound volumes in the bookcase. She sighed with relief. Opals were precursors of misfortune and bad luck. They might do her harm. She dared not tempt fate in any way, not now when she needed fortune to be kind.

Her father wept when he kissed her goodbye.

"This is a mistake, Inga! No good can come of it!"

"I can't explain. I need to be with him. He needs me."

"I need you!"

She wiped the tears from his cheeks and said nothing. What was there to say?

Grace stared in shock at Mickey. Skin so pale it was almost translucent, windswept dark blonde hair falling over her forehead, partially covering her face. She sat opposite, twisting her hands in her lap.

"I've been raped," Mickey said. "I need you to examine me. But I must tell you that I showered after the rape. I don't know what you'll find."

"Oh God, Mickey! Who? Who raped you?"

"You don't know him. I don't want to say."

"You've reported the rape to the police?"

"Yes. That's why I'm here. They need you to examine me for forensic evidence."

"Lord, I've never done this before! There's a protocol that needs to be followed. I should make an appointment for you to see the District Surgeon..."

"No! I couldn't bear that, Grace. I'd like you to do it. Please?"

"Sorry, of course I'll examine you! That was thoughtless of me. Did the rapist hurt you?"

"Bruises and scratches. A bump on the back of my head. Nothing serious."

Grace led Mickey to the cubicle and pointed to the gown hanging there. "Take off all your clothes and put this on," she said gently. "And while you're doing that, I'll call the police station and find out exactly what they need from me. Do you remember the name of the Detective you spoke to?"

"Detective Inspector Hector Jansen. He didn't believe me."

"Did he say so?"

"I could tell from his manner. His eyes. He was cold."

Grace drew the curtain and left Mickey alone to remove her clothing and slip on the gown.

The Inspector was helpful and courteous. "I'll fax through the sexual assault protocol," he said briskly. "It lays down guidelines for the medical examination and treatment. Look for bruises, marks, cuts. Take samples from places on the body that may have been in contact with semen. She had a shower; you may not find anything. She'll need medication to prevent HIV/AIDS or sexually transmitted diseases."

"Have you arrested the rapist?"

"No. I'm waiting for your report. Everything in good time."

"I'll send the report immediately, there won't be a delay on my side."

"Good. Oh, and see that she talks to someone. She needs counselling."

Although Grace was especially gentle, Mickey kept her eyes shut, tense and stiff during the examination. She answered Grace's questions tersely and offered little detail.

"You can relax now, Mickey. The worst is over. Get dressed while I write out my report. Take your time, I'll make a cup of sweet tea."

Mickey looked like a ghost slumped in the chair, eyes blank.

Grace gave her a handful of pills and a tumbler of water, watching as Mickey swallowed the tablets.

"You're in shock, Mickey. It's only natural: you've had the most terrifying ordeal. You must talk to someone about this. I have the name of a very good psychologist. I believe she can help you."

"I don't want to talk about it. I can't. I've said all I need to say. I want him punished, that's all."

"Well, you can leave that to the police. I don't think Detective Jansen didn't believe you. He seemed sympathetic. He was most concerned that you get some help."

Mickey looked away towards the window. "That's not how it is. Nothing is the way you think it is. Everything is a sham. Even God."

"Will you come and see me again?" The doctor's expression was troubled.

"Sorry, I don't want to. Thank you, but, honestly, there's nothing more you can do for me."

Grace watched Mickey walk towards the door. "I'd like to see you again. Please, Mickey. Make an appointment with my nurse."

Mickey turned the doorknob and was gone.

Ginny rode her bicycle to The Oysters and found Ian Frey wielding a hammer, smashing down a wall of burnt and blackened bricks. His face was streaked, his hair wild. "This used to be my workshop," he explained, wiping his hands clean.

"I heard about the fire. You're quite the hero! Everyone's talking about you!"

"I had help: the St Jude Fire Team, our neighbours; everyone played their part."

He looked expectantly at Ginny. "Fancy a coffee?"

They sat at the kitchen table. He offered shortbread and waited.

"You're probably wondering why I'm here? The thing is, I need your help. You know my son, Chris?"

"I don't know him well."

Ginny watched Frey's expression change: of course he knew Chris! Grace would have confided in her husband, told him she was treating Chris for AIDS. There was a good chance that a man like Ian might be homophobic: might hate homosexuals. Perhaps she'd made a mistake?

"I'm going to be honest with you!" Ginny's expression was earnest. "My son is very ill. Grace is his doctor, you probably know the details? Chris is resistant to all medication. It works for a while and then the disease mutates. Grace has tried every combination of drugs but we're running out of options. I believe we're nearing the end."

Ian frowned. He wondered why she avoided the name of the disease, was she afraid of uttering it aloud? "I don't understand why you're telling me this? What does it have to do with me?"

"Chris has taken on a commission. He's sculpting a two metre high angel from cedar for Edwina Hurley. I've told Chris that, given the state he's in, the job is clearly beyond him but he insists upon doing it. He says Edwina's set her heart on the statue."

Ian gulped his coffee and wondered where the conversation was going.

"Chris needs to rough out the basic shape in the trunk and, to do this, he'll have to use a chain saw clamped between steel discs. But he hasn't the strength: he could hurt himself. That's where you come in!" Ginny beamed triumphantly.

Ian stared, surprised.

"We need you to help with the initial stages of the carving. Use the chain saw to cut away excess wood. You're a skilled carpenter. You know about wood. You're strong and healthy."

"I'm no sculptor. I've never done anything remotely like this. Does Chris know you're talking to me?"

"Not exactly. It's my idea. He's too proud to accept help and worried about the integrity of the sculpture. But you could work on the carving with him and share the credit for the piece. He can't do it alone. Will you help?"

Ginny paused, breathless and hopeful. Ian chewed a thumbnail.

My life is changing, he thought. *None of this is my doing! I'm being swept along powerless to resist the orchestrations of some outside force, divine intervention or whatever it is that salvages the wreckage and sets a drowning man upon his feet again.* It had all begun with the bush fire. With the fearsome sight of advancing flames threatening his home, his family, their future. He'd been conscious of a moment of frozen indecision: the 'fight or flight' response of animals to acute stress. He'd stared at the oncoming wall of fire, heart drumming and, just like that, the old Ian had been returned to him with a surge of courage, confidence and the strength to easily vanquish the fire and turn what might have been a disaster into a personal victory. That had been followed by Edwina's haughty summoning of him to the post-fire crisis meeting of Environ where, through heavy-handed manipulation, she had bestowed upon him the dubious honour of the role of Chairperson of not one but two committees dedicated to the preservation of St Jude's environment. And now Ginny had delivered another unexpected bolt from the blue! The gods were playing games: unforeseeable and random, but games in which, with luck, he might be declared a winner, might come out of this better off than before. Someone or something had decided Ian Frey might be worth saving.

After a few moments, Ginny gestured with impatience.

His expression remained serious. "We need to get a few things clear. I haven't the first clue about carving an angel. I'd need to be told exactly what to do, every step of the way. I might make mistakes. Might do more damage than good."

She nodded, face lighting up.

"But, I must admit, the project sounds intriguing and you're right, I am a carpenter and I understand wood. I'd like to help. I'll do what I can."

Ginny jumped from the chair and ran to hug him, flinging her arms around his waist.

"You're a good man!" she cried. "A good man."

Ian watched her peddle away, grey-streaked auburn plait flying in the wind like a beacon. She turned and gave a happy wave, blowing a kiss.

He strode to the workshop and picked up the hammer. He felt alive.

"I'm back!" he said, beneath his breath. "I'm back!"

Chapter 5

Mickey and James

I saw Mickey looking white and dazed and noted with sadness that she was not carrying Folly in his pouch. I gathered that the worst had happened. "Are you ill?" I asked. She looked blank and uncomprehending. I tried again. "Mickey, tell me what's wrong? Has something happened to Folly?" Numb with misery, Mickey wept inconsolably like a child. I took her hand and we walked silently to my home where, after a while, she told me all that had happened.

"You shouldn't be alone at a time like this," I said, stricken with horror. "Have you spoken to your father? Would you like to call him now?"

"I have no father," she replied in a cracked voice. "I am an orphan."

I'd heard it said that the famous Michael Graham, alienated and removed from his eldest daughter, had made a life for himself in London with a new wife and a young family. But surely any parent would offer help and comfort at a time like this?

"Call him, Mickey," I pleaded. "Tell him everything you've told me."

"Don't speak of my father again!" she cried. "I am nothing in his eyes. I could be dead for all he cares!" She covered her face. Once she had quietened, I encouraged her to take a little food and drink and led her, unresisting, to my guest room where I covered her beneath a quilt and drew the curtains. She slept. Hours later she emerged, rested and calm. "I feel better," she said, gratefully. "Don't repeat what I have told you, I don't want everyone pitying me. I must be strong. There will be a court case. The rapist must be punished. Only then will I be able to go on with my life."

The nurse switched off the oxygen, removed the clear, narrow plastic tubes from James' nose and helped him sit up against a pile of starched pillows.

"Breathe normally. Deep breaths like this: in and out, in and out. Yes, just like that."

She glanced at her watch. "Your parents will be here soon," she said, kindly laying the back of her cool hand against his forehead. "Your fever's dropping. You're feeling so much better!"

How did she know how he was feeling? She poured cold water from a flask into a glass and handed it to him. "Small sips," she instructed. "Take small sips."

He did as she said, observing that her frilly nurses' cap sat upon her curly hair at a rakish angle, like a wafer stuck into a scoop of ice cream. He returned the glass and she set it carefully upon the shiny silver cabinet.

"Good boy!" she sang out as she marched from the room.

James felt guilty. He wasn't a good boy. He didn't feel better. He felt worse! Much worse. Dad and Caron were on their way to the hospital and he'd have to tell them what had happened. He'd have to explain why he'd run away. Then they would ask about the fire. What would he say? He could hardly believe, even now, that his small, innocent campfire, just a few burning sticks really, had set the whole estuary alight. It had happened in minutes. The flames had broken away from the ring of twigs and brushwood that he had padded with dry grass to make it burn more quickly, leaping and jumping, racing into the undergrowth. If he closed his eyes he could still see trees burning: flames skyrocketing through blackening branches, tearing through dry bush, making for the houses on the hill. He wondered if the houses had caught alight and burned to the ground? If people and animals had been hurt? His teeth began to chatter.

He had done something very bad. There was a good chance the police might arrest him and send him to prison for arson. Arson was when a person set fire to something on purpose. His fire had been a mistake; all he'd wanted to do was to cook a few sausages, but would anyone believe him?

He squeezed his eyes shut. "Back in time," he whispered. "Go back in time!"

He didn't have a wand or a book of spells but maybe wanting something really badly might make it happen? If only he could go back in time. Back to the day before yesterday: to the time before he had spied and heard about the baby, before the quarrelling, before he had decided to run away.

"Go back in time! Please!"

It would be like a video running in reverse…

The door burst open. His father entered and took three long strides to his bedside.

He bent and brought his face close. "Jamie, Jamie Boy! Are you all right? Tell me? Are you all right?"

James opened his mouth but couldn't speak.

His dad kissed his head and rubbed his back. "Can you breathe properly? Are you well enough to go home?

James opened his mouth again. Yes, he wanted to say, yes, please take me home but only a dry, scratchy, whispery noise came out.

His dad pulled back the bedcovers and lifted James in his arms, holding him to his chest.

"Thank God you're safe, Jamie," he said fervently. "As long as you're safe, my boy, nothing else matters!"

James looked over his father's shoulder to the empty doorway beyond.

He found his voice.

"Where's Caron?"

His father glanced around the room. "Did you have anything else with you, any other clothes? Anything?"

James felt his heart falling. Where was Caron? Why had she not come to the hospital?

"Is Caron at home?"

His father was silent. James felt as though he might be sick all over the bedspread, over the sheets, over the hospital pyjamas. Had Caron gone away? Gone because of what he'd done? Would he never see her again?

"Dad?"

"She's at home, Jamie. Waiting for you."

James leaned into his father's hard chest, pressing his face into the rumpled blue shirt as his father carried him swiftly through the hospital corridors, his shoes squeaking on polished floors. He felt as though he were a baby, as though he'd suddenly become small and helpless, his teeth still chattering with fear. His father had not said anything about him running away. Had not said anything about the fire. He dared to hope. Perhaps he didn't know about the fire? Perhaps nobody knew? Maybe he wouldn't have to tell? Maybe it could be a secret?

At home, Caron waited on the step, outside the front door. She ran and pulled him to her, hugging him hard. Her eyes were swollen. Her face was puffy. He submitted for a few moments and then squirmed away.

"James!" she cried. "James!" Her voice sounded like someone else. It seemed that, like him, she couldn't speak.

His father took his hand and led him indoors. "A bath first," he said firmly. "And then something to eat. You must be starving!"

The lamp was glowing in his bedroom: the bedclothes had been turned back, his blue and white striped pyjamas were folded on his pillow. A small, strangled cry rose in his throat. This was where he wanted to be: he felt himself filled with an unbearable longing for the cool sheets, the comfort of his overstuffed pillow, the place at the window where the curtains didn't quite meet, where the bloated moon shone through the pile of well-read books on the bedside table – how could he have ever left it behind? How could he have run away from all this?

She found her voice. "Let me do this," Caron beseeched. "Please, Alec!"

His father shrugged, not meeting her eyes. "I'll make some grilled cheese sandwiches," he said to James as he left the bathroom.

Caron helped James undress. He'd come home in borrowed, pale green hospital pyjamas. His clothes had been placed in a damp, brown paper bag. She said nothing about how dirty they were or how they smelled of fire and wood smoke and nor did she comment on his soaked Doc Martins. Barely noticing, she mechanically stuffed his filthy, wet clothes into the laundry hamper and turned on the bath taps.

She began unbuttoning the front of the pyjamas and then paused. "Do you mind if I help you?" she asked, guardedly.

Usually he would have minded, minded very much. Usually he dressed and undressed himself. He didn't like to be touched but tonight it didn't seem to matter. He still felt like a tiny baby that could do nothing for itself. A tiny baby with wobbly legs and shaky arms and a large head that bobbed upon a thin neck, like a balloon on a string. She soaped a facecloth and lifted his foot, bending over to wash it, but that was too much. He wrenched away, slamming his foot into the water, splashing walls and floors. "Don't *wash* me!" he cried in panic. "I can do that myself!"

She handed him the soap and cloth. He washed his right foot

carefully and then moved on to his left. When he was clean, Caron wordlessly handed the shampoo that smelled of ripe peaches. Finally, she spoke.

"Why did you run away, James?"

He poured a little of the shimmering pinkish liquid into his hand.

"You heard us quarrelling. Your Dad and I, was that it? Were you frightened?"

She knew, then. She knew why he'd run away.

He rubbed the shampoo into his hair. The air was fragrant with rich fruitiness.

She stared at the bathroom tiles. "I'm sorry, James. It won't happen again, I promise. No more quarrelling."

He didn't believe her. The house felt sad. His father was still angry. He wouldn't even look at Caron, wouldn't meet her eyes.

She held out a towel, warm from the heated rail. He dried himself and pulled on his pyjamas, his back to her.

"I can't find your Superman pyjamas," she said. "I'll look properly tomorrow."

He hung his head, ashamed.

"James?"

"I lost them," he confessed miserably. "I lost my asthma pump and my backpack and my favourite Harry Potter book. I took the sausages from the fridge."

He looked up sorrowfully. Lost he'd said. I lost them. That was not really true. Lost sounded as though these things might still be found. He hadn't lost anything. Everything had been burned in the fire. The fire he'd started. Didn't she know about the fire? Hadn't anyone said anything?

"None of that matters. All I care is that you're home again, safe and sound."

She held out her hand. "Let me wash your glasses for you. They're really dirty. Full of little black specks."

She turned to the basin, holding them beneath the running tap.

The little black specks would probably be tiny dots of ash. But she washed them all away, uncurious and unconcerned.

"I love you, James," she said solemnly, bending over the basin, polishing the lenses of his spectacles with a paper tissue. "You do know that, don't you?"

He looked at the back of her head. Without his glasses he saw a soft, misty shape: the brown of her hair bleeding into the smooth, pale pink of her neck.

There was something he needed to ask.

"If you love me," he said carefully, "why do we need a baby?"

Ian and Grace watched the sunrise from the deck, thighs touching.

"The depression's gone," he said. "If that's what it was. I feel like the old me."

She kissed his cheek.

"It was the fire, you know. The fire shocked me out of that dreary black fug. Made me see what's really important, what matters most. It's you, Gracie, you and the kids, our home, our life together. I've been a self-pitying sod, God knows how you've put up with me?"

"Phoenix rising," his wife said.

"What?"

"You know, that old myth. The Phoenix builds its own funeral pyre and throws itself into the flames. As it dies it's reborn: rising from the ashes to live again."

The tide was coming in. Light glinted off the water. Reeds swayed. A pile of uprooted, blackened, dead and dying Port Jackson Willows lay on the riverbanks, waiting to be hauled away.

Later that day, several members of Environ would be planting indigenous dune vegetation to replace shrubs lost in the fire. Ian was responsible for the operation and during the past few days had overseen the planting of over two hundred grasses and the same number of sea pumpkins. Today the group would focus on the hummock-shaped dunes fringing the estuary where hundreds of ericas, grassy fynbos and wart-stemmed pincushions would be introduced. In a matter of weeks, the area would be completely restored.

He could hardly believe how his life had turned around so that after working alone for so many years, he had become the man in charge with people deferring to him, waiting for his instruction, obeying his every wish.

He'd spent several hours a day with Edwina, learning the ropes. Yesterday she'd handed an armful of well-thumbed books on terrestrial ecology, estuary vegetation and coastal systems. "You get your nose into those!" she'd insisted. "You're still a novice with a great deal yet to learn."

She was a bossy old thing, but she had her heart in the right place.

"How did the fire start? Do you know?" she had probed.

He hadn't really thought that much about it. A stray cigarette tossed into the grasses perhaps? A campfire not properly extinguished? How could anyone know? The land was bone dry. It had been a long, hot summer. Not a drop of rain for months. It wouldn't take much to start a conflagration like that.

"No idea. A careless accident, I imagine."

"Not good enough!" Pursing ruby lips, Edwina had given a calculating stare. "I'd like to establish the cause of the fire. See what you can find out. Talk to people. Ask questions. Unless it's a case of spontaneous combustion, *somebody* is responsible!"

Detective Inspector Hector Jansen called Mickey at home and asked her to meet him at the police station.

She sat in his office, waiting. Light poured through the window illuminating a bronze plaque on his desk: '*Detective Inspector Hector Jansen*'.

The desk was neat and orderly. Yellow case files in date order; a pile of papers; some pens arranged methodically; a photograph, black and white, of a woman and child in a silver frame.

The Detective arrived half an hour late and sat at his desk, without an apology.

Opening her file, he glanced through it and looked up at her, expressionless.

"Mr Black has been released on bail," he said.

Mickey swallowed. "Why has he been released? I don't understand?"

"He has denied your charge of rape. He says sex was consensual. He also claims you were both drunk at the time."

"That's a lie!"

The Detective remained silent, impassive.

"What happens now?"

"In my experience, it often takes a long time for the case to go to trial. If we cannot find sufficient evidence to prove that you have been raped, the prosecutor may decide not to prosecute."

"How long will it take?"

"Months. Perhaps longer."

"What about my money? The charge of theft of ten thousand?"

"Mr Black denies that he stole the money from you. He says you paid a deposit to purchase materials for repairs. He claims he is in the process of working on the house and is willing to complete the job. If this is the case, Miss Graham, and the money was part of a legitimate transaction, we will have to withdraw the charge of theft."

"I don't want him to complete the job! Can't I make you understand? I don't want Jordan Black anywhere near my house! He is dangerous and violent. I want him to return the money he has taken from me."

Detective Jansen regarded her silently. He tapped his pen upon the desk.

"You're not going to help me, are you?" she flung at him. "He's going to get away with everything! Jordan Black is a rapist and a thief. You met him. You've spoken to him. You can see what kind of man he is!"

The detective lifted a brow. "Please understand that I will do whatever I can to help you, Miss Graham. However, there were no witnesses to this rape. Mr Jordan denies the allegation. The forensic evidence is inconclusive."

"What are you saying? You think I should drop everything? Walk away from this? Allow Jordan Black to go unpunished?"

"I believe it may be difficult to prove that you were raped."

"I see." Deflated, Mickey crumpled in the chair. Oh, it was all too much! It was all so hopeless, so terribly unfair. There was no justice in the world. The guilty walked the streets. The innocent were preyed upon. There was no one to protect you. Who could you turn to? Not to men like Inspector Detective Jansen. Men who wouldn't give an inch: colder than ice, harder than nails.

"You win!" she said, her voice shaking.

His expression remained neutral.

"Tear up the case dockets. I withdraw the charges."

"Is that what you want to do, Miss Graham?"

"No! It's what *you* want me to do."

She could not look at him. She stumbled from the chair. At the door, she turned. "Jordan Black will not go unpunished!" She flung the words at him. "Do you hear me? If I have to, I will make him pay for what he's done to me."

There was a knock. Ginny opened the door to find Inga, flowers in her arms. She thrust them at Ginny. A bouquet of lilies: plain, spotted and trumpet shaped, in a cone of tissue paper. "I have come to see Chris," she said with a wan smile. "I have been away. I went home for a few weeks, to visit my father."

"Oh, he's missed you!" Ginny beamed, burying her nose in the waxy blooms, opening the door wide and leading Inga to the sitting room. She disappeared for a moment, returning with the flowers in a dripping crystal vase. "How clever of you to bring my favourite flowers."

Inga sank into a comfortable, sagging chair covered with a patterned Indian throw. A large cat lay in a pool of sunlight, washing itself. There was a bowl of fruit on the table, a pile of art books, some sewing, a tray of tea.

"It's fresh. Can I pour you a cup?"

Inga sipped. "How is he?"

Ginny looked at her; such a beautiful woman, so graceful with those long legs crossed, her hair spilling about her face.

"I think I should warn you, he's not well. He's lost weight. You'll find him changed, I think. Try not to let him see your reaction, the shock on your face might be too much. I am always so careful to keep my face unemotional." She presented Inga with a calm, almost serene exterior.

Inga felt a tremor of fear. "May I see him?"

"Of course." Ginny picked up her sewing. The needle flashed. "I've been hoping you would return," she said, eyes on her work. "I know how fond you are of Chris."

"I love him!"

"I believe you do. And Chris loves you too. Not in the way you want to be loved, not sexually, but he has deep feelings for you."

"How do you know?"

"A mother always knows. Chris has loved very few people in his time: me, of course, and his grandmother, before she died. There was a man he loved profoundly, but we won't speak of that. And now there's you."

Inga studied Ginny thoughtfully. Her hair was tightly pulled back into a thick plait, tendrils waved about her face. Lines drooped from her mouth. Blue shadows from lack of sleep or worry, were etched beneath her eyes. She looked older since Inga had seen her last and very tired.

"What are you saying?" she asked, confused.

Ginny laid her sewing upon her lap. Their eyes met. "He needs you! Needs a friend: someone generous, kind and loving. Someone to talk to, confide in and trust."

She paused for a few moments. "But Inga, if you are that person – and I believe you may be, you'll have to be strong and steadfast. You'll have to be brave. There's so much to endure. So many dark days ahead."

"Why are you telling me this?"

"Because I want to be honest. You deserve that, at least. You should know what you're getting into. And, my dear, if you feel that you are not strong enough to cope, walk away now. Before he sees you. Before his spirits are lifted. Before he becomes too attached."

"You are frightening me!"

"I'm sorry." Ginny picked up her sewing. "I won't think less of you, Inga, if you decide to run from here now. It might be best to protect yourself from pain and sorrow."

Inga knew. "So he is dying, then?"

"Yes."

Inga became mute. She drummed her fingers on the arms of the chair. Tapped one small foot in a flat, black pump, the kind dancers wear. In a few moments, she would spring from the chair and fly away.

Ginny re-threaded the needle, knotted the cotton. The cat yawned. The door opened. Chris walked in.

"You're home!" he said. A radiant smile transfused his face.

Inga ran to him. She buried her head against his chest. She could feel his ribs. His skin burned with fierce heat. He pressed his lips to her head. She felt his hair brush her face.

"I'm glad you're back," he said, simply.

The next day, Caron and Alec avoided one another. That night he slept in the guest room, tossing and turning on the hard mattress; she wept in their double bed, but softly, so that James could not hear. The tension in the house was palpable. James retreated into his books, his telescope, his computer.

Finally, Caron could stand it no longer.

"Alec! We must think of James. This is no life for a child. The silence and anger between us is making him desperately unhappy. That's why he ran away in the first place. We can't go on like this."

"I agree."

"I'll do whatever you want, Alec. I want to be a good wife and mother. I want things to be as they were before. I want us to be happy!"

"You know what you need to do, Caron."

"An abortion? You want me to have an abortion?"

"Don't lay this on me! I didn't want you to get pregnant in the first place. You knew how things were. You went behind my back! This is all your idea, not mine. You must sort it out."

Caron placed her hand protectively upon her stomach.

"But, would it be so terrible? Another child? Why does everything have to fall apart like this? You know how much I want this baby. A brother or sister for James."

He flung his hands in the air. "I can't talk to you!" he said, stalking away.

Caron imagined the ten-week-old foetus in her womb. Smaller than a goldfish, smaller than a rose in full bloom, smaller, even, than the miniature conch shell. But it had a brain, a spinal cord and a beating heart. It waved its arms and legs. It swallowed and sucked its thumb. On the tips of starfish fingers were fingerprints. Minute, feathery impressions, barely discernable to the human eye, but there all the same. In two weeks the foetus would learn to curl its toes.

Caron called the clinic in Port Victoria and asked to speak to one of the staff on duty.

"I am ten weeks pregnant," she said. "I need to book an appointment for an abortion."

She could hear the nurse turning pages.

"What happens?" she asked. "Exactly. Can you take me through the procedure?"

The nurse spoke hurriedly: obviously busy and anxious to get back to work.

"For pregnancies of under fourteen weeks, you'll have the suction abortion. Your cervix is stretched open and a vacuum aspirator is inserted. The contents of your uterus are suctioned out and placed in a medical waste container. It's quick, relatively painless."

Caron gasped.

"We can see you on Friday morning," the nurse said. "Nine-thirty?"

She could not speak.

"Does that suit? Hello? Are you there?"

The foetus would be sucked out and placed in a medical waste container.

Caron replaced the phone quietly.

Standing in the artist's studio, Ian imagined the cedar growing in a dense forest, branches covered with spiral clusters of evergreen leaves.

"Why an angel?" he asked curiously

"Not just any angel," said Chris. "A *Guardian* Angel: a spirit to protect and guide. In this case, to light the way for Edwina Hurley."

Ian studied the clay model and detailed working drawings. "Never done this before. I'm going to work slowly," he said. "I don't want to take away too much of the wood. OK?"

Chris showed him how to use the chain saw. "Be careful!" he warned. "It turns at about twelve thousand revs per minute. And the wood chips fly! They can cut you to pieces. Use a mask and goggles."

Ian was surprised at how difficult it was to remove the excess wood without taking off too much and leaving the sculptor too little to work from. After three hours of cutting away at the wood with chainsaw and hatchet, he found himself sweating profusely, his neck stiff with tension, wrists throbbing with the weight of the saw.

"I had no idea how strenuous this is! Not a job for sissies, that's for sure!"

Chris shot a look.

"I didn't mean anything by that." Ian was embarrassed.

Chris ran his hands lightly over the roughly shaped log of cedar: the fine grain exposed to show the intricate whorls, knots and faint imperfections that would give this carving its unique character.

"This is good," he admitted. "I can work with it now, I'll take it from here. You've been a great help – how can I repay you?"

"Not necessary, glad to help. One question, though. Why sculpt in wood if it's so physically demanding?"

Chris picked up a gouge and began to chip away at the wood. "Wood is my medium. Unlike metal or bronze, wood is natural. Once I've sanded and smoothed this piece it will feel like satin. You'll want to make physical contact, to reach out and touch, caress and stroke."

Reluctant to leave, Ian stood for a few minutes, observing Chris working with careful precision, completely absorbed. The artist had turned inward, lost in the carving: unaware of Ian's continuing presence in the room.

This is it! Ian thought. *A true artist at work. A union of two free spirits, the sculptor and the tree that had once been alive and would now be brought to life again.* He imagined the cedar angel standing two metres high, keeping a vigilant watch over Edwina's magnificent garden.

The gouge had a steady rhythm. The chips fell like flakes. Soon the angel would reveal herself.

Chapter 6

Edwina and Mickey

The Environ Group were out in force, industriously engaged in replenishing the natural vegetation in the estuary so that, just weeks after the blaze, the sand magically sprouted sour fig, dune morning glory, seaside bean and sea pumpkins. That morning, whilst walking Angus on the beach, I spotted an elderly man and woman bending creakily over trowels as they dug and planted. I shouted 'Good morning!' and cheerily waved but they looked crossly away to show their displeasure at my idleness in the face of their unselfish, unstinting labours. It's a fact that St Jude's tree-huggers take themselves too seriously and this couple clearly felt I should be slaving alongside them but, for my part, I'd rather patiently wait for nature to send tender green shoots from blackened stumps and, in her own good time, restore the trail of devastation laid waste by the fire.

Ian, wearing twin hats: Chairperson of Environ and of the Save the Beach project was like a man possessed. He was everywhere. Supervising dune planting, overseeing removal of burnt branches and stumps and inspecting the construction of the seawall. Most of the community expressed relief at his appointments but there were others who commented that, for an ordinary carpenter, Frey had come up rather too quickly in the world, particularly for one who had never, so far as anyone knew, been a member of any local environmental group and whose grasp of St Jude's unique ecology was, to say the least, dodgy.

An official buff envelope arrived at the Grant household bearing the stamp of the Betty's Bay Primary School.

"Your test results!" announced Caron to James who was colouring a map of Africa and highlighting important areas of agriculture with a green felt-tip pen.

James peered over his glasses at the square envelope in Caron's hand. It seemed such a long time ago since he had written the mid-term tests in the school-hall at Betty's Bay Primary, almost another lifetime. He thought he'd aced the tests: they'd all been easy. He remembered the examination hall: rows and rows of desks, girls and boys in grey and white uniforms with laced shoes, everyone staring at his blue shirt and trainers, pointing, whispering, giggling. He remembered finishing long before the others and then fidgeting and kicking the desk until a teacher had scurried over and, frowning, held a finger to her lips. It seemed forever until the bell rang and she shouted, "Pens down, please!"

James thoughtfully surveyed the map of Africa and chose a brown pen to colour in key mining areas.

Caron sat at the table. "Shall we open the report?" she breathed. "Or would you prefer to wait until Dad comes home and we can look at your results together?"

"Dunno." He gave a shrug. It didn't matter. He didn't care about test results. His marks would be good; they always were. Caron would be pleased because she was his teacher, Dad would say that he was proud. They would smile and pretend to be happy. But they wouldn't look at each other. His father would look past Caron into the distance, and she would look past him. Their eyes would never meet. Did they think he didn't see? Their smiles weren't real, either. They would stretch their lips and show their teeth. And then they would speak in those pretend voices: loud and jolly, but not really.

What was real was the sound of whispering: Dad whispering to Caron when he thought James couldn't hear, Caron whispering back. Those low, sharp voices frightened him. His father slept in the spare room with the door shut. Caron slept in the upstairs bedroom but on her own. She cried sometimes, he could hear her through the walls, very softly, like rain or the wind. The pitiful sound of her crying made him sad: he felt as though something were sitting on his chest, something very heavy, making it hard to breathe.

Caron slit open the envelope and pulled out the crisp, folded pages. The paper crackled as she opened it and smoothed it flat with her hand. Her eyes ran quickly over the report. Her face shone. "Well done, James! You've got an A in almost every subject! Listen to the Principal's comment: 'A truly outstanding accomplishment from a student who has achieved the best results in his age group.'

She handed him the report. "*Best* in your age group!" she repeated. He saw telltale red staining her cheeks, a sure sign that she was pleased.

James took the report and placed it face down on the desk, hunting for a red crayon to colour in capital cities.

"James? Read your report. See how well you've done in all your tests."

He didn't look up. "I don't care!" he said. "Tests don't matter."

"Of course they matter! You should be proud of your marks. I know I am!"

She picked up the report, waving it at him. "Please, James!"

He scanned the neat, black, printed columns: "English: A, Maths: A, Geography: A, Biology: A, History: A, Art: B…"

The notes at the end of the report, written in thick, black curly handwriting by the school principal, faded to a blur. He didn't feel proud. Didn't feel anything.

"Very good, James!" he said, under his breath. He folded the report and lay it flat on the desk. He took up the red crayon again. None of it mattered.

The room was still. Sunlight played upon the polished sheen of the wooden table. Caron watched James colouring in his map, painstakingly following the lines.

Since that night, when he had been found hardly breathing and taken to hospital, James had been frozen. He hardly spoke. He ate little, hardly enough to keep a mouse alive. At night he often shouted or cried out in his sleep. It was happening again. He was turning inwards, shutting himself off from everything, from everyone. This was the way he'd been when she had first come to the house as a new bride, when she'd struggled to build a relationship with the boy whose mother had recently died, leaving him desolate and withdrawn. She'd worked so hard, they'd come all this way and now, just like that, they were back at square one.

Except it wasn't square one for her. Her feelings had changed. She wondered when they'd changed? When had she stopped seeing James as an unattractive, difficult boy, another woman's awkward child, and started to love him as her own? She'd known how deep her feelings ran that day when she'd woken and found him missing. She'd been filled with sudden terror, her blood turned to ice. In those first few minutes she'd known how much she cared. How she would have done anything – *anything!* – to find him and bring him home safely.

I must tell him that I love him! she'd thought. *He must know, before it's too late!*

And she had. She'd said the words, meaning them with all her heart but James, stiff and shut-away, had looked at her, no, looked *through* her as though he didn't believe her, didn't trust her.

And then that comment about the baby. "If you love me," he'd asked, "why do we need a baby?" She'd been at a loss for a few moments. The answer seemed incredibly important. He had stared up at her, waiting.

"A baby won't change the way I feel about you!" she'd replied. He'd gazed steadily until she had looked away. Was she being honest? How could she know how she'd feel when she had her own baby, her own flesh and blood? She'd said what she thought he wanted to hear, but she had no idea if it were true or not. And then he'd turned away and she had lost him again, lost her chance.

James whispered to himself. She inclined her head to listen and heard him spelling words aloud.

"Addis Ababa, capital of Ethiopia. *A-d-d-i-s A-b-a-b-a.*"

She grasped at a straw. "Do you know what that means? Addis Ababa?"

"Huh?"

She smiled. "It means 'new flower'."

He nodded. "New flower," he repeated softly.

She placed the palm of her right hand flat upon her stomach.

Poor baby, she thought. *Nobody wants you. Not your father. Not your half-brother. Everyone is afraid of you, afraid of how you will change their lives. But I want you. More than anything else in the world, I want you!*

Edwina's affairs were in order. In collaboration with her long-standing and trusted lawyers, Stanford Brown & Associates, she had revised and signed her last will and testament. The document included a great many generous donations to worthy charities and handsome gratuities to select, deserving individuals.

She had set up family trusts and apportioned the Hurley jewels, sharing them equally between daughters, daughters-in-law, granddaughters and female cousins. Valuable gifts of silver, pewter, crystal and china had been bequeathed to those few good friends Edwina believed might cherish such tokens of remembrance. An endowment of some of the finest items in the Hurley art collection had been made to the Port Victoria Art Museum and dozens of cartons of books were to be delivered to the St Jude Hospice after her demise.

Thomas was fully provided for and, once she'd gone, a sensible and responsible full-time nurse would move into the house as a salaried employee, to care for his every need. Edwina had interviewed several nurses for the post and chosen a competent, big-boned, fresh-faced young woman whom she thought would be strong and cheerful and know how to laugh and keep Thomas in good spirits.

The household staff: maids, gardeners, chauffeur and cook would all be kept on whilst Thomas lived, but after his death, the house would revert to the Hurley family in whose hands their fate would lie. In the event of their being dismissed, Edwina had made provision for a handsome annual stipend for each of the staff until their death.

She had also decreed that a section of the extensive garden at Hurley House should be cordoned off with a high white wall leading to a scrolling floral ironwork gate.

This would be conferred to St Jude as the '*Edwina Hurley Community Garden*' so that everyone in the village could enjoy its leafy splendour.

No stone was left unturned. Edwina chose a plain pine coffin and several rousing hymns for her funeral. She also set aside a rather fetching cream woollen suit with bone buttons in which she was to be buried and, since she would not be walking in them, made it known that she was to wear the elegant black leather Italian sandals with six inch heels on her long, narrow feet. In readiness, the family plot behind the local church was planted with white standard roses and her name chiselled on a simple slab of dove grey marble:

'Edwina Jane Hurley – Beloved Wife and Mother – 20.02.1935 –…'

The only unknown was the date, the exact day, upon which Edwina would finally die.

One detail remained outstanding: the angel. Weeks had passed and she had heard nothing from the sculptor, Chris. Local gossip suggested that he might be ill, confined to bed and unable to work.

"He's stick-thin and as white as a ghost!" reported her old friend, Laura Winthrop. "Near death's door if you ask me!"

Edwina bristled. "I suppose you're going around saying the same thing about me!"

"I have been telling folk that you're not long for this world," admitted Mrs Winthrop. "But I find that, of late, you're looking rather well. There's a touch of colour in your cheeks and your eyes are bright."

"You stupid woman! That's the fever!"

"Well, whatever it is. You're looking better for it!"

Edwina's chauffeur drove her to meet with Chris in his studio, at home.

She arrived unannounced. The house appeared deserted with doors locked and curtains drawn. Edwina rapped hard, several times, before Chris unlatched the door.

"I wondered when you'd come," he said, stepping back to admit her.

She barged in. "You owe me a Guardian Angel. I wish to see for myself what progress has been made."

Laura Winthrop had not exaggerated. Chris looked gaunt and walked as though his bones hurt. He led her slowly upstairs to his studio.

Canvases were propped up against the wall. There was an easel. A plain wooden table and chair. A bookshelf and a narrow daybed covered with a vivid quilt.

The carving stood before the window. It was still rough, but Edwina could easily discern the shape of the angel: arms raised, head back, wings folded. There was a distinct sharp, clean fragrance in the air. Edwina sniffed. Pine cones perhaps?

Chris gestured apologetically at the carving. "There's still a great deal to do. Days of work, weeks perhaps."

Edwina reached out to touch the sculpture. Her fingers caressed the wood.

"I have a question," she announced briskly.

He knew what was coming. "Yes?"

"Have you the strength to finish the carving?"

A shadow passed over his face. "I made you a promise. I intend to keep it."

Edwina sat upon the chair beside the table and picked up the miniature clay model, balancing it on the flat of her palm. It was perfect in every detail. She imagined it towering two metres tall in a sunlit garden. Sleek, statuesque, beautiful.

"You may think me a foolish old woman, but I have faith in your angel. Once she stands in the garden of Hurley House, I believe I may be able to rest, at last."

Silently, Chris picked up a chisel and began to work on the head of the carving.

Edwina observed the sharp, silver tool tenderly removing fragments of wood, defining a cheekbone, the curve of a cheek, the fullness of a lip. The eyes were flat indentations, waiting for life.

"Do you mind if I watch for a while?"

But the artist, engrossed in shaping the delicate features of the angel's lovely face, either ignored or did not hear her.

Edwina leaned back in the chair. Her eyes fell upon the quilt covering the daybed.

The colours dazzled: red, ochre, orange, purple and sage green. The design was complicated: interlinking circles and triangles. She half-closed her eyes and imagined a garden. The circles were flowers, the triangles trees. Probably sewn by his mother, Ginny, highly regarded as a skilled and creative quilter.

She turned back to the angel. The light falling from the open window formed a nimbus around the head. Even in its rough state, the figure was powerful.

Perhaps she fell asleep for a few moments? Perhaps the quiet, steady chisel tapping upon wood had been soporific? She woke to the sound of bees or wasps outside in the garden, buzzing amongst the delphiniums growing against the wall. Suddenly, unexpectedly and without warning, Edwina felt quite calm: her body flooded with a sense of extraordinary peace. She wondered at this sudden stillness. What had happened? Was it being in the studio, this quiet place, washed with silver light? Was it the sight of this young man, absorbed in work, carving the angel's features? Could it be the sound of cedar fragments hitting the floor, falling like raindrops?

Or did the pure and gracious spirit of the angel permeate the room and fill her with what could only be described as a sense of unblemished happiness?

One week later, Edwina arrived early for her weekly appointment with Grace.

"Could you shuffle patients?" she asked the nurse. "I must see the doctor at once!"

The doctor examined the patient carefully. "How are you feeling?"

Edwina dramatically removed the silk scarf concealing the tumour. "What do you see?" she demanded.

Grace closely scrutinised the ugly, inflamed growth. She blinked, confused.

"It seems smaller?"

"Yes! Yes! I haven't said anything to anyone, not a word! But, I agree, it appears to be shrinking!"

"Interesting."

" '*Interesting'?* Is that all you can say?"

"Don't get too excited, Edwina. Malignant tumours don't disappear."

Edwina reached for the scarf. "Here's what I know, Grace. The tumour is definitely smaller. And the pain is not as intense. Admittedly it's still there, but duller than before."

Grace frowned. "Are you sure?"

"Do you believe in miracles, doctor?"

"I believe in medical science."

"Every morning I force myself to look at this grotesque growth. I stand naked before the mirror and face my enemy. During the past week, I have seen this lump diminish. I've felt the pain fade. I can't explain it and, clearly, neither can you."

Grace gave a glimmer of a smile. "Tumours can be..."

Edwina held up both hands. "Hear me out, Grace. This might sound like the ravings of a mad woman, but I must tell you this. You may have heard that Chris Lourens, the sculptor, is carving a Guardian Angel for me? Yesterday I went to see Chris and, for an hour or so, I watched him at work."

Edwina dropped her voice to a theatrical whisper.

"Grace, whilst I sat in the studio, something extraordinary happened. A sense of peace descended. For a moment I shut my eyes, imagining my tumour. I saw the raw, red flesh melting away. I saw this ghastly, pitted orange giving way to healthy tissue. I saw myself becoming whole again, becoming well!" Edwina leaned forward conspiratorially. "What do you think of *that?*"

Grace gazed helplessly. "Oh, Edwina. What are you saying? Being in the presence of a wooden carving of a Guardian Angel has cured you? Is that what you're telling me?"

Edwina had the grace to blush. "I suppose you think I've lost my mind? A dying woman clinging to hope, the chance of a miracle?"

Grace considered. "Edwina, I don't want to be brutal, but, as you know, you're in the final stages of metastatic breast cancer. The cancer has spread to your lymph nodes and other parts of your body. So, even if the tumour appears to be shrinking, it doesn't mean your cancer has been cured, far from it."

Edwina's expression changed. The hopefulness waned. She opened her handbag and removed a gold compact, fluttering a powder puff over sunken cheeks. Grace heard disappointment cloud her voice. "You're right," she sighed. "I know you're right. Forget everything I've said."

She gave a wobbly laugh. "The doctor always knows best!"

Alec made an appointment to meet Ben Barker at his surgery. They shook hands. "Thanks for your time," Alec said. "I'd like to find out what happened that night, the night when you found James."

"Well, technically speaking, Lucky found James. We were on the beach. Lucky ran ahead. I lost him for a while. Then I heard him barking and when I finally reached him, Lucky was standing over James. He'd collapsed in the sand."

"He was having an asthma attack?"

"He was struggling to breathe."

"When you found him, how close was he to the bush fire?"

"Very close. The smoke probably affected his breathing."

"James ran away early that morning. By the time you discovered him, he'd been missing for over twelve hours. We were distraught, my wife and I, panicked and desperately worried. Thank God you found him!"

"I ran away when I was a kid," Ben grinned. "Took my bow and arrow and a loaf of bread. You probably did the same thing? Most kids…"

"No!" Alec was firm. "James is not like most kids. Running away is completely out of character. He's been unhappy lately. Stressed. I'm worried about him."

Ben nodded sympathetically.

Distracted, Alec Grant ran his hands through his hair. "Thing is, I think James may have had something to do with the fire in the estuary."

"I wondered about that. He might have lit a fire, the way boys do. Perhaps it got out of hand. These things happen. Have you asked him?"

"No, I haven't. He's been upset, I haven't wanted to make things worse at this point. But he has admitted to taking sausages from the fridge and I gather he meant to cook them over an open fire. The fire probably got out of control." Alec shuddered. "He might have been killed, burned to death!"

Ben gripped Alec's shoulder. "Put it out of your mind. Don't keep dwelling on it. What's done is done!"

"You saved my boy! If it wasn't for you, Ben ..."

"Not me!" Ben laughed. "That dog – the one who lives next door to you – he saved your boy."

Alec drove fast along the main road leading away from the village. He passed the Evans' dairy farm where plodding cows were being led to pasture. The farmer's wife pegged white sheets that flapped and danced in the breeze. Ordinary life, he thought. Some people have ordinary lives. Happy lives. He raced over the humped stone bridge above the Krill River where, far below, a small blue boat sailed towards the horizon. Tractors in the fields chewed up thick clods of earth, trailing billowing clouds of fine orange dust. A grey pony galloped alone in a field of clover.

It was a perfect day in every way and yet it might have been the end of the world.

The road disappeared beneath the wheels. Where was he going? He didn't know, didn't care. What did it matter? His life was a fucking disaster! Married to a woman he no longer loved. A woman carrying a child he didn't want.

James was taking the brunt of it all. Running away from home, what did that tell you? You didn't have to be a genius to work out how unhappy the boy must have been to have run off like that. He'd run away from the tension in the house, the non-stop bloody quarrelling. Even when they shut themselves in other rooms, spoke quietly or whispered, James seemed to know they were going at it ding-dong bells!

He'd never quarrelled with Deborah, well, hardly ever. They'd probably had a few arguments but it had all been over and done with in minutes. No coldness, no sulking, no moods that lasted for days the way they did with Caron.

The quarrelling was one thing, but Caron's never-ending lessons and tutorials were quite another. And yes, she might be, as she claimed, developing James' potential, teaching him to focus, achieving brilliant results, but what kind of life was this for a little kid? No school. No holidays. No friends to speak of. Not one! James was bright, brighter than other kids and Deborah had guessed at this from the first, had encouraged him to read when he was very young and understood that he might be more sensitive, more emotional than other kids, but something had happened to change James.

When had he become so insecure, fidgety, incredibly intense and anxious? When had he stopped trusting them; taking their word; believing what they said? The new James seemed overly suspicious of everything, calculating, even judgemental. And where did he go in his head when he got that blank look on his face: the look that shut everyone else out like a door slamming? Why did James often pull back from a hug or flinch when kissed, what was that about?

Alec pulled off the road and cut the engine. The mountains rose up before him. The sun melted into the clouds.

"What the hell am I going to do? Divorce Caron and bring up James alone? Or, give the marriage another chance and try to make a go of it?"

Alec looked at the valley lying below in the shadow of the mountains. A white farmhouse complete with picket fence set in a lush grove of orange and lemon trees, purple Bougainvillea spilling voluptuously over a brick wall.

One problem, one really big fucking problem! How could a man divorce his pregnant wife and live with his conscience? Was it remotely possible?

Caron would never have an abortion, she'd almost said as much. The baby was on its way, whether he liked it or not. You married for better or worse. You made a promise. Men who walked away from their responsibility were shits. The writing was, pretty much, on the wall. He was thinking in clichés, one after another but he knew one thing for sure: she would have that baby, a brother or sister for James and he would do his best to be a good and loving father. What else could he do? There would have to be conditions though. They'd have to agree to put an end to the arguments, the ongoing rows. She'd have to stop being so manipulative, compulsive and neurotic and, for his part, he'd have to learn to control his temper and stop flaring up at the least provocation. He'd have to learn tolerance. He'd insist on James going back to school and, with a new baby on the way, Caron would surely be in agreement? In any event, this aspect was non-negotiable. With James at school, mixing with other kids, having fun, playing sport, there would be a greater chance of his enjoying a normal, happy childhood.

He'd made the right decision, hell, what other decision was there with a baby on the way? Why then, as he turned the car back towards the village, did he feel so heavy? Heavy and numb with loss and despair "Oh Deborah," he sighed, and then put her out of his mind.

He imagined telling Caron of his decision. Her face would flood with relief. There would be tears. He saw himself opening his arms to her. Embracing her. And feeling only emptiness.

Mickey went to the church to pray. The church was familiar to her and yet it felt cold and dark. A bare interior, high white walls, a domed ceiling, Gothic windows. Dust lay thickly upon the pews. A bleeding crucifix on one of the walls. Prayer books and hymn sheets. A stiff arrangement of lilies in rank water.

Mickey knelt at one of the wooden pews and shut her eyes. She missed God. He had been a part of her life for so long: a clear voice in her head, keeping her on the straight and narrow path, taking the dutiful steps to ensure a bespoken place in Heaven.

Today she had come to the church to bargain with God. The terms of the negotiation were simple. If He came back into her life now, today, this very minute – she would forgive Him for deserting her in her hour of greatest need.

"Do you hear me?" she said, projecting her voice so that there could be no doubt. "Come back into my life and I will forgive you! We'll go on as before. The way it was. The way I want it to be again. I need you!"

Eyes tightly shut, Mickey waited for God's answer.

She heard the groan of the heavy iron latch on the door.

Soft footsteps as the Reverend Watson crept up the worn strip of carpet to the pew where she knelt. She recognised his muffled footfalls. Smelt the citrus aftershave he lavished on his jowls. The footsteps ceased. He hovered in the aisle, she felt a slight draft.

Mickey opened her eyes. "Reverend Watson?"

"Miss Graham. How nice. We've missed you."

She wondered exactly who the Reverend included in that magnanimous 'we'. Who had missed her? She attended church seldom and knew few of the parishioners who regularly prayed here.

Mickey rose from her knees and sat tiredly on the pew. She stared through the church window at the tops of the trees, green against the faded blue sky.

"Are you well, Miss Graham?"

"No. I lost my dog, Folly. He died."

"You have my deepest sympathy."

"And I have been raped."

She heard a shocked intake of breath. "Raped! In St Jude! I can hardly believe such a terrible thing!"

"Do you believe in retribution?"

"I beg your pardon?"

"An eye for an eye, a tooth for a tooth?"

"Ah! The Old Testament principle of exact reciprocity which believes that the punishment must be equal to the crime."

"Yes!"

"Personally, Miss Graham, I don't believe in the concept of vengeance. I prefer to be guided by Jesus' Sermon on the Mount. Do you remember? '*If anyone strikes you on the right cheek, turn to him the other also.*' "

"So you believe I should forgive the man who raped me?"

"Christianity teaches us to forgive those who wrong us, rather than seek retribution."

"That sounds like a cop-out. I prefer the idea of revenge."

"Pray for guidance. Turn to God, Miss Graham. Ask for wisdom, forgiveness and humanity."

"Yes, well, that's what I was doing. I was praying, before you interrupted me."

"I'll leave you then, shall I?"

"Please." Mickey knelt again and shut her eyes.

The Reverend tentatively cleared his throat. "If you ever need to talk?" he offered. "If I am able to provide comfort or solace of any kind? I am always here."

His footsteps shuffled away, the citrus fragrance faded.

Vengeance or forgiveness? *To err is human, to forgive divine.* Who said that?

She wasn't sure, Alexander Pope perhaps? Someone famous. Mickey waited to hear the voice of God. She would leave it in His hands to decide which path she should follow. She listened. She opened heart and mind. Minutes grew to hours. Her body cramped with stiffness and cold. Her neck hurt. Her attuned ears heard the murmuring of doves in the church gardens: birds scratching in the grass, feathers spread in sunlight. Heads bobbing, eyes shining: wings soaring to heaven.

Heaven. God. Gone from her life forever.

"I have lost my faith," she whispered aloud.

As she stood and stretched her stiff legs, she felt relief. The path was clear. The way ahead had been determined. *'An eye for an eye, a tooth for a tooth.'*

She walked down the aisle, pushed open the heavy door and left the church without a backward glance.

Chapter 7

Alec and Inga

I rose early the next morning and drank coffee on my deck on what promised to be another sublime day. The canal waters, as dark and still as a pool of spilled green paint, were suddenly churned by an inflatable boat heading towards the Serpentine Canal. I recognised the occupants as Chris and Inga; both were dressed in white, her hair tied back with a scarf whipping in the wind and he wearing a peak cap, the shadow falling over his face. I heard their voices, the rise and fall of laughter. She had her hands upon the wheel, he sat facing her, a sketchpad on his knees, drawing with quick, sure strokes. The boat hit a sandbank and he rose to stand behind her to navigate the shallow waters. She pressed against him as he bent to take the wheel and, as I watched, he leaned forward so that their cheeks touched. I knew, we all did, that Chris was gay and I was naturally surprised to see these two in such an intimate embrace. I could not tear my eyes away, staring until the boat turned the bend leaving wide ripples shattering the mirrored surface.

All day the memory returned: I kept seeing those two conjoined white figures and feeling envy for what I observed as the purest kind of love.

Sarah had faithfully promised Ben a tour of The Two Potters. A date had been set but when the time came she found she had to cancel. An antique shop in Port Victoria was closing and she had read that items for sale included tapestries, hanging lanterns, a set of eight coveted ladderback chairs, a French bread cupboard and a quantity of old pewter bowls and vases.

She called Ben to apologise. "It's too good to resist," she said. "I might be able to pick up some rare antiques for a song."

"Don't worry about it." He sounded weary. "Another time."

"Ginny could show you around?" she volunteered.

"OK," he agreed, flatly.

Ginny was delighted. "Ben Barker? What larks! It will be a pleasure to give him a guided tour!"

On the day, she unplaited her hair so that, taken back in two wooden combs, it rippled down her back. She twisted and turned in front of the long mirror. She didn't want to look ridiculous – not mutton dressed as lamb! – but perhaps she could yet get away with this cascade of hair?

She paraded before Chris. "Too much, do you think? Should I wear it in my usual plait? A French twist, perhaps?"

"It's beautiful," he said honestly. "Just as it is."

He observed her lovingly: she might have been a much younger woman in that tightly fitting jade shirt with the full-skirted striped cotton skirt, brown sandals on bare feet and that sumptuous curtain of unruly red hair tumbling down her back. He felt ridiculously proud that she could still, at her age, look so vibrant; that her hair, apart from a few strands of white should still burn with such colour.

"A visitor to the gallery," she explained. "I want to look my best."

"Anyone I know?"

She lifted her arms high above her head. "Darling! Look closely, here, at the tops of my arms. Are they too withered? Does the skin flap when I move them? Look, like this!" Bracelets jangling, she waved both arms wildly in the air.

He struggled to contain his laughter. "Ma, relax. You look lovely."

A van pulled up outside the gallery. His mother flew from the room.

Ben remembered almost nothing of Ginny. If pressed, he could conjure a vague mental image of a sad, tired, middle-aged woman. She'd been riding a bicycle and he'd given her a lift. At the time, she'd seemed pathetically grateful for this small kindness.

He hardly recognised the smiling woman who met him at the entrance of The Two Potters. She waved him inside, greeting him warmly. "Hello, Ben! Ginny Lourens. We've met. You kindly played Sir Galahad: gave me a lift on a desperately cold day!" Her eyes danced.

He was taken by surprise when she tucked her hand into his arm as if it were the most natural thing in the world and led him into the gallery.

He had an impression of high windows and a collection of framed oils, watercolours, pastels and ink drawings on freshly painted walls.

He was drawn particularly to one canvas: a portrait of a woman sewing, a cat supine at her feet. The woman's face was strong and handsome. A heavy braid hung over one shoulder. The artist had captured her full, sensual mouth, the planes of her face, a trace of pink in each hollowed cheek.

Ben's eyes moved from the painting to Ginny's lively face. "Self portrait?"

She laughed. "Oh no! I can paint, but nothing as fine as this. This is my son's work. You may have heard of Chris Lourens?"

Ben grimaced. "I don't know much about art," he confessed. "And no, I don't know the artist, but the likeness is very good. You look…? He faltered, trying to think of what to say that might please her. "*Serene!* You look very serene in this painting."

He saw a flicker of disappointment.

He kicked himself. "And lovely," he added. "Truly lovely."

She blushed, crimson flooding her neck, rising to her cheeks.

She spun away towards another painting and began a rapid commentary about the artist. He listened, without hearing anything she said. Her voice was quick and light, she laughed often. There was something about her? What was it? Her hands flew in the air as she gestured at a canvas of a seascape. She wore an armful of silver bracelets so that every movement was underscored by a series of jingling notes, as though a tambourine had been shaken lightly in the room. She laughed again, throwing her head back.

He knew suddenly. In spite of her performance, Ginny was nervous: as nervous and self-conscious as a young girl. But nervous of what, of *him,* surely not? Ben was amazed and then charmed. It had been a very long time, years, since any woman had responded to him in this way. He couldn't help it, he smiled widely. Ginny stopped speaking mid-stream and gave a quizzical glance. He realised the smile had been inappropriate. What had she been saying?

"Interesting," he tried. "Most interesting. Do go on."

"You haven't heard a word!"

"No," he confessed. "I'm sorry. As I've said, art is not really my thing."

"My fault! I'm sorry. I babble. Everyone says so. Once you get me started, I never stop. Are you interested in books? We have some fine limited editions I could show you?"

"Tell you what, I'd give my right hand for a coffee, that is, if you have time?" She beamed and, taking his arm again, swept him through a long, sun-lit room filled with carved wooden chests, pottery bowls, woven baskets and piled carpets.

He was impressed. "Where do you find all this stuff?"

"Oh, I don't. This is all Sarah's work; all her doing. I talk to clients and suppliers and give lessons in quilting and painting. It's Sarah who's the driving force behind the gallery, the real reason for our recent successes."

She led him to a small café, to a corner table piled high with new bestsellers. "Browse!" she demanded. "Browse away while I organise cake and coffee."

He watched her darting behind the counter: pouring coffee, warming milk, slicing cake. Her movements were light and deft. She hummed quietly, her lips curved into a smile. He wanted to plunge his hands into her thick mane of hair, bury himself in its slippery, rich, auburn sheen. He found that he was staring, gave himself a jolt and hurriedly picked up one of the books on display. He flipped through the pages and then, looking up again, caught her glancing shyly in his direction. He smiled and she dropped her eyes in confusion. *How strange*, he thought, *we're behaving exactly like a couple of teenagers.* He felt an unexpected fizzing of happiness. What was happening?

They sat on quaint, white painted chairs with legs like sticks of twisted barley sugar. She poured a jet of coffee into pottery cups and as he took the cup, their fingers touched. The air seemed charged. He felt the blood rush to his face. He caught her gaze. Christ! What *was* happening? He cleared his throat, opened his mouth to speak but as he did, Sarah appeared in the doorway.

"There you are! I've been looking all over for you."

She hurried towards them and, pulling out a chair, flopped down at the table. Her face was shining, her hair windswept. "Oh, Ginny, you're a darling! Thanks for taking care of Ben for me!"

Ginny wilted, he saw it happen, saw her sparkle diminish in seconds, her happiness fade. She forced a smile, pushed aside her untouched coffee and gave a glance at her wristwatch. "Look at the time! I'll leave you in Sarah's hands. It was good to see you again, Ben."

He stumbled to his feet as she rushed from the room. *Don't go*, he said in the secret part of himself that he kept buried away. *I haven't felt this way since God knows when. Don't go!*

Sarah's glowing face was expectant. "Don't keep me in suspense. Tell me. What do you think of the new gallery?"

Alec delayed returning home that evening: putting off "The Talk" with Caron. It didn't feel right, the timing was off. Tomorrow, over breakfast, he'd suggest she organise a sitter for James and they'd go out, just the two of them. Dinner at the Italian restaurant: pasta, wine, music, candles burning on the table. The setting was important. There was a far greater chance that on neutral ground, in a crowded restaurant, he'd be less likely to fly off the handle at a chance remark. He'd keep the discussion calm, constructive and amiable. They'd talk about the future, the baby, James returning to school, a change in attitude on both sides.

"The first chapter of our new life," he'd say and lift a glass of cold Chianti.

He called home to tell her he'd be working late. "Yes," she'd said stiffly. "Thanks for letting me know." That's how it was with them. They might have been strangers.

He worked on the plans for a new shopping centre, a modern glass and brick structure: sharply angled with a variety of horizontal and vertical planes below a shallow dome. He'd given the project to one of the junior partners, Jim Flint, who'd designed a dramatic foyer lined with pink marble. The young architect had talent, loads of it, but his work was too extreme for the simple, parochial tastes of St Jude. Alec had thrown the design back at Flint and asked him to rework the layout.

"Pink marble!" he'd said in disgust. "It's not a shrine for poofters!"

Flint had joined him in his office, the two of them revising the plans for an early morning client presentation.

Alec would never have admitted it, but he was jealous of Flint. He was unquestionably better looking than the stocky, swarthy young man whose thick black hair stood defiantly on his head like a row of short porcupine quills, but there was something about Flint. He was energetic and vital: a man of huge appetites. He ate and drank excessively without obvious ill effects and had a fearsome reputation as a womaniser. Alec had seen how the female staff of Grant & Associates behaved in Flint's company; like giddy lambs in the presence of a hungry fox.

"I've gotta go, Boss!" Flint pulled on a worn leather jacket. "I'm meeting someone."

Word had it that Jim was dating three women at once. Tracy, the young draftswoman with big breasts, pretty nineteen-year-old Simone, the nail stylist at the hair salon and the stunning, newly-divorced Barbara who, at thirty-five, had eight years at least on Flint.

Alec couldn't resist. "Who's the lucky girl then?"

Flint grinned hugely and ran a meaty paw through his prickly hair.

"Barbara Abbot!" He winked knowingly with furtive eyes. "We're meeting for drinks at the pub. Join us?"

Alec gave a sigh. "No can do. See you tomorrow," he said, returning to his computer.

He poured a mug of black coffee and printed out the plans. He tried to concentrate but couldn't stop imagining Flint and Barbara cosily together at the bar.

Flint flirting, Barbara teasing, eyes meeting, hands touching. He'd light her cigarettes, pour her drinks, solicitous and dazzling with boyish charm. Afterwards, they'd go to her place for coffee: his hands all over her, she moaning with pleasure. Lucky bastard! To be young and free, the world your oyster and women like Barbara for the taking. No promises, no commitments!

Was that it? Was that why he felt filled with an outraged sense of self-pity? Why he felt trapped in his humdrum domestic life?

He'd never been the Flint type. At Flint's age, he'd fallen deeply, madly in love with Deborah, settling easily, willingly even, into marriage and taking on all its responsibilities without ever mourning the loss of his independence. Then James had come along and, with him, the habits and routines of fatherhood had begun to define his life. After Deborah's death, when he might have played the field and had some fun with girls like Tracy, Simone and Barbara, he had, for better or worse, married Caron. Bottom line: he'd had his chance and blown it.

He stapled the plans, fitted them into a black folder and slid them into his briefcase.

Switching off the lights, he stood for a moment listening to the quiet monotonous hum of computers. *One life*, he thought. *One shot at getting it right. Time to knuckle down and make the best of it. You're not Jim Flint, you're a father with a kid who needs a happy, stable home. That's your priority: that's all that matters.*

Why, then, as he left the office, did he walk as though he were an old man carrying a weighty burden, a burden he'd rather not deal with: not now, not ever!

The next morning James woke and lay in bed watching the curtains billow in the breeze. There were shadows on the wall that changed as the curtain moved; one of them might have been a dinosaur with two heads that turned into a horse with a wild flying mane, racing above clouds, making for the sun. The curtains made a whispering sound but, aside from that, the house was silent. James listened. Usually, at this time, he could hear his father in the shower or the chink of china as Caron set the table but this morning there was only the sway and swish of curtains. He got out of bed and padded to the door, careful not to step on any of the cracks on the cool, shining floor tiles. Step on a crack and you would have bad luck!

He stood for a few moments in the doorway, listening keenly, hearing nothing.

He walked down the corridor, past the bathroom and spare bedroom, to the top of the stairs. From where he was standing, looking down the long flight, he could see that the door leading to the veranda was wide open. He heard voices: Dad and Caron's. Not whispering. Not shouting. They were talking in normal voices. Ordinary voices. Everyday voices. He let the sound of their conversation wash over him. He stopped holding his breath. Everything felt ordinary. The house felt ordinary. He tiptoed down the stairs, bare feet soundless on the carpet.

At the bottom of the stairs, he froze.

"I'd like that," Caron was saying, eagerly. "We haven't been out alone together for ages!"

"I'll make a reservation for seven thirty. Will you organise a sitter for James?"

James shuffled closer and craned his head. They were sitting together, side by side, on the garden seat on the veranda. There was a space between them and they were not touching, but it was the closest they'd sat for a very long while. There was a tray of tea on the table. Caron still wore her yellow quilted dressing gown; Alec was dressed for work. James took another step closer and bumped against the door.

"Hello, Jamie!" His father turned. "You're up early! Come and have a cup of tea with Caron. I'm off to work. Give me a hug!"

He briefly pressed against his father's white shirt. Caron said something, his father laughed.

Something had changed, he could feel it. Something was different. The air no longer hung heavily, didn't close in on him as though it might suffocate.

"Later, then?" his father said to Caron. She gave a nod, a smile. James caught their glance. They were looking *at* one another, and not looking away.

James lowered himself into the still-warm indentation his father had left upon the flowered cushions. He waved at his father's retreating back.

Caron passed a cup of milky tea. He sipped it, watching a red-winged starling snatching ripe mulberries from the hedge.

"Did you hear me, James? I said I thought we might take a walk, before we start lessons. Would you like that?"

"Not to the beach!" he blurted anxiously. "I don't want to walk to the beach."

"The village, I thought. We'll have breakfast at The Rambling Rose. Pancakes with syrup!"

"I'd rather have an egg. A boiled egg with toast."

"But, James, they make the most scrumptious pancakes. I thought we'd try them, for a change?"

"I'd like a three-minute egg. Please."

She laughed. "Whatever you want, James."

He could hear in her voice that she also knew that something had changed and the air was lighter.

He drank from the cup and swung his feet. The sunlight lit Caron's hair, turning it the colour of dark toffee. Birds were clucking, cheeping, drinking at the birdbath.

The red-winged starling sat on a twisted branch warbling its melancholy song: 'Peeeoo, peeeoo, peeeoo.' He could hear Lucky barking next door.

Everything was going to be all right.

Every evening, after sunset, once she had tidied the yoga studio and made everything ready for the next day's classes, Inga came to Chris. She always brought small gifts. This evening she had packed a square wicker basket with a light meal, a cold bottle of wine and two heavy goblets. She'd added a clutch of sandalwood candles and her favourite aromatherapy oils.

The drive from Betty's Bay to St Jude, along the farm roads, was always a thrilling journey for her holding, as it did, the pleasurable anticipation of seeing him again, putting her arms around him, touching him. She drove, filled with yearning, queasy with love, sick with the crippling fear of losing him.

They never spoke of his illness but she could see the toll it took in spite of the almost super-human spirit that carried him along, defying his obvious physical disintegration.

During the past week she'd guessed at the raw sores in his mouth: he spoke seldom and consumed only liquids. "Does your mouth hurt?" she had asked tenderly. "A little," he'd answered, and then changed the subject.

"So, this is taboo?" she'd asked. "We can never speak of your illness?"

He had taken her hand. "What good does it do?" he'd asked, hopelessly. She had shrugged. "Sometimes, it helps to talk. To get things out in the open."

"Not about this!" he'd cried. "It's agony. I'm sick of talking about this disease. It makes me self-pitying and morose. Makes me childish and needy. I start to fear the worst, to panic and lose my way. I don't want to talk about it, OK? Not with you."

The mood had been shattered: he'd turned away to work on the carving, silent and dismissive. That's when she'd learned that his disease was not a subject they would ever discuss, it would forever remain a mystery; something shameful and locked away.

Their evenings together were always the same, as a routine had been established.

First there was the warm welcome from Ginny: a kiss on her cheek, a light caress as she stepped aside so that Inga could walk up the stairs to tap on the closed studio door waiting for it to open, for the sight of his face, that slow, sweet smile. Inga would chatter mindlessly about her day: her students, news from Sweden, gossip from Betty's Bay and he would listen, working on the carving, his head tilted towards the sound of her voice.

Usually he had rested during the day, conserving his energy for the night when he always said he did his best work. In the early evenings he worked strongly, rhythmically, but the pace would slow as the hours passed. She would light candles so that long shadows flickered on the walls and unpack the hamper, setting out their meal on the table cleared of chisels, knives and mallets.

When she could see his energy flagging, she would firmly take a tool from his hands and lead him to the table to sit and rest. She would tempt him with a little soup: chicken broth or pureed vegetables. His eyes would turn to the carving and he would gesture, inviting her to comment on the work he'd done.

She would nod and murmur, "She comes alive! You have made great progress!"

She could see in his eyes how pleased he was with the statue, how proud he was of his work.

Even though she loved him and, wanted always to be completely honest with him, Inga knew she would never tell Chris how much she feared the angel.

Day by day, as he worked upon the carving, the angel did indeed seem to come alive. Her eyes were the worst! Those all-seeing, all-knowing eyes followed Inga's every move.

They pierced her heart; saw into her soul; guessed her secrets. It was impossible to hide from those eyes, no matter where she stood in the tiny studio, they found and sought her out.

The angel's arms appalled her. They were strong and sinewy, muscled like a man's limbs; they looked nothing like her own thin arms with their bony protruding wrists. The legs were rugged and muscular with well-defined calves, the legs of an athlete. *Not mine*, she thought, *nothing like my long, slender limbs, the ankles narrow, the feet well shaped and small. Whose legs are those?* The angel's wings were massive and so lifelike, each perfect feather interlinking the next that Inga felt, at any moment, they might stir and flap. The angel filled her with awe and horror. But how could she tell him that she saw something *terrifying* in the carving that had her face and hair and, unmistakeably, the body of a strapping Herculean man?

The question she wanted to ask but could not was: whose body is this? Not mine. Not yours. Is it his? The body of the man you loved once? Is this your way of remembering him? Have you created a monster with my head and his body?

At night, alone in her bed, Inga dreamed of the angel. The dreams were always the same. The carving had become human: wood made flesh. The angel's wings were beating, its mouth curled into a fiercely radiant smile. The angel carried Chris in massive arms as she soared into the sky. His was the body of a child; he looked weak, worn and defenceless. Gazing from below Inga called to him, "Don't leave me, Chris! Don't leave me!"

He seemed not to hear. The angel bore him away, their images growing smaller and less distinct as she sped them through tumultuously breaking clouds, towards Heaven.

All day Chris waited for Inga. Even when he was most engrossed in carving the statue Inga was not far from his mind.

In her presence he felt peaceful, she quieted his mind, clearing away the chaos of angry and bitter thoughts that confronted him whenever he found himself alone.

Every evening it was the same. He opened the door to her and, seeing her lovely face broken with a luminous smile, reached for her and with her arms clinging to his waist, he felt safe. As she held him all the fear and pain leaked away, leaving only stillness.

It returned once she'd gone. The anguish, all those unanswered 'why-me?' questions, his morbid fear of dying.

His mother watched them closely, covetously. He saw her hopefulness and felt pity that she should still be so innocent at her age, even after all they'd been through together.

"I know you can't be in love with Inga," she said, "but sometimes I feel you are. How can that be?"

He wanted to laugh. Wanted to tell her to grow up for Christ's sake and stop being such a romantic. How to explain such things anyway? How to tell his mother that yes, of course he loved Inga! Loved her like a dear friend, like a kindred spirit, like his own sweet sister? Loved her mightily because in her calm presence, he stopped thinking about how the disease would get him in the end, about making a pitiful mess of things when the time came. Then there was her boundless lust for life, her passion and energy and his hope that, if he kept her near, kept her close, some of that spirit might rub off and extend his own life.

All those who'd seen his carving seemed enraptured with the angel, even going so far as to bestow mythical, magical qualities upon it.

Edwina believed the angel might keep her safe and even his mother touched the wood reverently with only her fingertips.

Didn't they know that carving of the angel was nothing: a slab of wood, and nothing else?

The eyes were sightless, the wings lifeless, the feet would always be still. He admitted that while the craftsmanship of the piece was faultless – the work of a highly skilled carver – it had no spirit, no life.

Didn't they know that there was only one true guardian angel, a person of flesh and blood who had brought the unforeseen gift of love into his life when he expected it least?

Every night Ginny retreated downstairs, leaving them alone, sitting with her sewing in the darkened room, listening to their muted voices. She thought she could listen forever to Inga's lilting voice, her cadences, the trilling of graceful laughter and then Chris's: mellow, deep and slow.

She gave fervent thanks for this young woman who'd appeared like the answer to a prayer and she had such faith in Inga: faith enough to entrust her with the care of her precious son.

Ginny made a point of not invading their privacy. Once she'd taken up a tray of tea and found them together, Chris lying face forward upon the daybed, shirt removed, Inga massaging his neck and back with sweet oils.

She'd gasped aloud at the sight of her son's cruelly wasted body, his sharply defined vertebra, the arched shoulder blades. He looked like a skeleton, fleshless: a dying man.

"Oh, Lord!" she'd cried, unable to stop herself. "Oh, Lord, *look* at you!"

Inga had widened her eyes in warning and given a shake of her head.

"Tea!" she'd said brightly, masking Ginny's dismay.

They'd both glanced down but Chris had seemed oblivious, perhaps he'd been asleep? Ginny had laid the tray on the table and, tears welling, quickly slipped away.

Now she left them alone, never entering the studio without an invitation. Sometimes it was better not to know, not to see too much.

She waited each night for the voices to grow softer and finally to cease. Moments later Inga would creep down the stairs, carrying the basket. The two women would stand at the door for a few moments admiring the stars, talking of this and that. Often Ginny would reach out, touch her, "Bless you! Bless you, Inga!" They never spoke of Chris or his rapidly failing health.

Once Inga had left, the car lights disappearing around the bend, Ginny would return to the silent house and put herself to bed. In the last few moments before sleep took her she gave thanks for a young woman's infinite love and devotion that might yet cure her ailing son. This single thought, however fragile, gave comfort throughout the long night.

The next morning, the offices of Grant and Associates were consumed with the news. Jim Flint, driving home alone after two in the morning had rounded a sharp curve near the bridge over the river and lost control of his four-door silver-grey sedan, crashing into the metal guardrail. The vehicle had flown like a bird through the railing, rolling down a steep embankment and into the inky waters of the Krill.

Ejected from the vehicle, Jim Flint had lain broken on the road until four am, when the manager at the Evans' farm had stopped for a figure sprawled on the tarmac. He'd immediately called for an ambulance but by then, it was too late.

The hospital confirmed that Flint had died shortly after the accident, from massive head trauma and compound fractures in both arms and legs.

Alec, arriving late to the office after a client presentation, was the last to hear of the tragedy. He slumped at his desk, head in his hands, voices swirling around him. Tracy, the young draftswoman, was weeping. Telephones rang unanswered. Alec was conscious of a plunging sense of grief and yet, as he sat there, hunched over in shock, he wondered if the sudden, tragic death of the young architect conveyed a message of some kind?

A cup of hot, sweet tea was placed before him. A hand on his shoulder.

His secretary, sympathetic and concerned, offered tea. "Are you all right?" she asked in a low voice. "It's the shock. Drink this, you'll feel better."

He looked up at her. "I envied him! I wanted to be him! Be like him! Wanted his life. And now… *this!*"

Her face was confused. "But why? Why would you, of all people, envy the likes of Jim?" She bent closer. Dropped her voice. "He'd been drinking all night. We always said he'd go too far. It was bound to happen and now he's paid the price!"

Alec sipped scalding tea. He was right: there was a message in this tragic, unforeseen accident. A message for him. But he couldn't think straight. His brain felt numb. The message eluded him. "Christ!" he whispered. "I wanted to be Jim Flint and now he's dead!"

Chapter 8

Caron and James

I went to see Mickey at the Northwind Nursery and found it deserted.

I waited for a while, sitting on a bench in the dappled shade of leafy fruit trees, smelling the sweetness of wild gardenia climbing a trellis. The nursery appeared neglected. Falling leaves had blown into trembling heaps, plants drooped, a wheelbarrow was filled with hardening, fly-strewn compost. Rusted sheets of metal lay scattered and abandoned on the brick pathway. It was the sprawling herb garden that shocked the most. The earth was cracked from the heat; most of the herbs were dead or dying, their stems whitening, flowers fading and falling.

I noticed that the lovely white dovecot had fallen to the ground or been pushed over. The little wooden house lay in pieces, half-hidden in tall grass. Mickey arrived in her clattering old truck and saw me picking up fragments of wood. "He's been here!" she said, and led me to where an ancient, heavy Grecian urn lay cracked and broken, pitched off a wide stone pedestal. "That's his work too!"

"Who?" I asked, although I knew full well.

"Jordan Black, who else? He's trying to frighten me." I suggested Mickey come and stay with me for a few weeks. "Get away from here! Let me take care of you." She gazed blankly. "I have work to do," she said, dismissively.

I left then and when I turned at the gate I saw that Mickey was standing quite still, looking down at where the dovecot lay shattered in the grass, her face a mask of misery.

Caron sat on the veranda with James listening to the birds in the garden and wondering about her husband's invitation to dinner that evening. She'd been standing at the kitchen window when Alec came down. He was dressed for work, his briefcase under one arm, his jacket in the other.

"Caron, we need to talk!" he'd blurted. "We've got to find some way to work things out."

She hadn't dared to hope. They'd had this conversation many times before, without any kind of resolution.

He touched her arm. "I've got a few moments," he'd said. "Let's go outside, sit on the veranda?"

She had made a tray of tea and poured him a cup.

Avoiding his eyes, she'd leaned against the blue floral cushions, gazing at the violets growing at the edge of the garden path. He'd moved closer to her, his body turned to face her, his expression serious and intense.

"I've been thinking," he said. "About us. James. The baby…"

"Yes?"

"We need to get back on track, if we can. Make an effort to get along, if only for James' sake."

She wondered about the baby. Was such an effort to be made for the new baby too?

"James is coming down the stairs," she warned. She could hear his small, flat feet scuffing the carpeting.

"So?"

"He listens. Surely you know? I don't want him to hear anything upsetting."

"What about going out, then? Tonight, just the two of us? Dinner at the Italian place? We'll be able to talk without interruption." Caron kept her voice light. "I'd like that!" she'd said. "We haven't been out for such a long time."

Alec had picked up her cue. "I'll make a reservation for seven thirty. Will you organise a sitter for James?"

James had slipped and fallen against the door. "Hello, James!" Alec had said, as his son emerged looking sleepy and guilty.

Caron could see that the hopefulness she'd suppressed was alive in James' expression. His eyes moved hungrily from Caron to Alec and back again. He seemed to be measuring the distance they sat apart.

"Give me a hug!" said Alec and her heart broke to see the way James flung himself into his father's arms; burrowing against his crisply pressed shirt, his designer silk tie. Alec laughed. James looked up and gave his toothy grin. *If only*, she thought, *it was always like this. If only we were a happy, normal family.*

Once Alec had left for work, she suggested changing the usual routine and taking a walk to the village where they might have a breakfast together. Pancakes and syrup at The Rambling Rose, she'd said, thinking the idea might please him. His face serious, he refused pancakes and asked instead for a three-minute boiled egg and toast.

This was either James' way of controlling things or he really was a little old man in the body of a nine-year-old boy!

James coughed, spilling tea down the front of his pyjamas and splashing it onto the newly laundered blue cushions. She bit back a retort and turned her attention instead to the tiny brown birds balancing precariously on the edge of the birdbath, rocking up and down in unison. A starling burst into song.

The dog next door was making a racket and then, without warning, she felt a stab of unbearable pain.

"Ow!" she cried. "Oh, that hurts!"

James' eyes raked her face. "What's wrong?

"I've got a a tummy ache," she replied calmly. "Stay here James, I won't be a moment."

As she walked upstairs to the bathroom, the pain stabbed again and again.

She bent double, shocked and breathless. Liquid streamed between her legs and dribbled, sticky and warm, down her thighs. Hurrying into the bathroom she saw drops falling, staining the floor. She locked the door, lifted her dressing gown. Blood stained her legs, pooled on the bathroom tiles. *Oh*, she thought, dully. *This is what happens! This is how it ends. I'm going to lose this baby!*

She felt another cramp coming and before she doubled over she clenched her thumb between her teeth to stop from screaming and frightening James.

James wandered over to the birdbath for a better view but the birds flew away at his approach. He spotted an ants' nest and crouched on the wet grass to study it.

There were at least a zillion ants and they all seemed to be in a hurry: scurrying this way and that. Some carried tiny white grains into the nest, probably to feed the queen ant. A black ant crawled upon his hand and he bent closer. Three body parts, six legs, two tiny waving antennae. Imagine if the ant were huge! Say as big as a dog! Imagine it marching up with that sharp, jagged mouth, opening and closing, antennae wagging wildly in that creepy way…

"Hello, James! What are you doing?"

James looked up, squinting in the sunlight. Sarah peered down from above.

"Ants!" he mumbled. "I'm studying this nest. It's very interesting."

"Your pyjamas are sopping wet!"

"I don't mind."

"Where's Caron?"

He shrugged and lifted his hand to his face as the ant marched steadily across a finger. He held out the finger to show her. "This is a worker ant," he explained. "There are also scouts; they look out for enemies. And inside, down there, is the queen ant. She lays the eggs."

"Have you had breakfast?"

"I'm going to have a boiled egg." The ant tumbled from his finger. James bent to search for it, scrabbling in the wet grass.

"James, look, you're getting muddy: you know how you hate being wet or dirty! Let's go and find Caron."

James' face loomed inches above the ants' nest. "They're small," he acknowledged. "But they're *much* stronger than they look. They can carry stuff that weighs twenty times more than they do!"

Sarah held out her hand. Her face, framed by the sunlight, was dark. He couldn't see her eyes or mouth. He shivered and looked down again. The ants swirled before his eyes. "Ants are very clever," he continued. "They have the biggest brains in the insect family. That's why they can build such awesome nests."

He mumbled indistinctly, digging in the damp soil.

The front door was wide open. Sarah knocked. "Caron? Anyone home?"

There was a tray of tea on the veranda. She picked it up and took it through to the empty kitchen. Everything was spotless. Where was she? Alec had left for work earlier: she'd seen the car speeding away. Sarah stood at the bottom of the stairs and called "Caron!" The bathroom door opened a crack. "In here!"

Sarah dashed up the stairs; pushed open the door. The floor was spattered with blood, Caron's dressing gown stained with red splotches. Sarah felt ill: there was such a lot of blood, the hot, sickly smell of it everywhere!

"I'm having a miscarriage," Caron said in a small voice. Her face was grey. "I've lost my baby, I think."

"Oh, no! Who's your doctor? Grace Frey? Shall I call her?"

"I need to get to the hospital. But what about James?"

"Your husband. I'll call him!"

"Please don't. He has an important client meeting. Can you call an ambulance for me and take care of James?"

"God, Caron! This is St Jude! An ambulance could take forever! I'll take you to the hospital. James can come with us."

"I don't want him to see me like this!"

Sarah took a deep breath. "Caron, can you change your clothes? Have you any sanitary pads? I'll get James into the car. We need to leave as quickly as possible. Before it's too late!"

Caron clutched her stomach and moaned in pain.

"Let me help you," Sarah reached over and began to untie the bloodied gown.

Caron pushed her away gently. "I can do it. Wait for me in the car with James, please. Think of something to say to him. I don't want him frightened."

Sarah called Grace who met them at the hospital. Caron was wheeled into a cubicle. Sarah and James sat on chilly, green leather seats, in the hospital reception. She gave him a child's book to read and paged listlessly through tattered farming magazines.

Behind the cubicle curtains, Grace gently pressed Caron's abdomen. "How long have you been pregnant?" Her voice registered surprise.

"Fourteen weeks. I'm losing the baby, aren't I?"

"You might be. Cramping and blood loss are a sign that your womb is contracting," said Grace. Grave-faced, she gave Caron a pelvic examination.

The doctor's expression told Caron everything she needed to know. "Your cervix is open. You may have already passed the foetal tissue. Did you notice any clotting?"

"Yes, I saw clots."

"I'm sorry, Caron. You're having what we call an 'inevitable' miscarriage."

Caron looked away. "*Inevitable*!" She gave a hollow laugh. "That's apt! An inevitable miscarriage. I wasn't meant to have this baby after all!"

Grace took her hand. "You can always try again," she said comfortingly. "You've conceived once, which means it can happen again. When you've recovered from this loss, there's nothing to say that..."

"No!" Caron's voice echoed in the small room. "Nobody wanted this baby but me. And even I considered having an abortion! It's so ironic that my body has decided the baby's fate. Alec will be relieved. James, too. I'm the only one who will grieve."

Grace walked beside the gurney to the operating theatre, her heels clattering on vinyl. She spoke in a low whisper to a nurse about a patient who, hours before, had delivered a baby boy. Seeing Caron's haunted eyes she motioned to the nurse to be quiet. "Sorry!" she mouthed.

"Right, Doctor Frey, we'll take Mrs Grant off your hands now." One of the surgical nurses dressed in bright green and wearing a mask, dragged the gurney through the operating room swing-doors.

Grace bent over Caron.

"I'll see you later," she said, pressing her hand warmly. "Has anyone called your husband?"

A solitary tear escaped and slowly rolled down Caron's cheek.

Sarah called Alec at work. "I'm sorry," his secretary said, "Mr Grant is in a meeting. May I give him a message?"

"No. I must speak to him. It's extremely urgent. It's about his wife!"

After a brief pause the secretary put the call through to the boardroom.

"Caron is at St Jude's Hospital," Sarah said. "She's had a miscarriage. She's in surgery now."

She heard an audible intake of breath and then silence.

"Alec?"

"Christ!" He seemed unable to speak.

"You should be at the hospital with her."

"I'll come immediately. Where's James?"

"He's with me. I'll take care of him until you're ready to take him home."

"How is he? Is he all right?"

Sarah's voice was sharper than she intended. "James is fine, Alec! It's Caron you should be worried about."

"I am. I'm on my way. Thanks for letting me know." She heard him replace the receiver.

James stared at her. She knelt and pulled him close. His body felt as stiff as a board, unbending. His hands hung at his sides. His face was white and pinched.

"James, Caron is going to stay here, at the hospital, for a while. Dad will come later to fetch her and bring her home. We're going to spend the day together, OK? We'll go to the gallery. You can paint or make clay figures. Or help me sort books. There's lots to keep us both very busy!"

James blinked behind smeared glasses. "What's wrong with Caron?"

"She's not well, James. But the doctors at the hospital are taking care of her and she'll be home soon."

"But what's *wrong* with her?"

James had seen too much. He had trailed sadly, helplessly behind Caron who had taken that slow, stumbling, painful walk down the long hospital corridor to the waiting wheelchair. He'd heard her muffled groans and seen dark smears of blood on her shoes. What could she say to him? How should she explain what had happened? It had been a mistake to bring him to the hospital and subject him to all this. She should have found someone to care for him but it had all happened so quickly that there'd been no time to think.

And now, all these questions! For one blinding moment, she *hated* the Grants. Hated them for their miserable, dysfunctional and utterly un-private lives! Hated them for always dragging her into intimate and emotional situations where she was made to feel guilty, uncomfortable and out of place. Why couldn't they sort out their own messes? Why was she always the one left trying to explain things to James? Surely they didn't expect a neighbour to tell a little boy his stepmother had had a miscarriage? And where in heaven's name was that *insufferable* Alec, too busy to be interrupted, even when his wife had been taken to hospital!

Sarah shepherded James firmly away from the hushed waiting room towards the hospital swing doors. "Caron and Dad will explain everything later, James. We're off to the gallery. We'll stop on the way to change your clothes and collect Lucky. He'll be wondering where we are."

James looked desolate. He walked silently beside her in his still damp, muddy pyjamas. She took his hand. It felt incredibly small in hers.

"Is it my fault?" he asked tearfully. "Did I do something bad?"

Mickey was spying on Jordan Black. He was working at a house at Seal's Landing, overlooking the sea. A dilapidated wooden fence surrounding the house had been torn down and broken, splintered strips tossed willy-nilly onto a neighbour's verge. Black and two other men were digging a trench around the house in readiness for the erection of a high brick wall. Mickey concealed her truck behind a copse of trees and clambered down a steep cliff to where a narrow, winding fisherman's path curved below the rocks, in front of the house.

From her hiding place, she could see where Black was working. Shovel loads of earth were flung high into the air as the men dug the foundations for the new wall.

She heard Black shouting orders: his voice louder than the others, bullying them into working harder, faster. She heard spades striking rock, sharp metal ringing on stone. An articulated truck delivered pallets of red bricks. Another dropped off a load of sand and bags of cement.

Huddled between two enormous rocks, Mickey kept the house in her line of vision. She wondered whose house it was? It seemed to be shut-up: curtains half-drawn, doors and windows barred. Probably a holiday home, perhaps she might find out who the owners were and call them.

"I feel the need to warn you," she would say. "Jordan Black, the man working on your house is a known criminal. A thief. A rapist. A drunkard. He has a malicious heart. You can't trust him – he'll trick and steal from you. And, if he can harm you in other ways, he will. Is it wise to have such a vile man working on your property?"

Black gave a sudden shout of raucous laughter. The others joined in. Mickey clenched her jaw tightly, grinding her teeth with loathing.

If only he would die now, as she spied on him, killed by a fatal blow. She grimly considered the possibilities: a heart attack, a stroke, a bolt of lightening! A tower of bricks falling and crushing him to a bloody pulp? A tsunami? An earthquake?

"Die," she whispered, "die why don't you?" Perhaps her hatred would consume him?

Lately she had taken to dreaming of Black. The dreams were horrifying: each one the same. She had killed him and was struggling to dispose of his blood-soaked body. She dragged him this way and then that, looking for a grave, but as she tugged, parts of his body came off in her hands: a hairy arm, a leg, a severed hand. Once his shaved head had separated from his thick neck. She held it like a wet cabbage in both hands. She always woke from these dreams whimpering like a terrified child.

Recently there were times when she wondered if she were going mad. When her thoughts became a jumble, a rushing, whirling noise in her brain, voices in her ears, the chaos making her so nauseated she thought she might vomit. Sometimes she thought of herself as someone else. Poor little Mickey Graham who seemed so lost and alone. Poor little Mickey Graham who was nothing more than a tiny speck floating in the universe, whose life, really, was meaningless. Poor Mickey Graham …

But then she'd stop herself. *That's not me*, she'd tell herself. *I'm not lost, my life is not meaningless. I am a woman with a purpose.* She couldn't remember exactly when she'd made up her mind and decided exactly what her purpose would be. There had been a time, a few days perhaps, when she might, with brute strength, have pulled herself back into her old life, her Christian life, and turned away from what she could quite plainly see was a path leading headlong into destruction.

But the moment had come and gone and now, here she was, spying on her enemy and plotting revenge.

Alec paced the hospital waiting room until a nurse called him. He followed her, striding down antiseptic-smelling corridors to a ward where he found Caron alone in a narrow bed behind a blue screen. She'd been propped against a bank of pillows and given something hot and sweet to drink. Her clothes lay neatly folded at the end of the bed.

"We're waiting for Dr Frey," the nurse said. "Once she's given the all-clear, Mrs Grant can go home."

She left them together and when he could no longer hear the squeaking of the nurse's efficient rubber-soles. Alec took Caron in his arms. "I'm sorry, darling," he said gently. "I'm so sorry!"

Grace found them together; Caron weeping in her husband's arms, his face filled with sorrow.

"She's had a tremendous shock," Grace said to Alec. "She'll need time to get over this. There'll be a period of sadness, grief and depression. You'll need to be supportive and caring and work through this bereavement together."

"Of course."

"You'll have to explain what's happened to James,"

"What does James know? What did he see?"

"He was here, at the hospital with Caron. He won't know exactly what's happened, but he'll be frightened and confused. Don't hide anything from him. Talk about the miscarriage naturally and as simply as possible so that he understands."

Alec bit his lip. "This isn't going to be easy."

"It's not going to be easy for any of you," admitted Grace. "You'll probably also go through a period of mourning. It will take time for the whole family to come to terms with what's happened."

Caron blew her nose and dabbed at her eyes. She looked exhausted.

"Come and see me next week," suggested Grace. "And don't hesitate to call if you need me. I'll leave you to get dressed." With a quick smile the doctor left the room.

They stared at one another. Her lips trembled. "We won't talk about this, will we?" she said. "We'll pretend it never happened and go on with our lives, such as they are."

"Caron, of course we'll talk about it. We must."

"Oh, Alec. You sound so sanctimonious! You're not going to pretend you're unhappy at my losing the baby, are you?"

"Caron, I..."

"Doctor Frey might think you're going to go through a period of mourning, but we both know I'm the only one who will mourn the loss of our baby."

"Look, I'm desperately sad that you've had to go through this. It's the last thing I wanted to happen."

"That's not true. Don't you remember what you said?"

"I was angry, I said some things I didn't mean."

"What were you going to say to me tonight, Alec? Over dinner at the restaurant?"

"I told you. I don't want to go on like this. I want us to work together to try and save our marriage. There are ..."

"Were you going to insist on my having an abortion?"

His expression was anguished. "No! You probably won't believe me now, after this, but I could see how much you wanted this child. I was prepared to do my best to accept the baby, to be a good father."

"I wish I could believe that."

"You can! It's true. I swear."

She could not look at him. She reached over and picked up her blouse.

"I'll never know, will I, Alec? I'll never know the truth now."

He handed her the pleated skirt. He bent to pick up her shoes. They were spattered with dried blood.

"I don't know what to say, Caron."

"You never do." She zipped up the skirt and slipped her feet into her shoes. "I don't want to speak of this any more," she said.

He held out his hand. "Caron, please!"

She turned away and began the long, slow walk back along the antiseptic corridors.

He walked beside her, his hand pressed into the small of her back. The nurses waved goodbye. *What now*? he thought, a stone in his chest. *What do we do now?*

It was Ginny who took care of James that day. Ginny who, once Sarah had quietly explained what had happened, took James and led him to the café where she asked him to help her make breakfast.

"You must be starving! What about a boiled egg and toast with honey?"

James looked up, wide-eyed and silent. She gave him a fistful of cutlery and asked him to set the table. "Come back for egg cups and plates," she instructed and pushed him gently in the direction of the table.

Very slowly, James laid out the silver. Ginny handed plates and mugs. "Tea?" she asked. "Cocoa? Or milk?"

He shrugged listlessly.

Once the egg and toast were placed before him, James stared blankly at the food until Ginny cracked open his egg, cut the toast into tiny pieces and fed him as she might a small toddler. "Open wide, that's a good boy."

"I don't need to be fed," he said. "I'm nearly ten!" She handed him the spoon.

He ate mechanically, swallowing with difficulty. Milk spilled onto the floor where Lucky, lying beneath the table, licked it up.

"Caron's in hospital," he said, gravely. "I don't know what's wrong with her. I don't know when she's coming home."

"She'll be home this evening, I should think," said Ginny, matter-of-factly. "Your Mom and Dad will explain everything to you, I'm sure."

"Caron's not my Mom!"

"Well," Ginny said, diplomatically. "She's your step-mother..."

"It's not the *same!*" He sounded desperate.

Ginny cleared away the plates and, taking James' hand, led him to the tiny studio adjacent to the gallery, where she and Chris gave art and pottery lessons.

She helped James onto the high wooden bench and handed a lump of damp clay. "We're going to make a zoo!" she announced gaily. "I'll begin with a lion or two. Perhaps some baby cubs. What animal would you like to make?"

He miserably fingered the clay.

"A bear?" she suggested kindly. "A big, brown bear! Shall I help you?"

He nodded. Ginny tore off a piece and quickly, deftly, shaped a bear.

She chatted mindlessly as she worked, bracelets jingling. "Bears, as far as I can remember, have big, fat, cuddly bodies. The head is rather sweet with a tiny snubbed nose, long snout, round furry ears. They look rather like this, do you see? A bear's paws are huge. All the better for holding honey jars!"

"No!" James shouted.

Ginny jumped. "What's the matter?"

"Bears are nothing like that! You've made Winnie the Pooh! Proper bears don't eat honey from jars! They have powerful claws! They use them to climb trees and rip open beehives. That's where they get their honey!"

"I see." Ginny humoured him. "Tell me more."

"Well, bears aren't cuddly! They're dangerous. Some bears, like grizzly bears, can *eat* you!" He bared his teeth at her. "They have awesome teeth; sharp and pointed!"

Ginny laughed. "Well, since you know so much about bears," she said, "why don't you give me a big bear hug?"

By the end of the afternoon, Ginny and James had created an entire zoo. Some of the animals were misshapen and wobbly, others perfectly scaled miniatures of the real thing. Sarah was called to admire their work.

Flushed with excitement, James knelt on the bench, looking down at the tiny clay figures. His eyes behind his glasses shone with excitement. "This one is mine! That one is Ginny's!"

"Very good! Very lifelike!"

"Ginny's are better," he pronounced generously. "But I like my animals too – even if they are a bit lumpy."

"They're all wonderful!" admired Sarah.

"I'll fire them," said Ginny. "And once they're dry, we can glaze and paint them.

"Can you come again next week, James?"

"Cool!"

Sarah tapped at her watch. "Time to go home. You can stay with me until Caron and your dad return from the hospital."

Instantly, James stiffened. The light drained from his face. He tugged at Ginny's skirt. "Can't I stay here?" he whispered. "I like it here. I don't want to go home."

Ginny and Sarah exchanged glances.

He stood head hanging, shifting from one foot to the other. Ginny kissed the top of his head. "You can't stay here," she explained. "You've a home to go to and parents who love you."

Sarah manoeuvred James towards the door. Lucky, at his side, tail beating, nuzzled affectionately with a wet nose. The door banged behind them. James dragged his feet until they reached the car. Sarah helped him into the passenger seat and locked the safety belt.

Lucky sprang into the back, head through the open window, tongue lolling. They drove slowly home. Long shadows fell upon the grass. The sun was setting; the clouds tipped with scarlet, the sky lightening from blue to washed grey.

James, head averted, seemed close to tears. Sarah tried to distract him. "Look at the sunset, James! Those blazing clouds!"

He sniffed and swallowed.

"And see, that flock of birds flying up there? They're heading for those tall trees, seeking for shelter for the night."

"I don't want to go home," he said, plaintively. "Please don't make me."

Sarah's heart sank. Turning the corner she saw lights burning in the Grant's house, Alec's car in the driveway. She breathed a sigh of relief.

"It will be all right, James," she said. "Everything will be all right. You'll see."

But her words sounded hollow even to her own ears.

Alec's face at the door was drawn and strained. "We always seem to be in your debt," he said. "Frankly, I don't know what would have happened this morning, if you hadn't been there to help. We're immensely grateful to you, I hope you know that?"

"It's the least I could do. Is Caron all right?"

He pulled a face, gave a shrug. "As well as can be expected, I suppose. She's had a shock. It will take some time to recover."

Sarah gave James a little push towards his father. "Bye, James!" she said with as cheerful a voice as she could muster. "I'll pick you up next week so that you and Ginny can paint the animals in your zoo, OK?"

Before she turned away, Sarah watched Alec kneel to face James.

"Bad day, Jamie?" he whispered. James nodded solemnly. Alec pressed him close. "Don't worry, my boy," he said. "You're home now!"

Chapter 9

Mickey and Edwina

My latest book was done at last; published in hardcover and ready for shipping to bookstores. A book tour called me away from St Jude and I was caught up in the usual breathless whirlwind: racing from bookshop to radio station to my hotel for hasty interviews with journalists from local newspapers and magazines.

I was provided with a charming media escort with the unlikely name of Samara Starr who whisked me swiftly from one rushed engagement to the next so that I wouldn't get lost, or stuck in traffic, or run over time. Ms Starr, as the name suggested, glittered from her star-spangled eye shadow to her gleaming lips and drenched herself in so much expensive French perfume that there was always a prickly updraft of it in my nostrils. At one of the book signings, a disgruntled woman in a hat like an upturned bucket informed me that she had loathed my previous books but was "giving this one a chance." At a loss for words, I opened and closed my mouth like a goldfish but Tamara swooped to my rescue, snatching the book from her hand. "Don't do us any favours!" she snapped.

I was relieved, at the end of it all, to pack my good black suit and make my way home to St Jude where I am simply Rachael Wood, the ageing spinster who occupies the house on the corner of Mussel Street. Admittedly, there are a few in the village who read my books and are always keen to draw grammatical or factual errors to my attention. I suppose I might have one or two fans in the community but generally people know very little about who I am or what I do. This book might change all that, though. This book may well transform me from one perceived as faceless and unfathomable to a minor celebrity; at least in St Jude, where I imagine everyone will have an opinion and point of view about the content. We all have our own ideas of what happened that summer; this is what I know to be true.

Ben emptied Folly's ashes into a deep, square, silver cigarette box bearing the monogram 'RB' written in an elegant script. The box had belonged to his grandfather, Reginald Barker and, because it had sentimental value, Ben had toyed guiltily with the idea of giving it to Mickey. A cherished relic from the past, the cigarette box had been displayed on his crowded mantle for years. He squared his conscience with the fact that, since most of the Barker family were dead and gone, he was probably the only one who might feel the loss of it.

Ben had taken down the box that morning. He'd wiped away a fine coating of dust and polished it until it gleamed and caught the light. When he opened the lid he could still smell, after all these years, a faint aroma of very strong Turkish tobacco.

The dog had weighed very little: there was barely a tablespoon of powdery white ash, like fine sand, clotted with tiny bone fragments. He'd waited for the right time to bring the ashes to Mickey. Waited for her to regain composure; she would still be sad and grieving, depressed perhaps, but surely less emotional and overwrought by now?

Ben had a slightly creased Polaroid snapshot of a puppy in his jacket pocket, a scrap of a thing; one of a litter born seven weeks ago. All but this pup had found good homes. "Don't sell it," he had begged the owner. "I know of someone..."

He planned to show Mickey the photograph of the female pup. Surely she would lose her heart to this dog, how could she not? A Spaniel – liver and white, with a sturdy body, high domed head, long feathery ears and beautiful almond-shaped eyes.

Ben liked Spaniels. They were good dogs: intelligent, affectionate, obedient and loyal. The dog would make the perfect companion for Mickey. Take her mind off things, give her something to love and care for.

He drove carefully, the square silver box resting on his lap, avoiding potholes in the road. The sky was pewter shot through with purple, the sun as white as the moon. Perhaps it might rain later? There were acres of waving green fields to the left and right and, just ahead, the Evans' dairy farm where once he had stopped to give Ginny a lift on a cold and windy day. She'd made little or no impression that first time: indistinguishable from the dozens of tired women who came daily to his practice with a sick dog, a cat in a basket, or a bird in a cage. He'd recalled one thing, though. That thick, wiry plait of red hair and the way she had carelessly tossed it over her shoulder so that it had slapped against her back like coiled rope.

Since his visit to the gallery, Ginny had been on his mind: he could hardly stop thinking of her. He ran and re-ran the images over and over again. Saw her threading her arm through his, leading him into that long, dim room with paintings on the walls. Saw her laughing, her whole face alight. Remembered wanting to reach out and touch her slippery, rippling red hair, wanting to plunge his hands into its coolness. The way her silver bracelets cascaded like water. The way she'd glanced at him, lowering her eyes, blushing like a girl. He'd been unable to take his eyes from her, staring openly, captivated by her slight, shapely body, graceful arms and slender brown feet; the way she darted through the rooms, quick as a hummingbird.

There had been something there, something between them. He knew they'd both felt it. An immediate attraction, a pleasurable frisson, a *charge!*

It wasn't so very long ago he'd felt himself falling in love with Sarah but that had all been one-sided. Sarah had made it plain she saw him only as a friend and, from that time, had been at pains to distance herself. She'd built a wall between them; the relationship felt strained, less easy than before. At first he'd been wounded but what was the point of hurt pride if his feelings weren't reciprocated? He was learning to accept that he and Sarah would be as she said: "just good friends" – nothing more.

Ginny was different! Whatever it was that had passed fleetingly between them had felt like a miracle; a second chance for a man not yet passed his prime.

Why was it, then, that he had not contacted her since the day she'd given him a tour of the gallery? Once or twice he'd picked up the telephone, dialled the number, listened to the ringing and then, heart in his mouth, swiftly replaced the receiver. Had Sarah's rebuff destroyed his confidence? Was it getting older that made this kind of thing so hard? Had he lost his nerve? Why did he wonder, holding the phone to his ear, whether he'd completely misread the situation and seen something that wasn't there? Wasn't it possible that Ginny Lourens, co-owner of The Two Potters, felt nothing more for him than she did for any of those customers who received similarly delightful guided tours of the gallery? Imagine how foolish he'd feel inviting Ginny to dinner, say, or a walk on the beach and being met by a response of wide-eyed surprise, amusement, or, worst of all, *pity?*

When Ben pulled up outside the Northwind Nursery, Mickey was leaving the house.

She stopped and waited for him. He was shocked to see how thin she was, how wasted. There were bruised shadows beneath her eyes and she seemed to have hacked at her hair with something blunt.

"You're not well!" he exclaimed.

"Do you have something for me?" Her eyes had found the silver box.

"Folly's ashes."

"I've been waiting for them." She held out her hands.

"What will you do with them?"

"Keep them close."

She took the box from him, thoughtfully running a finger over the delicately intertwined letters. "RB?"

"My grandfather. Reginald Barker. It's his old cigarette box. I thought it might do for Folly's ashes."

"Don't you want it back?"

"You keep it."

"It's perfect," she breathed. "I will take very good care of it."

"How've you been?"

She shrugged, hugging the box to her chest. "As you see me."

"You've seen a doctor? Got some help?"

"I've seen a doctor. Who can help me? I must help myself."

There seemed nothing more to say. He fumbled in his jacket pocket and pulled out the photograph of the puppy.

"Look," he said, uncomfortably. "It may be too soon. I don't know. There's a puppy. A little female."

"No, thank you."

He thrust the photograph at her. "Don't be too hasty. Take the Polaroid. Think about it. She's a Spaniel. Eight weeks. Needs a good home. Let me know."

Mickey took the photograph and gave it a cursory glance. "Sorry!" she said. "I have something that I must do. I've got to keep focused. A puppy has no place in my life now."

He took a step closer, opened his mouth to object. She stopped him with a fierce stare. "Thank you, Mr Barker. Thank you for Folly's ashes and for the precious silver box. You've been very kind. I can't take the puppy. I hope you understand."

Mickey strode towards the truck, opened the door and climbed in. She settled Folly's ashes on her lap. He saw a white face at the window, a puff of black smoke from the exhaust, and then she was gone.

Edwina, fresh from her bath and wearing only a towel, wiped the steam from the mirror so that she could see herself more clearly. Taking a deep breath, she stepped closer, removing the towel so that it fell on the floor at her feet.

She gazed at her reflection.

"What do you think?" she asked the face in the mirror. "Am I insane or is the tumour smaller?"

The face in the mirror raised two sharply plucked eyebrows. The steam had made her hair frizz about her face, softening her countenance. Her complexion was still very good: a little washed out, perhaps, but that was to be expected. The weight loss suited, she thought. It firmed her jaw and honed her cheekbones so that they jutted rather elegantly. Her neck was ravaged and there was, sadly, nothing to be done about that other than conceal the crepe with flowing silken scarves. It was her body, however, that had betrayed her. All that thin, spotted, bruised, ageing skin hanging off her frame and the red tumour between her breasts. Such an ugly deformity: it made her freakish, grotesque, like something in a circus: '*The Woman with Three Breasts!*'

She placed the palm of her right hand over the growth. She enclosed it easily.

In the beginning, months ago, when she had forced herself to touch the tumour it had been akin to holding a throbbing grapefruit. Now the growth curved neatly into her palm, the size of a small orange and, while the tumour appeared distinctly enflamed, it no longer pulsed with angry heat.

"Smaller!" she whispered victoriously to the reflection. "Definitely smaller."

The mirror image smiled. The lips, without the usual brilliantly red gloss, looked vulnerable, thinner: the eyes showed naked hopefulness.

She leaned closer, the reflection growing larger. "It's shrinking," she confirmed. "Daily, it diminishes. A miracle is taking place, I'm sure of it. A *miracle!*"

She heard, annoyingly, a gentle, persistent tapping at the door.

"Edwina? Darling?"

She held her breath. *Oh, go away, Thomas. Go away!*

"Edwina? Are you all right?"

She barked from behind the locked door. "Why shouldn't I be?"

"You've been in there for such a long time. An hour or more."

Tightening her lips, Edwina hastily draped herself with the towel and opened the door a crack. "I've been soaking. A delicious bubble bath: a small indulgence. Do you object?"

His chins wobbled nervously at signs of her obvious displeasure. "No, of course not. Forgive me. Just an old worry-wart!" He struggled to turn the wheelchair.

She took pity. "Oh, come in then!" She opened the door wide.

"You're sure?" He looked happy, his vague eyes alight with pleasure.

"Yes!" she said, impulsively. "I want to show you something."

He manoeuvred the chair into the lightly steaming bathroom and smiled expectantly.

"My tumour," she said, dropping her voice a little. "I want to show you my tumour."

His face fell. His hands fluttered like anxious moths.

"Oh, dear!" he said miserably. "I'd rather not see. Don't show me. Please don't show me."

Edwina sat on the edge of the bath and buried her long, thin feet in the soft cream bath mat. Her eyes flashed. "Don't be silly!" she said, scathingly. "You don't understand, Thomas! The tumour is shrinking! It's smaller. That's why I want to show you."

"But..."

"My tumour was once the size of a large grapefruit. Now it has become a small orange. A Valencia! A Satsuma!" She pondered. "No! A Blood Orange!"

"A what?"

"A Blood Orange. You slice into a heart of deepest maroon."

"I don't understand? Your tumour is maroon?"

"God, you are irritating! Listen to what I'm saying and try not to be so obtuse!"

His face crumpled like a chastened child.

"I have spoken to Grace about this. I have informed her the tumour is smaller. She doesn't believe me, though she's seen the evidence with her own eyes. Doctors! They're all alike. They'll never admit that the body might heal itself without medical intervention. That miracles do happen!"

Thomas nodded doubtfully. "A miracle?"

Edwina dramatically lowered the bath towel and leaned forward. "Look, Thomas!"

He blanched with sudden shock. He flinched. Unthinking, he gasped. He lifted his trembling hands and covered his eyes. "Oh God," he whimpered.

Edwina covered herself again. She found she was shivering, suddenly cold. "You don't understand, Thomas! I am being *healed!*"

He gave a smothered sob. His shoulders heaved. His head drooped, exposing a scraping of thin white hair over a tender, pink scalp.

Edwina took his hands, drawing them away from his eyes. He blinked through tears. "If I'd known you were going to be such a baby, I would never have shown you."

"I had no idea!" he cried. "That monstrous growth. You've been so brave. I feel ashamed."

Edwina knotted the towel above her breasts. "You're being idiotic and sentimental. I wish I hadn't said anything. You've missed the point. I'm being healed, Thomas. I'm not going to die. A miracle is taking place. More cause for joy, I imagine, than tears?"

His eyes swam. "Poor you," he muttered. "I had no idea."

A long silence followed.

Edwina took a deep breath and flung open the bathroom door. She flapped her hands. "Off you go, Thomas. I must get dressed. Tell cook to organise breakfast on the deck, will you? I shall be down in half an hour."

He fumbled with the brake of the chair and looked up sorrowfully. "Is there anything special you'd like for breakfast?"

Edwina gave the wheelchair a push.

"Chilled fruit perhaps? Why don't you see if you can lay your hands on a couple of Blood Oranges?"

He turned, unsure, lips stretched into a sadly wavering smile as Edwina banged the door.

Mickey concealed the truck in the shade beneath the line of trees at Seal's Landing.

She opened the silver box and touched Folly's ashes with the tips of her fingers.

She'd thought the ash would be grey, like the dull ashes from a wood fire, but they were alabaster white, like finest beach sand, speckled with bits of bone.

She closed the box and pressed it to her heart. Tonight, at home, she would carefully place a delicate nail tip of the ashes into the silver locket. She would wear the locket about her neck and never take it off. They would be together forever.

The time before Folly's death seemed like another lifetime. She'd been a different person then. Life had been simpler. She'd had problems, of course, but nothing like those she now faced. How glad she was that Folly was not here to see how she'd changed. How she'd become this calculating, vengeful person who spent every waking hour spying upon Jordan Black and whose nightmares were coloured with brutal images.

Folly, gentle spirit, had anchored her life with goodness. Caring for him had made her kinder. Now that Folly had gone, now that God had abandoned her, Mickey knew she had grown hard, bitter and angry; the kind of person she'd once have feared.

She'd found herself turning away the kindness and generosity of others. From Rachael Wood who'd offered a sanctuary in her home. From Ben Barker who'd given a valuable silver box and offered her a puppy. Only yesterday, Edwina had telephoned and asked for her help in laying out a kitchen herb garden at Hurley House.

"A Knott Garden," Edwina had said in her haughty voice. "Do you know the term?"

How condescending she could be, Mickey had thought, *perhaps it was having all that money, all that breeding, perhaps that's what made you behave as though you were the Queen of England.*

"It's an intricate, formal herb garden," Mickey had replied. "Designed to resemble a classical tile."

"Very clever!" Edwina had applauded. "Right up your street, I thought! It comes, of course, with a generous budget."

For a few moments, Mickey had been tempted. Once she'd have given God all the credit for the Knott Garden and even though she now knew better, she also knew that working on the garden would be one way to restore some kind of normality to her life. She'd be spending time at Hurley House again. There would be a routine to shape her days and nights. The project might last for several weeks. A generous budget would give her the means to finally repair the roof, and the staircase.

She'd imagined laying out a perfectly rectangular space defined by low hedges of rosemary and thyme. She would create the design's symmetrical curves and scrolls with lemon verbena, fennel, marjoram and mint.

She would fill the spaces between with small white pebbles. There would be narrow brick paths dividing the beds. She would sew the beds with white begonias and erigeron…

"I'm sorry," she'd said. "I have my hands full. Another time, perhaps?"

She'd put Edwina's offer out of her mind; she had no time to think about gardens, herb or otherwise.

Mickey quietly locked the truck and crept noiselessly over the sand towards the rocks. She planned to clamber, unseen, to her hiding place where she would spend the day secretly observing Black and his team at work on the garden wall.

The men had not yet arrived. The site was deserted. Shovels and picks leaned against the walls. One of the builders had left heavy mud-caked boots and a torn sweater on the scuffed wooden steps leading to the veranda.

Mickey climbed the stairs. The veranda was wide and shady, littered with old pieces of furniture. A wooden rocking chair; bleached by wind and sun; two faded teak recliners and, between them, a flat wicker basket filled with sandy shells. There was also a lobster pot; a winding coil of boat ropes; a string hammock, grey with dust and an empty pagoda birdcage swaying from the rafters.

On impulse Mickey lowered herself into the fragile chair. She leaned back, rocking, gazing out at a small sandy cove crowned with beach plum. A collapsing wooden fence bound together with rusted wires had been erected in a half-hearted attempt to protect the tiny inlet from erosion. She checked to make sure that her hiding place amongst the rocks was barely visible from the veranda, safely concealed from Black and his team.

The rocker creaked on the wooden deck. Backwards, forwards. The hypnotic motion made her sleepy. The sun was hot upon her skin, scorching her hair. There was the tang of salt in the air and the blue sky above was so pale as to seem transparent.

She wondered, wistfully, what it would be like to be one of the family spending long and peaceful holidays in this old house? She could almost see them; these shadowy figures, their lives so rich and full, so different from hers.

The house was silent but for the creaking rockers and the muted thunder of surf on rocks. With the family in residence, the quiet would be shattered by a noisy hubbub; people talking and shouting; children laughing; dogs barking; music playing.

She imagined their lives. Picnics on the tiny beach; bathing in the sea; bonfires at night. Children fishing in the tidal pools for limpets and mussels; adults relaxing together on the sweeping veranda or bobbing to sea in a sailing boat, trailing hands and feet in the cool water. Afternoons spent reading or napping in one of the dimly lit bedrooms with the shades closed against the sun.

Mickey rose from the chair and, rubbing at the dusty glass, peered through one of the sliding doors. The curtains inside were partially drawn but she could make out a cosy arrangement of wicker and rattan chairs stuffed with faded cushions and draped with shawls.

A bookcase haphazardly filled with paperbacks and piles of magazines. Fishing rods against the wall. A clutch of paraffin lamps on a table. A fireplace filled with logs, ready for burning. Mickey closed her eyes, imagining them all here together.

Unexpectedly she felt overwhelmed with a sad yearning, an ache for... For *what?*

What filled her with such longing? A normal family life, was that it? A husband, small children? Summer holidays in a house set high above the sea where everything felt safe; where people might be happy together?

Mickey shook herself, impatiently. Too late! Too late for any of that!

She scrambled down the wooden steps, crossing the rocks, making for her hiding place. *Don't do this,* she said to herself grimly. *Don't lose sight of your plan. Don't let misgivings throw you off track. Only one thing matters now, only one thing!*

That afternoon Edwina had invited friends for a game of tennis. She couldn't play herself but could watch and perhaps she might umpire.

It had been months since they'd all enjoyed the tennis court at Hurley House and Edwina missed the fun and excitement of the game; the laughter, good-natured teasing and camaraderie of the old girls, together again after so long.

She had planned the afternoon with great care and asked the cook to prepare strawberries and cream and tall jugs of iced lemonade to be enjoyed in the shade of the spreading trees.

"Very Wimbledon, don't you agree? So appropriate for such a lovely summer's day!" The cook, a sensible soul, had suggested that tea should also be served and perhaps cream scones or cucumber sandwiches for those who might feel peckish after the game.

Edwina spent time deliberating what to wear. White, of course, for tennis, even if she was merely one of the audience.

She pulled out a hanger draped with white linen trousers, perfectly creased and worn, with a narrow belt of silver links. That would do. She wasn't sure whether she should wear the cotton blouse with the French lace collar or the simple, ivory sports shirt? She settled upon a classic silk blouse with a high neckline. Earrings. Flat pumps. A bracelet of bone and gold. Her trademark scarlet lipstick and a feathering of blusher on each cheek.

"Tell me how I look?" she asked Thomas, not really caring, the mirror told all she needed to know.

"You look a picture!" he said admiringly. "Delightful, my dear!"

"I hope you're going to change?"

"Oh?" he glanced at his crumpled blue shirt; his old-fashioned tweed trousers bagging around his ankles; ancient, scuffed leather shoes.

"A white shirt perhaps? Clean tennis shoes?"

"But, I'm not playing?"

"Of course not! And neither am I. But we must dress the part, Thomas! Standards must be upheld. An effort must be made, don't you agree?"

They arrived promptly at three o'clock. Marjorie and Eleanor, Belinda and Amelia who were to play doubles, and Sharon and Elise, who, with Edwina, would make up the audience watching the game. They were laughing and talking all at once like a lot of fussing hens.

"Just like old times!" cried Edwina, holding out her hands to them. There were fluttering kisses and careful hugs and she was conscious that they touched her lightly, delicately as they might a newborn baby.

Thomas arrived wearing something entirely unsuitable with an unflattering hat upon his head. He beamed as Marjorie and Amelia planted hearty kisses on his cheeks, and Belinda bent to fling an affectionate arm around his shoulder.

"Darling Thomas!" said Sharon. "How handsome you are today!" Elise tucked a daisy in his buttonhole.

Thomas preened, looking up at them from below his flopping brim and showing large yellow teeth in a wide and happy grin.

Edwina bumped his wheelchair roughly down the garden path, leading them all to where the table was laid for tea beneath the trees.

The game began. The girls played with a bold and vigorous rhythm as though they'd been practicing for months. Edwina was envious. They looked so strong, bursting with life and energy. Marjorie, as usual, was hitting powerful, deep shots to the corners. Amelia's weak backhand had improved and Eleanor's tactic was obviously to hit balls with little depth and force so that Belinda couldn't return them.

The audience shouted advice, groaned, cheered and clapped loudly.

"Such fun!" said Edwina. "I've missed our games."

It was more than that, though. She missed the girls. Missed their easy chat, the jokes and gossip and it grieved her that, lately, they seemed to all have drifted apart; each going their own way.

Belinda hit a deep lob over Eleanor's head.

Impressed, Edwina clapped loudly. "I'm astonished at how well the girls are all playing," she said. "They haven't practiced for ages!"

"Oh, but we play together every week!" said Sharon.

Edwina looked stung.

"We haven't wanted to impose," Sharon hastily explained "You've been so ill. We felt it best to leave you in peace. We play at the club every Wednesday afternoon. You're most welcome to join us, whenever you're feeling well enough!"

"Thank you," replied Edwina stiffly.

It was inevitable, she supposed, that now she was thought to be dying that friends would stay away and resume their lives without her. She wondered why she felt so hurt.

The excitement of the occasion ebbed, leaving her inexplicably weary.

The sun was hot, the thwack of ball against racquets hypnotic, her eyelids drooped. She wasn't sure for how long she dozed but when she awoke the game was over and they were all seated around the tea table.

She heard ice tinkling in glasses, tea being poured. Their voices were pitched low, almost a whisper.

"She's lost so much weight!" hissed Marjorie. "She's as thin as a rail!"

"It's desperately sad," murmured Belinda. "What does the doctor say, Thomas? What is the prognosis? How long does she have?"

"Months, I think," said Thomas. "But Edwina is confident that she will outlast us all and I'm happy to say she's been feeling a little better lately."

"Feeling a little better!" Sharon's voice sounded shocked "I've never seen her look so drained and weak. She's utterly worn out, poor thing!"

Elisa jumped in next. "She's not herself! Those heavy shadows beneath her eyes. And then, to fall asleep like this, in the middle of a match!"

Edwina joined them at the table. "It's the morphine!" she said, curtly. "It makes me nod off, sometimes."

Conversation turned to the garden; they twittered on about how lovely it was with all the flowers in bloom, the leaves in bud, the fountains spilling, fish darting in the ponds, birds singing in the trees.

Edwina sipped black tea and waved away offerings of scones and sandwiches.

Their voices faded; she heard only background murmuring, they sounded like a lot of barnyard hens clucking and cheeping. She regarded each face.

Belinda with bouffant hair and puffy cheeks was a Chinese Silky. Tiny, trim, beady-eyed Sharon a feisty little Bantam. Those muscular thighs and rounded bosom made Elise the perfect Cornish Hen and dull Marjorie was, of course, a faded farmyard fowl. Only Amelia, smiling kindly at Edwina from across the table, remained herself.

Cluck, cluck, cluck! Meaningless words from sharp, pointed beaks. These old friends had moved on with their lives. They were playing tennis doubles once a week at the club. They spoke in whispers about her failing health and feigned sympathy but she could not detect even the slightest concern in their voices. Her illness had made her an outcast, overlooked and ignored, soon she would be entirely forgotten. So much for friends!

"I'm not dead yet!" She'd spoken her thoughts aloud, without thinking.

Startled, the hens stopped talking at once.

"What's that, darling?" As always, Thomas appeared confused.

"I made the point," Edwina, enunciating each word clearly, "that I am not dead yet!"

Cluck, cluck, cluck! What did she mean? Of course she wasn't dead yet? She was, in fact, looking very well indeed. They were just remarking, how well she looked for one who, well, had been very ill indeed. And then of course there was always medical science, technology, miraculous advances in cures and treatments, one should always hold onto hope… Cluck, cluck, cluck.

They fell silent and left very quickly after that. Collecting racquets and balls, rummaging for handbags beneath the table. Sympathetic looks were directed at Thomas, his hand was warmly pressed, his ear whispered into. Edwina's cheek was effusively kissed. They waved and waved.

Edwina watched them go. She would probably never see any of them again and, at that moment didn't much care.

The shadows lengthened. Cold teacups and crumb-littered plates were carried indoors. The sun began to sink.

Edwina pressed her hand against her heart. She felt it beating strongly, pulsing with life: blood pumping powerfully through her veins, coursing through her body.

"I'm not dead yet!" she shouted triumphantly. How wonderful it was to be alive on such an evening as this? She reached out her arms, embracing the setting sun, the wind shaking the leaves, the canal water lapping against the stone wall, the flowers closing petals in readiness for the night.

Edwina pushed the wheelchair, walking with easy strides across the lawn towards the light from the open doors.

Thomas glimpsed a face filled with strength and purpose. Thank God. He'd been desperately worried. That extraordinary outburst at the table! Her words, heavy with bitterness, flung at them all with such intensity. The girls had been shocked. They'd practically run from the garden and who could blame them?

Oh, she was so hard to fathom sometimes. But look, here she was, his beautiful Edwina again, restored and full of life.

Thomas smiled with relief. "You're very much alive, my love," he said thankfully.

Chapter 10

Chris

"Why is there only emptiness
when the end inevitably arrives?
Eyelids pressed shut, world blanked out
heart stilled, brain shut down,
muscles stiffened and cold.
Where is the endless corridor
leading to the all encompassing light?
Why are they hiding, those angel choirs,
When they should be beckoning
Towards forgiveness?
Who has silenced the sweet music of harps
Plucked by invisible hands?
And where is God's promised love,
Enfolding like a silken shawl
As the gates swing wide?
Why is there only emptiness
When the end inevitably arrives?"

Dawood Hill. Poet Laureate. 2006.

Our village is, as you know, named after the Apostle Saint Jude Thaddeus, the Patron Saint of the Impossible – the Saint called upon when all other Saints have turned a deaf ear. The Saint of 'lost causes' and 'cases despaired of', Saint Jude's help is expected at the last moment; a true miracle, a blinding flash of redemptive light appearing only when the last vestige of hope has faded.

There were many in our village who might have prayed to St Jude at that time.

Many whose lives, suddenly, had changed inexorably; who battled demons and disease and had lost their faith or spirit, or both. How many heard their cries for help, I wonder? And, if not St Jude, then who was there to comfort them in their hour of greatest need?

When, at last, the angel was finally done, Chris collapsed with exhaustion. He took to his bed and slept for days. He shook with fever and sank into vivid dreams from which he emerged with a face as starkly white as the bed sheets. Ginny summoned Grace, who listened to his racing heart; his shallow, rasping breaths indicating early pneumonia settling in his lungs. She helped him sit up and took his temperature.

"You've stopped taking your medication," she said, shaking the thermometer. It was more a statement than a question.

"Yes." His mouth was studded with painful ulcers. A furious rash peppered his arms and legs.

"Why?"

"The medication does nothing for me. I'm getting worse. My body is collapsing, you can see for yourself. And the pills make me feel like shit! I can't work with all those chemicals in my system. I'm better off without them."

"But you're not! If you continue taking your medication you have at least a fighting chance. New cures are being developed. New treatments. New options. We must be patient!"

He closed his eyes, blocking her out.

"Chris?"

"I've lost the will. I'm tired, Grace. Tired of living like this. I don't know why this is happening to me, but I do know I'm a lost cause. I can't go on. I haven't the strength."

"So, you're giving up?"

"Yeah. If that's what you want to call it. The fight's gone out of me."

"But what about your mother? Inga? The people who love you? Make an effort, Chris, if only for their sakes!"

"That's unfair, Grace! I've made a huge bloody effort. Lived with this disease for years. It's killing my mother, watching me die a slow death. As for Inga, do you think I want her to see me like this?"

Grace bit her lip. "Go back onto the treatment," she pleaded.

He turned his head towards the window, towards the angel's face.

The doctor stared at him helplessly for a few moments before becoming matter-of-fact, her face inscrutable. "Well, here's what we have to deal with now. Your lungs are inflamed. You have an upper respiratory infection. It may be nothing, a cold perhaps, but there's a chance of early pneumonia. I'm going to prescribe medication to treat the infection. You *must* take this. Do you hear me, Chris?"

"Yeah." His voice sounded flat, disinterested, weary.

Grace scribbled on her prescription pad, tore off the sheet and placed it on the table, weighted with a chisel.

The angel stood before the window, her face tilted towards the light.

Grace reached up to touch the angel's uplifted arms. The wood was as smooth as silk. She ran her palm over the limbs: the clearly defined muscles, the deltoid running from the shoulder down the arm, the taut biceps at the front of the arm, the triceps at the back. The wrists were thick, like a man's, but the hands were slender with long, tapered fingers. Both hands were open, fingers curling, reaching out. At the tip of each finger was a perfect nail, short and blunt.

"Your hands," she said, turning to Chris.

His face broke into a slow smile. "Inga's face. My hands and feet. The limbs and torso carved from memory. Someone I once knew. She's a very strange hybrid."

Grace touched a foot. It was long and slender with a high arched instep. She admired the complex arrangement of bones, muscles, tendons. It was anatomically perfect and utterly beautiful.

Inga's face? She studied it. Was this Inga's face? Deep-set eyes with heavy lids: a generous, full-lipped mouth, half-open. A wide brow, strong chin, small ears, half hidden behind backswept, flowing hair. The face was powerful and commanding. The Inga she knew was softer, the cheeks slightly fuller, nose smaller, chin more delicate.

"Edwina Hurley believes your angel is capable of miracles," she said lightly.

"So I've heard."

"She says the angel is curing her; healing diseased tissue; shrinking her tumour." Grace smiled to show how ridiculous she thought this was.

His eyes were closed. His chest rose and fell rhythmically. His hair fell forward over his face. His hands lay on the quilt; an artist's hands. A deep sense of sadness stole over her. What a waste of a young, talented life.

She glanced again at the angel and it seemed as though the angel stared back. For a moment, barely a few seconds, she imagined the angel trembling with life: breath flowing from her mouth, a pulse beating in her neck.

Grace picked up her bag and fled.

Minutes later, facing Ginny, she regained her composure. "He's stopped taking his medication," she said quietly.

"Yes, I knew that."

"But do you also know that without anti-retrovirals he'll get progressively worse? It's happening already: the virus is taking over, his immune system is breaking down. He already has a chest inflection, possibly pneumonia. I've written a script. We may need chest X-rays. You'll have to monitor him, make sure he takes the medication."

Ginny nodded numbly. "He's giving up. I've seen it coming. Seen the signs for some time. And who can blame him?" She stopped. The lump in her throat, making it impossible to speak.

Grace shook her head in sympathy. What was left to say?

Caron had also taken to her bed. She drew the blinds and crawled beneath the bedclothes, burrowing in consoling darkness. Since that day in the hospital when she had wept upon Alec's chest, she'd been unable to cry. She felt hollow, as though her heart had been removed; leaving her chest cavity empty, her body flattened by despair. She'd dreamed of watching her stomach gently swell, her breasts grow full, blue veins visible beneath creamy skin; the aureole growing darker, spreading like a flower. But now, too soon, she'd reclaimed her body. It felt familiar, the arch of her rib cage, the concave stomach, the sad deflated breasts. As she withdrew to her bedroom, the skies opened and a sullen rain fell, unusual for mid-summer, but strangely appropriate Caron thought, for this time of mourning. The rain fell over the fields in great, grey sheets, numbing the cow's grazing in the Evans' pastures, drenching the newly planted dune olive and Cape beech trees at the estuary, soaking through the sand to sandstone and shale beneath. Rain dimpled and muddied the waters of the canal, left potholes in the roads and drowned the golf course.

For four days, Caron floated between deep sleep and moments of wakefulness until the fifth day when she decided that enough was enough. She rose early and stood in the shower, punishing water beating down, as hot as she could stand, until her skin steamed.

She shoved her pyjamas in the hamper and dressed in a soft shirt and denims, tying back her damp hair with a ribbon. She had lost four days of her life and remembered nothing. She had no idea how Alec and James had coped with meals, schoolwork, housework. She'd heard muffled noises behind closed bedroom doors. Rain drumming upon the roof, spattering against the windows. Cupboards opening and closing. Dishes clattering. Water running in the bathtub. A car in the driveway; coming and going. The front door, opening and closing. A gentle tap upon the bedroom door, the creak as it opened and then swung shut.

Sometimes she'd woken to find a tray on the bedside table. Cereal and juice. A sandwich, curling at the edges: a cold cup of tea, skin floating on the surface.

She'd left the trays untouched and eaten nothing, drinking only from the cold tap in the bathroom.

She opened the blinds; threw wide the windows, pulled sheets off the bed. She tiptoed downstairs carrying an armful of laundry and saw through the half-open door that James was still submerged beneath blankets. The door to the spare room was also shut; Alec, probably sleeping.

The kitchen was dusty; dishes in the sink, the floor not properly swept, the counter scattered with breadcrumbs. James schoolbooks were spread on the table, his crayons spilling from the box, a jar of muddy-coloured water with a paintbrush. She ran hot water in the sink, squirted in dishwashing liquid and threw the sheets in the washing machine. By the time Alec came down, dressed for work, she'd pegged the laundry on the line, washed the kitchen floor and made a pot of freshly percolated coffee. She poured a cup. He took it gratefully.

"You're looking a little better," he said, hesitantly.

"Yes. I'm feeling it."

His face relaxed slightly. "We've missed you. Both of us."

"How've you managed?" She was curious.

"I took a couple of days off work and when I went back, I took James with me. It wasn't easy but we coped."

"What did you tell him?"

"That you were sick."

"Did you explain? About the baby?"

"No," his expression was sheepish. "I wasn't sure what to say. I thought, perhaps, we might do it together."

"I'll do it. I'll tell James today."

"Caron, we need to spend time together, talk things over. Find a way to move forward."

She gazed levelly. She had heard him say exactly this before; on that morning before she'd lost the baby. Didn't he know the moment had passed when they might yet reclaim something of their marriage?

"Do you remember saying that you didn't love me?" she asked. Her face was impassive, her eyes stared through him.

"I remember saying something like that in the heat of the moment. I didn't mean it."

"I think you did." Her voice was calm. "I've been thinking, Alec. I've decided I can't stay in a one-sided relationship with all the loving on my side and nothing on yours. It's too painful."

His face contorted. "This is about the baby, isn't it, Caron? We're never going to get past this, are we?"

"It's about *us!* The baby is only a part of it. If we're honest we've been unhappy forever. James is caught in the middle of all this: and he's suffering, just as much as you and I. I've tried to be a good mother but I don't know how to reach him. He's too shut away!"

Alec's expression hardened. "What are you saying?"

"I'm leaving you, Alec. I have some money saved; enough to get by. I'll find a job teaching at a school somewhere."

"For Christ's sake, Caron!"

They heard James thumping down the stairs. He pushed open the kitchen door and stood in the doorway. "Are you better?" he asked in a small voice.

Caron smiled. "Yes. Much better."

James ran to the table and shuffled amongst his books so that they slid across the surface and crashed to the floor. He found what he was looking for and held it out to Caron, his face breaking into a radiant smile.

"I made this for you!" he said proudly. "It's a 'get well' card."

Caron took the folded piece of paper. On the front was a carefully coloured drawing of a woman wearing a yellow dressing gown, slippers with pom-poms on her feet. In one hand she held a bunch of flowers. There was a round orange sun in the sky: whipped cream clouds and a blue bird flying overhead. The woman held the hand of a small boy. The boy's hair stuck straight up on his head and he was looking up at the woman's face. In the crook of his other arm, the boy cradled a tiny baby. All three figures were smiling widely.

Caron opened the folded paper. Inside, in large, colourful letters, James had printed:

'PLEASE GET BETTER SOON! WITH LOVE FROM JAMES.'

Caron opened her arms. James rushed into them, butting his head hard into her stomach. They stood there, holding onto one another.

Sarah called Mickey and asked her to meet her, that morning, at The Two Potters.

"I'm sorry," said Mickey. "I'm busy."

"I have some money for you," said Sarah. "Quite a lot. Your range has sold out. I need more stock."

"I'll come and get the money," Mickey said, "but I can't supply any more herbs. They've all died."

Sarah had heard people talking about Mickey. Ben had told her about Folly and there were rumours that she'd been ill, but nothing prepared her for the sight of Mickey walking into the gallery. She looked gaunt and her hair had been cut short in an ugly, ragged style that made her look years older.

Seeing Sarah's expression Mickey stopped. "What?" she demanded.

"I'm sorry!" Sarah took her arm. "It's just that you don't look well."

"I've come for my money."

"Yes, of course. Have you time for a chat?"

"What do you want to talk about?"

"I've had a few ideas, I'd like to share with you."

"I'm busy. I told you. I don't have time for this."

"Fair enough. But I have coffee brewing and some of Ginny's famous bran muffins." She took Mickey's arm and led her towards the café.

Mickey ate and drank ravenously.

"You're not sleeping?" asked Sarah, cautiously.

"Not much. Bad dreams."

"And not eating much, either?"

"I have no appetite. Well…" Mickey gave a glimmer of a smile. "Not usually. The muffins are very good, though."

"Have you seen a doctor?"

Mickey scowled. "Everyone asks me that. As though doctors hold the cure for everything. Yes, I've seen the doctor. No, the doctor can't help me."

"But, if you're sick?"

"I'm sick at heart," Mickey said. "Sick to my soul. It may not look it, but my body is very strong."

"I'm sorry about Folly," said Sarah, tentatively. "I have a dog who means the world to me. I'd be distraught if anything happened to him."

Mickey's eyes were still, grey pools.

"But, well, life goes on. Ben told me about a puppy..."

"You don't understand," said Mickey. "This is about more than Folly!"

Sarah waited.

"I was raped!"

Sarah's hands flew to her face.

"Raped by a man who has stolen money from me and damaged my home. He can't get away with it. He must be punished."

"Have you reported this to the police?"

"The police! The police don't care. They won't help. They don't even believe me."

"But ..."

"Sarah, this is my business. I don't want to talk about it any more. Have you got my money?"

"Yes. But, Mickey, I'd like to help, if I can..."

"You can't. Please don't say anything else. And don't tell anyone what I've said."

Reluctantly, Sarah got up and walked through to the gallery with Mickey following.

A customer stood waiting for attention. The woman was large and wore a red caftan hung with ropes of wooden beads. Her face pouted with displeasure. "I've been waiting for ten minutes and more!"

Sarah's tone was apologetic. "How can I help?"

"An armoire. Ideally an antique. Do you have any in stock?"

"An armoire?"

The woman sighed. "Large cabinet with panelled doors. Adjustable shelves and drawers inside. Horizontal pediment on the top and arches between the legs."

"Yes," Sarah's expression was thoughtful. "I know what it is. I was wondering where you might be able to find one."

"I want an imposing piece. Preferably something in maple or cherry."

"It will be difficult to find a genuine antique. But you could have one made. There's a very good carpenter working for a builder by the name of Jordan Black. Have you heard of him?"

The woman shook her head.

"Black has a small warehouse on Otter Lane where you can order custom-made items of furniture. It's worth a visit."

Sarah scribbled the address on a slip of paper and gave it to the woman.

She turned to find Mickey gaping at her. "A warehouse? I didn't know Jordan Black was manufacturing furniture?"

"It's very small operation; the warehouse is probably more of a shed. The carpenter is called Wayne or Wade?"

Mickey tried to think. That day, when they were both working on the roof of her house, Black had introduced her to a short man with a scruffy red beard and ponytail. "My sidekick, Wayne," he'd said.

"Wayne," she murmured. "Not Wade."

"Yes. Well, he's an excellent carpenter. They're producing some well-crafted pieces. I've sent a few clients to see them. Why are you interested?"

"I've worked with Jordan Black on a couple of projects. I'd like to get in touch."

"You'll find Black at the warehouse every night, after seven."

"Thank you!" Mickey sounded grateful.

Sarah opened a desk drawer and removed a sealed envelope. "This is what we owe you."

Mickey took the envelope and, without glancing at it, stuffed it in her pocket.

Sarah walked her to the door.

"I wish I could help, Mickey."

"Oh, you have! You've been very helpful."

Sarah frowned. "I don't see how."

Mickey turned to face her. "Trust me," she said. "You've been a great help."

On the way home, Mickey drove past the warehouse in Otter Lane.

There was a hand painted sign outside: '*Jordan Black: kitchens, cupboards, custom-made furniture. Enquire within.*'

Sarah was right. The warehouse was small. A simple wooden shed with a pile of smooth planks at the entrance. Mickey stopped outside. Heart pounding, she knocked quietly at the door. No answer. She knocked again and then pushed the door open. It swung easily. There was no one inside. A work-bench with a gleaming, sharp-toothed circular saw, rows of shelves, carpenter's tools, tins of paint and varnish, the carcass of a wooden cupboard, three half-finished wooden chairs.

In the gloom at the back of the shed she could see a narrow bed, a table holding a paraffin lamp, empty beer cans, coffee mugs, a flask. There was a lock on the inside of the door and a large metal bolt. A length of fraying rope. Paintbrushes were soaking in a bucket of cloudy turpentine.

All these things she consigned to memory.

So, this was where he came after working on site. Where he met with Wayne to check on the day's progress. Where customers like the one in the gallery might commission furniture: an expensive armoire in cherry or maple. Where life, for Jordan Black, went on as usual, untouched by what he had done to her.

Mickey was conscious of the deep silence of the shed, the pinyesmell of wood shavings, the sharp odour of paint remover.

Jordan Black had hurt her, had destroyed her life. Now it was her turn.

Ginny called Ian and asked him for his help moving the angel from the upstairs studio to Edwina Hurley's garden.

"It's heavy," she warned. "You'll need four men, at least."

Ian went to see the angel to feel the weight of her and consider how best to transport the carving from that small space in the studio, down the steep flight of stairs and then to Hurley House.

Inga met him at the door and led him upstairs to where Chris was sitting in a chair, with a sketchpad on his knees.

"I wish I could help," he apologised ruefully. "I've got a damned infection; some kind of chest cold. I'm no good to anyone at this point."

Inga, easy and graceful, stood beside the carving. "You like it?" she smiled.

Grace had said that she found the angel too life-like and strangely frightening.

"I felt uncomfortable," she had admitted. "I couldn't wait to get away from those terrifying eyes!"

But Ian was drawn to the angel. The face was kind, filled with compassion and tenderness. You could spill your heart and be forgiven. You would feel safe in the embrace of those powerful arms. Grace was wrong, there was nothing here to fear: only a well-sculptured piece, a good likeness of an angel, if such a thing ever existed.

"I envy you," he said, turning to Chris. "To be able to carve something as fine as this."

"Have you ever tried?"

"Who, me? Hell, I'm a humble carpenter, not a sculptor!"

"You work in wood. It's a start. How do you know what you can do until you try?"

Ian laughed. "I know," he said.

He tested the weight of the sculpture. It would be impossible to carry the statue down the narrow, curving staircase without damaging it. "I suggest we tie her with ropes and lower her from the window."

Ian called the builder, Jordan Black, and asked for his help. The man was as strong as a bull; if anyone could help assist with the heavy carving, he could.

"OK," agreed Black. "I'll bring two of my men."

They unscrewed and removed the windows and carefully bound the angel with thick rope. The plan seemed safe; two men above holding the ropes, two men below, guiding the statue to the ground. Ian and one of Black's men turned the angel on her side and, panting with exertion, heaved the carving through the open window. Ian struggled. The statue was heavier than expected; his muscles ached trying to balance the massive weight of the carving so that it didn't fall crashing to the ground.

When he first saw it, Black had given the carving only a cursory glance. It seemed to be a life-size figure with wings. Wings? A Greek God? Something like that.

It was when the statue was being lowered that Black recognised it as an angel.

As he watched, the figure, caught between taut ropes, began to sway, lightly at first, and then, lurching heavily from side to side.

"Watch it! he shouted. The head of the angel swung inches from his face.

"Easy does it! Easy!"

He reached out and held the head, steadying the sculpture and, as he did so, looked into eyes like ice. He gasped. The eyes were the coldest he'd ever seen: broken splinters sharp enough to pierce through skin, muscle and soft tissue. His legs shook. He relaxed his grip on the rope. Suddenly, the carving dropped a full half metre. Black ducked, bellowing in terror as the figure swung towards him. Those eyes, those cold, bloody eyes!

He fell to the ground, face forward, the breath knocked out of him, waiting for the weight of the wood to squeeze the very life from him.

"Close call!" shouted Ian. "Are you OK?"

Black looked up. The angel hung above, the ropes held tight.

He got to his feet and grabbed the rope he had dropped. Together the men lowered the angel safely to the ground.

As she lay on the grass, he dared to look at her eyes. He drew close. Heavy, drooping lids, pupils staring. Sightless. He ran his hands over the face. Up close he could see wood grain; see where a sharpened chisel had cut to create the swelling of an eyelid, the flair of a nostril, a curl of hair.

He laughed. The sound echoed; edged with hysteria.

Ian thumped him on the back. "Bloody hell!" he said. "A few inches more and you'd have been a goner."

They wrapped the carving in sacking, carried it to the truck, and heaved it in the back.

As he drove off Black found his hands quivering uncontrollably on the wheel.

"You all right?" asked one of the men.

Black gave a mirthless bark of laughter. "Angel!" he said. "Call that an angel. The fucking thing nearly killed me!"

Chapter 11

Grace and Inga

Edwina Hurley sent invitations to attend the formal unveiling of the statue in her garden. She wore a hat – a frill of tulle dappled with purple violets – and looked, in her flowing lilac chiffon, like the mother of the bride. Surrounded by luminaries and friends who flocked to see the famous 'Guardian Angel', Edwina was in high spirits, basking in the warm glow of the limelight. Word had it that she was in a grateful state of remission and photographs taken that day show her looking not unlike her old self: laughing, eyes sparkling; the very picture of good health.

Inga was there to apologise for the absence of the guest of honour, Chris Lourens, and explain that a chest cold kept the artist in bed on this late summer's day.

I thought it a pity that Chris missed the cheers and thunderous applause that arose once concealing drapery was removed to reveal the angel in all her glory: the heel of one elegant foot poised in readiness to soar into the heavens.

I knew that Inga had been the model for the angel though, frankly, I found little similarity between the young woman who seemed so light and fragile, walking with a dancer's grace, compared to the proud majesty of that splendid Atlantean creature.

The angel seemed to hold Edwina in thrall; she remained at her side throughout the ceremony, lovingly stroking the satiny smooth limbs, as though drawing strength from the figure. "It's not real, you know!" said a child who'd been absorbed, watching as Edwina fondled the angel. Edwina, who was not particularly fond of children, leaned towards the boy. "How could you possibly know?" she hissed. The boy fled. Edwina called for more champagne.

Grace took a brief leave of absence from the surgery and a locum by the name of Dr Adrian Lawrence was brought in from Port Victoria. A solid man wearing a grey pinstripe, the doctor appeared both prosperous and professional and gave a stiff, formal bow when they were introduced.

Grace's secretary, the formidable Mrs Stanley, seemed unimpressed by the good doctor. Instead of welcoming him with a coffee served, as usual, with a sliver of her own home-baked shortbread, she merely pointed at the hissing percolator.

"What's wrong?" whispered Grace. "Why don't you like him?"

"Oily!" she pronounced. "And too smooth by far! Not to be trusted, in my opinion."

"Oh please!" begged Grace. "Please be kind. It's only for five days!"

Mrs Stanley wrinkled her pointed nose and gave a sniff. "I'll try," she said, "but I can't promise."

The next morning Ian and Grace slept in until late. Grace woke first and watched light stream through the blinds and fall to horizontal lines on rumpled sheets.

She tried to remember when she'd last felt so peaceful, so happy. The children were shouting in the kitchen: Annie Hook, in charge of breakfast, would probably make oatmeal or eggs boiled too lightly, something they wouldn't eat.

Grace opened her mind to the possibilities of the day. Perhaps they would walk with the dogs to the village and buy fresh croissants and eat them on the deck, watching the swirling canal waters rise with the incoming tide. They could stretch out on wooden recliners and read or drive to Betty's Bay to visit the nursery and buy plants. She was excited at the prospect of uprooting the dead and dying shrubs that had been destroyed by the bush fire and starting afresh. A new garden, something different, wild and wonderful spilling over with boldly clashing colours.

They could invite friends to a long overdue dinner: she'd make a fragrant curry and that wonderful lemony dessert and set the table outdoors. They'd laugh and talk, drink too much red wine and stay up late.

She felt her husband's hands on her. "What are you thinking?"

She turned to him. "I'm thinking of all the wonderful things we could do today."

He kissed her neck, pulling her close. "Such as?"

"This will do," she breathed, kissing him back. "This will do for starters!"

That afternoon, Grace, in muddy shorts and a stained t-shirt, was kneeling in the garden, planting white and blue agapanthus, when she received the call.

"He can't breathe, Grace! He can't breathe!"

She recognised Ginny's emotional voice. "Ginny! I'm sorry! I'm on leave. Can you call the locum? His name is Dr Lawrence. He'll know exactly what to do. I've left copious notes."

"Oh, please, Grace! Please come right away. I can't call anyone else! It's you he trusts! He won't see anyone else, won't let them touch him."

"But, Ginny ..."

She heard ragged weeping.

"I'll call the ambulance," Grace sighed. "And meet you at the hospital."

Grace left the hospital late that night after Chris had finally fallen asleep. An intricate web of fine, clear plastic tubes leaked oxygen and medication into his blood stream. Inga sent Ginny home to rest and kept a lonely vigil at his bedside. She faithfully copied the notes that the doctor had written in her careless black script on the patient's records, clipped to a board hanging at the base of the narrow cot.

"The diagnosis of Pneumocystis pneumonia (PCP) due to Pneumocystis jirovecii has been confirmed by a chest x-ray showing widespread pulmonary infiltrates and a low arterial oxygen level. This diagnosis is definitively confirmed by the pathologic identification of the organism in the patient's sputum."

Inga turned the chart towards the bed so that Ginny might be spared confusing and dismaying details of her son's illness.

The next morning Chris was sleeping when Ginny crept into the ward: her arrival coinciding with an avalanche of hospital staff wielding humming floor polishers, buckets and mops. "Rest, my dear!" she said to Inga. "It's my watch now. You're exhausted! Go home and sleep." With superhuman effort, Mrs Lourens had pulled herself together. She'd applied makeup and wore a lime scarf cheerfully threaded through her hair. Only her swollen eyelids gave her away. She came prepared, carrying a basket containing coloured squares for a quilt she was making, a thermos of creamy pumpkin soup for Chris and bed socks for his cold feet. "You needn't worry, I won't fall apart," she whispered to Inga. "I can't afford to. He needs us to be strong."

Inga sped home to the studio where, yesterday, she'd posted a note on the door cancelling the week's lessons. She'd offered no explanation and ignored the dozens of concerned or curious messages left on her answering machine.

Showered and wrapped in a bathrobe, Inga typed *'Pneumonocytis jirovecii'* on her laptop's search engine and almost instantly discovered that this was a "yeast-like fungal micro-organism, commonly found amongst patients with a weakened immune system".

Her eyes skimmed the site until she found the sentence she sought; *"Prior to the development of effective treatments, PCP was a common and rapid cause of death in AIDS patients."*

Inga stared at the page, the words bleeding one into the other, meaningless yet terrifying at the same time. There was a picture of a chest X-ray, the negative image of the lower part of the lungs grown opaque and misty with an invasive white fungus. Another sentence leapt into view: *"the disease attacks the fibrous tissue of the lungs leading to significant oxygen deficiency which can be fatal if not treated aggressively."*

Was the disease being treated aggressively? Dr Frey had said she was 'cautiously optimistic' that the medication would reduce inflammation. What did that mean, 'cautiously optimistic'? Was it the kind of thing doctors said when they weren't sure what was happening?

If Ginny had not been with her at the time, Inga would have asked the doctor for the truth. "Is this the end?" she would have said. "Will this pneumonia kill him?"

But how could she have voiced such a question with his mother in the room?

How had it happened? Only a few days ago he'd been carving the angel and while she'd noticed his voice had been rough and hoarse and he'd had a dry cough, there'd been no sign, no warning that he would suddenly collapse, grow blue around the mouth and fight to draw breath.

She had not been with him on the day of his collapse. He'd asked her to attend Edwina Hurley's unveiling of the angel: to be there on his behalf. "Are you sure?" she'd asked, ridiculously pleased. "What about Ginny? Surely it would be better if your mother were at the unveiling. She knows more about art, about your work than I do. She is the one who should go."

"You're the inspiration for the angel," he'd said gravely. "It must be you."

She'd been so proud to represent him and hear such generous praise from all those who'd flocked to Edwina's garden. Words like 'masterful', 'ingenious' and 'adroit' were used. Chris was declared an extraordinary artist and there were many who rhapsodised about how 'lifelike' the angel was, whatever that meant, for who amongst them had seen an angel in the flesh? Photographs of the figure had been taken from every angle and one ambitious photographer had scaled the twisting branches of a wild fig tree to capture an image of the sculpture from above so that it appeared as though the angel were ascending. The photographs would appear in the art section of the local newspapers accompanied by a profile of the sculptor.

Inga had collected a slim sheaf of business cards from journalists, writers and art collectors, all eager to meet Chris and discuss the possibility of interviews or future commissions.

The day, however, belonged to Mrs Hurley. St Jude's patroness of the arts posed for the cameras, issued wise and witty comments to the press and rejoiced in the euphoric warmth of public adoration. To Inga, watching from a respectful distance, Edwina seemed to have fallen in love with the statue. She kept one worshipful hand upon a limb or an outstretched wing as though fearful of letting go. Thomas, in his wheelchair, an arm's length away, wore an expression of abject dismay.

"This is a happy occasion!" Inga had reminded him. "Why do you look so tragic?"

"I worry about her," Thomas had confessed miserably. "She has such faith in that angel!"

He'd motioned Inga to draw closer so that he could speak without being overheard. "She believes it has divine powers," he'd whispered softly. "She thinks it's destroying her cancer."

"Is that such a bad thing?" Inga had asked innocently.

"I've seen the tumour!" Thomas had seemed upset. "I've spoken to the doctor. The cancer has spread. Edwina refuses medical treatment. She cannot be cured. It is only a question of time."

"But faith!" Inga had exclaimed. "Faith can perform miracles!"

He'd seemed on the verge of tears. "Forgive an old man for being such a pessimist but I don't share your belief. There will come a time when Edwina sees the cancer is invincible and nothing can cure her. Tell me, what am I to do then?"

Inga had given a sad smile. "I speak only for myself," she'd said.

"But I believe when the end is near, love and comfort are all we have to offer."

Edwina had taken Inga's hand and drawn her away, introducing her to a visiting artist from Port Victoria who had expressed a desire to meet the famous Chris Lourens. It was Edwina, however, who did all the talking, extolling the many virtues of the young sculptor. Observing her, Inga had seen a perfectly poised woman wearing a frilly hat at a rakish angle. Her laughter was giddy and merry. She had a healthy bloom in her cheeks. Her eyes glowed. The artist from Port Victoria had been charmed and, mouth agape, listened entranced to Edwina's happy patter.

Whatever Thomas thought, *something* had changed Edwina and 'whether it was faith or the angel or a miraculous triumph of mind over matter'; she'd never looked better.

One of the last to leave, Inga had driven to the Lourens' house brimming with the anticipation of recounting the gratifying response to the angel! She'd also considered how she might broach the subject of Edwina and her miraculous recovery. Faith, she would say, had cured her! Chris had lost faith in everything: medicine, the doctor, in his own ability to keep going on, and of putting one foot before the other.

He refused outright to take the daily handful of tablets that she laid out for him with a glass of water. Deaf to her pleas and Ginny's tears, he ate only specks. He would not go out or see friends. "Look at me!" he'd said. "They'll run a mile!" Habit alone made him pick up his sketchpad but his pencil drawings were unfinished; Ginny's silver dimpled thimble, a half-eaten apple, the silken folds of a scarf strewn on a table, a necklace of beads.

"When I look at him now," Ginny had said, "I see a man waiting to die!"

Inga had carefully rehearsed what she would say, repeating the words to herself. "Edwina has such faith! She believes her cancer can be cured. And you should see her! Mrs Hurley is vibrant and strong. She is *healthy!* She has transformed herself. You would never know, to look at her now, that she was once knocking at death's door!"

Perhaps her tale of Edwina might inspire Chris? Perhaps he would see that it was not yet too late and, with faith, almost anything was possible.

How could she have known she would return to find an ambulance parked in the driveway and Ginny blubbering like a child as paramedics fitted Chris with an oxygen mask and helped him onto a stretcher?

Ginny had stayed with Chris, in the ambulance, as Inga followed the speeding vehicle to the hospital. She'd been surprised to discover how calm she felt, how composed. She'd remained at the reception desk slowly filling in forms, providing the patient's details, all those she could remember, leaving blank spaces for those she could not. They told her he'd been taken to a private ward on the third floor and she'd climbed the stairs, rather than taking the elevator, stopping at the hospital gift shop to buy a posy of flowers and a bottle of iced mineral water. It was only when she'd reached ward 34C and stood for several minutes outside the closed door that she'd realised she'd been too afraid to turn the doorknob and walk inside. Too afraid of what she might see and how she might respond.

Dr Frey, emerging from the room with another doctor, had saved her from herself.

"Oh good!" she'd said. "He's asking for you, Inga. You can go right in!"

No one would ever know what courage it took for her to walk into that pale grey painted room. She entered, guarding her expression, keeping her face neutral, shaping her lips into a tender smile. She saw him return the smile, behind the oxygen mask. She saw the smile in small wrinkles radiating from the side of his mouth, and his eyes. Ginny had one of his hands in hers, gripped with fierce intensity and Inga, setting aside the posy and bottled water, took the other hand, her smile widening as he weakly squeezed her fingers, his eyes upon her.

It was only after that long vigil watching Chris sleep fitfully through the night, that Inga remembered Edwina's grand unveiling. She'd told him nothing of the praise he'd received or the number of people who wished to meet him, shake his hand and congratulate him on his fine sculpture. None of that seemed to matter any more.

And as for *faith!* Faith might cure Edwina and it might even move mountains but what kind of fight could it put up in the face of the deadly '*Pneumonocytis jirovecii'*; an organism surviving in a weakened immune system, attacking fragile lung tissue and thickening tiny honeycombed air sacs so that precious oxygen no longer flowed from them into his blood.

Love, then, would have to do, in lieu of faith. And she had more than enough of that to give. He would need love in abundance to keep him warm, keep him comfortable, keep him free from harm while he still lived and breathed, safe in her care.

St Jude's relatively small, fifty-six bed hospital was not only full but short staffed and, for this reason, the year's intake of inexperienced young student nurses were given more responsibility than they deserved.

St Jude's senior nurses were easily identified by their large square caps, burgundy lapels and a quantity of badges and medals denoting courses and exams taken and passed, affixed to bosoms large and small. Student nurses, however, wore tiny caps wobbling like white moths upon their heads and went without lapels and merit badges. Junior nurses were also made to wear unflattering, thick, white pantyhose and white lace ups while senior staff wore hose tinted the shade of a bronzed summer tan and polished brown shoes.

Most of the young nurses were easily identified by their expressions of baffled confusion as they tore from ward to ward, answering bells, carrying bedpans, following swiftly on the heels of galloping ward sisters and doctors on rounds. Student nurse, Kat White, was given responsibility for monitoring the patient in ward 34C and alerting the senior staff on duty as to any changes in his condition.

Since she had only been working at the hospital for four months, Kat had no idea what *Pneumocystis pneumonia (PCP)* meant but there was no mistaking the words HIV/AIDS on the patient's card.

"Oh, shit!" she said in alarm. "Mr Lourens has AIDS!"

Sister Sinclair regarded the young nurse with eyes like slits. "Is that a problem, Nurse White?"

"Uh, no. But…"

"So there is a problem?"

Nurse White gulped. "No, Sister!"

"Good! You are responsible for monitoring the patient's vitals and closely observing his IV lines. The treatment must be delivered slowly and intermittently throughout the day. Make sure Mr Lourens is breathing comfortably at all times. If you are concerned about anything, call me immediately! Is that clear, Nurse?"

Kat White nodded quickly: no sense in pissing off Sister Sinclair this early in the morning and facing the danger of being banished to the sluice room and made to scrub bed-pans all day.

Creeping on the thick soles of her ugly white shoes, Kat sidled into ward 34C and removed the chart from the end of the patient's bed. The patient was asleep. There was a woman sitting in a chair beside the bed, his mother probably, sewing a blanket of coloured squares. The woman looked up.

"Hello!" she said, cheerfully. "I'm Ginny Lourens. Who are you?"

"Kat White," she said, automatically. "Um, I mean Nurse White. Or, rather, Student Nurse White."

"Kat? Short for Katherine, I presume? What a lovely name! And what are you going to do to my son, Kat?"

"I'm going to take his vital signs," she mumbled.

"His what?"

"Temperature, respiratory rate, pulse rate and blood pressure," she reeled off.

"But you're not going to wake him up to do that, are you?" His mother's smile was dazzling.

"Yeah. I have to."

The smile disappeared. Mrs Lourens brows met, her expression darkened. "No, my dear, you're not. His vital signs, if that's what they're called, were taken just one hour ago. If you examine that chart that you are holding, you will see that his condition is steadily improving. Listen to his breathing! Can you hear? Slow and steady. He's just fallen asleep again and I don't want him woken up!"

"But, Sister said …"

"Sister Sinclair? Sister Barrie? Oh, I shouldn't worry about them. We've had a long chat this morning and we all agree that, along with the treatment Chris is receiving, sleep is the best cure for him." The smile flashed briefly, coldly.

Student Nurse White was at a loss. She wasn't sure who she was more afraid of: Sister Sinclair or the little Mrs Lourens? The woman sitting opposite had eyes that glinted like steel.

"I'll be back in one hour," Kat said as firmly as she could, and then disappointed herself by adding, "If that's OK?"

"Thank you, Kat!" Mrs Lourens picked up her sewing.

Exactly one hour later, Kat White returned, with a slightly firmer tread. She'd have to take the patient's vitals this time or it was bedpans for sure!

Mr Lourens sat up against a hill of pillows. His mother was fussing with the bed linen; peeling back the heavy counterpane. "Oh, hello Kat. Just in time! Chris is hot, it's the fever I expect, and these blankets are too heavy. Just sheets, I think, to cover him. Do you agree?"

"Um, yes, I suppose so."

"I've opened the windows to let in a little fresh air. Do you suppose you could fill this flask with fresh water? Iced, if possible?"

She thrust the flask at Nurse White who took it and, sighing loudly, disappeared from the room. No doubt about it! Mrs Lourens was going to be a regular pain in the arse.

Sister Sinclair stopped her as she was returning hastily from the kitchen with the flask of iced water. "How is our patient?" she asked, crisply.

"Um, he's awake and sitting up."

"And his vitals?"

"I'm about to take them, Sister."

Sister Sinclair glanced at the watch pinned on her bosom and pressed her lips into a thin line. "I'd like to see the patient's chart," she said. "Please bring it to me."

Kat White dashed into ward 34C. Mrs Lourens, sitting on the edge of the bed, was massaging her son's foot.

Kat grabbed the chart. "Sorry!" she said. "I've got to take his temperature!"

Mrs Lourens held up a hand. "Can it wait a moment?" she asked pleasantly.

"No! It can't. Sister's on the warpath!"

The patient laughed. "Ma! Leave the poor girl alone, will you. She's got a job to do."

He opened his mouth and stuck out his tongue. "Where's your thermometer?" he asked, pointing.

Kat slipped the thermometer into the patient's mouth and, with one eye on the second hand of her watch, carefully placed index and middle fingers on the radial artery to take his pulse.

"Your pulse rate is improving!" she announced with what she hoped was an authoritative voice, and neatly filled in the correct column on the chart.

Happily, Kat looked up to smile at Mr Lourens and saw his face, properly for the first time. She blinked. She flushed. She looked away.

The patient was incredibly good looking! Better than Brad Pitt. Better than Jude Law. Better than, well, than just about any man she had ever seen in real life or on the screen.

Chris smiled and absently swept back a lock of soft blond hair that had fallen over one eye. Kat's fingers trembled as she wrapped the blood pressure cuff around his arm, just above his elbow. She inserted the earpieces of the stethoscope, placing the bell over the brachial artery. She could feel her skin burn.

Sister Sinclair's head appeared around the open door.

"Nurse White! The chart please!"

"One sec! Almost done!"

Sister Sinclair darted a look across the room. "Two minutes!" she said. "I'll see you in the staff room."

Inflating the cuff, Kat White listened to the brachial pulse. She found it hard to concentrate. Systolic pressure, diastolic pressure. Oh, it was all so confusing, particularly with the patient's eyes on her. She deflated the cuff and started again.

"Anything wrong?" His voice sounded sympathetic.

"I'm making a mess of this. I need more practice."

He placed his hand on her arm. "Relax," he said. "Don't worry about Sister Sinclair. Do it carefully and slowly."

Kat nodded gratefully and repeated the procedure, writing her findings in the next column on the patient's chart. "Blood pressure still a little high," she mumbled, apologetically.

"What's next?"

"Um, respiratory rate. Except, I'm not really supposed to tell the patient that I'm measuring breathing. Sometimes, when they know that, they slow the breaths down. So, could you please breath normally for me, as if you didn't know I was counting?"

Chris breathed quietly.

Kat counted his breaths for fifteen seconds and multiplied the number by four.

"Normal!" she announced. "That's awesome!" She filled in the last column and, chart in hand, bolted from the room.

Ginny rolled her eyes. "I'm not sure I have much confidence in that dizzy little thing," she said.

Kat brushed her hair and glossed her lips before she went in to check the IV lines in 34C, later that afternoon. She was deeply disappointed to find another woman in the ward with the patient and his mother. The woman was beautiful enough to be a model; super thin with amazing cheekbones and long blond hair, pinned up in a sprouting twist at the back, falling around her face in the front. She wore no makeup.

Kat chewed her lips, removing the slick of shining gloss.

The woman looked up as she entered and held out a slender hand. "You are Kat," she said, "and I am Inga. I am very pleased to make your acquaintance."

Her voice was foreign but Kat couldn't place the accent.

"Student Nurse White," said Kat, shaking her hand.

Kat saw the fleeting look of amusement that passed between the patient and the woman called Inga. Flustered, Kat checked the IV lines. One of the treatment bags was almost empty. Ginny indicated the bag with a wave of her hand.

"Please call Sister Sinclair," she said. "No offence, Kat but I would feel more comfortable if she changed the bag."

Head down, Kat left the room to summon Sister. "Mrs Lourens says she would rather you changed the IV bag," she said, miserably.

Sister Sinclair lifted bushy brows. "Oh, would she indeed?"

A compromise was reached with Sister Sinclair barking instructions at Nurse White, while patient and visitors quietly observed the proceedings.

The Sister's voice boomed in the small room. "Shut off the IV line using the control clamp."

Kat's fingers shook with nervousness and shame. "This one? Oh, no, this one. Sorry!"

"Now, clean the Y-port with alcohol."

"The, um, Y-port?"

Sister Sinclair jabbed an irritated finger to indicate.

"Connect the medication needle to the port. Inject the contents slowly. Slowly, Nurse White. Do you understand the meaning of s-l-o-w-l-y?"

Kat's could feel her face turning a shade of tomato.

"Now, disconnect the syringe and remove it."

Kat looked up, syringe in her hand, for a sign of approval.

"Reopen the IV line using the control clamp, and reset the flow. Got it, Nurse White?"

Kat nodded meekly as Sister Sinclair swept away. Kat's bottom lip trembled. Surely she wasn't going to cry, not with all these people watching! The tears spilled. "Oh shit," she said, angrily rubbing her eyes.

Mrs Lourens jumped from her chair with a sorrowful cry and pulled Kat into a tight embrace. Her wiry red hair smelled of lemons, her silver bracelets dug painfully into Kat's arm.

"Oh Kat!" she exclaimed. "I'm so sorry, my dear! Poor, poor you! Sister Sinclair is a battleaxe. A Tartar! I had no idea. Forgive me for being such an interfering busy-body!"

"No," mumbled Kat. "I couldn't have done it on my own. You were right to call Sister. I'm a junior. I've a lot to learn."

The woman called Inga removed a silver flask from a bag and jiggled it. "I have iced tea!" she smiled. "Will you join us?"

Kat sipped the drink, eyes straying to their beautiful faces; to the patient, so handsome she could hardly bear look at him. To the foreign woman with her lovely shining face. He loved her, she loved him; you could see it in the way they looked at one another, the way their hands touched, the way they sent messages with their eyes, no words necessary. And then there was Mrs Lourens: the kind of mother who wore a luminous green scarf in her hair and fought to the death to protect her son. How lucky they were! How charmed their lives! How dull, in comparison, her own dreary existence seemed.

Afterwards, at every chance, Kat drifted into ward 34C to monitor vitals, check the IV lines and then, as the patient's health progressed, simply to be with them all as though, if she stood amongst them and breathed the same air, some of the love they shared, some of their happiness at being together, might rub off on her.

Chapter 12

Sarah and James

Summer was passing; I could feel it in the cold snap at dawn before the sun warmed the day and in the dank, chilled evening mist that floated like a wraith above the canal.

I enjoyed my morning walks with Angus all the more knowing that soon it would be still dark at this hour with a raw wind blowing. We always followed the same paths towards the beach; hopeful that the tide might be out and we could walk on the sand towards the estuary. At high tide, when the beach became impassable, we steered our walk towards the village where we often met up with Sarah and Lucky. There were many in St Jude who seemed in awe of Sarah.

Her home, once a humble holiday cottage, was now considered one of the finest in the village and then there was the miraculous change she had wrought upon The Two Potters; transforming the tired gallery into St Jude's favourite meeting place. I know that many envied Sarah. Attractive, confident and successful; she seemed to have it all. For my part I thought her a sad figure: too isolated for one still relatively young and full of life. She had a few friends: the Lourenses and the Grants, particularly James, and then there was Ben Barker. Many of us had hoped that a romantic relationship might be hatching between Sarah and Ben but nothing came of it, chiefly, I suspect, because she still mourned the loss of her husband. Had I been a close friend I'd have suggested that it might be time to leave the past behind and move on with her life, but, we were merely nodding acquaintances at that stage and it was not my place to dispense romantic advice.

Sarah had stopped dreaming of David. She missed those dreams. She kept a nightlight burning so that, before she slept, she could gaze at his one-dimensional smiling face in the photograph at her bedside, hoping the image might come alive in dreams.

Sometimes she dreamed she was searching for him: driving across endless flat highways or striding through empty fields, calling his name. Sometimes she thought she saw a hint of him: the back of his head, that way his hair stood up from his crown, the black windcheater he'd loved to wear, his hand carrying his worn leather briefcase with the initials inscribed in gold. But then the picture would dissolve and he would fade away.

There were times when she felt herself floating towards wakefulness because Ben had drifted into her sub-conscious when David should have been there instead.

There were often new dreams now: dreams that no longer included her husband.

The dreams were ones in which she found herself hunting for a shop she couldn't find, where sale goods were on offer; priceless antiques to be had for a handful of coins.

She wondered why her subconscious mind deliberately chose to fill her brain with images of shopping rather than obey her desire to dream of her beloved husband and decided that it was probably because she knew for certain that David had finally left Peace Cottage.

She could hardly remember when she'd last heard his voice or felt his presence even though, from habit, she spoke to him as she went about her chores.

She missed their old life: missed their conversations, and even their arguments. They'd disagreed on almost everything: art, food, music, décor, fashion, films, books. Cappuccino versus filter coffee. Stainless steel versus oak. Cashmere versus wool. Comedy versus drama. His view, her view; the ongoing tussle that could never be resolved without a compromise on her part.

A friend had visited; dropping in, unannounced from the past, astonished at how much Sarah had changed and the new directions she'd taken since her retreat to St Jude.

"All this!" the friend had said, her circling hand encompassing the house, the garden, the large dog on the antique rug, the gallery order books on the coffee table and even Sarah's flat moccasins. "It's amazing!"

Sarah had smiled hesitantly, wondering what, exactly, was so amazing?

The friend had taken great care to explain. "There's none of David's influence in this house," she'd said, approvingly. "Not a scrap.

It's all you, Sarah, every bit. He'd have made the house more modern, more masculine. The garden would have been a lot of brick paving and big planters."

The friend had warmed to her theory. "As for the gallery, well, imagine David's reaction. He'd have been outraged at the idea of you working in retail. *In a shop!* And a dog! A great big, hairy dog at that! Come on, he'd never have allowed it!"

"What are you saying?"

"Only that I'm proud of you!" The friend's face had beamed approval. "You've become your own person, Sarah. David was always so *controlling* ..."

"I loved him!" Her instant rebuke was a warning.

"Oh, I know that. We all did! But he had you right here, under his thumb!" She demonstrated: her thumb on the coffee table, grinding into the polished veneer.

Sarah felt defensive, protective. "He was a *wonderful* husband!"

"I'm sure he was. But now you have a life of your own and..."

"A lonely life. I miss him still" There, she'd said it. For all the so-called accomplishments, for all the great strides she'd made, she still felt incredibly lonely without David. She felt half a person, really.

A flicker of annoyance had passed over her companion's face.

"David's gone, Sarah. He's not coming back. You've made friends, surely? Any men friends?"

"One. But he is just that, a friend."

Seeing her wistful expression, the friend had softened. "Give it time," she'd advised. "Put yourself out there. Circulate. Meet people. You'll find someone. I guarantee it. But, Sarah, don't, for God's sake, *wallow!*"

"Wallow?" She felt indignant.

"You know what I mean. Indulge in self-pity. Become a recluse. Imagine no man could ever replace David."

"That's not wallowing," Sarah had said softly. "That's the first stage of widowhood."

"Point taken," her friend had smiled, "but now it's time for act two!"

It was not long after this conversation that Ben had appeared in Sarah's confused nightly dreams and, though she woke from these flooded with a pervasive sense of disloyalty, she wondered if her subconscious were prodding her with unsubtle messages; perhaps it *was* time to move on with her life?

On an impulse, Sarah called Ben at home early one morning, before he was due to depart for the surgery, and invited him to dinner. "I'm in the mood for an old fashioned roast chicken with gravy, potatoes and steamed vegetables. Will you join me?"

There'd been a long pause that had taken her by surprise. "Ben? Are you there?"

"Thanks, Sarah but I've a very full day ahead and I'll probably be working till late tonight. Dinner sounds tempting but I'll have to pass. Sorry!"

"Tomorrow, then?"

There was another pause. "I can't commit to anything right now. I'll call you, if I may, when I have some free time. Is that OK?"

After the call, Sarah surprised herself by feeling hurt. Something was wrong, that much was obvious. Ben had turned her down flat and his voice had sounded… what? Remote? Disinterested?

That day, moving between the rooms of the gallery, opening boxes of new stock and ordering books, Sarah carried a tight kernel of unease in her breast. She set out a Chinese Tiffany lamp on an antique silver tray and draped a bolt of Ghanaian cloth, hand-woven with gold thread, over a chair, but her heart wasn't in it.

She knew why Ben had spoken in that detached voice, rejecting her invitation. She'd pushed him away so often he'd probably grown tired of waiting for her to come to her senses. Perhaps he'd met someone else? A sensible woman who appreciated the warmth and affection a good man like Ben had to give.

Lucky sat at her feet, mouth open, staring up with liquid eyes.

"Why is it," Sarah asked the dog, scratching the space between his ears, "that we never know what we truly want, until it's too late?!"

James hadn't seen Caron for five whole days and had missed her more than he thought possible. The door to the bedroom had been kept shut and only his father had gone in with trays of food and cups of tea.

"She's resting," he'd whispered to James as he closed the door behind him and James had taken that to mean that he was not to enter the quiet, darkened room until Caron felt well enough to see him.

James had missed all the things Caron did that he'd never really noticed before. The kitchen had grown untidy; dishes and mugs left in the sink and dust on windowsills. There'd been a brown ring around the bath, the towels had a funny wet smell and his Dad left piles of newspapers, just anyhow, on the coffee table.

The mess had given James a headache and made him sulky and miserable. He'd tried to keep his bedroom clean, made his bed every morning and put his pyjamas in the laundry hamper as Caron had shown him but the hamper had overflowed with unwashed sheets and his dad's shirts and stuff and then he'd run out of clean pyjamas and had to wear t-shirts and shorts to bed.

Meal times had been the worst! His dad hadn't known that he liked the crusts cut off his toast triangles, his egg boiled for exactly three minutes and then perfectly cracked with a sharp knife so that the top came off cleanly like a little Chinese hat.

James had secretly thrown two breakfast eggs away because his father had walloped them with a teaspoon so that the yolk had spilled over onto the shell in little sticky streams of thick yellow that made him feel squeamish. He always had a half a glass of milk and two oat biscuits at eleven o'clock but his dad had forgotten his mid-morning snack and when James reminded him had tossed a bar of chocolate.

James had been mildly shocked. "I don't have chocolate as a snack," he'd said. "It's not allowed. Too much sugar is not good for me."

"Not true! Chocolate is packed with energy!"

James had slipped the chocolate bar into his pencil case and taken two biscuits from the tin in the pantry and put them on a plate.

He'd poured exactly half a glass of milk and had taken the plate to the table where he'd nibbled the biscuits slowly. "When will Caron be better?" he'd asked, mournfully.

His dad had also been hopeless with schoolwork. He'd set up his laptop at one end of the kitchen table and positioned James at the other with his books, maps and crayons. Eyes on the computer screen, he'd absently given James a few simple projects. He'd asked him to draw things, set a page of very easy maths equations that a baby could do and then suggested that he write a story.

"What kind of story?"

His father had gazed, distractedly about the room. There were birds cheeping in the trees beyond the window.

"Write a story about a bird," he'd said.

Puffing out his cheeks, James had sighed heavily and kicked the chair. "Which bird?" he'd asked patiently.

"Any bird. Use your imagination!"

"The African Hoopoe?"

"The, ah, *what?"*

"A bird with a crest like a Red-Indian headdress and a long, sharp curved bill. It has a brown body and black and white wings and it makes a noise like this: 'hoop, hoop, hoop'!"

"Good! Write a story about the African thingamajig."

James had been annoyed. "The African *Hoopoe*, dad! Everyone knows what it's called. Anyway, what kind of story do you want me to write?"

There'd been a note of exasperation in his father's voice. "An exciting story. The kind you'd like to read."

Frowning, James had scrutinised his father's face. "You're not very good at this," he had decided, finally. "Caron is better. Much better."

His dad had laughed. "Give me a break, James," he'd said. After that they'd gone outdoors where his father had rigged up a new basketball net above the garage. James had missed the baskets, every one. He'd seen how disappointed his dad had been. "You'll get better!" his father had promised. "You need more practice. We'll play every afternoon when I come home from work."

Going to his dad's office at Grant and Associates had not been much fun either.

His father had spent most of the time in meetings in the boardroom and James had been consigned to a desk in an empty office.

The office had once belonged to someone called Jim Flint who had died in a car accident. Mr Flint's stuff was still in the room; there were packets of cigarettes in the drawers, a silver lighter, a black leather diary with a photograph of a girl in a bikini marking one of the pages, some used airline tickets and a box of black pens for drawing.

James used one of the pens to write the story about the African Hoopoe.

He turned the story into a murder mystery: *"The African Hoopoe was found dead, hanging from a branch in the thorn tree."* he wrote. "*It had a noose around its neck. Somebody had strangled it.*"

"This is pretty grim!" his dad had said, reading with a troubled expression.

"I wrote it in Mr Flint's office with one of his pens," James had explained. "It feels sad in there."

After that, James had been given a table in a narrow office with his dad's secretary who, busy with telephone calls, faxes, photostats and endless trays of coffee for the boardroom, had left him alone to his own devices. That's when James had secretly drawn and coloured the card for Caron.

That morning, James had awoken to the sound of their voices. He had run with expectant pleasure down the stairs and into the kitchen where Caron stood at the sink wearing a blue shirt with a ribbon tied in her toffee-coloured hair, looking the way she usually did.

He had jiggled from one foot to the other. "Are you better?" he had asked.

"Yes, much better!"

The kitchen windows had been wide open, the floor shining. The dishes in the sink had been washed and put away. Coffee bubbled in the percolator.

James had scrambled amongst the things on the table, found the card and thrust it at Caron, watching her expression intently. Her face had grown softer as she'd gazed at the drawing. She'd gathered James into her arms. They'd stood together for a moment before he'd pulled away. She'd smelled of soap and detergent.

He'd felt suddenly happy. "I missed you!' he'd blurted.

Later that day, Caron took James outdoors and they sat against the cushions on the garden seat in the shade of the veranda.

"I want to talk to you about the baby, James." Something in her voice had made him look up, at her face.

"You remember the day Sarah took us to the St Jude hospital?"

He nodded, looking away.

"Well, I was sick because the baby died, James. It died in my uterus, before it could be born."

He remembered red blood staining her dressing gown, splotches of blood on her shoes, the hot, sickening smell of it.

He remembered coming home from the hospital and going up to the bathroom to change and seeing red on the floor tiles. Sarah had sent him to his bedroom and when he'd come out, the floor had been cleaned.

"Why?" he asked, eyes searching the sky. "Why did the baby die?"

“I don’t know,” she said honestly. “It was very tiny, not yet properly formed. The baby might have been sick. Or perhaps my body wasn’t strong enough to feed and care for it properly.”

James stared hard at a billowing, white cumulous cloud.

“Remember when you planted vegetables in the garden, James?”

Tiny seeds they’d dropped into the soil. Small green shoots emerging. The tomato plant with vigorous, twisting leaves and small, hard sour green tomatoes. He remembered.

“Well, as you know, some of the seeds grew to become healthy plants and others didn’t. Those seeds weren’t strong enough and so they died. The same thing happened to the baby.”

He thought about what she was saying. The baby hadn’t been strong enough and so it had died. She wasn’t having a baby any more.

“Remember the Cape Robin’s nest?” Caron added. “Two of the eggs opened and tiny fledglings emerged. But there was one egg that never hatched. You kept it for a while.”

A small fragile egg wrapped in a blue sock. He’d hoped that if he kept it warm the chick would survive. But the egg had grown cold and he had buried it finally in a flowerbed.

“Will there be another baby?” he asked.

“No.” One word spoken very softly. She started to say something else and stopped. He wondered if she were going to cry. He looked at her face. She took his hand.

He wanted to pull his hand away but left it there to comfort her because she looked sad and lost. He tried to make his hand feel friendly.

James was the first to break the silence.

“I wrote a story about an African Hoopoe,” he told her. “It’s a murder mystery. Dad doesn’t get it, but I think you’ll like it.”

“Intriguing,” she said. “A murder mystery about a Hoopoe. Why don’t you read it to me?”

He found the story on the kitchen table and brought it out and began reading: *“The African Hoopoe was found dead, hanging from a branch in the thorn tree. It had a noose around its neck. Somebody had strangled it.”*

Her face wore an expression of delight. “Excellent beginning, James!” she smiled. “I love it already! Carry on…”

It was the dream that showed Mickey the way. She dreamed of an inferno, possibly Hell, where flames consumed everything living and thick smoke and specks of floating ash filled the air. When she woke, Mickey knew what had to be done.

She also knew for certain that the vision had not been inspired by God or the Devil, but by her own all-consuming desire for revenge. If she had, however, still been in communication with God, if they'd still been close, their covenant not broken, Mickey knew He would have given her vision a Godlike nod of approval.

God, however, had made it clear that he had other fish to fry and so, as far as Mickey was concerned, she was wholly responsible for extracting a tooth and an eye from Jordan Black.

God would not be permitted to take any of the credit for his punishment.

The small warehouse in Otter Lane where Jordan Black, along with his sidekick, Wayne, produced 'kitchens, cupboards, custom-made furniture' was central to the vision. Since she had first discovered the shed, a veritable hive of industry, she had driven past the warehouse every day. Sometimes she cruised past two or three times a day. Though it was risky, Mickey often parked the truck some distance away and, with her hat pulled low over her face, sauntered slowly past the open door of Black's workshop.

She heard the high-pitched whine of the electric saw slicing cleanly through planks of wood, rap music booming from a cassette player, and bursts of male laughter.

The air was filled with dust: curling wood shavings pirouetted before her eyes.

There was a sharp odour of paint: someone wielding a spray gun, blasting white gloss onto cupboard doors. Once, she'd seen the woman from the gallery – the large matron who'd enquired about an armoire. The woman had been in conversation with the red-bearded cripple, Wayne, and Mickey had heard her loudly describing the cupboard that she wanted made "in maple, or cherry."

Mickey observed it all: recording every detail. She purchased a black, hard-covered exercise book and made copious and accurate notes.

A battered blue Toyota dropped Wayne in Otter Lane every morning, promptly, at eight o'clock. The Toyota, driven by a thickset man Mickey recognised as one of Black's bricklayers then drove off, presumably to one of the sites where the team was working. Wayne, together with two other carpenters, spent the day inside the shed, producing furniture to order. They took a lunch break at one and sometimes gathered outside to share a flask of tea at three in the afternoon. Black arrived at the warehouse, usually after six in the evening, and spent half an hour or so with the men, sharing a six-pack of cold beers. Once or twice Wayne and Black had worked together until after seven, but generally the shed was locked for the night by then.

Mickey drew an asterisk on a page and inked it heavily. Beside this she wrote: *"Thursday 12th, after midnight "* – the date and time when she would get her own back on Jordan Black. She closed the book with a sigh of relief. So, there it was!

The dye was cast; the way forward pre-ordained. She had committed herself to a vision of vengeance that would, in all likelihood, consign her to hell if there were such a place, but it was a small price to pay for getting even with the man who had become her worst enemy.

When she returned home that evening, Mickey found Ian Frey perched upon her roof, nailing down the last of the sheets of corrugated iron that had lain untouched upon the garden path.

"What are you doing?" she shouted, peering up at him.

"Fixing your roof!"

"Oh, please come down!" she called, her voice torn with emotion. "Stop what you're doing and come down from there!"

"Almost done!" She heard the sound of nails hammered through corrugated iron into wood.

"Come down! Come down!"

Frey climbed backwards down the ladder, carrying a hammer. He turned and grinned. "I heard about your roof," he said. "Black's a bastard! I couldn't leave it like that." He seemed to be waiting for her thanks.

"Why?" She cried. She bit her lip to control her voice. "Why didn't you let well enough alone?"

"I don't understand?"

"I wanted it left! I wanted to go to sleep beneath that great yawning hole and wake looking at the sky above. I wanted the roof left as it was – *for a reason!"*

"What reason? What reason could you possibly have to leave your roof like that? It's dangerous. Winter's on its way. The rains will come soon and then what? The house will be flooded!"

"Good! Good!" Her voice was a wail.

Ian frowned. He stepped closer and examined Mickey's face. "What is it? Tell me? I don't understand."

"Jordan Black did this. I wanted it left, just as it was, so that I could keep it alive."

"Keep what alive?"

"My hatred for Black."

"Mickey, look, I may be talking out of turn …"

"And I wanted people to see something of the damage he's done so they'd understand and not judge me too harshly. The roof was *evidence!*"

"Mickey …"

She held up her hand. "Don't say anything more. Please."

"You need help. You need to talk to someone about this."

Mickey composed herself. He saw her shoulders rise. She stood straighter. Lifted her chin. "I don't need to talk to anyone, that's where you're wrong. I know exactly what to do to resolve the situation. I want to be left alone, that's all! Is that too much to ask?"

He shrugged. "I didn't mean to interfere. I only wanted to help." He picked up his tools.

She looked up at the roof, the iron sheets neatly bolted down; a good job.

"Thank you!" she said, grudgingly. "I didn't mean to be rude. I am grateful, it's just that I wish people would stop trying to help."

She cried then, soundlessly squeezing out tears. It had been such a long time since she'd wept, she'd forgotten how.

He put his arms around her and she leaned against his hard shoulder, resting there as her tears dampened his shirt. She felt his huge hand rhythmically patting her back. He smelled of something familiar and clean like the expensive soap her father had used so many years ago. "Lock up the house and come home with me," he said, soothingly. "Have dinner with us. Grace will be home by now."

She was torn for a few seconds. Her cheek still rested on his shoulder. A curl of his thick hair brushed her face. She wished she could stay there, pressed in the comfortingly deep curve between his shoulder and neck, even as she put her hands upon his chest and pushed herself away.

"I can't," she said, simply. "But thank you."

Once he'd gone, she felt desolate. *How strong am I, really,* she wondered, *if a kind deed, a consoling word, a sympathetic hand touching me can make me fall apart like this?*

That night Mickey dreamed again of the inferno. She saw a tower of flames consuming a wooden structure; glass showering from windows and glittering in the night like stars. She saw the blackened carcasses of cupboards and chairs silhouetted against a frieze of shooting flames and spiralling smoke. An armoire made of maple or cherry crumpled like paper and fell to charred dust.

Waking, Mickey remembered the dream clearly. But what did it really mean? Was the inferno a symbol of punishment, of fire and brimstone to be meted out for Jordan Black or did it represent the eternal hellfire and damnation waiting for Mickey Graham?

James dreamed of tomato plants. They climbed with twisty stems up wooden stakes towards the sky, waving hairy leaves in the air, like grasping hands. Clusters of hard, green tomatoes grew as he watched, ripening in the hot sun so that they became first pale yellow, then orange, then shiny red.

James picked the tomatoes, filling a basket. It was only when the tomatoes began to wail and scream that he saw they were all babies' heads; mouths open wide, like chicks, clamouring for food.

Sarah dreamed that her arms were filled with candlesticks and picture frames, with books and silk shawls, Toby jugs and pewter bracelets.

David was in the dream: walking away down a labyrinthine corridor and all that she could see was his disappearing back and a sprout of reckless hair waving from the top of his head. She tried to run after him but her feet were rooted and, though she called his name over and over again, she couldn't hear her own voice above a whisper. She stood there, hugging her bulky bounty and watching her husband grow smaller until he faded from sight, gone, gone, gone!

Chris dreamed that he sat cross-legged upon the jetty looking down into the deep, green, still waters of the canal and saw his own face reflected there. The day was hot: the sun burned his skin. The water, cool and silken like the softest sheets beckoned invitingly. He submerged both feet, breaking the surface of the water with concentric ripples. His legs next and then his torso. He felt the water breaking over his shoulders so that only his head was free. He floated peacefully, drifting like a leaf, a bobbing blossom, upon the shimmering water.

He woke, yearning for the weightless sensation of being carried along by the graceful ebb and flow of endless tides.

"You've been dreaming," Inga said, lightly stroking his hair. "You were laughing in your sleep!"

Chris closed his eyes, drawing himself back into the dream towards that still place where water embraced his feeble, tired body like cool satin. The hospital ward faded, Inga's face dimmed and all that remained, all that he could clearly see was the bleached and cloudless sky above, as the water flowed sweetly over his head.

Chapter 13

Ginny and Chris

I had a sense, as we went about our lives, that we were all waiting for something to happen. It was like that unbearably pregnant pause before a summer thunderstorm when the steaming air is so electric it crackles with static and everyone waits, holding their breath for lightning to snake across the sky, the clouds to burst and rain to finally plummet to earth. We were locked in that quiet pause until, one by one, a series of events took place that would culminate in the tragedy that motivated me to write this book in the first place.

At the time, I made a few predictions. I was convinced that poor, obsessive Mickey would make herself so ill she'd have a nervous breakdown. I feared the inevitability of Chris succumbing to the virus that daily sapped his life and strength. I thought there may be some truth in rumours, spread mainly by Alec's secretary, that the Grants were soon to proceed with a divorce. And all of us waited for brave Edwina to face her certain fate. Some of my predictions were correct: others were not.

There is a fine line drawn between the normal and the insane, and Mickey discovered the line sometimes faded so she wasn't always sure which side she was on. There was no doubt that her world had grown more disordered, her thoughts more chaotic as though violins were being noisily tuned inside her brain, but for much of the time she also felt completely in control of her life and the events that she fastidiously set in motion were neither random not meaningless.

There was a sudden interest in her health and well-being from people who'd never before been troubled by whether she swallowed vitamins or had sufficient sleep or a friend to confide in. '*Someone to talk to*' seemed to be generally considered as the primary cure for all her problems and by that, she gathered that the 'someone' referred to was either a psychologist or psychiatrist: certainly one involved with treatment of mental disorders. Didn't they realise she was not mad, not losing her mind? Often she thought she'd never been more sane!

Mrs Hurley called frequently asking for help in the garden but it was all a ruse and Mickey could see right through it. Edwina was obviously responding to rumours that Mickey appeared to have lost her marbles and was attempting to toss a life raft.

Ian Frey had taken it upon himself to repair her roof and Mr Barker had called again to find out if she'd changed her mind about the puppy. Sarah, visiting the nursery to purchase plants, had overpaid for a dozen root-bound fig trees, long past their best and dropping leaves. She'd pressed a wad of crumpled notes into Mickey's hand. "This is too much!" Mickey had objected, counting the money, but Sarah had driven away before Mickey could return any of it.

She knew, of course, everyone was trying to be kind but found their unwanted attentions both annoying and humiliating and decided, in future, not to answer either the door or the telephone. There was a job to be planned and executed and a grave danger that the generosity and kindness of well-meaning people would prove a distraction and might even achieve the unthinkable and draw her off course!

The little black book proved invaluable. The first few pages were dedicated to the comings and goings of those who worked at the warehouse in Otter's Lane. The next few pages detailed items that filled the warehouse.

All Mickey had to do was shut her eyes, and one by one, images of items in the shed floated from her cortex to the blank canvas behind her eyelids. Mickey couldn't help but laugh. It was as though every detail regarding the interior of the carpenters' shed had been burned into her brain. If she'd been playing a memory game she'd have won top prize. Mickey drew a column and wrote down each item, printing carefully. A workbench. A silver circular saw. Shelves against the wall. Carpenter's tools. A tower of paint tins. Paintbrushes soaking in a bucket of turpentine. Piles of wooden planks. A bed and table. Paraffin lamps. The door locked with a bolt from the inside; a padlock on the outside. *A coil of fraying rope near the door.* The rope was important. She underlined the word 'rope'.

She'd had a good look at it: two or three metres of twisted, intertwined hemp, the thickness of a small finger, sprouting fine, twisting fibres.

The items of furniture in the shed changed from day to day. Yesterday, four finished cupboards had been piled into the back of a truck and carted away.

The wood for the armoire had been delivered. The client had inspected it; caressing the grain with a plump, white hand and had seemed well pleased.

There was a second column in which Mickey attempted to gauge the value of the contents of the workshop. She had no idea how much a circular saw might cost but there was no doubt that the collective tools, furniture and materials alone would add up to the sum of ten thousand and probably more. She wrote 'ten thousand +' and gave the column a well-satisfied tick. On the next page Mickey wrote the word: 'Purchases' and scribbled a brief list of requirements: two metres of rope, one gallon drum of petrol, one pair of gloves, a flashlight.

She added the date at the bottom of the page: Wednesday 11th. One more day and the plan would be executed. Justice would be served!

Discharged from hospital, Chris rested at home in the narrow bed, beneath the flowered quilt. Divested of the angel, the room seemed lighter and more spacious.

Ginny told those who called to enquire that Chris was 'recuperating' and would soon be well enough to get out and about. She used a special voice for telephone calls: an octave higher with a tone that aimed at briskly efficient cheerfulness.

Inga also played the game. She imagined herself through a make-believe camera lens, performing like a seasoned actor. She practiced her expression in the mirror, aiming for a look of smiling serenity. She laughed often with an upward ascending trill of happiness that, with any luck, might fool all of the people, all of the time. She dropped the mask only at the end of the day when she returned home to the loft above the yoga studio and collapsed. That's when she knew, with the sharp clarity that comes after midnight, that her father had been right and she should *never* have fallen in love with Chris.

That time before they'd met seemed, in retrospect, relatively happy and carefree. She'd been content enough with her life. Certainly she'd been free from pain.

And how did one deal with pain? How did one conceal it?

Crying was out of the question. Crying bruised her fine skin, reddened and thickened her eyelids. Crying made her ugly. And what message did her tear-ravaged face hold for Chris and Ginny? That she had given up and expected the worst to happen? That she waited, as they all did, for him to die?

Her father had surprised her. She'd written to confess she should have listened to him, should never have lost her heart to a dying man for now, here she was, torn in pieces and filled with anguish at watching the man she loved slowly lose the will to fight for life.

"*You will have to be strong,*" her father had replied. *"He needs you. It's too late to indulge in regret. Be brave and true and do what needs to be done. You said he saw you as his Guardian Angel? Well, the part is yours my darling and now you must play it through to the bitter end."*

The tone of the letter was confusing. Was the good professor rebuking her as he might a disobedient and wayward student and telling her to lie upon the bed she'd made for herself? Or did her father understand and sympathise? Did he feel love and pity for his daughter and the man she loved?

She wasn't exactly sure of his meaning but her father's words articulated something she knew intuitively to be true: *she* – Inga Johansson – was his guardian angel. Happenstance had brought her from her home in Sweden to the remote village of St Jude to stand at the side of the man she loved as he neared the end of his life.

There was nothing to be done but to obey her father. She would play the part to the end and only when it was done, would she cry.

Edwina paid a visit to the Lourens' home, bringing a jug of black bean and bacon soup and a white orchid in a vase.

Ginny led her upstairs to where Chris lay sleeping.

"I won't disturb him!" Edwina reassured his mother. "I'll sit here for a little while, in case he wakes."

Ginny left them together. Edwina listened to Chris' steady breathing and the gentle ticking of the bedside clock. Outside, on this perfect summer's day, she could hear the murmurs of sparrows, weavers and thrush in the garden as they fluttered from leafy trees to the feeding tray where Ginny had laid out seed, crumbs and ripe fruit.

Edwina's eyes flitted between the patient and the open window.

She had never noticed before, but Chris had a look of Christ about him. Christ on the cross, the suffering Christ. Long, curling blond hair, beautiful mouth – gentle in repose – those heavy-lidded closed eyes, the high, domed brow. She'd seen the same tragic face on so many alter walls in dim, hushed churches.

He stirred and opened his eyes. "Edwina?" He seemed surprised.

She leaned forward. "You must never lose hope!" she whispered fiercely. "You must hold onto life for as long as you can! You must fight! Fight this disease!"

He closed his eyes.

"Do you hear me, Chris?" Her face was very close; he could smell a cloying whiff of gardenia in her perfume, the rope of beads hanging around her neck brushed his hand, icy to the touch. "Don't give up!"

He nodded, too tired to talk. How to explain? How to tell Edwina that he was no longer afraid of dying; it was life he feared. And pain. His own pain and theirs: the pain he knew that Ginny and Inga were hiding from him.

Perhaps he slept again for a few moments, as he surfaced to find Edwina roughly shaking his arm. "You have all the time in the world to sleep when you're dead!" she hissed. "Listen to me! You are alive! Use your stamina, your energy, your *faith* to heal your body."

"Faith?" The idea was laughable. "I have AIDS, Edwina! How can you speak of faith?"

"Do you believe in miracles?" Edwina vibrated with intensity.

"I know what you think," he said. "You're dead wrong. I'm beyond faith and miracles. And, frankly, I'm too tired for this conversation."

He dozed off, her voice still echoing in his ear. Afterwards, he remembered snatches. The angel. God's divine messenger. Tumours shrinking. Cancer destroyed. Tissue healing.

When he awoke, none of it seemed real. "I had a weird dream about Edwina," he told his mother. "She was ranting about the angel and about faith. She seemed hostile; she shouted at me to wake up and fight."

His mother brought Edwina's soup on a tray and set the orchid on the table beside his bed. *How strange*, she thought, *that Chris should have consigned Edwina's passionate message to a dream.* Ginny had stood outside the bedroom door listening to Edwina, fingers tightly crossed, hoping against hope that her son might be inspired by Edwina's conviction to rally; to swallow the handful of brightly coloured tablets that offered some small resistance to the virus; to build his strength and, yes, as Edwina had pleaded; to fight for life.

But no, even now he was pushing away the soup after just a single mouthful.

Suddenly overcome with fury, Ginny picked up the tray, spilling soup onto the white sheets. "Look at you!" she cried. "Surrendering, so meekly, like a lamb to the slaughter. Edwina is right. Where is your fight, your courage? Why don't you care any more?"

His eyes remained closed but she knew he'd heard her. The fury boiled and spilled. The face on the pillow, lying there, might have been a face in a coffin. Cadaverously pale. Emotionless, expressionless, shut off from the world. Away from her.

"Already dead!" she shouted recklessly. "You might as well already be dead!"

She swept from the room, tears swimming, bumping blindly down the stairs.

In the kitchen she leaned against the stove where moments before she'd heated the soup "Oh, what have I said?" she whimpered. "How could I be so cruel?"

Grace arrived to find her whey-faced, dabbing her nose and face with a tea towel. "I can't bear it," she hiccupped. "Can't go on any longer! This is much harder than I ever imagined!"

Grace set her bag on the kitchen table and filled the kettle. "Tea?" she asked, quietly. Ginny nodded and sat stiffly on one of the chairs, twisting the towel.

Of course she knew that, in her own kitchen, she should be setting the tray for the doctor and not the other way around, but she felt as though if she got up now, her knees would buckle and she would fall to the floor.

Grace tossed teabags into two mugs and added boiling water. She found the milk in the fridge, the sugar in the pantry. She pulled out a chair and, sipping the scalding tea, motioned Ginny to drink.

"It's going to be hell," she said firmly, "but you've got to be strong. You can't give way, Ginny. It's not an option."

Ginny nodded. "I know." The hands kept twisting the towel.

"Talk to me. Tell me how you're feeling."

"Betrayed!" Ginny's answer was a shout. "I feel *betrayed!* Chris has turned his back on life, on me, on Inga! He's refused the medicine and eats hardly anything. He won't get out of bed. Won't draw or paint. He just lies there, waiting for the end. I'm so angry, Grace. I could kill him!"

"He's been through a lot, Ginny. Been ill for years. And he's been unlucky. His resistance to anti-retroviral drugs has made it impossible to control the virus. The side effects of the drugs have been intolerable. He's had to face so many disappointments..."

"Grace, I know all that! God knows I'm his mother. I've been through this nightmare journey with him. I know he's suffering! Know his body is breaking down. But I want him to *want* to live! Is that too much to ask?"

Grace shook her head.

"And now there's Inga. The girl is hopelessly in love with Chris. This is tearing her apart, I can see it!"

"I'd like to prescribe a short course of anti-depressants for you. Would that help?"

"Trust a doctor! You're going to turn me into a zombie to get through this?"

"Very mild anti-depressants. They'll help you get up in the morning and put on a cheerful face. They won't turn you into a zombie, I promise."

"Sorry!" Ginny clapped her hand to her mouth. "The most awful things keep flying from my mouth. I've been cruel today. I can't help myself."

Grace held her with a serious gaze. "I can't tell you how to get through this, Ginny. I can offer support and sympathy and, if you need it, some tablets to calm you. You're his mother and he needs you. You'll have to find the strength from somewhere."

Ginny drained her mug and set it firmly on the table. "Thank you, Grace. I needed that tantrum. Needed to get my anger and frustration out in the open and have you to tell me to pull myself together. If you think they'll help, give me a few happy pills. They can't do any harm, I suppose."

Ginny got to her feet. "Right, do you want to see the patient now?" She picked up the doctor's bag and, with a courageous smile on her face, ascended the stairs like the warrior Queen Boadicea going into battle.

Caron left James at the gallery with Sarah and drove to Betty's Bay Primary School, where she had a late afternoon appointment with Mrs Morris: James' ex-teacher.

With the exception of the soccer team who were practising on the field, the school was deserted: the parking ground almost empty.

She crept down the corridors to class 4A, where Mrs Morris sat at her desk, marking a pile of exercise books in a room that smelled of chalk dust.

Helen Morris fumbled beneath the table for her shoes and slipped them discretely onto her bunioned feet. "I must congratulate you!" she said, her face breaking into a smile, as Caron eased into the chair opposite. "You've done wonders with James! His marks are excellent. As you know, I'm no great fan of home schooling but perhaps, in this case, I was wrong. A boy like James clearly needs that unique, individual attention you can provide in a nurturing home environment and where he works at his own pace…"

"Mrs Morris…"

"Helen, please call me Helen."

"Helen, we've decided that it would be better for James to return to school. That's why I'm here. I'd like to enrol James in your class from next term."

"But why?"

"We feel – his father and I – that he should spend more time with other children of his age. He needs friends. And Alec would like him to participate in a variety of extra-curricular activities and sports. Soccer. Cricket. Swimming."

"I see. Well, of course the school will be delighted to accept James again as one of our pupils. Such a bright boy! I must admit, though, that I'm surprised at your change of heart. You've had such rewarding success with home schooling James."

"Success? Yes, his marks are good. But, as I say, we think James would be happier in a more normal school environment where he has the opportunity to mix with other children."

Helen Morris observed Caron Grant closely. Her face was pale and strained: she sat nervously on the edge of the chair, tapping the toe of one shoe on the linoleum.

How long, she wondered, had it been since Alec Grant had removed James from school in order to have the boy home schooled by his new wife? Less than a year?

At the time, Helen Morris had been strongly outspoken about the folly of such a decision. She'd taken herself to the Headmaster's office to object. She'd railed long and loudly about James, who had, not so long ago, lost his mother, poor child, and whose life would now be further disrupted by being *wrenched* from a stimulating classroom to a situation where he would be closeted, day after day, with that very uptight Mrs Grant who'd never had any children of her own was certainly not equipped to handle a sensitive and clever child like James!

She had been wrong though and she didn't mind admitting it.

The first evidence she'd had of this had been at the Betty's Bay Spelling Bee where James had surprised her with newfound confidence and maturity. The boy who had calmly spelled difficult words in the harsh glare of stage spotlights and an atmosphere thick with tension was a very different James to the remote, solitary, nervous child she'd had in her class. If he hadn't made that slip at the end, he'd have walked away with the trophy! And then, marking his end of term test papers, she'd found James' work to be far superior to that of his peers. She'd written glowing comments on his report. James was more creative with a wider vocabulary than the average nine-year-old. He displayed reasoning powers and problem-solving ability. He appeared to grasp concepts and principles quickly and comprehend readily. Mrs Grant had done so much with the boy…

"Helen?" Caron Grant seemed impatient.

"Sorry! I was thinking about James. He doesn't make friends easily, but of course you know that. And as for sports activities; swimming, cricket, soccer!" Helen gave a humourless laugh. "Well, his interests are more intellectual. Chess. Astronomy Club. Natural History. But, again, as his step-mother, you know all that."

"Yes, but his father would like him to…"

"In my class I found it difficult to get James to concentrate unless the subject really grabbed his attention in which case you'd get eight pages instead of the required two. He's always been a dreamer, but, based on his test results, you've improved his ability to focus and his memory recall."

Other things she remembered clearly were that James had been manipulative, moody and impossible to discipline. But how could one mention such things without causing offence? She looked up to meet Mrs Grant's anxious gaze.

"What does James think about coming back to school?"

Mrs Grant's foot began to tap the linoleum again. "We haven't spoken to James yet. I needed to make sure that he would be accepted back in the new term. There's no point in raising his hopes only to dash them."

Helen Grant folded her arms and leaned forward. "I'm going to be absolutely honest with you," she confided. "I've seen a positive change in James since you've been working with him. He shows initiative and originality far beyond his years. He's more confident and appears much happier than…"

"He's not happy!" The sentence, blurted, lay between them.

Mrs Morris kept her face impassive. "Go on," she said.

"Only that. He's not happy. We've had problems. Things haven't been easy."

"Well, things are never easy. And James is a very different child. He needs special care, special understanding and attention."

"It's more than that." Mrs Grant clearly wanted to explain further, but stopped herself. "It's – *personal.*"

"Ah!" Helen Morris wrinkled her lips into a tight bow. She understood. She'd heard rumours. So there *were* problems with the marriage then. Problems between Alec and Caron Grant with James stuck in the middle; the way that children inevitably were. The sympathy drained from her face.

She peeled back the paper on a tube of mints and popped one into her mouth so that it bulged in her cheek. She gave a weary, wheezing sigh.

"Well, in that case, James must come back to school, of course. And the sooner the better, I expect?" Her tone was brusque.

"The new term would be best for James. We've fallen behind, a little, with the curriculum. I'd like to have him ready."

"One question!" Mrs Morris pushed back her chair. "What if James doesn't want to come back to school? Have you thought about that?"

"It's not an option," Caron replied, guardedly. "But I have no doubt he'll be more than happy to return to Betty's Bay Primary School."

"And you? You've spent so much time with James. Instruction, research, preparation, teaching. You'll miss all that. What will you do with your time now?"

Caron let the question hang there, annoyed. Her voice tightened. "I have some plans." She stood. "Thank you for your time, Mrs Morris, uh, Helen. We'll be in touch." She left the classroom without a backward glance.

Helen Morris gathered up the pile of exercise books and folded them into her worn, leather sling bag. She shut the classroom windows and draped her beige cardigan over her shoulders. James Grant had sat in the third desk on the right, in the front row. Tiny Kayleigh Platt sat there now. She was no trouble. Kayleigh would have to be moved so that James could sit at the front again, right under her nose where she could keep a careful eye on him. Things would not be easy if there were problems at home. That non-committal remark of Caron Grant's: "I have some plans."

How cold she was! Was there a suggestion of a separation or a divorce in the offing? Was the boy to be left motherless again?

"Poor James," Helen sighed aloud. "Poor, poor James!"

Ben mustered the courage to call Ginny and invite her to dinner.

He could tell the call had taken her by surprise. "Oh," she'd said. "Oh, how lovely!" And then, silence.

"Tomorrow evening? Say around seven?"

"I'd love to come." She'd sounded flustered. "Oh, please believe me, it would be so good to get out for a bit. But my son, Chris is ill. I don't think I can leave him although, of course, there is always Inga so perhaps…?"

He waited, hoping.

"But, it's probably not a good idea." Her voice was filled with regret.

He took a breath. "I'm sorry. Another time, then?"

"Such a pity. But, yes, another time. And, oh Ben …"

"Yes?"

"Thank you for asking me!"

She put the phone down. "You'll never guess!" she said to Chris. "Ben Barker phoned."

"Who?"

"The Vet. Ben Barker."

"Oh, yes. What did he want?"

She giggled, bright spots on each cheek. "He invited me to dinner. The French place, that new restaurant in the square."

His eyes widened. "Great! When?"

"Oh, no, darling. I can't go. But I'm so *thrilled* to be asked. You've no idea. It's been years and years since any man…"

"Why can't you go, Ma?"

"How could I possibly leave you alone? I wouldn't dream of it. My conscience would never allow it!"

"Oh for God's sake. Forget your conscience! Go and have some fun for a change. Inga will be here, and anyway I can look after myself. Call him back! Tell him you'll accept his invitation."

"Darling boy! I'm flattered beyond words: Ben is such a nice man. But my heart's not in it. I'd be thinking about you, worrying myself silly."

He looked at her sadly. "And what about me?"

"What do you mean?"

"What about what I want? Doesn't that matter? I want you to go out, Ma. I want you to have a good time. More than anything in the world, I want you to be happy!"

"Yes, I know that, darling. But..."

"Call him back. Say you'll go. Please, Ma. Do it for me."

She picked up the tray. She gave a quick smile. "I'll think about it," she promised and fled.

How could he understand? He had no idea how much of her energy and strength he consumed so that there was nothing left for anything else. The call had been a surprise; Ben's voice, the unexpected invitation. For a moment Ginny had felt herself flooded with joyful anticipation, with lightness and, yes, with gratitude.

She'd even felt a surge of triumph knowing that she had not imagined Ben's interest in her, there *had* been something between them and he had sensed it too.

And then the moment had passed and she had expelled a quiet breath and replied that she would love to come but Chris was ill. And that was only half the truth for he was not only ill but also dying and it would be utterly insane to go out and leave him, even with compassionate Inga at his bedside.

"Call him back. Say you'll go." Impossible. Impossible to consider dressing up with jewellery, perfume and high heels and trying to have an intelligent conversation, to sip wine and eat expensive French food when her mind, her heart and every throbbing fibre of her being remained upstairs in the studio where her son was confined to a narrow cot bed. "Do it for me!" he'd said. She would do anything for him. Anything but this!

The telephone rang.

She reached to pick it up, her hand hovering above the receiver. Suppose it was Ben calling to invite her at another time? What would she say? A second refusal and he'd never call again and that would be that.

She picked up the phone.

"Ginny, it's Ben. I've had an idea. If your son is ill, perhaps I could bring dinner to your house and we could eat in? How does that sound?"

There it was again; a vein opening and filling her body with unforeseen happiness. "Oh," she said breathlessly. "What a good idea!"

He laughed. "Snails in garlic butter, coq au vin and some unpronounceable French dessert. The restaurant can make up a take-away meal for me. Do you eat snails?"

Snails! Dismal little rubbery things: not worth eating and much happier on a leaf or a patch of lawn.

"I adore them!"

"Seven o'clock, then?"

She took the stairs two at a time and arrived at his door, panting .

"What shall I wear?" she cried. "I want to look absolutely stunning."

He grinned. The boyish smile lit up his white face: his eyes shone. "The green velvet," he said instantly, "with the lacy black bolero. Silver sandals. The black onyx earrings."

She burst into tears.

"What's the matter?" He patted the bed. "Sit here, tell me?"

"How shall I live without you?" Her voice dropped to a whisper. "Tell me, *how?*"

She held him. Skin and bones, feverish to the touch. She pressed her face to his heart to hear it strongly beating, listened to his breathing, feeling his chest rhythmically rise and fall.

He pressed his lips into her hair. "Get the velvet and try it on for me. Oh, and let your hair down."

She smiled up, gratefully.

When she'd left the room, he lay back against the pillows. He hadn't been able to get the words out but at that moment, with her head on his chest, he'd wanted to tell her things. Tell her he'd had a good life, perhaps not as long as he would have liked, but good. He'd known love and happiness: it surrounded him still and how many people could say that? He wanted her to know that she'd been the most devoted mother anyone could wish for. "My rock," he'd wanted to say. "My inspiration. My source of loving kindness and comfort." The words had been there, at the tip of his tongue, but his throat had knotted with emotion. He could never get them out: his voice would break, she would dissolve into tears again and the moment would be lost forever. Much better to write down what he wanted to say and leave the message behind so that she could read it, afterwards, and know the true depth of his feelings for her.

When she returned in the green dress, they both saw that she'd lost weight; the dress was too big, and her thin, naked arms looked exposed through the revealing lace of the black bolero. She stood before him, like a young girl, as he pulled the fabric this way and then that, issuing instructions: a stitch here, another there, the straps lifted slightly, the bolero replaced with a soft shawl.

"How beautiful," he said, his voice catching. "How beautiful you are in every way!"

Chapter 14

Mickey

Friday morning dawned. I sat on the deck watching a pair of glossy, black plumed cormorants pirouetting like sleek dancers in the canal as they dived for fish.

Later I heard that a pod of dolphins had been sighted near Granny's Pool and whales seen near the harbour mouth, spouting from their blowholes and performing mid-air arabesques, high above the waves. I remember thinking that morning that, in a world made up seven-tenths of salty water, ours was by far the sweetest curve of any coastline. I remember feeling blessed with good fortune to live in such a charmed seaside village, a peaceful, natural paradise that had, so far, managed to avoid most of the problems troubling the rest of the world. If I had to find one word to describe the essence of St Jude I think, at that time, I might have chosen the adjective: 'safe'. But that was before. Before the news broke. Before we all heard what had happened late on Thursday night. Before life altered in St Jude so that, for a time afterwards, none of us felt safe.

Mickey changed her routine that day. She went out early to walk on the beach and clear her head. It was important that she remain completely in control: her mind set upon the single action to be undertaken after midnight. She felt almost robotic, as though she were bloodless, her flesh turned to steel, her joints to smoothly greased bolts. She had not eaten for a while, for days, perhaps – and yet in her light-headedness, she felt empowered, as though she might walk forever without stopping.

The sea was clean: the water deep blue fading to turquoise and the white hot sun glared so fiercely that to look at it would sear your eyes. Once she'd have tilted her head towards Heaven for a sign from God, seeking His blessing. Now she didn't much care whether He approved of what she was about to do or not. Nothing mattered but that Jordan

Black should be punished for what he'd done. Once it was all over, perhaps she would become herself again? Perhaps her head would stop whirring like wasps trapped in a bottle? Perhaps she could stop obsessing about Black, about the rape, the money he'd stolen and get on with her life, such as it was?

The seagulls were fighting over a dead fish, making a din and on another day, had things been different, she might have sat on a rock and watched them, but not today. She hardly saw the swooping flights of oystercatchers drifting in with the incoming tide. Today there was only the satisfaction of striding across miles of wet sand, watching her footprints disappear behind her as though she had never been there, never existed and repeating one single thought: *After midnight, it will all be over!*

Jordan Black and his partner, Wayne, had a meeting that morning with a client who was kicking up a stink because an armoire she had ordered was still not finished. The client, whose name was Mrs Oates, was a fat old bitch with an axe to grind and Black would have given anything to have told her to fuck off, but for the fact that she was prepared to pay ten grand for the armoire which would clear a minimum of three grand profit and that was not the kind of money to be sniffed at.

"Let me do the talking," he instructed Wayne, who shuffled into a dark corner, relieved not to have to open his mouth.

On this particular occasion, Mrs Oates was accompanied by Mr Oates, who looked like a sad grey elephant, right down to the longest hooter Black had seen on anyone's face, poor sod.

Mr Oates hung back, behind his wife, clearing his throat and swivelling his eyes.

Black could see right away that the old geezer wasn't going to be the problem but charming the old cow so that he could get his way was not going to be easy.

Mrs Oates launched the attack. "You promised the armoire would be ready by the end of the week," she said in her snooty voice. She waved in the general direction of the cupboard standing, half finished in the gloom of the shed. "Do you call that *ready?*"

"I said we'd try our best," said Black amicably, "but what with late delivery of the cherry wood and a couple of problems with..."

"I'm not interested in excuses," snipped Mrs Oates. "Those are your problems, not mine."

"Yeah, but…"

"My problem is a houseful of guests arriving tomorrow. I *must* have the cupboard. It's not negotiable. You will have to work overtime."

"Look, Mrs Oates. You don't want Wayne to compromise on the quality of the workmanship…"

"No, I most certainly do not."

"Well, it's not possible to finish by tomorrow without…"

"Listen to me, Mr Black!" Mrs Oates narrowed her eyes so that they took the shape of small black almonds resting on doughy cheeks. "If the armoire is not ready by tomorrow you may cancel the order and refund my deposit."

"Yeah, but you want a quality job, don't you?"

"I will not accept anything less than a quality job! If the armoire is not made exactly to my specifications and my very high standards, I will simply walk away from it."

Black and Mrs Oates glared. He was the first to drop his eyes.

"OK!" he shrugged. "We'll do our best."

"I will be here at noon – no later – to collect the armoire. Don't let me down, Mr Black!"

Mrs Oates swept away with Mr Oates plodding uncertainly behind her. Black noticed that his loose grey suit, worn shiny in the seat, gave the unmistakeable impression of a sagging elephant bottom.

"Shit!" he groaned. "Shit! Shit! Shit!"

"Can't be done," mumbled Wayne, emerging from the shadows.

"That's where you're wrong!" barked Black. "It has to be done. You heard the old bitch! Not negotiable."

Wayne's face crumpled. "I can't. There aren't enough hours…"

"Aw, don't have a hernia! I'll help you, OK? We'll work through the night. With two of us on the job, we can finish by twelve tomorrow, no problem."

"Well, with two of us, maybe?" Wayne's face cheered slightly.

"Good! Now you're talking!" Black pounded him on the back and Wayne jolted forward as though he'd been shot. "You get right onto it!" Black instructed. "I'll be back in a couple of hours. No flies on us. We'll show the old cow what's what, eh?"

Mickey returned home from the beach late in the afternoon. She took a shower to wash away the sand and grime and shampooed her hair. She brushed it carefully, studying her face in the mirror. Mickey Graham. Who was she? The face was familiar but the person inside was not. The eyes staring back looked, what? Flat? Cold? No, scared. Yes, that was it – the eyes were terrified, the pupils huge. It was still, however, the same face. The nose a little beaky, the mouth pinched, lines drooping sharply downwards. The chin as stubborn as ever. Her hair a mess: she remembered hacking at it with a pair of blunt scissors and now could do nothing with it. The brush, when she stopped brushing, was clotted with fine hair: was it falling out? Yes, come to think of it, it looked thinner, her scalp visible in one or two places. Perhaps, afterwards, it would grow back, or perhaps not? Anyway, she wouldn't think about that now.

Mickey dressed in a clean white t-shirt and tracksuit pants and then made tea and toast to keep her strength up although, even now, she wasn't the least hungry.

She washed the mug and plate and wiped the kitchen counter. Six o'clock.

She loaded the back of the truck with flashlight and gloves and the gallon drum of petrol into which she'd dropped the coil of rope. She placed the black book on top of the drum although she had little need of it now and slipped a new packet of matches into her pocket. She touched the locket that hung about her neck. God had gone but Folly was there and she would draw courage from his presence.

Six twenty. Time was dragging. She felt tired suddenly. Sick with exhaustion. Feet dragging, she climbed the stairs and collapsed on the bed.

Perhaps it was the late nights, the constant worrying? Perhaps it was the long trudge across the sand and the fresh air? Whatever it was, she could hardly keep her eyes open. She decided to close them for a few moments, not long. She would rest until it was time to leave, no harm in that. Almost instantly, she fell deeply asleep.

There was something very satisfying in working together on the armoire.

Wayne, of course, was the real carpenter and so the tricky parts, like the door mouldings and arches, fell to him, but Black had a hand in cutting and sanding the adjustable shelves and edging them with cherry veneer.

They worked without stopping until almost six when Black remembered that the liquor outlet on the corner would be closing soon and, downing tools, sped off to buy cold beers and four cheese burgers with fries to keep them going. When he returned, Wayne saw that Black had also bought a couple of half-jacks of whiskey.

"Better lay off the booze," he suggested, wolfing down a burger, "got a long night ahead of us!"

Black laughed and cracked open a can of beer, handing it to Wayne. "Yeah," he said. "That's why you'll need this! Keep your strength up, eh?"

They were hard at it again by seven and making good progress.

An argument ensued at eight fifteen when Black told Wayne to make the door mouldings simpler. "We'll be here all night," he burst out, "if you don't speed up. Cut a couple of corners, eh? It doesn't have to be fucking *perfect!*"

"But, Mrs Oates said she wanted mouldings like gothic windows. You heard her!"

"She can have her bloody gothic mouldings – but they don't have to be that gothic. Use your head. Keep it simple, stupid!"

He could hear Wayne muttering under his breath as he clamped the doors in place with brass hinges.

"And belt up, will you!" – he threw in for good measure. Black poured himself a shot of whiskey and gulped it. He followed it with another. He saw Wayne watching and tossed the bottle to him. "This'll ease the pain!" he grinned.

By ten, two six-packs consumed and both whiskey bottles emptied, the armoire was nearing completion. Classically proportioned with three adjustable shelves, a removable clothes bar and four drawers, the armoire was practical yet refined. The arches between the legs were graceful, the horizontal pediment had an appealing assertiveness and the piece de resistance was a large antique brass key to lock the cupboard.

"Genius!" slurred Black. "Bloody genius, that's what you are!"

Wayne, whose eyes were crossing, stepped back to admire the cupboard and, stumbling, knocked over a jigsaw that clattered to the floor.

"Mrs Oates has got her assertive arches and graceful pediment!" he announced, with pride.

Black laughed drunkenly. "Nah! She's got her graceful arches and assertive pediment!" He advanced upon the armoire with a screwdriver but Wayne stopped him. "Call it a night?" he suggested, slumping to the floor. In minutes he'd fallen asleep. Black bolted the door of the shed shut, blew out the lamps and stretched, full-length, across the bed. He'd catch forty winks, he decided, and once he'd sobered up, take Wayne home with him. A couple more hours of sleep, a hot shower and they'd be as right as rain. Ready to face the dragon and tell her to her fat face that if she didn't like the armoire, she could stuff it. The armoire was fucking fantastic, a regular work of art and he could probably sell it to that posh chick from The Gallery for a lot more than ten grand! That would show Mrs Fucking Oates!

The silvery light of the moon through the window woke Mickey.

She sat up with a start, squinting at her watch. Eleven thirty! She was late! How had she fallen asleep at a time like this? After all her careful planning?

It was absolutely critical to get the job done shortly after midnight, well before any of the dairy trucks were on the road, before fishermen made their way to the harbour mouth where the boats waited.

She splashed her face with cold water and brushed her teeth. She pulled on a jumper and laced her feet into soft, worn tennis shoes. She'd chosen the shoes because they allowed her to walk soundlessly and were so old the imprint had long faded from the sole. Anyone studying footprints left behind at the scene of the crime would find nothing to incriminate her.

Her throat was dry, her heart pumping. She drank a glass of water and stood for a moment taking deep breaths to calm herself. Her fingers found the locket. She held it tightly. "Give me strength," she murmured. "Give me courage." Perhaps she imagined it, but Mickey felt suddenly composed, her mind stilled. She pressed the locket to her lips. She was ready!

The truck started first time and she eased in the clutch and drove slowly through the gate, freewheeling silently for as long as she was able. If any of the nosy neighbours heard her clattering truck on the road at this time of the night, it wouldn't be difficult to put two and two together later.

The roads were dark but for the light of the moon and the yellow, sulphurous glow from a few streetlamps, buzzing with moths and flying beetles. There was no sign of life and no lights flickering in windows and it seemed to Mickey, as the truck lurched hesitantly along, dim headlamps cutting through the darkness, that she was the only person awake in the village. Even so, her eyes nervously swept the empty streets and side lanes, just to be sure.

She pulled up in Otter's Lane, outside Black's warehouse, at twenty past twelve.

The building was deserted and in darkness. She sat staring at the familiar shape of the shed, listening to her booming heart echoing in her ears.

Her hands clutched the steering wheel as though they'd been glued there.

"Come on, Mickey," she said aloud. "Get it together, will you!" She tried to make her voice sound tough but it came out a cracked whisper. Another time, she'd have laughed at how pathetic, how weak she sounded, but this was no laughing matter and so she rubbed the silver locket instead. The sight of a lean grey cat slinking in the shadows across the road stirred her into action. She opened the door of the truck, wincing with every creak, and left it slightly ajar. She crept noiselessly to the shed and stood there for a few moments, her ear pressed to the door, her shoulder leaning into the wood.

She heard crickets singing in the brittle grass. Large, black flying beetles swooning against the still burning headlamps of the truck. The sound of her frightened panting. The shed was silent.

Mickey returned to the truck and reached into the back for the gallon drum of petrol, flashlight and gloves. With a glance at the sky, she put back the torch; the moon shone so brightly she could see everything quite clearly. She slid the gloves onto her hands and then carried the petrol drum to the shed and set it on the ground.

She knelt and fished out the length of petrol-soaked rope from the drum, keeping it at arm's length so that there was little danger of splattering her clothing with the fuel. She closed her eyes, remembering the exact layout of the interior of the warehouse. The bolt of rope was kept near the doorway, on the right. One metre or so away from the rope stood an apple green plastic bucket filled with turpentine and soaking paintbrushes. Behind the bucket, a tower of unopened paint tins balanced precariously to the left of a bulky pile of newly sawed wooden planks.

Mickey snaked the wet rope beneath the opening of the door so that it coiled inside the shed. She retracted a length of it, a metre or so and, as she did so, heard something. A noise! What was it? She tried to quiet her breathing, suddenly harsh and loud. Perhaps she'd heard her own rasping breaths? Was that it?

Her fingers shook. The rope quivered like a live thing in her hands.

She clambered to her feet and stepped away from the shed. She looked right and left. A light breeze was stirring. Dried leaves scuttled across the road. The crickets fell silent.

"Get a grip!" she muttered. "Get a grip!"

Mickey picked up the petrol drum and poured some of the liquid over the length of rope so that it pooled beneath the door, flowing like a stream of black ink into the shed. There! Her chest was bursting. She stopped holding her breath and grabbed the petrol drum, ran to the truck, threw it in the back and then climbed inside. She turned the ignition, the engine caught quickly, and reversed the truck so that it faced the road, ready for a quick getaway. She secured the handbrake and left the engine running.

Returning to the shed, Mickey glimpsed the reflection of the moon shimmering in the inky pool of petrol. She gasped. The sight of the white shape, pure and innocent, filled her with horror. Her cheeks blazed. Her legs shook so much she could feel her whole body swaying. She heard a voice.

"Don't do it, Mickey!" the voice said. "Turn away now, before it's too late."

God? Was God speaking to her again, after so long? She listened. "You'll live to regret this," the voice said.

She could hardly believe it. "Now's a fine time!" she said, indignantly.

"Turn away! Turn away!"

"An eye for an eye," Mickey replied stoically. "A tooth for a tooth."

"Turn the other cheek!"

Not God's voice, then but, in fact her own. That cowering, shrinking, tormented part that kept surfacing, breaking into her consciousness, trying to ruin everything. The part that watched and judged and disapproved and, at this precise moment, quaked with naked terror.

Mickey used the reflected full moon, trapped on the unbroken surface of the fuel, as her gleaming bull's eye. She took the matches from her pocket, lit one, and tossed it into the puddle in which the rope lay. There was a sudden, satisfying spurt of pale blue flames. The flames danced merrily along the length of the rope towards the door. In seconds they'd ducked beneath the gap, tearing into the shed. She felt a flush of triumph. It had been so easy, so simple that it was laughable. If she hadn't been quivering like a leaf she might have shouted something into the night: something dramatic and appropriate but her mind was a blank and all she could come up with was a faint whispered: "I said I'd get you back!"

The shed would burn to the ground in a few hours. Jordan Black would lose everything: tools, supplies and whatever items of commissioned furniture had been kept inside. The value of the contents would be at least ten thousand, and there was something sweet about making him suffer such a loss; a true case of the punishment fitting the crime.

Before Mickey ran towards the waiting truck she saw, from the corner of her eye, that the large, industrial strength steel padlock hanging on the outside of the shed door had not been locked but swung open on the latch.

Black awoke, befuddled and woozy with booze, He heard shuffling outside the warehouse and wondered if the cat he'd sometimes seen, darting like an arrow across the road, had scratched at the door to get in.

Then he heard voices. Or was it only one voice? He strained to hear but the voice, if it was one, was mumbling and incoherent. A tramp perhaps: a loony looking for a place to crash?

His mouth was as dry as a parrot's cage and he had a mother of all headaches.

He sat up on the bed and kicked at Wayne. "Get up!" he urged. "Someone outside!"

"What? What?" Wayne rubbed his eyes.

Black listened keenly. "Might be a break-in!"

They sat unmoving, ears tuned to muted scuffling outside.

Wayne picked up the jigsaw. He handed it to Black. "Use it as a weapon!" suggested Wayne.

Black flicked his lighter and lit a lamp. It gave off a pale, smoking light. He narrowed his eyes, squinting at the door and then uttered a mirthless laugh.

"Ha! Door's bolted inside," he said, relaxing. "Nobody can get in. Fort bloody Knox. We're safe!"

"Can you smell anything?" Wayne asked, wrinkling his nose. "Smells like…"

And then there was a God almighty explosion.

Mickey sat in the truck, waiting to release the hand brake. The unlocked padlock on the outside of the door made no sense. Why would Black leave the warehouse unlocked? He'd never done such a thing before. Every night the lock had been secured, the door firmly bolted against intruders. Unless? Unless? No! It didn't bear thinking about. Surely there wasn't anyone *inside?*

She leapt at the sound of a shattering explosion. The wooden shed erupted into a shooting jet of flames. It all happened so quickly: a matter of minutes, that's all. Before she drove away Mickey saw the roof and walls began to cave, falling as easily as if the fragile structure had been made from matchsticks.

Her ears were filled with the crackling, hissing and spitting roar of the fire and as she put her foot on the accelerator, immediately before the truck jolted away, she thought she heard the agonised sound of screaming from within.

A fisherman, leaving early to get a head start, was the first to see the fire engulfing what had once been Jordan Black's warehouse in Otter's Lane. He noted that a second blaze, moving with rapid speed, was making its way towards the boat yard. The fisherman made three calls on his mobile phone: the fire brigade, the police and the owner of Luxury Boats Inc. and, within half an hour, a team of fire fighters had been assembled and were aiming hoses at the shed and damping down the boat yard before it caught alight.

Hours later, as smoke-blackened firemen were picking their way through the remains of Black's property, they discovered two bodies, charred beyond recognition.

Mickey remained surprisingly calm. She found the strength to dig a deep hole at the back of the nursery, beyond the herb garden and near the compost heap, where she buried the petrol drum and gloves. As an afterthought, she tossed her tennis shoes on top of the drum, just in case. Once she'd filled in the hole, the earth covering what she came to think of as 'the burial site' looked too fresh, too chocolaty brown amidst the parched grey, so she dragged two large potted ferns from the front garden and placed them on the newly turned soil. She threw down gravel, leaves and a few twigs for good measure. Once she'd buried the incriminating evidence, she hosed down the tyres on her truck so that they could not provide any clue as to where the vehicle had been parked and then cleaned out the back of the cab. Detecting a whiff of petrol, she scrubbed the floor of the cab with a heady combination of soap, bleach and household cleaner.

The truck looked suspiciously clean and so she flung a few bags of potting soil in the back and a couple of sacks of fertiliser. It was then she remembered the little black book. Where was it? She knew she'd taken the book with her. She clearly remembered placing it on top of the petrol drum – but she couldn't recall seeing it after that and, hadn't buried it with the other items.

She searched the truck: front and back. She searched again and found nothing.

Oh God, she whispered from habit. Oh God. Where was the book? Had she dropped it? Would someone find it and read it? Would they hand it to the police?

Panic flooded Mickey. She felt, for a giddying moment, as though she might faint.

She held onto the side of the truck to steady herself before inevitable blackness descended. She felt her knees give. She swayed. The sensation passed.

She tried to think. Where could it be? She retraced her steps to the back of the house, to the burial site. She combed through the truck again. She crawled beneath the truck. She found nothing. That's when she knew that she would have to return to Otter's Lane and search for the book. Back to the scene of the fire! The scene of that noise she'd heard as the roof had fallen in. The noise that sounded like terrified screaming from within an inferno. She found the presence of mind to wash her face. She changed her clothes, pulling on a clean t-shirt, denims and trainers. She sat on the edge of the bath and covered her face with her hands. If only her heart would stop banging against her ribcage. If only her mind would stop racing so that she could *think!*

A crowd had gathered in Otter's Lane. Cars parked anyhow. People standing, gawking at the still smoking blackened heap that was all that remained of Black's furniture warehouse. Mickey joined the throng. She stared at the charred ruins. There was the smell of acrid smoke in the air. She could hardly believe she had done this. Razed the building to the ground. The contents of the shed – she knew each item by heart -- had been reduced to this insignificant, blackened mound.

She turned to one of the spectators. "What happened?" she asked, feigning ignorance.

The man shrugged. "Probably left a lamp or candle burning. Whole place went up in minutes."

She kept her voice level. "Was anyone hurt?"

"They found two bodies. Taken them to the mortuary."

"Oh God. Two? Two bodies?" Her voice sounded hysterical.

"So they say." The man stared.

Mickey swallowed. "Do they know who they are?"

"Not yet. Jordan Black is probably one of them. That's his warehouse."

"Jordan Black?" She said the words aloud. Jordan Black, dead?

"Local builder," the man explained, "made furniture to order on the side."

Her head began to swim. Her skin prickled. The heap of black and smouldering debris reeled before her eyes. She was going to faint, she could feel herself losing consciousness.

"You feeling alright?" That stare again.

"Uh, yes. Bit of a shock."

She staggered away on wobbling legs.

She heard her name called.

"Miss Graham!" A heavy hand reached for her arm. Fingers dug into her skin.

She turned. Fleshy face, brutal hair cut, narrowed, all-seeing eyes.

"Detective Inspector Jansen," she said, weakly.

"I'm surprised to see you here," he said, wasting no time.

"Why?"

"How did you hear about the fire?"

Her throat was very dry. She opened and closed her mouth. She swallowed. "Talk," she mumbled, at last. "Talk in the village."

His eyes bored through her.

She rallied. "How did these people hear about the fire?" she burst out. "Dozens of people. Why don't you ask them?"

"I will," he said levelly. "I will be conducting a thorough investigation."

"How did the fire start? Do you know?"

"Too early to say. I don't wish to speculate. There will be a comprehensive forensic investigation. Arson experts will be summoned."

"Someone mentioned a candle? A lamp left burning?"

"Perhaps. As I say, I don't yet know how the fire started."

She couldn't help herself. "Do you suspect foul play, Inspector?"

"Not at this stage."

There was nothing more to say. She turned. Her head would not stop spinning. Her mouth felt stuffed with cotton wool. She took two faltering steps away from him.

"Miss Graham!" There it was: that commanding voice. He *knew*. Detective Inspector Hector Jansen knew that she had set fire to Black's warehouse and, in the process, killed two people.

She felt his heavy, meaty hand upon her arm again and then she fainted.

Chapter 15

Mickey and James

When we first heard the news that Jordan Black's warehouse in Otter's Lane had burned to the ground, the fire was seen as an unfortunate accident. But then two bodies were discovered and taken to the mortuary where Black's gold chain, ruby ring and distinctive dental work identified the larger of these as his. Since Wayne Miller, Black's carpenter, was missing it didn't take much to confirm that his was the smaller of the corpses. Following a hunch, Detective Inspector Jansen immediately cordoned off the area and assembled a team of forensic experts to search for evidence of arson.

The gruesome fire at Otter's Lane became the talk of the village. It was well known that Black had any number of enemies but who amongst them hated him enough to want him dead? And who was cruel enough to murder the men in such a grisly way? It was not until much later that any of us connected this terrible incident to Mickey Graham.

When Mickey regained consciousness, she was helped to sit up by a young policewoman who suggested she rest her head between her knees until she felt steadier. Detective Jansen was nowhere in sight. Mickey sat on the ground, head down, staring at the earth beneath her feet. "Sorry!" she said, leaning away from the policewoman and vomiting onto the road. She retched shamefully until tears poured. The woman kindly kicked sand over the vomit and handed her a tissue. "Would you like some water?" she asked and went in search of some.

Mickey was not deceived by the policewoman's apparent concern. The Detective had probably told her to take Mickey into custody. She would be led into one of those cold, dark rooms with mysterious two-way glass where she would be interrogated until she confessed. A tape recorder would be placed on a table and switched on. Questions would be fired regarding her whereabouts and whether she had an alibi to confirm that she had, as she claimed, spent the night at home. There was, of course, no such person but, unless one of her neighbours had heard the truck starting up or someone had seen her in the vicinity of the warehouse, nobody could verify that she had *not* been at home during the time in question.

It was well known that she was a sworn enemy of Jordan Black – but surely she was not his only enemy, a man like that probably had dozens.

The problem was the black book. She'd lost it somewhere. Possibly near the warehouse. There was a chance she'd dropped it when she'd lifted the petrol drum from the back of the truck. It might have fallen to the ground unnoticed. The area surrounding the warehouse was sandy with very little shrubbery. The book would have been easy to spot. Perhaps it had been discovered by a fireman or one of the police and given to the detective? There was enough evidence in there to find her guilty of setting fire to the shed. It was not such a leap to therefore assume that she'd plotted and executed the murder of the two men.

She'd be arrested, found guilty and imprisoned in a tiny cell for the rest of her life.

The policewoman tapped her lightly, offering a bottle of cold water. "How are you feeling now?" She was very young and seemed sympathetic.

Mickey lifted her head slowly. "A bit better, thanks." She swallowed small sips.

The policewoman helped Mickey to her feet. "I'll give you a lift home," she said.

Mickey could hardly believe her ears. "Did you say *home?*"

"You can't drive in this condition. My partner will drive your truck for you. Are you pregnant? Is that why you fainted?"

Mickey stared. "Uh, no. I'm not feeling well, that's all."

"Do you need to see a doctor?"

"No, thanks. I need to get home and sleep, I think."

The policewoman gave a nod and led Mickey to her car.

"Did Detective Jansen say anything about me?" Mickey asked.

"Yes. He did." The policewoman opened the car door. "Oh, have you got the keys for your truck on you?"

Mickey fumbled in her pocket and handed her the bunch.

The policewoman tossed the keys to one of men and jerked her thumb in the direction of Mickey's truck. "Follow behind us!" she shouted.

Holding open the car door she looked expectantly at Mickey. "Get in," she suggested, patiently.

"The detective," Mickey reminded her. "What did he say?"

"Oh," the policewoman smiled. "He said I had to look after you. Told me to make sure you got home safely."

"Detective Jansen said that?"

"Yes."

Mickey sank into the passenger seat. "I'm grateful," she said, relieved beyond words. "I didn't think you'd be so kind."

James knew things were different. Something was changing. Had changed. The quarrels between Caron and his dad had stopped but they spent a lot of time shut away in different rooms in the house, talking, voices pitched so low he couldn't hear a word they said.

Sometimes, after he'd gone to bed, they went into the garden, carrying chairs to the far side of the deck. He saw them from the gap in the curtains at the window of his bedroom. Caron sitting up straight with her hands in her lap, his father leaning towards her. They kept their faces close but never touched.

Because they were so far away he couldn't hear what they were saying and they seemed to talk for hours. Often he lay in bed half-hearing a stream of words floating up from below through the opened windows, bubbling, gurgling and lapping around him, flowing beneath his bed, spilling over the blanket so that sleep came with a swishing sound, like water in his ears.

He wanted to tell that he'd stopped listening behind doors and spying on them. Spying was no fun. You heard things you didn't want to know. Things that stayed in your head long after you wished they'd go away: things that made you miserable.

He'd also noticed that, when they were with him their voices sounded different. Caron kept hers light so that it skimmed the air.

Dad's voice was loud and happy, as though he were an actor reading lines in a play. All these things were worrying, mostly because he couldn't work out why things were so different.

It was like doing a jigsaw puzzle. You'd get to that part where the puzzle was coming together and then you'd find a piece missing, like a bit of blue sky, the hardest piece to find and only when you'd finally fitted the piece into the right place did the picture start to make sense.

Because he knew that everything was changing, James had made an effort to be good.

He ate all the food on his plate at mealtimes, even broccoli and peas, and drank his milk. He tried to concentrate during lessons and didn't read past bedtime. He even tried not to keep changing his clothes every time there was a little spill on them. The funny thing was that nobody seemed to notice how much of an effort he was making.

The puzzle came together on Friday morning, after breakfast.

They asked him to join them on the veranda as though it were a Saturday and not a weekday. Caron and Dad sat together against the blue flowered cushions but not close enough to touch. Their faces were serious. His father invitingly patted a seat but James sat on the front step, a little way away from them. He wrapped his arms around his middle, stared at the blue and brown stripes on his socks and waited for the sky to fall.

Dad leaned forward, "James, how would you like to go back to school? To Betty's Bay Primary?"

James opened his eyes wide. He glanced at Caron. She looked down at her hands in her lap and fiddled with her wedding ring, turning it round and round on her finger.

The question frightened him. *Would you like to go back to school?* He wasn't sure whether this was a trick question. They'd never spoken about his going back to school before. He wondered if Caron were upset with him? Perhaps she didn't want to teach him any more? His father waited, face expectant, half-smiling as though he'd offered James a treat of some kind.

James felt a dark sadness coming over him. He chewed his thumbnail. It *was* a trick question. If he said yes, he did want to go back to school, Caron would be angry. If he said no, his father would be disappointed.

"James?"

"I don't know," he said truthfully, not looking at either of them, staring at his socks that had slipped around his ankles. Why did socks always do that?

He had a thought. "Do you *want* me to go back to school?"

Dad and Caron shared a look.

"Don't you miss your friends?" his dad asked, carefully.

James thought. He hadn't had many friends when he'd gone to

Betty's Bay. Anna and Jeremy, he'd missed them in the beginning, but not any more.

They had new friends now. When he'd written his end of term tests in the school hall, he'd waved at Anna but she hadn't waved back. She'd looked away. She'd been sitting next to a fat girl with freckles. She'd whispered to the girl who'd turned and stuck her tongue out. "Baby!" the girl had said. "You're a big baby!" Since the fat girl didn't know anything about him, he guessed Anna must have said something about him being a baby.

"I don't have friends," he said.

"Well, that's because you're not at school. You've lost touch. But you'd like friends, wouldn't you? Of course you would! Everyone needs friends."

James spat out a sliver of thumbnail. "What I don't really understand is why you want me to go back to school?" he repeated, solemnly. "Have I done something wrong?"

That look passed between them again. Caron twisted her wedding ring. "No," she said, firmly. "You've done nothing wrong. Nothing at all."

His father cleared his throat. "It was a kind of experiment, Jamie, being taught at home. And you've done extremely well: your test results are excellent. But you've had to give up so much. Friends, as I said, and the opportunity to mix with other kids. And I'd like you to have the chance to play sport: cricket, soccer, swimming."

James frowned. His glasses slid down his nose. Pushing them up he sighed. "I hate sports," he said. "I've told you that, over and over again. I keep telling you, Dad, but you never listen. *You* like sports, I don't. I specially hate basketball!"

He could see his father trying to be patient. "OK, James. Forget about sports. What about going back to school. How do you feel about that?"

He wasn't sure. He hadn't thought about school for ages. In the beginning, when they'd made him leave Betty's Bay Primary to be taught by Caron at home, he'd been miserable.

He hadn't liked Caron then and hated her bossing him and telling him what to do. He'd missed Mrs Morris and the classroom. Missed Chess Club and Astronomy. Missed school holidays. But then…

"Talk to us, Jamie."

But then he'd started to enjoy lessons with Caron. He found he liked doing interesting projects and keeping a Nature Book and going to pottery and painting classes at the gallery. Caron made maths easy. She let him spend loads of time doing research on his computer and looking through his telescope and reading all the books he wanted. And no sports! That was one of the best things about being taught at home. No cricket or soccer or swimming. Or PE classes where other kids laughed at him and made him feel clumsy and stupid.

He turned to Caron. "Don't you want to teach me?" he asked. He watched her face intently for clues.

"I might have made a mistake," she admitted. "Taking you out of school, away from your friends."

She brought her hands together like two halves of a shell closing.

"Perhaps you do need to be challenged by other children of your age in a stimulating school environment? Perhaps you need to have more *fun*, James?"

He met her eyes. He understood. "You don't want to teach me any more," he said, with finality.

"That's not true…"

He shrugged. "Will I be in Mrs Morris' class?" he asked gravely.

"Yes, for the last term. She's looking forward to your coming back."

So, Mrs Morris knew. When had they gone to see her? Why had they not told him? Why had it been kept a secret until now?

Worms slithered in his stomach: he felt the painful pull of them. Caron and his dad weren't *asking* him whether he wanted to go back to school, not really. They were *telling* him he was going back to Betty's Bay Primary for the last term. That's what they'd been talking about at night on the deck, their chairs turned so that he wouldn't be able to hear. More changes were coming. He'd be going back to school. Caron wouldn't teach him any more. It would be like before…

He saw it all in a flash as the last piece of the puzzle, that chunk of blue sky that nobody could ever find, fell into place and everything suddenly became clear.

"Are you going away?" he asked Caron.

Startled, she blinked. She darted a look at his father. She moved her wedding ring up and down.

His dad jumped to his feet. "It's late!" he said, reaching for his briefcase. "We'll talk again, Jamie."

Caron started fussing with the tea things. James yanked up his socks and picked at one of the brown threads, pulling it slowly undone.

So it was true, then. Caron *was* going away. It would be the way it had been after his mother died when there was just James and his father. He'd be going back to Mrs Morris' class where Anna and Jeremy were not his friends any more and where it would be like being the new boy, with everybody staring and whispering. It was his fault Caron was leaving them. He'd done a lot of things he was ashamed of. He counted them on his fingers. Number one, he'd lost the Grand National Spelling Bee on purpose. Number two, he'd run away from home. Number three, he'd started the fire that had almost burned down the houses above the estuary. Number four was the worst thing he'd done. When Caron was having the baby he'd wished it would go away and not be born.

James heard the drone of a honeybee. There it was, under his nose, throbbing in the heart of a purple waxy flower. Caron had once told him that the markings on a flower were like beckoning landing lights on an airport runway. Those shimmering lights guided landing bees towards the pollen. James peered closely. The bee was covered with fine, fuzzy hairs that shivered with an electric charge. It was this burst of quivering energy that sucked the pollen from the flower. Soon, the bee would fly to another purple flower where it would drop its cargo of pollen on the stigma. That's when the magic of pollination would happen. He watched four gauzy, transparent tiny wings beating together as the bee lifted into the air and flew away.

Dimly, he heard his dad saying goodbye. Felt his father's hand on his shoulder, gripping. "We'll talk again, Jamie." The words sounded sorrowful. He heard the car starting up, backing away.

Caron stood behind him.

"Shall we go inside, James?"

He didn't answer. He dipped his nose into the flower like a bee's proboscis. When he squinted he could see fine grains of soft yellow pollen sticking to his nose.

The worms in his stomach began to twitch. All the feelings were coming back. Things were changing. Caron was leaving. He was going back to school. He hated being James Grant. He'd rather be anyone else, even a honeybee. At least a bee could fly.

Caron gave a cry. James looked up to see her wedding ring flying from her finger. It spiralled at an angle in the air for a moment before dropping with a ping onto the deck where it rolled like a golden hoop until it encountered the deep, dark space between two bolted wooden planks and vanished from view.

They stared dumbly at one another before Caron began, hysterically, to laugh.

Mickey cried in the shower. She'd never intended to kill Jordan Black or harm a single hair on the head of his sidekick Wayne.

The plan, so carefully considered, had gone terribly wrong.

In setting fire to the warehouse, she'd somehow murdered two men. She could hardly believe it!

No one would believe that the murders had not been premeditated or that she was not a heartless, cold-blooded killer seeking revenge.

She kept waiting for a banging at her door. The police, stern-faced and grim. She'd be handcuffed and taken away into custody. There would be a trial.

The black book would give her away but there was also her behaviour before the fire when she'd freely told a number of people she wanted to punish Jordan Black and made her feelings about him quite plain. Her hatred of Black would make her a key suspect. Why had she not thought to keep her mouth shut?

Detective Inspector Hector Jansen with his inscrutable face and dead eyes knew what she had done. Knew she alone was the guilty culprit. He was simply biding his time; gathering irrefutable evidence that would condemn her for all eternity.

If only she could go back to the time before she'd thrown the match into the shimmering pool of petrol. There'd been a silvery moon reflected in the pool. A voice telling her to turn away. If only she had listened. If only she had got into her truck and driven away. If only she was that person again; Mickey Graham, whose heart had been filled with hate but who had not yet committed an unforgivable crime. She shut her eyes. The door would have been locked from the inside. Petrol, paraffin and paint ignited in a fountain of flames. Black and Wayne trapped, powerless to do anything but scream in terror and pain. She'd heard the screaming as she'd driven away. Could hear it still.

Mickey sank on the cold, wet tiles. She tipped her head back. Scalding tears ran into her hair, her ears. "Oh God," she prayed. "Please forgive me. Please help me. *Please, please, please!*"

Prison awaited. What was the word they used? *Incarcerated?* She would be incarcerated, the word sounded almost medieval, along with other women who'd brutally murdered husbands, boyfriends perhaps even their own children. Prison, with only those terrifying women for company – would be her life until death.

"Oh, God. *Please, please, please!*"

Detective Inspector Hector Jansen rang Edwina Hurley's doorbell and heard, in the distance, a lively snatch of Westminster Chimes. The door was opened by a maid who stepped back at the sight of the burly, uniformed policeman waiting on the front step.

"Is Mrs Hurley at home?"

"Um, who shall I say is calling?"

The maid bolted to the conservatory where Edwina was potting up double begonias. With undisguised excitement she made her dramatic announcement: "Detective Inspector Somebody Jansen is here to see you!"

Edwina's lips tightened as though she were sucking a lemon. "*Somebody* Jansen? Odd appendage, wouldn't you say?"

The maid gave a shrug. "I didn't catch his first name," she said, unconcerned. "Shall I show the detective into the library? Or the …"

"Oh, bring him in here," Edwina replied, pulling off her gardening gloves and untying an apron printed with red and yellow tulips. "I don't think we need to stand on ceremony. I can't imagine what the detective wishes to discuss, but I expect the meeting will be brief."

The detective was a big, shambling man with large red ears and an unflattering hair cut. "I apologise for disturbing you, Mrs Hurley," he said politely, "but I wonder if you might spare me a few moments of your time?"

"Of course," Edwina graced him with her most charming smile. She led him to a circle of wicker chairs nearest the window and sank into one of them.

"I gather you've heard about the fire in Otter's Lane?" he asked, flipping open an official looking notebook and clicking a silver ballpoint.

"Fire? I can't say I have. What fire?"

"Jordan Black's warehouse was burned to the ground two days ago."

Edwina frowned. "I am sorry to hear that," she said, stiffly.

"Mr Black and a carpenter, by the name of Wayne Miller, were both killed in the blaze."

"How shocking!" Edwina gave the detective a penetrating glance. "I gather you don't believe that the fire was an accident?"

"We have opened an investigation into the possibility of arson."

"I see." Edwina pondered for a moment. "But, this line of questioning, Detective? What has it to do with me?"

"Mr Black worked for you, I understand?"

"Yes, for several months. He constructed the decking for a new wing of Hurley House. Built walls, laid paving. I found him hard working and reliable. His fee was more than reasonable."

"He has a reputation for being something of a trouble-maker and a con-man. Jobs left unfinished. Materials charged for and not purchased. That kind of thing."

"So I've heard. But that was not my experience."

"Do you know whether Mr Black had any enemies?"

Edwina wavered for a moment before collecting herself. "Well, Detective, if, as you say, Black was perceived as a confidence trickster, I imagine the man had many enemies."

"I mean *specific* enemies, Mrs Hurley? Do you know of anyone who may have wished to harm Jordan Black?"

Mickey's face flashed into her mind for a second. Mickey hated Jordan Black. Mickey most certainly wished harm to come his way.

"I'm sorry," she said, with what she hoped was an apologetic smile. "I knew little of Mr Black's private life. I have no idea who might be included amongst his enemies."

The detective seemed disappointed. He used the silver ballpoint pen to scribble on the page of his notebook and then snapped it shut. Edwina was surprised; surely their conversation had yielded nothing worth noting down?

Edwina rose from the chair with fluid elegance. "If that's all?"

She politely accompanied him to the door.

He handed a card with a mock bow. "If you think of anyone, or if anything comes to mind that you feel may be useful to our enquiries..."

Edwina smiled. "I shall contact you immediately."

Once the detective had departed, Edwina telephoned Mickey. The phone rang unanswered. It had been doing that for days. She returned to the conservatory where she pulled on her gloves and resumed her potting. The news was most disturbing. Jordan Black, dead! His carpenter, that frail, crippled man with a limp, also dead! The warehouse burned to the ground!

The detective had not mentioned names, but she wondered if Mickey was a suspect.

There was no doubt Mickey had been behaving strangely. Many said she seemed disorientated. Some said she looked depressed and exhausted. She'd lost weight and then there was her hair! The fact that she'd chopped it off was a sign, surely, of some kind of instability. The nursery garden was an absolute disgrace – plants dead and dying, weeds everywhere.

Edwina had offered Mickey several jobs to keep her occupied but she'd flatly turned them down. Good jobs, rewarded with a handsome fee. The Knott Garden, a vegetable garden, monthly maintenance of lawns and flowerbeds at Hurley House. Mickey had made the excuse she was too busy to take on any of Edwina's projects, but busy doing what?

Edwina heard the wheelchair. Thomas appeared wearing, of all things, a baseball cap: a violently yellow cap with a royal blue tick on the front.

"What have you on your head?" she asked, querulously. "You look ridiculous!"

"Oh, do you think so?" Thomas scowled like a sulky child. "I thought I looked rather good." He turned the peak of the cap to the back of his head so that the adhesive strap ran over his domed forehead. Sparse, white hair sprouted above the strap.

Edwina clenched her jaw. "Thomas!" she said firmly. "You are not a teenager. You are an old man. A very old man as it turns out. And branded baseball caps do not suit old men. Please take it off at once!"

"You're in a mood, I see," said Thomas. He gave her a sweet smile. "I shall return later," he promised, "once you've got over yourself."

The wheelchair spun cheekily.

"You're right!" Edwina announced. "I am in rather a state. I have a pain at the back of my eyes. I feel the onset of an attack of migraine." She held a dramatic hand to her head.

His face dropped. "Are you feeling ill again?"

"Aside from a racing heart and a thumping head, I am the very picture of good health. This is not about me, Thomas. I have a ghastly suspicion that Mickey has done something dreadful!"

He leaned forward, curious. "What has she done?"

"I might be wrong, but I have a hunch she may have killed Jordan Black and one of his carpenters."

"Good God! You can't be serious!"

"It may have been an accident. Murder seems out of character for such a gentle, Christian soul. Perhaps she meant only to torch the warehouse?"

"She burnt his warehouse?"

"Possibly. I don't know for certain. However, Mickey's behaviour of late has been extremely..."

"What has this to do with you Edwina? Stay out of it."

"Don't be such an old goat, Thomas. How can I turn my back on Mickey? She needs my help now more than ever!"

Edwina ripped off her gloves and flung them carelessly upon an upturned plant pot.

"Are you coming, Thomas?"

"I'm not sure helping a murder suspect is wise," he countered, mildly. "I'm fond of Mickey, as you know, but my instinct tells me that, if murder is involved, it might be an idea to keep my nose clean. That is, if you don't mind, my dear?"

"As you wish. But, Thomas?"

"Yes, dear?"

"Remove that cap and give it to the gardener. I don't want to see it again. Ever!"

Edwina rapped at Mickey's door for several minutes but there was no reply although the clapped-out truck stood in the driveway and it was obvious she was at home, hiding inside.

"It's me, Mickey!" Edwina shouted. "Open the door! Please let me in! I *must* talk to you."

There was no response.

Edwina picked up a handful of gravel and hurled it at the kitchen window.

"Mickey! Open the door! It's Edwina. I must talk to you!"

There was a noise inside like rats scuffling. The door creaked open slightly. "Go away!" Mickey pleaded in a tearful voice. "Please, go away and leave me alone."

Edwina gave the door an almighty shove so that Mickey, taken by surprise, staggered backwards and Edwina fell into the house.

She stumbled forward, almost falling and then righted herself, clutching the edge of the door, and panting hard.

They stared at one another.

"Good grief," Edwina cried. "You look like death! I've been calling. Why don't you answer? What's the matter? Talk to me!"

Mickey sobbed desperately into her hands.

Wrapping her ropy arms around the weeping woman, Edwina held her close for a few moments before dragging her inside and bolting the door.

"We don't want anyone to see or hear us," she whispered, leading Mickey, unresisting, into the kitchen.

"Sit!" she commanded. "And do try to stop crying, if you can. I have a headache and that noise is not helping."

Her eyes flew about the dusty room: a kettle, mugs, a jug. She lifted the jug and sniffed. The milk was sour, almost curdled.

"Black tea with sugar," she decided. "Good for shock."

The tea canister was empty and the inch of coffee in the bottom of the jar was rock solid. Edwina discovered a bottle of dark cocoa and, by happy accident, an unopened tin of condensed milk.

It would have to do. They sat wordlessly sipping mugs of hot, sweet cocoa.

"If you're feeling up to it," said Edwina at last, "I'd like you to tell me what has happened."

"I've murdered Jordan Black and a carpenter called Wayne Miller," said Mickey, dully. "I burned down Black's warehouse and they were both killed in the fire."

"I thought it might have been you," replied Edwina calmly. "May I ask why you did such a thing?"

"It was an accident. Not the burning of the warehouse, I did that on purpose. Black raped me. He owed me money. I wanted to punish him. I hated him, well, you knew that, but I didn't intend to kill him. I'd no idea they'd be in the shed that night. Detective Inspector Jansen knows what I've done. I'm waiting for him to arrest me. He'll send me to prison for life."

"Tell him the truth. Tell him it was an accident!"

"He knows about the rape. He'll think the murder was premeditated."

"Deny it. Admit you intended to burn down the warehouse to extract punishment for crimes committed against you. But that you had no idea…"

"Edwina! Listen to what you're saying! He won't believe me."

"But, if it is the truth?"

"Since when does truth matter? I told him I was raped and he didn't believe me."

Edwina walked to the window and stared blankly through the dirty panes at the sky beyond. She'd promised to help, but *how?* She knew Mickey well and might offer to be a character witness? She could testify that Miss Graham was deeply religious: an upstanding, hard working young woman of integrity and compassion.

All that was true. Mickey *was* a good woman. Her beloved dog had died. Black had raped her. She had, for a while, lost her mind.

Edwina sighed. She felt helpless. "Perhaps," she said, thoughtfully, "the better option might be to deny everything. The fire, the murders – everything! They can't pin this crime on you without evidence. What evidence do the police have? Did anyone see you? Were there witnesses to your setting fire to the warehouse?"

"No. I don't think so. I didn't see anyone."

Edwina paced the kitchen floor. "Black had many enemies. I gather that a few of Black's ex-clients had contacted lawyers with a view to suing the man for broken contracts, unfinished jobs; that kind of thing. I've heard the man was a thug. There are tales of pub brawls, drunkenness and fistfights. Why should you, of all people, be the primary suspect in this affair?"

Mickey gazed like a hopeful child and then her face fell. "I'll tell you why!" she cried. "I kept notes in an exercise book. I made a list of the contents of the shed. I worked out the value of things. Wrote a shopping list of stuff I needed to set fire to the shed. I had the book with me on the night and afterwards I couldn't find it. I may have dropped it. The police may already have it."

"Have you tried to find the book?"

"I went back, next morning but the police were there. It was impossible to do a proper search."

"A small, black exercise book you say?"

"Yes. With a red spine."

"Does it have your name on it?"

"No."

"Well, it might be anyone's then!"

"My handwriting, though."

"True. Tell you what, I'll search the area and see if I can locate the book."

Edwina took one of Mickey's limp, cold hands and held it tightly.

"Take my advice," she said, firmly. "Build your strength. Good food and sleep. The next few weeks might prove difficult and you're in no condition to deal with any kind of stress. Have you money?"

Mickey nodded and pressed Edwina's hand. "You're a good friend," she said. "You have no idea…"

"The book! With any luck, I might find it! " Edwina unbolted the door and sailed out with a purposeful stride.

In the silence of the kitchen, Mickey dared to hope.

She knelt, pressed her hands together beneath her chin and closed her eyes.

If she were given a second chance, she would dedicate her life to finding the path to redemption. She would repent her crimes. Begin again, from scratch and try to be a good person. It was almost too much to hope for but perhaps, along the way, she might even find God again? Until then she would have to endure this time and learn to breathe again.

Chapter 16

Caron and Ginny

Gossip in the village was rife. There was intense speculation as to who was responsible for the deaths of Black and Miller. The scene of the crime had been cordoned off with official-looking yellow and black striped tape and a stone-faced team of forensic and arson experts were on site, scrabbling soberly amongst the charred remains, bagging and identifying burnt scraps and items that might be considered as potential clues.

Reporters from The Herald, The Clarion and The Witness eagerly descended upon the village to report on the twin murders and to interview 'man of the moment', Detective Inspector Hector Jansen. It was said that the detective claimed that 'significant progress had been made with the investigation' and hinted at the distinct possibility of an arrest within the next few days.

Caron knew she'd lost James, lost him forever, and no amount of kindness would ever win him back. She'd broken his trust with the secret visit to Mrs Morris, and after that talk on the veranda she'd seen James turning inward again.

Caron found herself back at the beginning, behaving as she had when she'd first met James: unsure of herself, trying too hard, treading on eggshells, uncertain of what to say and how to say it. That hard-won, easy familiarity that had lately grown between them had gone, probably never to return.

He hardly looked at her anymore. His eyes slid away from her face and fixed themselves instead on anything else: birds on the fence, ants trailing across floorboards, anything but her. Even when she demanded: "Look at me, James!" he would squint from the corner of an eye, refusing to turn his full gaze upon her as though he couldn't bear to look. She lay awake at night, sick with herself for hurting and betraying him, aching at the thought of leaving him and moving on with her life.

"I would stay for James," she'd said to Alec. "Only for James. Our relationship is over and done with, but I would I do it for him."

"Do it for both of us," he'd replied. "We both need you."

"Need is one thing. It's love I want!"

"But I do love you."

Liar! He'd spoken the truth that time when, in a spurt of fury, he'd admitted to never loving her, to marrying on the rebound too soon after Deborah's death. The words had cut like glass. Why was it, she'd wondered, that she was always the one who did all the loving but was never loved in equal measure? Every relationship had been the same; her coming off second-best.

"You want me to stay to take care of the two of you," she'd said, matter-of-factly. "To run your life smoothly. It's easier that way. But, Alec, a relationship based on convenience is not enough for me. It can't be enough for you, either, and you can see what it's doing to James!"

She'd worn him down. They'd retreated to the deck to talk. After a while their conversations had flowed one into the other like an endless river of words. She'd spoken without bitterness, without rancour, often thinking things aloud in order to work through them herself.

In the end she got him to agree that perhaps a separation might be the best course of action. Perhaps they were, after all, incompatible. Certainly the unhappiness and rows were not conducive to happy family life.

His face, that last night. He looked drained and exhausted.

"Have it your way!" he'd said, throwing his hands helplessly in the air. "I can't keep begging you to stay, Caron. Your mind is made up. You've found all the reasons in the world to leave us. For my part, as I've said umpteen times, I am willing to try again. Ready to make compromises and work together so that we can both get what we want from our marriage. But your heart's not in it. You've moved on. The only thing left to do is to pack and leave."

She remembered at that moment, looking back at the house: at the ribbon of light from the window; the line of dark trees against the wall; the shadow of rhododendron bushes and thinking how lovely it all looked, how much she would miss it, this home that had never really been hers.

They agreed, for James' sake, to behave as normally as possible until Caron's final departure. They slept in the king-size bed, both clinging to the edge of the mattress, careful not to brush against one another, even in sleep. Plans were made. There was the offer of a teaching position for Caron in Port Victoria, starting in the new term. Alec had heard of small, newly modernised apartment, close to the school, available for a reasonable rental. He'd promised a generous monthly allowance until she was financially secure and able to stand on her own two feet.

In turn Caron had promised to find someone responsible to handle the housework and help James with homework. He was old enough now to take the bus to school and daily extra-curricular activities would last until three in the afternoon. Alec made a commitment to reduce his working hours and be home by five, at the latest.

It was all very civilised: a perfect example of two mature adults making the best of a dreadful situation. It was also the best-kept secret in St Jude.

Only two people knew what was happening, although it was becoming clear that James had somehow tumbled on the fact that Caron might be leaving them and there was no doubt that the canny Mrs Morris had more than an inkling that all was not well in the Grant household.

James pulled a shutter across that part of his mind that knew Caron would be going away and kept it tightly closed. He decided not to think about it. Change, the idea of it, made him fearful. He tried to keep everything exactly as it was in his bedroom and had grown agitated, close to tears even when Caron, dusting his room, had rearranged the pile of books beside his bed. "This one belongs *here*," he'd fussed, sliding the larger blue Atlas at the bottom of the pile, the smaller Roald Dahl stories above then *White Fang* and the book on Aircraft and Space Craft. "Harry Potter is *always* on top!"

"Sorry," Caron had said, earnestly. "It was a mistake. It won't happen again."

But it did. When he went into the pantry at snack time to take two oat biscuits from the canister on the third shelf from the bottom near the nuts and raisins, he found it missing. He hunted through the pantry in a panic, looking for the white and silver biscuit container on all the shelves he could reach before bursting into tears. Caron found him sobbing in the kitchen and swooped upon him sorrowfully. "James! What is it? What's the matter?"

"It's not in the right place," he hiccupped. "Everything's changing, nothing's the same. I want things to stay the *same!*"
"I washed it," she explained, reaching for the canister on the draining board. He ran from the kitchen. Nothing was as it should be. *Nothing!*

James had a musical box his mother had once given him for Christmas. A china figure of a brown bear wearing pink Wellingtons stood on the top, splashing in a painted puddle near a bed of waving blue hollyhocks. The bear was dressed in a yellow raincoat and had a large waterproof sou'wester on his head, with two holes for his furry ears to stick out. A prim white china duck strutted behind the bear. When you turned the silver wheel on the bottom of the box, the bear and duck whirled in slow circles to the music of *Singing in the Rain.*

The musical box stood on the white painted chest of drawers until the day James had been unable to find the biscuit jar when he also discovered the musical box was missing. "Where is it?" he cried, accusingly. "My bear and duck musical box? It's not where it should be. Why have you moved it?"

Dismally, she'd sat him down. "I had an accident," she said ruefully. "I was cleaning the chest and bumped it." She showed him the white duck, one webbed foot missing, in the palm of her hand. "I'm going to glue it back on. You'll hardly notice, I promise!"

He'd bit back tears. "It'll never be the same. It's broken now! Don't touch my things! Did you hear me? Don't touch my special things!"

When the musical box reappeared on the chest with the prim white duck marching behind the bear, it did look almost the same but for a faint crack near the webbed foot and another where the tip of a shattered hollyhock had been re-glued.

James turned the silver wheel and the yellow-clad bear and white duck spun together, the same, but different. Nothing was as it should be.

To stop thinking about things that were making him miserable, James decided to write a book. After lessons and during free time in the late afternoons, he began a story about an alien from outer space who'd been sent to earth on a mission.

The alien was nine-years-old but had really lived for thousands and thousands of years and knew far more than anyone else on planet earth. His name was Jim and he lived with a family who believed he was their natural-born son and had no idea they were harbouring an alien in their home.

The alien pretended to be like everyone else but he was different. His brain was highly advanced and he had compound eyes like a bee, cleverly hidden behind what appeared to be normal human eyes. The alien's penetrating eyes could see everything. They could see when a person was lying. They could see when a person was pretending, like when somebody laughed without meaning it or said they were sorry when they weren't. They could see right through secrets and lies.

The alien had tiny suction cups on the heels of his feet and these permitted him to grab a landing spot on the ceiling and hang on, like a circus performer dangling upside down on a trapeze.

From this elevated position, high above everyone else, Jim the alien could look down at the world and observe everything that was happening. This gave him an advantage because nobody thought to look for him on the ceiling and so he was always hidden and always safe.

James loved writing about Jim. He finished the first chapter and began a second that was all about the alien going to school. When he described the school he thought it sounded very much like Betty's Bay Primary and so he made the school a red-bricked building in a desperately cold place where it always snowed and where trees looked like black skeletons. Jim the alien was not popular at school: nobody understood him because he was different. He could slide upside down like a shadow on ceilings, see through people and ace tests but he could not catch a ball. His alien hands were boneless, like jelly fish. Balls dropped right through them.

James called the book *'Jim the Human Alien'* because he thought he might like to read a book with that name.

When he accidentally left one of the pages from his first chapter with his homework on the table, Caron found it and read it.

He came upon her crying quietly, the page in her hand, and snatched it away. "That's mine!" he shouted angrily. "It's not schoolwork! It's *private!*"

The page was wet. Tears had wrinkled the paper. He couldn't be bothered copying out the page again and so he laid it carefully beneath his dictionary to flatten it and, when it was dry, stapled it to the manuscript he kept hidden in his pyjama drawer, where nobody could find it.

He wondered what it was that had made Caron cry and read the page again.

He'd written an amazing adventure about a super advanced alien, disguised as a boy, who was trying to survive on earth with a weird family who didn't understand him. What was sad about that?

Chris had a coughing fit the night Ben came to dinner and so, when he arrived, Ben found Ginny in a state.

She'd had no time to change into the green dress and shawl and was still in the crumpled peasant skirt and paint-daubed white blouse she'd worn to art class that day. Her hair had been pulled back into a tight plait, frizzing about her face which was bare of makeup.

Ginny knew she should never have left Chris but he'd seemed so well that morning and insisted she take the class as usual. But when she returned, late in the afternoon, later than her normal hour, she'd found him in the bathroom, leaning over the basin, coughing his lungs out.

"I'll call Grace!" she'd said, face draining. "Wait here, darling, I'll call Grace!"

"Christ sakes! No!"

She'd turned, alarmed.

"It's a cough! Stop running to Grace with every little problem!"

He'd leaned over the basin again, waiting for the next paroxysm and that's when she'd seen bright spatters on the enamel.

"Blood!" The word came out a scream. "You're coughing *blood!*"

The doctor arrived within half an hour. "You're not over the pneumonia," she'd said calmly. "Your lungs are still infected. I'm prescribing a course of antibiotics. If there's no improvement we may need to admit you to St Jude's for intravenous therapy."

Ginny had rushed to take the script to the pharmacy and Grace had picked up her bag to leave.

He'd stopped her. "I'm not sleeping!" he'd said. "Can you give me something?"

She had gazed at him levelly, eyes searching.

"Not sleeping?"

"No. Insomnia. I'm awake most nights."

"But you're sleeping during the day?"

"Yeah. Sometimes."

"Perhaps if you tried to stay awake..."

"Grace! Give me the fucking pills!"

Resigned, she'd flopped on the bed, rummaging in her bag and pulling out a silver foil package. "I'll give you six tablets, that's all!"

"Six! What good are six tablets?"

"It's not the answer, Chris."

"Who says? Who says it's not the answer? It's quick. Painless. Neat."

"I do. I say it's not the answer."

"And *this* is?"

Grace had popped six pink tablets from the foil and set them on the bedside table.

She'd taken a breath. "It's hard, Chris. The hardest thing you'll ever have to do. I'll help you as much as I can but I won't give you the means to end it all. I can't. It goes against everything I believe in. Do you understand?"

"No, I bloody well don't. You'd prefer a drawn-out, lingering, painful death? Is that it? A bottle of pills, that's all I ask. Nobody need know. It'll be like falling asleep. I'll be there and then I'll be gone."

She'd shaken her head gravely. "Not ethical. Not on my watch,"

"Other doctors do it! I've heard of doctors who dispense drugs to make it easier. Have you no compassion?"

"I'm sorry, Chris." There'd been a wistful note of apology in her voice. She'd rested her cheek against his for a moment before leaving the room.

He'd broken down then: crying into the bed sheets, muffling the noise of his awful weeping.

When he heard his mother running up the stairs, taking them two at a time, he'd taken a harsh breath, wiped his face with the sheet and swallowed the unshed tears. They lay like a dead weight imprisoned in his chest.

Ginny had held out a tumbler of water and three green and white striped capsules. "Thank God for Grace," she said fervently.

When the doorbell rang, moments later, Ginny was in the kitchen heating soup for Chris: chicken with vegetables, very nourishing, if only she could get him to swallow a few mouthfuls.

The sound of the bell took her by surprise and then, with a start, she remembered. Ben with the happily anticipated take-away dinner from the French restaurant!

She ducked to squint helplessly at her distorted reflection in the silver saucepan bubbling on the stove. What a fright! Dutch doll spots burning in each cheek. Nose like a beacon. Paint streaks on her blouse, her oldest leather sandals on none-too-clean feet.

She ran to the door and, attempting a welcoming smile, swung it wide open.

He'd dressed for the occasion in a white shirt with a tie, a jacket and pressed trousers with sharp creases. He smelled of aftershave, something pine-fresh and clean and held a tray laden with silver containers.

"Ben!" she cried. "Forgive me, I'm a sight! I've had no time to change. Chris is ill. He's had an attack of coughing. The doctor's been. Oh, do come in. Perhaps you could put the tray on the counter? I'm heating soup, not that Chris will eat it, he never does, but I must try to get him to take some nourishment..."

She noticed Ben's face wore a slightly amused expression and realised she was babbling; babbling like a brook. She took a deep breath. She spun around and opened the fridge, taking out a bottle of chilled white wine. She linked her arm with his and led him to the sitting room.

She pointed at the drinks tray. "Help yourself, please. The wine is good or you might prefer gin or brandy or a dry sherry? There's cold water and ice in the fridge, if you need it. I won't be long. Soup for Chris first and then I must change so that I look less like a bag lady. Can you spare me a few minutes?"

"Of course," he said, smothering a laugh, and picking up the bottle of wine.

"Ben's arrived! I've made the most awful impression," Ginny sighed, handing Chris the tray. "Look at me! Dragged through a hedge, backwards!"

He balanced the tray on his knees. "He's seen you before, as I recall, Ma. And if your appearance puts him off, he's not worth the trouble."

"Can you manage to eat a little, darling? I must fly. Ring the bell if you need me."

She dashed away and he could hear her in the next room, tugging open cupboard doors and drawers, slamming them shut again, muttering and sighing and then, from the bathroom, the sound of water rushing into a basin.

To please her, he drank half a bowl of soup and ate a little bread and then lay back against the pillows, waiting for Inga's light tread on the stairs.

Ben opened the wine and poured a glass, feeling instantly at home.

The room was inviting. A scrawny tabby wound itself sinuously around his legs, purring deeply.

His eye was drawn to a group of photographs in antique silver frames, lined upon the mantelpiece. He examined each minutely. Scenes from a life: a bald baby in a high chair, trying to drink from a plastic cup. A young Ginny, hair tumbling, in a bathing costume at the beach, the baby straddled on one bony hip.

A blond toddler wobbling on a new red tricycle towards the camera. Ginny in a tinsel crown, decorating a Christmas tree. A grinning schoolboy in a new uniform: knobbly knees, sharp elbows.

The graduation shot: an incredibly handsome young man in black gown and tasselled mortarboard. The same young man, arm in arm with an attractive older man, squinting, laughing into the sunlight. This last photograph was black and white, grainy and shot by someone with a good eye for composition. He'd heard rumours Ginny's son was gay: perhaps this was his partner? No sign of the husband and father anywhere.

Stepping back from the photographs, Ben had a sudden urge, quickly dismissed, to set down the barely touched wineglass and stride from the living room into the hallway, escaping through the front door and into the night.

There was an entire life here, on the mantelpiece. How to connect, at this point, with someone who'd been married, had a child, been divorced or widowed, now living alone but not alone, surrounded by memories, broken dreams, fading photographs, regrets?

'Baggage' they called it – what an apt expression for the mounds of stuff people dragged through their lives. Ginny came with baggage and a sick son besides. And he had his own set of bulky suitcases filled with the dreary detritus of a failed marriage. It made him tired thinking of it all.

He sat on the edge of the seat of a faded chintz armchair, surveying the room.

The moon floated through the window. The coffee table held a vase of dried twigs, two volumes of poetry and a sewing basket, the lid half off so that he could see cotton bobbins and a length of slippery red fabric. The room was hung with paintings now half in shadow so that rich colours glowed from the rough, unplastered surface of the walls. A low desk littered with bits and pieces, piles of letters and a gleaming brass bowl filled with seashells.

"I like it here," he said, when she returned, at last. "It's comfortable. Reminds me of my grandparents' home."

"Oh?" She wasn't sure how she should take the comment. Was he inferring the room was old-fashioned: the furniture worn and threadbare?

She waited for him to pour her a glass of wine but he paged absently through one of her poetry books and so she poured one for herself.

"Cheers!" she said brightly. "And welcome."

He fumbled for his glass, picked it up and held it aloft. "Cheers!"

"I've left you alone too long," she said, reading his subdued, reflective mood.

He replaced the book and sat up straight, collecting himself. "You look lovely. I like your dress. Blue suits you."

She held up a wide swathe of skirt. "It's green. Jade, I think? Or chartreuse?"

There was a silence.

"Your son," he added, politely. "How is he?"

"A little better." She gazed forlornly. "Do you mind if we don't talk about Chris? I don't particularly want to drag you into all of this. My life, I mean. It's complicated. Well, all lives are, I suppose, but mine is particularly so at this point. The less you know, the better!"

Had she read his mind? Had he shown her, somehow, something of the dread he'd suddenly felt at the idea of becoming involved with a woman with a history?

"Very well." He hoped he didn't sound too relieved. "Dinner and light conversation," he suggested.

She lifted her glass and drank from it. "Where shall we begin?"

They talked of this and that, nothing in particular and nothing too personal.

The village. His practice: the life of a farm vet. Dogs and cats. The gallery. Her love of art. Conversation was easy and she made him laugh.

At length, they wandered to the kitchen to re-heat the now-congealed meal.

She laid the table and set a vase of garden flowers on a blue cloth. Her movements were as graceful as he remembered from their meeting at the gallery. There was something innocent about Ginny, something fragile and vulnerable that filled him with a surprising tenderness. He'd never felt this way about any woman before. Something brave and strong there too: he found himself captivated by her determined, smiling face; the way she worked so hard to appear cheerful; those full, upturned lips; laughter lines criss-crossing from her eyes; the defiantly happy way she hummed as she busied herself, gathering cutlery and crockery.

It was while he observed her swallowing the snails, one at a time, with a large gulp of wine to chase them down – as though she were taking bitter-tasting pills – that he felt, again, the faint stirring of desire.

He took her unfinished plate and scraped the contents onto his own.

"How did you know?"

He placed his hand upon hers. "Just a hunch."

She dropped her eyes and gently extracted her hand. "I've been so excited," she confessed honestly. "So happy, thinking of this evening; seeing you again and sharing this meal together. But now that you're here, sitting opposite me, I know I'm being unfair. You've come into my life at the wrong time." She paused and swallowed a mouthful of wine. Flustered, she fanned her face with a napkin.

"I haven't been completely honest about my son, Chris. He's dying. The doctor thinks we may have a few months, no more. When he goes, I'll be a complete mess, probably never recover from the loss. I can't imagine life without my boy. You've never had children…"

Her lips trembled, her voice cracked. "Anyway, what I'm saying, Ben, is that I like you very much and I hope you can see that. But, as far as a relationship is concerned, our timing is seriously off and…"

"May I say something?"

"Yes, of course."

"Let's take it slowly. One day at a time. Let's get to know one another."

She blushed hotly. Had she put her foot in it again? Both feet? Was she reading too much into his presence in her kitchen, the dinner he'd brought? Perhaps he had only friendship on his mind, nothing more? Had she made a complete and utter fool of herself? She lifted the napkin and flapped it in front of her face to cool down.

He saw her squirming in embarrassment and guessed what she was thinking.

He took her hand again. "I'm attracted to you, Ginny," he said quietly. "You are a beautiful woman."

Gratitude flooded her face.

He leaned across the table and kissed her mouth. Her eyes opened wide.

They pulled apart and stared and then leaned close again.

She parted her lips and felt the soft sweetness of his mouth on hers.

"Oh dear!" she said, head swimming. "I thought…"

"Hush! Don't say anything more!"

Chris heard of Inga's shoes on the stairs and felt a rush of pleasurable anticipation. She slipped noiselessly into the room, leaning over the bed and dusting his face with feather light kisses, her cool fingers smoothing back his hair. She said nothing: the only noise in the room coming from a breeze loosening leaves in the trees.

He spoke first. "I've been waiting for you. Lying here, listening for the sound of your footsteps."

Her face glowed.

"I've grown too dependent upon you. I worry I may become a burden."

She laced her hands around his back and pulled him forwards so that she could shake out the pillows and turn them over. She motioned that he sit up straight and rest against the pillows.

"Inga?"

She lifted a finger to her lips, closed his eyelids gently. "Breathe in," she instructed quietly. "Calm your body. Inhale through the centre of both nostrils."

He straightened his spine against the pillows, rested the soles of his feet flat on the mattress, as she had taught him, inhaled deeply.

"Release your breath. Breathe out. Exhale through your nose. Slowly."

He breathed out.

"Allow your mind to follow your breathing: in and out. Inhale to the count of five; one, two, three…"

A sense of peace filled him, as it always did during these sessions.

"Exhale to the count of five. Be still and listen to the rhythm of your breathing. Allow your mind to follow your breath …"

The sound of her voice soothed him. His chest rose and fell.

Inga believed that yoga breathing exercises strengthened his respiratory and immune system and promoted healing. Perhaps ithey did, perhaps they did nothing more than fill him with a sense of peace and stop his brain working overtime. He always felt more relaxed after each session.

"Breathing in, I calm my body. Breathing out, I smile. Dwelling in the present moment…"

Sometimes he fell asleep. Sometimes she made him lie prone, face forward on the mattress, massaging his neck and back, calves and feet.

He had grown ashamed of his body. Ashamed of the way his flesh had become slack, hanging from his bones, darkly bruised in places, as fine tissue paper.

Her movements were never painful: the touch of a mother's loving hand upon a sick child. She always knew what he needed most. His hair washed or brushed. Another blanket. Clean pyjamas. Bed socks. A glass of ice water. The window opened or shut.

"You're a witch! How do you know? How do you *always* know?"

Her answer was a shrug. She knew because she knew. She knew because she loved him. She knew because it was easy to imagine how restless and uncomfortable he might feel on crumpled bed linen in an airless room. How his tender skin might chafe against the weave of sheets. How his heels might throb, his bones ache. How his mouth might become dry, his teeth furred, his throat parched.

Later, after the routine breathing exercises, the careful massage and all the thoughtful chores she gave herself to make him more comfortable, Inga would light candles and open the curtains so that they could more easily see the star-studded sky.

She would sit beside him, her cheek pressed against his chest, listening to his breathing, telling him tales of her childhood in her singsong accent until, he fell asleep.

Tonight, though, she found herself distracted by the sight of six pink tablets on the bedside table. "What are these?" she asked, pointing.

"Uh, pills."

"Yes, I can see that. What are they for?"

"To help me sleep."

He could see her digesting his answer.

"What are you thinking? Are you planning to take your own life?"

"One day, perhaps. When I can bear it no longer."

He studied her for expressions of shock, disappointment, grief.

She looked at him trustingly, nodding very slowly. "I will help you," she offered.

He could hardly believe it. "You will?"

She nodded. "When it becomes too painful to bear. I will do all I can to help you."

He told her then of the recurring dream he had, night after night. A boat drifting out to sea. The water beckoning invitingly, glittering with reflected sunlight. A graceful dive into the water; his body floating: as light as a leaf, carried on swift currents. The sensation of sinking: the water closing above his head and then peace, silence, nothingness.

"What does it mean, this dream?"

"A fantasy version of death, I think. The version I would choose if I had a choice."

"You would *drown?* But that is horrific!"

He pondered. "Drowning implies a struggle; suffocating in water, fighting for your life, gasping for breath, your limbs kicking and threshing. My version is much gentler. It's like falling asleep in water."

She shuddered. She had a sudden, terrifying image of his body fished from the sea. Sand in his eyes; weed in his hair; skin bleached the colour of old fish bones.

She took his hand. "Don't speak of it!"

His expression was impossible to read but there was something in his eyes, something so wretched. "Please, try to understand..."

"When I was a girl, growing up," she said, "we had a summer house in the Swedish archipelago where the wind blew so hard that I often thought our little wooden chalet would lift like a kite and soar high into the sky."

He settled back against the pillows. She nestled close: he could feel her lips moving against his breastbone.

"Our summer home was once a fisherman's cottage and so it always smelled faintly of crayfish but there was also the sweet smell of red clover from the garden..."

This nightly storytelling made him feel like a child at bedtime. His lids dropped, her voice caressed like a lullaby. She told her stories simply, with images that came alive so that he saw them clearly, like a favourite film played in his mind.

He imagined her as a white-haired sprite clutching a fishing net on a stick and peering into icy rock pools slippery with seaweed. He saw the Swedish sun gleaming weakly, seagulls soaring between tall boat masts. He smelled salt from the sea, and heard, like music, the cry of sandpipers on the wind.

They left at the same time. Ben politely walked Inga to her car, parked outside the gate. She observed a tall, rangy man with an intelligent, kind, weathered face.

He saw a beautiful young woman with fine features and long limbs. Up close though, in the pool of light from the garden lamp, she looked drained.

"Inga," she said, proffering a hand.

"Ben Barker."

"You are Ginny's friend." Her voice was foreign.

He liked the sound of that. "Yes," he said, with a smile. "Ginny's friend."

She leaned towards him slightly. "You will need to be strong," she said gravely, her eyes dark, expression intense.

"I see," he said, idiotically.

He stood unmoving until she'd gone. He stared at the blackened shadows of the garden and thought that the girl had clearly known something He would have to be strong to face all that lay ahead, particularly if the tragedy of a young man's death was on the cards, but Ginny would be worth it.

From what he'd learned about love, and he didn't, even at his advanced age know a lot, sacrifices were needed and there'd be storms to get through but a second chance like this, a chance at mid-life love when you thought it unattainable, a dream – he could hardly believe his luck!

Chapter 17

Edwina

With Jordan Black out of the picture, Ian's life changed. Suddenly he was in demand. His telephone rang off the hook. He was swept along on a tide of Black's unfinished building projects that were urgently requiring his management skills. There were also any number of unfulfilled orders for kitchen cabinets and custom-made items of furniture from Black's clients, some of whom had once been Ian's clients before they'd turned their backs on him.

He thought he might pick and choose the best of these, the jobs with the largest budgets, the most time available, but it seemed he had no time for anything other than juggling the interminable requests of the Save the Beach project with a full-time commitment to the Environ group. On top of this, he was answerable to Edwina who seemed to have become a tyrant and a bully. Whilst he was probably, on some level, flattered to have his reputation restored, Ian's life appeared to have gone to the dogs. "Feast or famine," he was heard to mutter and those who congratulated him on this deserved rise in status found him distinctly resentful of his sudden and unasked-for celebrity.

Ian had a meeting with a Mrs Oates who had called and said she needed to see him urgently.

"This is in connection with…?" He'd taken to keeping a diary and scribbling down names and details of jobs required. He was not used to so many calls, so many strange names and phone numbers, so many quotes to be written up and everything wanted yesterday.

"An armoire," Mrs Oates said. "Mr Black was making one for me before his unfortunate…"

She arrived promptly at the appointed time. Ian showed her to his new workshop, furnished now with a functional desk and two good chairs in a business-like nook where he might meet clients and discuss their particular requirements.

Mrs Oates was very specific about what she required. She drew an armoire in the air. Her pale, plump hands were expressive: she might have been conducting an orchestra. He tried to follow what she was saying. Something about gothic mouldings? She slashed the air like a Japanese kung fu artist. He listened carefully. An *assertive* horizontal pediment? What was that? He watched transfixed.

The hands formed wave shapes. Seeing his blank expression, Mrs Oates repeated the shapes in the air; the fingers swept a gracious curve before his eyes.

"Sorry?" he admitted. "I'm a bit lost here."

"Graceful arches between the legs," she snapped. "Like this..."

The hands floated again, drawing in mid-air.

He didn't get it. He had no idea at all what she might be getting at. He picked up a pencil and made a rough sketch. "Armoire. Classical proportions? Three shelves? Four drawers?"

She peered at the drawing. She frowned. Her nostrils flared.

"Nothing like that!" Her voice grew shrill. "Much more refined. More *tasteful.* And where, pray, are the gothic..."

He tried again. Another piece of paper. He added fiddly details although he had no idea what shape gothic mouldings on a door might take.

She shook her head with impatience, expression petulant.

"Too simple! Too plain!"

Ian pushed pencil and paper away. "Have you a photograph of the armoire? A picture? A drawing? Something I might copy?"

"Mr Black knew exactly what I wanted without a photograph. He understood my vision completely!" She scowled darkly, brows drawn.

"I'm sorry, Mrs Oates. You might be better off looking out for an antique. Have you tried the gallery?"

She made a fist and pounded his desk. "I started there! They put me onto Jordan Black. Why is it impossible to have a simple armoire made to order?"

Ian pushed back his chair. "Probably because it's not simple," he said. He kept the tone of his voice pleasant and professional. "I'm sorry. I can't help." He led her, muttering crossly, to the gate. "Good luck!" he shouted as she stamped away.

He had new respect for Jordan Black. How had the man put up with all this crap?

And then there was Edwina who was on his case, night and day.

Sometimes she called him after ten in the evening when he was either in bed or preparing for bed.

"We must schedule a meeting!" she'd said last night, without introduction. "There's talk of a nuclear power station to be built not far from St Jude!"

"A nuclear…?"

"A government project. Part of a fuel-diversity plan. We must get everyone together to warn them. We must contest the plans. Conduct our own environmental impact assessment…"

"You want to schedule a meeting with Environ?"

"Good gracious, no! We need to get everyone from the village to attend! I propose we use the village hall as the meeting place. Set up the gathering as a matter of great urgency!"

He'd been dumbstruck. "How do I do that?"

"Posters! Leaflets! E-mail! Telephone! Get onto it immediately, Ian. There's not a moment to be wasted!"

The next morning, Ian visited Hurley House and found Edwina in consultation with a Professor Jacobs, a proponent of nuclear power. Edwina was making notes.

"Morning, Ian!" she sang out. "I'm engaged in some preliminary research. Professor Jacobs has agreed to be one of the speakers at our meeting. He tells me that nuclear power plants provide as much as seventeen percent of the world's electricity!"

Wordlessly, Ian pulled out a chair and sat.

The professor, a burly man with a shock of grey hair, gave a polite nod. He continued itemising the benefits of nuclear power on stubby fingers. "Produces very little sulphur dioxide, nitrogen oxides, volatile organic compounds or greenhouse gasses. Is arguably the best base-load alternative to coal…"

Edwina sniffed. "You're saying nuclear energy is *safe?"*

"Yes."

"The Chernobyl disaster? Tons of toxic radioactive dust scattered into the atmosphere. And the more recent incident? A Japanese nuclear power plant stricken by an earthquake? Hundreds of barrels of nuclear waste tipped over! Radioactive water leaking into the Sea of Japan! You call that *safe?"*

Ian sighed. Edwina was just getting into her stride. The meeting might go on all day. Might go on forever.

"May I interrupt?" he blurted, feeling like a pupil in a classroom.

"What is it?"

"I can't do this, Edwina. Sorry. It's beyond me. I'd like to help but I honestly don't know the first thing about nuclear power plants ..."

"Listen then and learn!" Her tone was knife-sharp.

"No!" He held his ground. "You don't understand! I can help build sea walls to prevent erosion. I can replant dunes with indigenous vegetation. Hell, I can save penguins drenched in oil. Any fool can do any of those things. But I can't organise a meeting and invite the village to discuss nuclear power!"

"Why ever not?"

"I'm a carpenter! I haven't a clue about posters, leaflets, all that stuff. I'm not that person. You need someone with organisational skills."

"What are you saying?"

He shuffled his feet. "I've thought about it. I'd like to be part of the team," he said. "But I can't be the team leader."

Her expression was ferocious. "I see," she said, swinging her pen like a metronome.

He spoke in a rush. "I took over this position because you were ill. Everyone thought you were dying. You, yourself, said you were on your way out. But not from where I'm standing! You're looking pretty good: strong and healthy. All your faculties intact."

Her expression lightened. "Go on."

"Well, in my bumbling way, I'm saying I think you resume the positions of Chairperson on both committees. You should organise the nuclear power plant meeting. People listen to you. Face it, Edwina, you're the best person for the job!"

"Hear, hear!" said the professor.

Edwina blushed prettily. "You may have a point," she conceded. "I am feeling well: extremely well, in fact. I suppose that, in the short term, I could take on my positions as chair. There's no science to organising a nuclear debate meeting in the village hall; just common sense and connections."

He breathed a sigh of relief. Thank God for that. He pushed his chair back an inch or two.

"Not so hasty, Ian!"

Why had he thought he would get off so easily?

"I have agreed to take back responsibility in the *short-term* mainly because I find you have a great deal to learn. I sincerely hope that you will be active on both committees? My right-hand man, if you will. I will organise attendance and itinerary but your presence at the nuclear power plant meeting is imperative."

He felt himself slump like a schoolboy in the front row; reprimanded for misbehaving; cowed by the dead weight of responsibility falling again upon his shoulders.

"I suggest you listen to what the good professor here has to say and learn something about the subject of nuclear power plants."

Edwina tore several sheets from her notebook and passed them to him with a pen.

"Take notes!" she instructed.

The professor cleared his throat and resumed his lecture.

Ian felt a headache coming on.

Thomas, who had not been invited to attend the meeting with Professor Jacobs, sat alone in the garden in a fit of pique. He sulkily observed a party of chattering, red-faced mousebirds through his binoculars. The birds were feasting upon ripe mulberries, high in the branches, their beaks stained black with dripping fruit juice.

It was the closed door he objected to most: Edwina, the professor and Ian Frey together in private consultation regarding the matter of the nuclear power plant.

As a matter of fact, though by no means an expert, he himself knew something about nuclear power and believed that he might have made a valuable contribution to the discussion.

There was no reason why he should not have been invited but more and more. Edwina excluded him from such things, as though he were little more than a child unable to participate in adult matters. His deafness was probably the reason but he was not stone deaf and, if his hearing aid were finely tuned, was certainly able to gather the gist of most conversations.

"Why am I treated as *persona non grata*?" he asked Edwina when she came out to join him in the garden.

"What do you mean?"

"That meeting you've just had, regarding nuclear energy and the proposed plant: a subject close to my heart. Why was I not invited to attend?"

"I had no idea you were interested."

"You didn't ask."

"Well, why didn't you say? Why not simply join us?"

"Humph!"

"Oh don't sulk, Thomas!"

He lifted the binoculars and trained them on tufted heads of the mousebirds, they looked like punks with cheeky Mohawks.

"Where were you last evening?" he enquired. "You went out. Where did you go?"

She became flustered. "Ah," she said, stalling for time. "I had to do something for a friend."

"Who?"

"Mickey, if you must know."

"I don't understand. What did you have to do for Mickey?"

"Something personal, Thomas. Something private. Certainly nothing I care to discuss."

He lowered the binoculars with an expression of triumph. "See!" he accused, in his wavering old-man voice. "This is exactly what I mean! You are keeping things from me. Secrets. You no longer confide in me. You shut me out of everything important!"

She poked him on the arm. "You are being ridiculously tiresome!"

He felt stung with the injustice of it all. Why must she always speak to him as though he were a juvenile? Thomas wheeled the chair in the direction of a short flight of steps and a path leading to the Koi pond.

He braked and poised the chair nimbly at the edge of the steps. What now? From the corner of an eye he saw Edwina rising to her feet, her face twisted into an expression of annoyance.

Perhaps, if he were careful, he might manoeuvre the chair down the steps, and, with a little luck, arrive at the stone path. From there it was plain sailing all the way to the pond.

He clattered noisily down to the first step before the wheels slipped and the chair was hurled into the air, crashing on the third step and landing upside down, wheels spinning, in the centre of the stone pathway.

Winded, Thomas lay on his back, arms and legs waving in the air and looking, he supposed, like an upturned beetle. If his dignity weren't so wounded, he'd have laughed out loud.

With a high-pitched scream, Edwina flew to his side. "Thomas! Thomas, my dear! Are you hurt?"

He let her suffer for a few seconds before replying. He let out a pant and then a stifled groan. "No, I don't believe so. Only my pride."

She helped him to his feet. They limped together to the garden bench beneath the wild fig tree. He was conscious of a dull ache in the small of his back and a nasty twinge in his right knee.

"You're looking pale," she said anxiously. "Are you sure…?"

"I'm perfectly fine!" He gathered himself and gave what he hoped would be perceived as a brave smile.

He lowered himself creakily onto the bench and she sat beside him.

"I went to Black's warehouse to look for a book for Mickey," she confessed. She twisted her hands in her lap. "A book that, in the wrong hands, may seal her fate."

"Go on?"

"The book seems to have been kept as a record. Mickey said she'd written things in it that would clearly identify her as Black's killer. She lost the book on the night."

"Did you find it?"

"No. I searched everywhere. Someone has picked it up."

"I see." He heard the pious tone in his voice.

"I don't believe you do, Thomas! It was an accident. Black raped her. Stole money. She wanted him punished. How could she know Black and Miller would be sleeping in the warehouse that night!"

"What are the chances of Mickey being found guilty?"

"It all hinges on the book! If the police have it, Mickey is done for!"

"Be careful what you wish for…" he said, thoughtfully.

"What's that?"

"You know the phrase: 'Be careful what you wish for, lest it come true?' Well, Mickey wanted Black punished and she got her wish."

The party of mousebirds burst from the mulberry trees into the sky. Thomas took one of Edwina's hands in his own. "Friends?" he asked, beseechingly.

"I need your help!" Edwina replied, impulsively. "This nuclear power plant. We'll need to know the pros and cons of nuclear energy if we're to put up a fight against the erection of a reactor near St Jude. I've made a start but there's a great deal of research to be undertaken, data to be collected…"

"Ah!" His eyes glinted behind his spectacles. "Right up my street!" There was a show of yellow teeth, a quiet chuckle. "The world's reserves of fossil fuels are running out," he said, boastfully. "They will be burned up within fifty years. However, there are large global reserves of uranium…"

"Don't tell me you're in *favour* of nuclear energy?" She was astonished.

"There are benefits, obviously. But, I agree, we don't want a plant erected anywhere near St Jude. Do you remember the disaster at Three Mile Island?"

She didn't, really. Not the details, anyway. He waffled on, filling her in, losing her along the way. How surprising! Perhaps it was Thomas: timorous, vague, academic, partially deaf Thomas, who might be the one to lead the vanguard? To champion the rights of the residents and thwart government plans to erect the plant.

Edwina embraced him, clutching at a tangle of bristling tweed and cotton and feeling chin stubble, hot breath and slippery silk tie against her cheek. She gave him a kiss that missed his lips and landed on his chin.

"You're sorry, aren't you?" he said, grinning like a wicked elf. "You know you've been unkind. You're making it up to me?"

Edwina rose to her full height and held out a hand to help him to his feet. She would say nothing more. The not-quite-there kiss would have to do as an apology.

That night Edwina tossed and turned. She hadn't told Thomas how appalled she'd been at the sight of the ugly, blackened space that now took the place of the warehouse – the area now festooned with fluttering yellow tape and an official sign reading: '*No Admittance. Police Enquiry Underway'!*

She remembered visiting the carpenter's shop once before and being impressed with how neat and orderly it had been. A set of kitchen cupboards, newly finished, had been waiting for collection. A simple design, painted white with good silver handles, she'd admired the craftsmanship, and the detailed finishes.

But now there was nothing left, nothing but a blackened pile of rubble, the smell of smoke still lingering and two bodies lying in the mortuary.

Edwina had taken a stick to rummage amongst dried and dusty shrubs in the area but there'd been no sign of a small black notebook with a red spine.

She'd telephoned Mickey late that night. "Nothing!" she'd admitted. "I've found nothing! The book is not there. I'm sorry."

Edwina had heard Mickey's rough breathing for a few moments before she'd whispered 'thank you' and replaced the receiver.

Edwina wondered what she would do in Mickey's place, waiting for the police to pounce? Flee? Yes, she would flee rather than face life imprisonment. Leave the country? Was that possible? Did Mickey even have a passport?

Edwina could easily provide sufficient funds to facilitate the establishment of a new life in a foreign destination, but was Mickey up to it? She looked sickly and frail, traumatised by the horrifying chain of events that had led her to commit this crime.

Edwina pushed back the bedclothes and thrust her feet into satin quilted slippers. She flung a peach silk peignoir over her shoulders and crept quietly from the bedroom. The angel! It was time to commune with the angel. Perhaps she might help?

It was dark in the garden, the air soft and cool. The angel, lit by a meticulously positioned white spotlight, was poised between heaven and earth, face uplifted. Edwina stood on tiptoe so that she might place her right hand in the angel's hand. The hand felt hard, damp and chilled, mottled with blisters of dew. Edwina gripped the wooden fingers tightly. There was so much to say, so much help required. There was Mickey's life and death crisis. There was also the terrifying possibility of a nuclear power plant erected near St Jude. There were profound thanks to be offered. Thanks for cancer in remission, for newfound energy and stamina, for months, perhaps, of precious life ahead. She knew she'd been given a gift but the clock still ticked. There was no stopping time from marching towards the inevitable.

If the angel could assist Edwina in making a difference, in changing lives and outcomes, well, how very gratifying that would be as a legacy to be remembered by.

Mickey stood in the house her father had given her during what seemed like another lifetime, and imagined it without her. The rooms empty, gathering dust. Strangers living here, going through her things. Her meagre possessions would be fascinatingly elevated to the position of 'items that had once belonged to a murderer'. She imagined a film crew photographing things she'd left behind once she'd been sent away to prison. She imagined what people would say about her. '*Spinster, in her forties*'. '*Reclusive lifestyle*'. '*Eccentric and troubled personality*'. '*Once deeply religious, appeared to suffer a loss of faith'. 'Compulsive, obsessive nature'.*

They'd paint her as the local crazy lady and people would make that finger-whirling motion at the side of their heads whenever her name was mentioned. They'd say she deserved her punishment and forget about her before the year was out.

Mickey sorted out her life. She wrote a will leaving the nursery, its contents and any money remaining in her account to the St Jude Animal Shelter.

She cleaned cupboards and packed in boxes all the clothes she hadn't worn during the past twelve months and dropped these off at the St Jude Hospice for their monthly jumble sale. She bundled old magazines, newspapers and everything broken, stained or rusted in voluminous black garbage bags and deposited these at the tip along with all the plants and shrubs that had died while she'd been looking the other way.

She cleaned the house, swept and mopped floors and shone windows so thick with grime and sea-salt that she had to do them twice. She spent an entire day polishing the stained glass window cut in the shape of a sun rising above a sapphire sea. She laundered linen and towels and packed everything in mothballs in a cupboard leaving a duvet and one pillow on the bed, and a single towel hanging on a hook behind the bathroom door.

She polished her desk, tore letters into shreds and bagged in plastic her unfinished manuscript on the natural wilderness of the Eastern Cape.

When she was done, Mickey started on the nursery garden, sweeping, raking, forking and fertilising. She watered plants and hosed paths and walls and even, for good measure washed off the 'Northwind Nursery' sign that had become white with bird-droppings and sticky with spiders' webs.

The industry focused her mind on something other than the murders and made her so tired that she was able, late at night, to fall into bed and sleep solidly until morning.

Two days passed. Three days. Five days since she'd set the warehouse on fire.

She bought all the local newspapers and read them from cover to cover. According to reports, the police were still hard at work collecting evidence. Enquiries were progressing well. The articles concluded with the damning sentence that the police were confident of an early arrest.

Every day Mickey waited for the sound of their knocking on the door, for her heart to fall like a stone and for life, as she'd known it, to end.

Detective Inspector Hector Jansen read the reports from the arson and forensic teams but they told him nothing that he didn't already know or guess at.

After conducting intensive tests, the Forensic Science Laboratory concluded that inflammable liquid had been poured outside the warehouse from a container, most probably a bucket or jerrycan. The fuel had flowed beneath the front door reaching inside the building. At this point the liquid had been set alight.

The report confirmed the evidence of a trail of burn markings from *outside* the shed leading to the door, indicating a deliberate arson attempt.

The intensity of heat and the severe damage caused to material objects was a consequence of the combination of the fuel with the highly flammable contents of shed: paraffin, turpentine, paint, machine oils, lumber, rope etc.

The report concluded that the warehouse door had been securely barred from inside and, since the blaze had engulfed the front of the shed, the two imprisoned men had been unable to escape the deadly flames.

The detective was cautious about how much information he should divulge and, no fan of local reporters ("bloody bunch of vultures!"), he kept press briefings short and to the point.

That woman from *The Herald*, Jessica somebody, was a particular pain in the arse with her non-stop phone calls and sudden, unannounced appearances at the station.

"Do you have a suspect yet, Inspector?"

"We are pursuing our investigations and will let you know in due course."

"Is that double-talk for you haven't got a clue who the arsonist is?"

Jessica somebody was way off the mark. In fact, Detective Jansen had a very good idea who might have started the blaze and murdered Black and Miller.

The suspect he had in mind had both motive and inclination and recently had been heard to make several threats against Black.

The detective was, however, biding his time. The criminal justice system had to be held to the highest possible standards. Science and reliable evidence had to be used to prove guilt or innocence. There was no point in rushing these things. Investigations were underway, evidence was being gathered and very soon an arrest would be made.

The next morning Edwina slept late whilst Thomas enjoyed a rare, solitary breakfast.

He was given a glass of freshly squeezed orange juice with which to swallow the combination of salmon oil, Omega 3, multi-vitamins, Echinacea and cod-liver oil Edwina insisted was the 'fuel' of life. As usual he was given a bowl of natural yoghurt with bran and raisins to keep him regular. Since Edwina was not in evidence, Thomas also requested a cup of strong, black filter coffee and a large blueberry muffin that he happily consumed with lashings of forbidden butter.

He was licking the last of the delicious crumbs from his knife when Edwina burst into the dining room.

"I've had an idea!" she said, pulling up a chair and emptying bran flakes into her bowl. "You need a computer boffin to do your research."

"Research?"

"Data collection on the nuclear power plant! Don't tell me you've forgotten already?"

"No, dear. What's wrong with the library?"

"Out of date and far too slow. No, as I said, you need a computer boffin to access the latest information on nuclear energy."

He felt a sudden sinking of spirits. Was she going to spoil his fun and mastermind the research?

"James Grant. I suggest you ask James to help you with this project."

"But he's a child. No more than nine or ten!"

"And, I believe, a computer whiz. Most children are. I'll get onto Caron immediately after breakfast and ask if James can assist with your research."

Thomas considered. "I'd prefer to handle it my own way, if you don't mind," he said, huffily. "I'm not sure I need a child to help me access information."

Deftly, Edwina tossed a handful of multi-coloured vitamins into her mouth and chased them down them with half a glass of skim milk. "Don't be such a fuddy duddy! It's all there, on the Internet. James will show you how to find all you need in a nanosecond!"

"A *what?*"

But Edwina was on the move. There was a flurry of floral skirt as she left the room.

Thomas felt grieved. Perhaps he should not have volunteered? Perhaps he should have left her alone to do it all herself. Now there was the computer to worry about: mind boggling with its own uniquely foreign language and dizzying speed and here he was, relegated to position of onlooker and observer with a nine-year old boy executing the research, providing the answers and making him feel like a forgotten relic from another age. Oh, it was too humiliating for words!

"Would you like to help Mr Paton conduct research into nuclear power plants, James?" Caron, one hand placed discretely over the telephone mouthpiece, asked the question.

"Nuclear power plants?" James tasted the words. Nuclear was a word he knew how to spell, and not everyone did. Nuclear had something to do with the atom. There were nuclear bombs and nuclear weapons. There were nuclear reactors that had meltdowns. He nodded. "Cool!" he said.

At exactly noon, Edwina's driver dropped Thomas, in his wheelchair, at the Grant household. Caron answered the door and helped him inside.

James' computer and printer had been brought down from his bedroom and positioned, for convenience, on the large table in the kitchen, where they would have ample space to print out as many pages of research material as might be required.

James got up as Caron wheeled Thomas into the room. Thomas gave a wave and, for good measure, a wink. He remembered James from the Spelling Bee. The boy who wore glasses, had a mouthful of braces, legs like sticks and a wilful cow's lick of hair, reminded him of himself at that age.

"Thomas Paton, at your service!" he announced.

The boy stared openly. Caron nudged him forward. "James?"

He remembered his manners and stuck out a hand. "Pleased to meet you, Mr Paton," he said, obediently.

"I understand you're a computer whiz?"

"Boffin," said James seriously. "The correct term is boffin. And yes, I think I am. Well, for my age I am, anyway."

"Good. I wish to research nuclear power plants: the pros and cons thereof. Do you know anything about the subject?"

"I know what happens when you have a nuclear meltdown! You die! Radioactive rays kill everything!"

Thomas chortled. "Perhaps we should start right there," he said. "With the cons – the arguments against nuclear power."

They sat together at the computer.

"What are you doing?"

"Googling!"

"What's that?"

James explained patiently. "I'm using the Google search engine to find out about nuclear power plants. See? Which of these sites would you like to visit?" He read from the long list.

"My word!" said Thomas, wheeling closer to the screen. "How impressive! May we visit them all?"

Four hours later, James and Thomas had amassed a significant pile of computer printouts on the subject of nuclear power.

"I don't know when I've enjoyed myself more!" Thomas was flushed with excitement. He hunted for an appropriate comment. "Thanks, Bro!" he said.

James giggled. "Pleasure, Dude!"

The car arrived. Caron helped wheel Thomas outside. James and Thomas shook hands. Thomas appeared reluctant to leave. "Do you play chess?" he asked.

"Yeah! Chess is brilliant!"

"Ah. Good. Would you like to have a game with me?"

"Wow! Yes. I'd like that."

"I must warn you, though. I am a self-proclaimed grandmaster. I shall beat you hollow!"

"Grandmaster? Is that like a chess champion?"

Thomas gave a modest nod.

"You don't have the Harry Potter Chess set, do you?" James asked hopefully.

"The what?"

"There's a life-size chess game at the end of the film of *The Philosopher's Stone* and you can get this super chess set…"

"No, alas. No Harry whatsit chess set. A conventional board with traditional pieces, will that do?"

James nodded vigorously. "When can we play?"

They set a time for the end of the week.

James waved happily as the car exited the gates.

Caron and James smiled at one another before James remembered. The light in his face dimmed, he turned away. She followed him indoors. She watched him walk up the stairs to his bedroom and shut the door behind him.

How extraordinary it was, she thought, *that he could give himself so completely to a total stranger and yet offer nothing to her.*

She filled the washing machine with a load of laundry and switched it on. Perhaps it was simpler, she reasoned, to be friendly to someone he didn't know, someone who didn't have the power to hurt him or destroy his trust?

She stood in the kitchen thinking jealously of the two of them: the old man and the boy, together at the computer, faces shining, the easy laughter, the teasing.

At that moment, with only the liquid churning of the washing machine to break the silence in the empty room, she thought she'd never in her life been lonelier.

Chapter 18

Mickey

There was a meeting at the village hall to discuss the proposed nuclear power plant.

An angry buzzing, as people lead into the hall, gave an indication that everyone was up in arms and ready for a fight and it took Edwina five loud thumps of her mallet to quieten them all so that the first keynote speaker was able to make himself heard. Professor Jacobs, presenting the case for nuclear energy as an alternative power source was booed and shouted down five minutes into his talk. He tried again and again and then, patience exhausted, leaned into the microphone and shouted: 'Bollocks!' Grabbing his notes from the podium, he stormed off the stage. Edwina valiantly sounded a military rat-tat-tat with her mallet but the rambunctious crowd were not to be silenced.

Like a lamb to the slaughter, poor Thomas was wheeled to the podium, a sheaf of papers trembling in his hands. The microphone was lowered. He tapped on it nervously. "Can anyone hear me?" he quaked. Surprisingly, the frenzy subsided as all eyes turned to Thomas. "Ahem!" he cleared his throat, jumping as the noise bounced back like a tennis ball. He winced, expecting laughter and, when none came, silently shuffled papers and then, a drowning man, clutched at the microphone and blurted: "Ladies and gentlemen, I am honoured to be here today…"

Perhaps they felt sorry for Thomas? Perhaps it was his close association with the formidable Edwina? In any event the turbulent crowd stopped raging like a nest of angry wasps, to hear what he had to say.

Thomas began shakily, his faltering voice growing loud and then fading to a whisper. "Speak up!" they cried.

He paused, took a deep breath and then, gazing into the audience as Edwina had suggested, imagined a field of green cabbages. 'A great leveller, works every time', she'd said, and surprisingly, it did.

Aided by pertinent facts from global research, Thomas presented a concise, balanced picture of nuclear power, ultimately drawing the conclusion that, as a high-risk technology with the possibility of an accident or radiation exposure, a reactor in the area would be potentially disastrous for the vulnerable community of St Jude.

He warmed to his subject, bellowing into a microphone that popped with every hissing sibilant. "Imagine, if you will, a meltdown! Radioactive isotopes released into the atmosphere, swept along on our gusting south-westerly winds! Toxic radiation polluting our water resources: spilling into sea-beds, gushing into dams and poisoning canals. The deadly spread of cancer, radiation sickness, genetic mutation!"

Carried away with the drama of it all, Thomas drummed upon the lectern.

The audience applauded, whistled and stamped their feet in unison.

He wound down, at last, to a conclusion. "We cannot counteract the risk of global warming through the expansion of nuclear energy," he trumpeted. "Energy conservation and wind, sea and solar power are safer, cleaner ways to fight climate change. Our immediate challenge is to face our ministers and lobby against the erection of a nuclear reactor near St Jude! Are you with me? Eh? Are we ready to fight!"

As one, the audience rose to its feet and roared their approval.

It was, Thomas decided afterwards, a conquest! Members from the audience clustered about him, swarming the stage, nudging his chair, reaching out to shake his hand as though he were a soccer star or a pop idol.

One woman admitted she'd found his talk 'inspirational'! "Lucky Edwina," she'd whispered, her ample bosom grazing his arm.

There were questions, dozens of them and he was grateful to know the answers, well, most of them anyway, the others he took a brave stab at and hoped for the best. Afterwards, as the hall slowly emptied, Thomas remained behind with Edwina, Ian and half a dozen or so stragglers, too exhilarated to call it a night and return home. One of the committee ladies brewed tea in the urn and offered coconut biscuits from a packet. Rather modest fare, he thought. Surely French Champagne in fancy glasses might have been more appropriate for such a victory.

He was puffed with pride, panting with exhaustion. "I think that went rather well, don't you?" he asked, eyes blazing.

Edwina toasted him with her mug. "Well done!" she cried. "You were very Winston Churchill!" she smiled. "Rousing! You had them all right there!" She exhibited the palm of her hand. "Eating your every word. I felt prouder than you can imagine, my dear."

Inwardly, Thomas rejoiced. He nibbled a stale biscuit. You never know, he thought, if he played his cards right, later, once they were home and in bed, he might get lucky!

Mickey faced the day with a black sense of foreboding and, sure enough, at nine thirty that morning, a white and blue police car pulled up outside the nursery.

She saw the car from the window: saw two blue-uniformed figures inside and, moments later, heard the knocking she'd been waiting for. She walked calmly to the bathroom and brushed her teeth and then splashed cold water over her face before opening the door.

It was the nice policewoman, the one who had brought her home after her fainting spell. "Good morning," she said with a pleasant smile. "Detective Inspector Hector Jansen has asked me to accompany you to the police station so that you may assist with our routine enquiries."

Here it was, the anticipated day of reckoning. Her mouth felt dry. She asked if she might bring a bottle of water.

The policewoman nodded cheerfully and waited until Mickey emerged carrying the water and a sweater. Suddenly, in spite of the warmth of the day, Mickey had gooseflesh on her arms and legs.

She was made to wait on a hard wooden bench until the detective was ready.

He loomed in the doorway and motioned her wordlessly into his office. She was surprised. She'd thought she would be taken into a room with two-way glass and interrogated there until she admitted to her crime.

Detective Inspector Hector Jansen sat behind his desk. He removed a silver pen from his pocket, clicked it several times and tested the point on a pad of white lined paper. When he finally looked up, his expression was blank. Mickey searched his neat desk for the black notebook. She saw a pile of stacked papers, some cardboard files, a saucer filled with paperclips and a mug containing coffee dregs.

"Morning, Miss Grant," he said shortly. "Do you know why you are here?"

"To assist with routine enquiries. That's what the policewoman said."

"We have some questions regarding the matter of Jordan Black and Wayne Miller."

"Oh, yes?" Her voice came out a croak.

"As you know, Mr Black and Mr Miller were killed on the night of Thursday 12th, when their warehouse burned to the ground."

"So, I've heard."

"We have reason to believe that the warehouse was set alight with the deliberate intention to murder Black and Miller."

Mickey swallowed. She kept her face composed and impassive.

"Was it?" she asked, innocently. "I thought the fire had been an unfortunate accident. I heard mention of a candle left burning?"

"The fire was not an accident. Forensic evidence proves conclusively that the warehouse was set alight by a person or persons who wished to murder Black and Miller."

"I see."

The detective clicked his pen. There it was again, that inscrutable expression, those dead eyes. He had a dark mole at the corner of his mouth. It sprouted one long, fine white hair.

Mickey shifted in her chair. "I don't understand," she said. "Why are you speaking to me about this?"

"Where were you on the night of Thursday 12th, Miss Grant?"

"Do you think I set the shed on fire? Am I a suspect in your enquiries?"

"Please answer the question. Where were you on the night…"

"At home. I went to bed at nine and slept through the night."

"Can anyone corroborate this?"

"I live alone, as you know. But, if you ask them, my neighbours will tell you that I spent the night at home."

"I have asked. Your neighbours cannot say for sure whether or not you were at home on that particular night."

"Can they say, for sure, whether I went out?"

"One of your neighbours says he might have heard a van starting up at around midnight."

Mickey was stunned. She'd been so careful. Let in the clutch and free-wheeled down the road. She hadn't even switched on the headlamps. How could anyone have heard anything? The detective was bluffing. He had to be!

"Not me," she said. "Not my van. I was asleep at that time."

The detective made an illegible note on the pad. He looked up. "We have spoken to a great many people during this enquiry," he said. "Several have mentioned your name as a likely suspect."

She swallowed the lump in her throat. "Why? Why me?"

"You had the motive. You opened a rape docket against Jordan Black. You accused him of stealing a considerable sum of money from you. On several occasions, you were heard to threaten Black with punishment."

"Who says?"

"Our sources are, naturally, confidential. But, have you forgotten Miss Graham? You made a threat against Black in my presence. As I recall, you said you would make him pay for what he had done to you. I remember your words clearly."

"I was emotional. Overwrought. I don't remember what I said."

"I see. Most convenient."

They stared at one another. Mickey felt an unexpected surge of hope. He had nothing! Nothing at all! Jansen suspected her of the crime but had no corroborating evidence to convict her. The black book had not been handed to the police, not yet anyway. As far as the neighbours were concerned, it was their word against hers. Nobody had seen her committing the crime. If she could just keep her wits about her!

She sat up straighter and spoke firmly. "Look, Detective, do I need a lawyer present? Do you have any evidence to prove I was the person who set fire to the warehouse?"

"We are still conducting our enquiries, Miss Grant. We are in the process of collecting evidence. But I must warn you. You are considered one of our suspects in this felony."

"May I go now?"

"Yes, you are free to go. I would, however, caution you against leaving St Jude for any period of time in the immediate future. You will be called in again, to assist with our investigations. Is that clear, Miss Grant?"

"Yes, Detective. Very clear."

She pushed back the chair, hearing the legs scrape against the floor and walked to the door.

"Miss Grant!"

She froze.

"Is this yours?" His voice was smooth. She stood still, her back to him, too terrified to turn and face him. He had the black book. He'd saved it until last.

"Miss Grant?"

Her legs shook so that she could hardly stand. She turned slowly to find him pointing at her green sweater, half hanging off the back of the chair.

She looked up with dazed relief. He scowled, puzzled.

She snatched up the sweater. "Thank you!" she said and ran from the room.

Mickey called Edwina from a pay phone in the village. "They have no evidence yet," she whispered. "Not real, concrete evidence, anyway. They haven't got the black book!"

"Thank God!" Edwina cried. "Perhaps…"

"But, Jansen knows, Edwina! He knows I did it! He'll do all he can to find me guilty."

"But, if they have no evidence…"

"He's on the case. He'll find the evidence, whatever it takes! He hates me! Wants me convicted for murder."

"Calm down, Mickey!"

"Didn't you hear what I said, Edwina? He knows! Jansen knows I killed…"

"Hush, Mickey! Keep your voice down. Can anyone hear you?"

Mickey slammed down the phone. Edwina held the faintly humming receiver in her hand and felt acute despair. You could claim to be hopeful and put on a bright face but life got you in the end. It would certainly get Mickey.

A series of terrifying images swept through her mind: the flash of fire in the dead of night. Frozen bodies on a steel shelf in the mortuary. The policeman's knock at the door. The purposeful glint of handcuffs. Mickey's pitiful sobs as she was led away.

Edwina walked through the open French doors, down the steps, along the paved pathway to where the angel stood, bathed in sunlight and dappled shadow.

There was a white dove resting upon the tip of one of the wings.

Edwina flapped her arms. "Shoo!" she cried, "shoo!" The bird flew off.

She gazed up at the tilted face: the angel's expression of celestial beatitude.

"Don't you care?" she accused. "Why aren't you trying to save Mickey?"

Edwina touched her breast, reassured by the hard, flatness of the tumour, still there, but as benign as a dying fruit; not growing, no longer throbbing with tearing pain.

"Please understand," she begged. "I'm grateful for all you've done for me. But Mickey needs your help now. Surely you've more to give?"

Sarah knew she had no reason to feel jealous of Ginny, the poor woman's son was dying of AIDS and what could be worse than that? And yet she was jealous.

Ben and Ginny had become friends and probably more than friends. They were seen together often. Sharing an evening meal in one or other of St Jude's limited restaurants. Walking on the beach. Sailing the inflatable dinghy. His truck often parked outside the Lourens' house.

Still religiously faithful about walking Lucky two or three times a week, Ben no longer invited Sarah to accompany him.

"I never see you any more," she complained.

"I've been busy. The surgery. Farm work. This and that, you know how it is?"

Yes, she did know. Now that Ginny was in the picture Ben had dropped her like a ton of bricks. It was her fault. She'd made it abundantly clear she wasn't interested in romance, but what of friendship? Was she no longer considered a friend?

"How've you been? Are you well?"

He gave an open-faced smile, brown eyes gleaming. "Never better!"

"I'm glad!" Of course she wasn't, not really, but he looked so happy.

"You and Ginny," she said, clumsily. "I've heard."

He looked uncomfortable.

"And, well, I wanted to say I'm pleased for you both."

"Thanks." He gave a formal nod and took the dog's leash.

She felt a pang of disappointment. She'd hoped he might talk to her and say, perhaps, that he and Ginny were just good friends but his silence on the matter spoke volumes.

She watched them walk away: the tall rangy man and the dog bouncing at his side, looking up adoringly with a wagging plume of a tail held high.

So, she'd lost him. He hadn't waited for her to get over David's death, get used to the idea of a loving relationship with another man. He'd moved on. He'd chosen Ginny over her. She found it baffling.

How was it possible to be attracted to such different women? Ginny, with her long unruly red hair was impetuous, girlish, arty – given to wearing full gypsy skirts and musically tinkling silver bracelets. She was older than Sarah and not as pretty although who knew what men liked when it came to a woman's looks?

That night she told David.

"I'm sorry I pushed Ben away," she admitted. "I wish I'd told him to wait until I was over you. But I didn't. I said I could never love anyone else."

She addressed David's photograph hoping he didn't feel betrayed but he had to know that she was ready now to consider the possibility of another man in her life.

"Do you mind?" she asked. The image in the photograph stared at a point somewhere beyond her left ear. She moved the picture so that their eyes might connect. His lips were set in a perpetual expression of joy: one eyebrow frozen in constant amazement, a lock of hair pasted forever over one brow.

How could he mind? David was dead!

Next morning Sarah heard footsteps on the path. The knocker banged. She opened the door to find Caron with James.

"Any chance you could take James to the gallery with you for a few hours this morning?" Caron asked. "I have an appointment in Port Victoria. I'm sorry to spring this upon you without notice ..."

Lucky jumped up, licking James' face, barking excitedly. James fed the dog a biscuit from his pocket.

Pleased, Sarah invited James into the house. "Have you had breakfast?"

"Cereal and orange juice," James replied. "What are you having?"

She toasted a loaf of currant bread and served it with gooseberry jam. He ate hungrily. He showed her his manuscript. "It's a book," he explained. "A book about an alien from a distant galaxy who comes down to earth to live with a family. They think he's one of them, but he's not."

Sarah flipped through the stapled chapters. "May I read it?" she asked.

James considered the question, chewing his lip. "I suppose so," he said, finally. "But don't get jam on the pages!"

The story was well written: imaginative, descriptive and sensitive. It was clear, from the outset that 'Jim the Human Alien' was a barely disguised James and the family in the story, his own. There was a mother who gave Jim everything he needed but found him impossible to love because, of course, he was an alien, and different from other boys. There was a father who loved Jim but didn't understand him for the same reason. There were 'so-called' friends who were jealous of his super powers, jeered and labelled him a freak and a nerd.

Jim yearned to return to his alien family and real home in a distant galaxy but he'd been sent on an important mission to discover everything he could about earthlings and so he had to remain where he was no matter how lost and lonely he felt.

Sarah finished reading. She closed the manuscript. She composed herself.

"It's not a sad story," James said, reading her expression. "It's an *adventure!*"

"It's a little sad," Sarah said. "In parts."

"Do you like Jim, the alien?"

"Very much. I feel I know him quite well."

"That's the thing about aliens. You never really know them. You think you do, but you don't. They're not like other people, they just pretend to be the same."

At the gallery, James sat at Sarah's desk. "Chapter five!" he announced with a note of pride. He bent over the manuscript, tongue protruding, glasses sliding down his small nose, filling the page with his large, blocky, childish handwriting: lost in the fantasy world of his own creation.

"How is he?" whispered Ginny.

"I don't know," Sarah answered honestly. "He seems cheerful enough but, as you know, James is quite good at pretending. I have a hunch something's wrong, but I can't say for sure exactly what it is."

"Why not speak to the Grants – Caron and Alec?"

Sarah considered the question. "It's not my place," she said, at last. "And, anyway, I believe the parents are a real part of the problem!"

Ginny seemed about to say something. She opened her mouth and then closed it. She turned away and then, on impulse, turned back.

"Do you mind?" she said, in a rush. "Do you mind about Ben?"

Sarah gave a wary look. "I'm happy for you," she said. "He's a good man. Decent, kind, generous and loyal."

"Oh, I know!" Ginny's smile was tenderly protective. "Ben's wonderful! He's all those things and more! But, you were friends first: you and Ben. Nothing serious, you said, nothing romantic between you. I hope you don't think…"

"Ginny!" Sarah tried to stop the flow of words. "Ben and I are friends. Lucky is the link holding us together, there's nothing more. I'm glad you've found one another. Really, I mean it!"

Ginny hugged her. "Thank you, Sarah! I'd hate anything to come between us. I value your friendship so much!"

Sarah felt Ginny's bony arms around her waist, her face looked up, luminous with happiness.

"I'm pleased for you," Sarah repeated stiffly. "For both of you."

When Sarah took James home, he stuffed his manuscript into his backpack, bending it double, squeezing it inside.

"Careful," she warned. "The pages might tear!"

James pulled the leather straps tighter.

"James?"

"It's top secret!" he mumbled. "My manuscript. I don't want anyone else to see it!"

"But you let me read it!"

He shrugged. "You're my friend."

Alec opened the door and produced a dazzling smile. "Hi, Sarah! Thanks for taking care of Jamie. He loves spending time with you, don't you, boy?"

Sarah regarded him coolly: crisp white shirt, discretely patterned silk tie, gold cuff links. Carefully tousled hair, the faint suggestion of a beard growing in giving that unshaven, macho look men thought made them look heart-stoppingly attractive.

How had handsome, supremely confident and smooth Alec Grant ever produced a son like James?

"Come in!" he invited. "Have a drink. Caron will be home soon."

"Sorry! I can't stay." She knew she'd sounded abrupt, rude almost.

She bent and hugged James, whispering in his ear. "Thanks for letting me read your story," she said. She thought of the right word. "It's awesome!"

She walked down the garden path. She heard Alec's voice.

"Come and tell me about your day. Tell me everything. I've missed you." His voice was bluff and hearty.

She remembered a sentence from the book. She tried to recall the exact words.

"The dad didn't really know how to talk to Jim," James had written. *"So he used a pretend-happy voice because he thought that was what Jim wanted to hear. Underneath, though, Jim knew that the dad was a very sad person and that his real voice, if he ever used it, would be sad too."*

Grace sat at the bedside of a patient who, at thirty-six, had terminal cancer, and when she died would leave behind three children and a loving but inadequate husband who'd never changed a nappy, boiled an egg or helped with homework.

"It's not fair," said the woman, whose name was Hannah Green.

"No," Grace agreed, "it never is!"

"Not death!" said Hannah. "Not dying at thirty-six, although that sucks! No, what's not fair is that I've had a blameless life. I've been the good girl: the perfect mom, the loving, devoted wife. I've never got drunk or smoked pot or had sex with a man who wasn't my husband. Never been on an overseas holiday. Never binged on chocolate. Never even gone to sleep without taking my makeup off first!"

"What are you saying?"

"I wish I'd done some of those things. If I'd known how short life was going to be, I'd have had more of a good time. Let it rip! Been the party girl."

Hannah Green's words remained with her and that evening Grace returned to the private ward with an iced bottle of expensive dry champagne and a box of Belgium chocolates.

She gave the patient a paper cup and filled it with champagne before pouring some for herself. "Here's to being party girls!" she said.

Grace got home late and a little tipsy to find the children asleep and Ian frying bacon and eggs for supper.

"Bad day at black rock!" she said, by way of explanation. "You?"

"Not bad. Edwina on my back, but that's normal. Three new jobs! An order for a..."

"We should let rip more!" Grace cried, gripping his shoulders.

Ian laughed. "What's got into you?"

"Life! We're not having any fun! We might be dead tomorrow!"

He placed the plate before her and passed the rack of toast. "Speaking of 'dead'," he said, "Edwina Hurley looks pretty terrific for one who should have shuffled off her mortal coil!"

Grace snorted. "Mrs Hurley is riddled with cancer! Her tumour has metastasised. Millions of malignant cells have been released into her bloodstream, forming new tumours..."

"I don't know, Grace. That's not what it looks like from where I'm standing. Is there any chance Edwina might...?"

"*What?* Been cured by an angel? Oh, please Ian! Don't start all this spiritual, heal-thyself, black-magic crap!"

"OK, I admit, it sounds far-fetched. But, if you could see her!"

Grace popped a forkful of bacon into her mouth and chewed. "Mrs Hurley is in remission," she said finally. "It's that simple."

"What does that mean?"

"Edwina has been given a moment of grace. Time to sort out her affairs and enjoy the halcyon days before they disappear forever."

"How do you explain it? Medically, I mean."

Grace wished her mind were not so muzzy from champagne. The wilting party girl was ready for bed. "I honestly don't know," she said, pushing away the half-finished meal. "The tumour appears to have regressed without chemotherapy or radiotherapy or any drugs at all, apart from painkillers. Some doctors think spontaneous remission is the body's war against cancer."

"You don't?"

"Not really. Perhaps Edwina's own antioxidant defences and DNA repair enzymes are giving her a brief time-out before the final summons. Who knows?"

Ian washed the dishes while Grace lay back in a deep bubble bath, a rolled up towel behind her head, and thought about Hannah Green and Edwina Hurley and why it was that a young woman with a surgically removed cancer who'd undergone months of chemotherapy was dying while the indomitable Mrs Hurley still danced on table-tops blowing party squeakers?

Hard to believe, but Chris also seemed to be in some kind of remission. He found he had an appetite, not much of one admittedly, but more than before. He also had a renewed interest in his art, in painting. They rigged up an easel at his bedside with a chair and some cushions and he began a series of preliminary sketches.

The paintings he'd done before: the portrait of Ginny, the seascape and the angel were gifts for his mother. He wanted desperately to paint a canvas for Inga as a parting gift and something she could keep to remember him by.

He wanted to paint something meaningful and wasted a day or two trying to think of the perfect subject before it came to him: something from her childhood, from the Swedish landscape, from the stories she whispered before he fell asleep each night.

"Close your eyes," he commanded. "You're a child again. Tell me what you see."

So many things. Tall white windmills. Abandoned silver grey barns. Pebble beaches and towering cliffs. Boathouses falling to crumbling ruins. Black headed Arctic terns perched upon grey boulders. Herons rising above church steeples. The clear glass of iced lakes.

"What colours do you see?"

She held her breath. "Blue," she said. "And grey."

He mixed a pallet. From midnight blue to arctic grey and every shade between.

He painted wild herons soaring above water. The first grey light of day: a lonely, wind-torn landscape with a vestige of a pale moon hanging above a horizon of frosted trees. With the last brush strokes, he felt the illness creeping back.

"This is yours," he said. "A gift for both of us."

She looked questioningly.

"I never thought I'd paint again," he explained.

The work was not his best and he signed it without the usual pride but with relief and thankfulness that he'd been able to give her something of himself, something from his heart, before it was too late.

Chapter 19

Chris

Neither Black nor Miller appeared to have traceable families or friends and so their funerals were bleak affairs, hardly attended although there was a police presence in the form of Detective Inspector Hector Jansen and a couple of his men who were there in an official capacity. The two graves lay side by side with simple granite headstones chiselled only with name and date of death details since nobody knew anything more about the victims.

Edwina sent generous wreaths of white lilies to rest on both graves with a simple message wishing 'peace at the journey's end'. I wondered about the incongruity of Edwina's funeral flowers and put it down to good manners and a brief relationship with Black who had been her builder of choice in the restoration of the new wing of Hurley House. Afterwards though, when I knew more, I thought Edwina's gesture might have been more out of guilt than sympathy.

Edwina awoke with a message pealing in her head. The message came directly from the angel and, though it seemed odd and unexpected, she acted upon it immediately.

She visited Chris at home, startling Ginny with a loud hammering on the front door. "Not a good day!" said Ginny apologetically, opening only a crack.

Edwina swept inside. She thrust a large pot of blue delphiniums into Ginny's reluctant arms and bolted up the stairs.

The curtains were drawn, the room dim and cool. Chris appeared to be sleeping.

Edwina flung herself noisily into the chair beside the bed and cleared her throat.

His eyelids flickered. Wasting no time, she got straight to the point.

"I see you're unwell," she said. "I know I shouldn't disturb you. But Mickey is in trouble and I have a sense that you may be able to help her."

Chris gazed at Edwina uncomprehendingly before closing his eyes again.

She shook his arm gently. "Don't sleep," she begged. "Please stay awake. This is important. Mickey needs your help!"

He lifted his lids, swallowed once or twice, struggled to sit up.

She handed him a tumbler of water and waited while he sipped.

"Start again," he suggested, his voice scratchy and dry. "At the beginning. You're not making sense."

"I had a message," Edwina said. She spoke clearly, enunciating each word so that he could hear her properly. "A message from the angel…"

"Oh, Edwina! Not the fucking angel again!"

She laughed. A shuddering trill of relief that he still had some life in him although he looked, frankly, like death warmed up.

"Yes!" she admitted. "The angel and I have been in regular communication. I asked her to help Mickey. The angel told me to visit you."

He gave a faint glimmer of a smile. "You're nuts! Take a look at me, Edwina? If I can't help myself, how can I help anyone else?"

"You're not looking your best," Edwina admitted, patting his hand in sympathy. "But the angel was most specific."

"She *spoke* to you?"

"Yes."

"You saw her lips move? Heard an angelic voice ringing in your ears?"

He tried to laugh and coughed instead. His body heaved and shuddered.

Edwina thumped his back, her hand connecting with a fragile framework of protruding bones. She drew back horrified. "Lord! Did that hurt?"

"Everything hurts!"

"I'll be honest," Edwina confessed. "I was frankly surprised at the suggestion that Mickey should talk to you. I don't have the faintest idea how you can offer help in your present state. But, as I say, the angel was…"

"Don't say another word about the blasted angel. What's wrong with Mickey? Why does she need help?"

"You haven't heard?"

"Heard what?"

"About Jordan Black and Wayne Miller?"

"Oh, yes. The fire. Bloody horrific way to meet your maker!"

"Hideous!" Edwina agreed sadly.

"Go on," he prodded. "I still don't see…"

She blurted it out at once. "The police believe Mickey set fire to the warehouse. That she intended to murder Black and Miller. She is their prime suspect."

"Why Mickey, of all people?"

"It was an accident! Black raped Mickey and stole money from her. She burned his shed as an act of retribution. She had no idea the men were inside at the time."

"Christ!"

Edwina stood and paced the room, heels clicking wooden boards. Distractedly, she scraped her hands through her hair.

"I don't know why the angel led me to you but she did and I have such faith in her! There must be a reason. Think for a moment. Is there any advice you might give Mickey? Anything you might say that …"

He rolled his eyes. "What advice can I give? How can anyone help Mickey after what she's done?"

Edwina stood at the window. "My own view is that she should make a run for it," she said. "Get out of the country and go into hiding. Though I fear it's too late. Mickey's been warned not to leave St Jude. If she disappears, the police will alert airports, trains, bus stations. There's probably no way out, not now."

She stood silently peering through the lightly misted window. Birds were cooing in the rafters. The canal water swirled beneath a bobbing rubber dinghy tied to the jetty. A garden chair had blown over. The wind was coming up, leaves clattering in trees. The visit had been fruitless: a wild goose chase. What could he do or say? She should leave the poor man in peace. She turned. He seemed lost in thought.

"I've had an idea," he said, slowly.

She waited, heart thudding.

"I'll need to think it through though."

"Yes?"

"Tell Mickey to come and talk to me."

"Ha!" Edwina uttered a mirthless laugh. "I knew it!" she cried in triumph. "I wasn't wrong about the angel!"

Chris responded with a typically sweet smile.

"If you could place your faith in her," she urged. "If you could..."

"Goodbye, Edwina." He gave a mock wave.

"Dear boy!" She kissed him on both cheeks. "Thank you!"

He called out as she reached for the doorknob. "Wait!"

She turned.

"A favour for a favour. Do you have any sleeping pills?"

"Yes. I believe so. Why?"

"May I have them?"

She narrowed her eyes. He gazed back guilelessly.

There was a moment of doubt and concern, quickly banished. She understood perfectly. She herself had considered sleeping tablets as a painless way to end it all when the time came and who was she to sit in judgement? A dose of sleeping tablets was far more civilised than a gun in the mouth, a hose from a car exhaust, a draught of rat poison.

"I shall have them sent over tomorrow, will that do?"

He gave a grateful smile.

When James arrived at Hurley House he was shown into the library where Thomas waited patiently with chessboard and pieces laid out for their game.

Thomas rubbed his hands with elfin glee. "Ready to play the self-proclaimed Grandmaster of St Jude?"

"Ready!" said James, sliding into the chair opposite.

"I warn you in advance! I have learned from the greats," Thomas grinned. "Boris Spassky, Anatoly Karpov and the finest of them all: Bobby Fischer!"

"Who?"

"Bobby Fischer! Became a Grandmaster at age sixteen. What do you say to that?"

"Pretty good," said James. "Can I be white?"

They played until James found his king under attack with no way to counter and Thomas whooped: "Checkmate!" at the top of his voice. "You should have moved your king out of check. Or moved a piece between attacker and king."

"Thanks," said James. "I'll try to remember next time."

"Next time," said Thomas, "I shall teach you some interesting opening and defence moves. '*The Sicilian Defence*' for starters, I think, and then '*Queen's Gambit Declined*'."

"Wow!" breathed James, thrilled. He held out his hand for a high five. Thomas, after a moment of bafflement, reached out and slapped it hard.

They went outdoors for cranberry juice and fairy cakes at a table set out near the fishpond. James concentrated on peeling the paper from a pink cupcake without getting crumbs over his clothes.

"This is the biggest house I've ever seen," he said, conversationally. "Are you very rich?"

"Hurley House belongs to Mrs Hurley," explained Thomas. "I'm a special friend so she kindly allows me to share board and lodging."

"Mrs Hurley is a bit scary," said James, taking a small bite of cake. "Sometimes, when I see her, I feel like hiding away."

"I agree! I feel the same way myself. She's terrifying! But beneath that ferocious exterior lies a heart of purest gold."

They chewed companionably.

"You've got crumbs on your mouth," said James, touching his top lip. "And your tie."

"Most kind!" Thomas fluttered a hand in the general direction of his face and flapped his tie.

"You are schooled at home, I believe?"

"Yeah."

"When I was your age, I had a governess and a tutor who taught maths and science. Who teaches you?"

"Caron. My stepmother. She's a good teacher." He sighed and kicked the table leg. "I'm going to school again next term. To Betty's Bay Primary School, Mrs Morris will be my teacher."

"I see." Thomas looked quizzical. "May I ask why?"

James gave a helpless shrug. "My dad and Caron say it's because I don't have friends or play sports but I hate sports and the only friends I had were Anna and Jeremy, and they're not friends any more."

"Do you want to go back to school?"

James shook his head. "I did, in the beginning, but not any more. I'm used to learning at home. I do all my own research on the Internet and read zillions of books. I have art and pottery classes at the gallery. I keep a nature book. We also do stuff like astronomy. I have my own telescope!"

"You're interested in astronomy?"

"Yeah! Caron took me to the Planetarium – that was awesome!"

"Why don't you talk to them? Tell your father and stepmother you'd rather be schooled at home?"

James kicked furiously at the table. Thomas passed the plate of cakes. James chose one with white icing and silver sprinkles. He licked at the top.

Thomas waited, patiently. He tipped the jug of cranberry juice and poured another glass.

"I think Caron is going away," James said, in a small voice. "I think that's the real reason why they're sending me back to school. It's not really about sports and friends, it's because Caron won't be living with us any more."

Thomas pulled a face. "It all sounds rather complicated."

"It is!" James agreed. He stared down at his plate. "They fight a lot, Caron and my dad. Mostly about me. I haven't been on my best behaviour this year. I've done some things I wish I hadn't. I ran away. There was a fire. And then a baby that died before it was born. That made Caron sad. She cried a lot."

"Oh dear. Dear, dear me." Thomas was at a loss. "I'm sorry, my boy. Very sorry indeed." He removed his spectacles and polished them with his tie. "I'm not sure what to say..."

"That's OK."

Thomas spotted a Paradise Flycatcher and used the sighting as an opportunity to change the subject. "Hear that?" he asked, cupping a hand behind his left ear.

James listened.

"Paradise Flycatcher. Makes a wonderful noise. *Wheeoo-wit, wit, wit, wheeoowit!* One of my bird books describes it as a 'ripple of tiny laughter'. Are you interested in birds, James?"

"I think so. I like watching them."

"Perhaps you might like to join me for a spot of bird-watching one of these fine days?"

James grinned and aimed a sharp kick at the table. "Brilliant!" he said.

That night, over supper, Caron asked James how he'd enjoyed the game of chess with Mr Paton.

James concealed a floret of broccoli beneath a slice of potato and swallowed a small mouthful of chicken. "Mr Paton is a self-proclaimed Grandmaster," he replied with a glance at Alec. "He beat me. Next week we're going to play again and then, one of these fine days, we're going bird-watching."

Alec looked bemused. "You're a funny little guy," he said, shaking his head.

"Who, me?"

"Yes. How old is Mr Paton?"

"Pretty old, I think. But he's cool too. He's learned chess from the greats. From Boris Spassky, Anatoly somebody and Bobby Fischer, who was a Grandmaster at sixteen. He's going to teach me some opening moves and one day, if I can improve my game, maybe I can beat him!"

"I don't know much about chess," Caron offered, "but there are some excellent sites we could visit where you could learn strategies to help you win."

James speared a carrot and stuffed it in his mouth.

"If you're interested?" she added.

"James? Caron is speaking to you."

"I already know most of the sites," he mumbled.

"Well, that's good!" she said with forced cheerfulness. "Would you like a bowl of ice-cream? Vanilla, your favourite?"

James craned his head to stare at a spider crawling on the ceiling. "No, thank you."

Caron collected the plates and took them into the kitchen.

Without a word, James stole upstairs to his bedroom and closed the door.

He selected the well worn *Harry Potter and the Prisoner of Azkaban* from the pile on his desk and within minutes was completely engrossed.

That night, James dreamed the running-away dream again.

In his dream he filled his backpack with cupcakes and chess pieces and caught Harry Potter's enchanted triple-decker. "Destination?" asked the conductor. "Far away!" shouted James. The bus moved like lightning: banging, jolting and leaping through the streets. Mr Paton, waving from the top deck, was one of the passengers and Lucky was there too, barking his head off. Caron tried to stop the bus by holding out her arm as it approached but James shouted at the driver to go faster and Caron was left behind, a dot in the distance growing smaller and smaller and then disappearing completely.

The next morning James awoke feeling sad and ashamed.

There was the smell of toast from the kitchen. He found Caron laying the breakfast table. She tipped cereal into his bowl and passed the milk jug. "Did you sleep well, James?" she asked quietly.

He kept his eyes on the sugar bowl. "Maybe we could visit some of those chess sites today?" He spoke through a mouth of cornflakes. "I need to find out about an opening move called '*The Sicilian Defence*'?"

"I'd like that," she said, startled, happy. "We'll begin after breakfast!"

Mickey waited. She waited for the mournful sound of police sirens advancing.

For Detective Inspector Hector Jansen bawling out her name at the door: "Miss Graham! Miss Graham! Open up!"

She was ready. The house and garden in order. Papers left neat and tidy in the drawer. She'd sewn a sprinkling of Folly's ashes into a sachet made from strips of worn pillowcase and pinned this to her underwear.

In prison the silver locket would be taken into safekeeping but surely if she explained that these were the beloved ashes of an only child she might be able to hold onto a simple sachet? She kept her Bible close. If she were imprisoned for her life there'd be time to try and rebuild her relationship with God. Faith was probably the only thing that would help her survive the terrifying ordeal. She'd pray for forgiveness. God knew that the murders had been a terrible mistake and would surely find it in His heart to forgive her.

The phone rang. She jumped. She picked up the receiver and held it trembling to her ear. She waited to hear the detective's hard, curt voice.

"Mickey, it's Edwina!"

The call was confusing. In a rush, Edwina told her to visit Chris Lourens. "He wants to see you. He may be able to help."

The notion was ridiculous! Chris was ill. She'd heard he might even be dying.

"How can *Chris* help me?"

Edwina sounded impatient. "Please, Mickey! Go and see him at once."

"But what will I say?"

"Chris said he had an idea. Something he needed to think about. He's had time, more than twelve hours now, to hatch a plan to help you."

"Shall I go now?"

"Yes! Immediately. I shall call later."

Mickey replaced the receiver, tears of gratitude stinging her eyes.

She could hardly believe it. In spite of the unthinkable crimes she'd committed, helping hands were being offered by those few who still believed that she might be worth saving.

Ginny, warned by Chris to expect a visit from Mickey, showed her to the room at the top of the stairs. "Edwina sent me," Mickey said as though it were a secret code for a rite of passage that would gain her entry.

Ginny stood listening at the door for a few minutes, hearing soft murmuring. Her suspicious were alerted. Something was happening. This was the second unexpected visit in two days!

Edwina had arrived unannounced and stayed too long, leaving Chris exhausted beyond words. Now, here was Mickey sent by Edwina. Edwina was up to something. Ginny had widened her eyes at Chris as she'd led Mickey to the bed, shooting him a look that said: 'Why is she here'?

"Mickey's a friend," Chris had explained. "She's heard I'm ill and come to offer condolences."

"Is this true?"

Mickey, who'd looked frightened out of her wits, said yes.

"But what has this to do with Edwina? Why has she sent you? What's going on?"

Chris erupted in a bout of painful coughing and, when he'd recovered, Ginny's relief in seeing him breathing normally made her forget the question.

"I'll leave you two together then, shall I?" Ginny bustled anxiously from the room, hovering outside the door for a few moments, hearing nothing.

Chris, probably aware of her lingering presence, spoke more softly than usual and Mickey's low whispering was unintelligible.

Inga arrived at her usual time to find Mickey in the chair beside the bed.

She saw at once Mickey had been crying; her lashes clumped with tears.

"Mickey is in trouble," Chris explained. "I thought we might be able to help her."

Mickey told Inga of the rape, the theft, her vision of punishment; the shed and all its contents going up in a blaze; the men dying in an accident that would haunt her forever.

Inga listened, her eyes never leaving Mickey's face. "I believe you," she said. "Others will too. You have a good face. You will not be convicted of this crime."

Mickey gripped Inga's arm. "I've said things. Made threats. People have heard me. I'm a *suspect.*"

She told Inga of the police enquiries, the forensic and arson experts and the detective who knew she had the motive for the crime and was, even now, searching for evidence to convict her.

Chris gestured at Inga. "We might be able to help, Mickey. I've thinking about our plan..."

She lifted her finger to her lips. "Our *secret* plan?"

"Yes. There's a way we could include Mickey."

Inga recoiled, shocked. "No!"

Mickey sat up straight in the chair. "What plan?" she cried, afraid.

Chris and Inga were silent.

"I don't understand," Inga said. "What are you saying? Tell me!"

Chris struggled weakly to pull himself up against the pillows.

He turned to Mickey. "I've been dreaming," he said. "Perhaps it's the pills, the medication, I don't know. I keep having a recurring dream..."

Ginny, listening outside the door, heard voices rising and falling, one at a time: Chris, Inga, Mickey. She didn't realise she clenched her teeth, a tight knot in her chest, until Chris laughed and she expelled her breath, feeling her body relax. *What's the matter with me*? She thought. *Why am I listening at doors? Why should there be anything suspicious in this gathering of friends? Why doubt Edwina Hurley's good intentions?*

What was the harm in Chris surrounding himself with those who cared and comforted him as the end grew closer?

Ginny slipped downstairs, her careful footfalls placed so softly that the wooden floorboards did not give even the smallest creak.

Inga and Mickey left the house together.

Mickey, nervous as a cat, shuddered at the sudden rustling of lavender bushes. "I'm afraid," she whimpered.

"Yes." Inga nodded sympathetically. Briefly she touched the curve of Mickey's cheek.

"You're not alone. I am also afraid."

"I'm not brave enough to go through with this," Mickey stuttered.

"You and Chris are both so strong. I'm weak. I can't even think of it."

"You'll find the courage."

Mickey shook her head helplessly. "I won't!"

"Then you must face a life in prison. Are you brave enough for that?"

"No," Mickey said, knowing herself. "I'm not."

Inga embraced her lightly. "You will be surprised," she said in her low voice, "at how brave you can be when you have to be. When you have no other choice."

She waved a graceful hand in parting.

At home in her loft, Inga considered accidents and their meaning.

Chris had chosen a lover who, many years ago, had unknowingly infected him with a deadly virus. By accident, Mickey had killed two men.

An accident of fate had brought her from far-off Sweden to Betty's Bay where Chris had walked into her studio and seized her heart. A random accident, nothing more, had thrown Chris, Inga and Mickey together at this point in their disparate lives.

Inga clearly understood her role: she was charged with his loving care.

But what was Mickey's purpose in the plan?

Mickey was an unexpected complication: the result of an old woman's confused meddling and the pity of a dying man. Mickey, frail and close to collapse, might yet ruin everything for all of them.

"I'm afraid," Mickey had said. Her honesty had allowed Inga to confess her own fears. "You're not alone!" she'd cried. "I'm also afraid!"

Afraid was such an unsatisfactory word. A word that barely described the intense fear she felt leaking from every pore. She wasn't ready. Would *neve*r be ready. She loved Chris too much to let him go and yet, in this matter, as in the other, she had no say. Chris, with the heart of a lion was ready to die, ready to face the kind of death that would cause the least amount of pain both to himself and those who loved him.

It was Chris who'd orchestrated every detail of the plan. She would be called upon to play her part and would do her best.

"You cannot do better than your best," her father had always said, at different times in her life.

He'd said those words when, as a child, she'd stood on stage to play the violin; when she'd written her school and then university examinations; when she'd braved her first job interview.

She ached for her father. Ached for the comfortingly solid bulk of him, the warmth, the fragrance of Cuban cigars caught in the expensive fibres of worn jackets, his habit of rubbing a lock of her fine hair between thumb and forefinger as though it were a strand of silk.

She took out her wallet and removed a fading snap taken of the two of them playing croquet on a patchy lawn outside the summerhouse. How old was she then? Seventeen perhaps, hopeful and innocent in the ways of the world.

She placed the photograph beneath her pillow and lay, fully dressed, on the bed.

"You will find the courage," she'd said to Mickey Graham.

And, like an obedient child Mickey had taken a deep breath, believing her.

And her own courage, Inga wondered? Where would that come from when the time arrived? Would she draw the strength from Chris?

Or would it come from somewhere deep within where her inexhaustible love for him still flowed, would forever flow, like a boundless river?

Chapter 20

Mickey

Immediately after the event, the fire at Black's warehouse made front-page news.

*There were black and white photographs of the incinerated shed and poor, grainy likenesses of Black and an extremely youthful Wayne Miller. The story even made local TV news with a grim-faced Detective Inspector Jansen promising that every effort would be made to find the arsonist who had murdered two men in what appeared an act of cold-blooded revenge. After ten days, with no fresh information to hand, the story headlined: '**Police confident arrest will soon be made**!' had been reduced to a single column of type at the bottom of page two. As the case appeared to go cold there were many in St Jude who believed that, thanks to police bungling, the guilty culprit or culprits had got away with murder. I also judged Jansen's bellicose guarantee of a pending arrest to be more bluff and bluster than substance but, as it turns out, I was wrong.*

Detective Inspector Hector Jansen was taking his own sweet time.

There was, of course, some pressure from above, specifically from the Chief Inspector, to announce an arrest, but Jansen had no intention of being pushed and possibly making a mistake. The press was, as always, a thorn in his side.

Wherever he went, there they were, baying for information and making sarcastic jibes about the fact that he was not yet able, for all his specialist arson and forensic teams, to reveal the name of a possible suspect.

He fobbed them off with the usual bland statements: "The investigation is progressing well," and, "Our recent enquiries have yielded valuable information."

Two weeks after the fire, Jansen arrived at the deserted station one morning before six and made himself a mug of heavily sugared black coffee.

He paged again through the bulky Black/Miller file, surveying the information.

All the evidence suggested a clear-cut case of arson with the intention to murder Jordan Black. The carpenter, Wayne Miller, he suspected, had been an unlucky victim, his death a trick of fate: wrong time, wrong place.

Elbows on the desk, head in his hands, Jansen re-ran the tape in his brain, going through the sequence of events once more. He could see it all so clearly.

After working late that night, the two men had, for some reason, decided to sleep in the shed. There was a very good chance, given Black's reputation, they'd been drinking and were not in a fit state to drive home. They'd bolted the door from the inside. The murderer had been stalking the men, waiting for just such an opportunity. Forensics pinpointed his or her arrival on the site to be at roughly midnight, or there about. Petrol had been poured from a portable container beneath a gap in the barred door and into the warehouse. The petrol had been ignited and the warehouse – a veritable tinderbox of inflammable materials – had gone up in seconds with the men trapped inside. They might have awoken and seen the flames. Might have tried to escape through the exit blocked by a raging fire.

The heat would have been intense: there would have been loud explosions.

With any luck, the victims would have been asphyxiated by black smoke before being burned alive.

There were two possible culprits.

One of Black's ex-clients: a man by the name of Sol Isaacs had had a fight with Black and come off worse in the scrap.

Black had undertaken to build a deck for Isaacs who'd paid the money upfront. Months had lapsed. Isaacs had made a series of threatening phone calls. When Black failed to respond, Isaacs had taken legal action: a lawyer's letter had been sent demanding that Black erect the deck in three weeks or repay the deposit. Three weeks later, Isaacs had smashed a fist into Black's face giving him a black eye. Isaacs had been taken to hospital with a shattered collarbone and several broken ribs.

Afterwards, Isaacs had been heard to warn that Black hadn't seen the last of him and he'd get his money back, if it was the last thing he did!

Sol Isaacs had a sound alibi for the night in question. He'd been with friends at an anniversary party until well after midnight: his statement corroborated by the invited guests. Of course they could all be lying, but Jansen had a feeling that Isaacs was innocent. He didn't strike him as a man fanatical enough to plan murder as a form of revenge.

It was the second suspect he had his money on!

Mickey Graham claimed Jordan Black had raped her. She'd also accused him of stealing the sum of ten thousand, paid as a deposit. In addition, there'd been, as far as Jansen could deduce, a degree of intimidation on the part of Black. He'd started work on Graham's roof and left it unfinished. Materials – rusted sheets of corrugated iron, difficult to move – had been thrown on the path and left there. Graham had threatened to punish Black for all these actions and, in Jansen's view, she was more than capable of doing so.

Sol Isaacs and Mickey Graham were like night and day. Isaacs was all talk and bluff and no balls. Mickey Graham, however, was a case of still waters running very deep.

There was something in her eyes! Jansen had seen it before with convicted criminals. A madness that took hold. An insanity that drove them to commit terrible crimes as a way of getting back for past hurts and grievances.

Mickey Graham fitted the profile of the killer: she had the motive and he'd seen, with his own eyes, that she had the intention.

Jansen had spoken to many people who knew Mickey Graham. Some had been guarded in their responses, others less so. Generally, most felt that Mickey had a breakdown of some kind after the death of her dog. They said she'd stopped eating and become ill and irrational. Some used the word 'obsessive' to describe her behaviour. Others said she looked 'haunted'.

The most credible witness had been the local minister, Reverend Watson.

The Reverend had divulged that Mickey Graham appeared to have recently experienced a loss of faith and struck him as a deeply troubled young woman.

He said she'd asked whether he believed in the idea of 'an eye for an eye, a tooth for a tooth.'

Jansen had been surprised at this disclosure. In his experience, men of God refused to reveal information given to them in confidence.

"What did you say?" Jansen had asked the minister.

Tightening his mouth, the Reverend had replied piously. "I told her to pray for guidance and forgive those who had sinned against her."

Grace Frey, the doctor who had examined Mickey after her rape, had been less forthcoming.

"I don't understand what Mickey has to do with your investigations?" she'd said. "Is she a suspect in the case?"

Ignoring the question, Jansen had asked the doctor to describe Mickey's frame of mind after the rape.

"As you might expect!" the doctor had snapped. "Shocked, frightened and clearly distraught." Grace Frey had given Jansen a penetrating stare. "You saw her yourself, as I recall. How did you find her?"

"As you describe."

"Normal response for a rape victim, wouldn't you say?"

Jansen had asked if, during the consultation, the patient had made any threats against Black.

Grace had given a narrow-lipped smile. "Mickey did not disclose the name of the rapist. But I'm not surprised to hear it was Jordan Black."

Later, Jansen had questioned the doctor's husband, Ian Frey, who had volunteered to repair the roof at Northwind Nursery.

He'd found Frey equally unhelpful.

"What do you mean, 'how did she seem'?" he'd asked irritably.

Jansen had been very patient. "I am making enquiries into Miss Graham's state of mind at the time."

"Black left a hole in her roof! I fixed it. She was grateful. That's it."

Frey had half turned away, signalling an end to the exchange.

Jansen had persisted. "Did she appear distressed? Did you find her…?"

The doctor's husband had frowned, obviously annoyed. "She appeared as distressed as you or I would be in the same situation."

Jansen had waited, pen poised.

"What do you want me to say? I'm not a shrink. I've no idea about Mickey's state of mind but I would say, all things considering, she seemed naturally upset."

At that point Jansen had snapped his notebook shut and, with a polite bob, concluded the interview.

Reviewing the file that morning, Jansen came up with nothing new.

The problem was one of insufficient evidence. There was nothing yet to positively confirm that Graham had been guilty of the crime. And while there were witnesses who might concur that her behaviour had recently been that of someone in the throes of a nervous breakdown, there were others, like the doctor and her husband, who flatly denied Mickey's behaviour was unusual, given the recent events in her life.

A neighbour had said he thought he'd heard her truck starting up before midnight on the night of the fire, but when pressed admitted he couldn't be one hundred percent sure. There was the fact that Jansen himself had seen Mickey nosing around the crime site on the morning following the incident. Her appearance had been a surprise; she didn't strike him as the kind of individual who would hurry to the scene of an accident.

However, it was in the instant when, after calling out her name, she'd fallen down in a dead faint that he'd known, deep in his gut, that Mickey Graham was the person they were looking for. All that remained was to find the evidence that would prove her guilty beyond any shadow of a doubt.

By ten that morning, after a brief visit to the local magistrate, Jansen had organised a search warrant and gathered together a team.

He briefed them carefully. They were searching for the container that had held petrol used to ignite the fire. If forensics could prove that the container had been taken to the site on the night of the fire, they would have the evidence they needed.

Mickey Graham looked as though she had been expecting them. Calm and expressionless, she opened the door and stepped aside to let them in.

Jansen showed her the search warrant.

"What's that?"

"It gives me the authority to conduct a search of these premises. If we discover the evidence we're looking for, I'm authorised to seize it."

"You think that I killed Black?"

"Did you?"

"I am innocent. I don't know what you're looking for, but you won't find it here."

Mickey sat on a chair in the kitchen and watched as the team conducted a sweep of her home. The house was sparsely furnished: cupboards almost bare. Not many places to hide a petrol container. They bagged only two possible items: the largest of the saucepans discovered beneath the sink and a yellow plastic bucket from a broom cupboard.

The team moved outdoors to conduct a punctilious search of the nursery grounds. The search took three and a half hours during which time an empty paint drum and a large tin can containing fertiliser were confiscated. At the end of the search, Jansen knew it had been a pointless exercise.

Mickey Graham had moved outside to sit on a garden bench pretending to be engrossed in a book. He watched her candidly. Her eyes were everywhere. She chewed her fingernails. That calm exterior must have cost her something: the woman was a shattered bundle of nerves. She was also one step ahead of them – the petrol container was obviously not on the property. It had been hidden somewhere else. Thrown into the sea? Buried perhaps? It could be anywhere.

"Are you done?" she asked, watching the team load the bagged items into the police car.

"Yes. Thank you for your co-operation."

"Found what you're looking for?"

Jansen allowed himself a small smile. "Perhaps," he said. "Perhaps not. But I will find what I am looking for, Miss Graham. You may trust me on that."

She met his eyes unflinchingly. "Good luck," Mickey said and walked inside.

She began trembling the moment they'd gone. Her hands shook so much that when she picked up a glass to fill it with water it fell from her fingers and smashed to splinters. "Oh God," she breathed. She walked shakily to the back of the garden, beyond the herb bed, near the compost heap where the two large potted ferns stood atop the grave in which she had buried the petrol drum, the gloves and her old tennis shoes. She saw at once that the team had been there.

There were footprints in the soil: clear imprints of heavy, police issue boots.

The gravel had been disturbed, dried leaves trodden into the earth. Someone had moved the rake and spade. One of the men had kicked the soil to test for firmness.

Oh yes, they'd been scrupulous in their poking, prying and burrowing, but they hadn't thought to drag away the pots and see what lay beneath. The pots had not been moved, not even an inch.

She felt weak: stunned with relief. The feeling gave way to a sense of lightness, then gratitude, then utter incredulity at how slip-shod, how careless their search had been. They'd stood on the exact spot where she'd buried the evidence!

Detective Inspector Hector Jansen knew she was guilty but couldn't yet prove it.

He had no tangible evidence. No petrol drum. No black book.

Mickey dared to hope.

Bojangles, Ginny's cat, had suddenly taken to sleeping with Chris.

Every night he made his way up the stairs and scratched at the door until he was admitted. In a single bound he leapt onto the bed where, after a thorough and lengthy grooming, he pressed himself against Chris and began to sing with such intense rough, throaty purring his entire body vibrated like a tuning fork.

Often Chris woke to find Bo sitting like a dead weight upon his chest, kneading with chunky paws; eyes blazing; whiskers trembling; the gravel-throated purring interrupted only with frantic, high-pitched chirping whenever the cat spotted a bird at the window.

"Take him away! I don't want him!" he told his mother. "He's hot, sheds tons of fur, has claws like needles, takes up too much space and never stops with that infernal purring."

"He loves you," Ginny said, tenderly stroking the cat. "He wants to be with you."

"Why? Why now?"

The cat knew, of course. Knew he was on his way out. Cats had this second-sense, along with their nine lives. The singing: vigorous, sonorous and unceasing was Bo's final tribute; the feline version of a funeral march, a true expression of melodic cat compassion. Turned out of the room, Bo sat at the door, scratching and mewing until Chris relented and let him back in. The cat was clearly here to stay until the bitter end.

It was when Bo began to dim into a marmalade fog that Chris discovered his eyesight was fading.

There was a kind of film over his eyes so that he saw everything as though through gauze, details blurred, colours muted, edges softened.

Light hurt his eyes. Streaming through a window it fragmented into such white-hot brightness he had to close his eyes against the glare.

The onset semi-blindness was unexpected and devastating. Worse, he thought, much worse than all other symptoms of the disease now raging out of control.

The coughing, drenching night fevers, eczema, mouth ulcers, pain in his joints and agonising bouts of shameful diarrhoea were *nothing* compared to blindness. Blindness, for an artist, was death.

While he could still see, he wrote a letter to his mother in which he begged her to be happy.

"*Your happiness,*" he wrote, "*means more to me than anything in the world.*"

He begged for her forgiveness and understanding: thanking her for a lifetime of love and devotion and for all the gifts she'd bestowed along the way.

"You are part of my blood, my bone, the air I breathe. You live in my mind and heart. You've given me life and love and all that matters most. You've taught me to be the best that I can be. My inspiration, my hope, my solace…"

Re-reading what he'd written, he thought that a stranger picking up the page would guess it a letter written to a lover rather than a declaration of love from a son to an adored mother.

He placed the sealed letter in an envelope and slipped it into a book of pencil drawings he'd sketched of Ginny.

When the time came, he'd leave the book where she would find it. It might be some consolation in the dark days following his death.

True to her word, Edwina had sent a plastic sachet containing thirty pale blue sleeping tablets concealed in a tin of boiled glucose sweets. His mother had innocently placed the tin at his bedside with a comment about Edwina's thoughtfulness.

That evening Inga found him with the packet in his hands. He held it up for her to see. "Enough to kill a horse," he said, instantly regretting the crassness of the remark.

She gazed sadly at the blue tablets. "Mrs Hurley?"

"Are you ready, Inga? Are you strong enough to go through with this?"

"Are you?"

He pressed his lips to her hand. "I'm ready," he said, meaning it.

He heard her reply in her cheerful stage voice. "Then I am also ready. Ready whenever you need me." The words were a lie, and he knew it but he let that go.

Sometimes it was necessary to lie to those you loved.

Downstairs, in the kitchen, Ginny made vegetable soup.

Meticulously she washed and peeled the vegetables and then diced or sliced them as required, keeping her eyes upon her busy hands. These small, brown, freckled hands appeared to have a life of their own: surely her brain was not ordering them to expertly chop vegetables into neat cubes or thin, flat discs?

I'm not myself, she thought. Her brain seemed to function only in the simplest way.

It allowed her to manage basic, undemanding physical tasks: housework, gardening, cooking and caring for Chris. But did not permit much else. She couldn't have a meaningful conversation without crying. Could not sleep through the night.

Could not quilt, knit or sew. Could not read a book or a newspaper or watch television. Painting, teaching, working in the gallery were out of the question.

"Forgive me?" she'd begged Sarah. "My heart is not in it. Can you manage without me for a while?"

Sarah knew what she was going through; how hard it was. Sarah had lost a husband to a brain tumour. "Take all the time you need," she'd said, voice softened with sympathy.

Ginny browned the onions until they became soft and touched with gold. She tossed in carrots and celery and then coarsely chopped potatoes, chunks of zucchini, slivers of brilliantly green beans, and three cups of chicken stock laced with gobbets of fat.

She stared into the bubbling broth and felt such agonising pain that she pressed her hand to bosom. "What?" she asked herself impatiently. "What's wrong with you?"

Of course she knew exactly what was wrong. This pain that assaulted her in the region of her heart was grief. Here she was, already grieving the loss of her son, while he still lay sleeping in the upstairs room, still alive, not yet dead.

"Time enough to mourn afterwards," she whispered aloud. "Don't give way now. Hold on!" Easy to say but how could she stop grief welling up inside?

She added a tin of peeled Italian tomatoes to the soup and a few generous tablespoonfuls of tomato puree. Seasoning to taste. The steam billowed fragrantly into her face as she stirred, tasted, sniffed. Anyone seeing her at the stove would think her busy and preoccupied, nurturing mother caring for her son: organised, practical, sensible.

She set the lid upon the saucepan and turned down the heat. The soup would simmer for an hour and then she'd pour a little into a bowl and take it up on a tray.

Inga found her weeping over the tray, the linen cloth with the lace edge blotting her tears.

"Hush," she said, as though talking to a child. "Hush, now."

"How can you bear it?" Ginny sobbed.

"We must be brave for Chris," Inga urged. "Only later, once he has gone, can you give way to sorrow. But for now, he needs us both to be strong!"

"But this is killing me!"

"Think of him! However hard it is for us, it is much worse for Chris."

Ginny bowed in shame.

"Come," said Inga, her voice cajoling. "Take him some of your very good soup. He will feel better if he eats a little."

Ginny turned back to the stove and stirred the soup. She poured a little into a bowl and gave the tray to Inga. "You go. I'll be up in a bit," she said, with as much cheer as she could muster. "As soon as I've fixed my face!"

Detective Inspector Hector Jansen knew something about psychology.

Without a shred of incriminating evidence his only recourse was to see if he could get Mickey Graham to admit to her crime. The challenge was to achieve a voluntary admission without applying any degree of stress or pressure or being seen to intimidate the suspect. Intuition told him that Mickey, for all her bluff, was only just keeping it together. She'd been through a lot and though she tried to come across as a pretty cool customer, he'd seen another side to her that hinted she might be ready to crack.

He found her bagging leaves when he pulled up outside the nursery next day.

"Miss Graham," he said, "would you mind accompanying me to the station?"

Her eyes grew large. "What for?"

"I would like some information from you."

"I've told you all I know."

"And I require a set of your fingerprints."

She chewed her lip anxiously.

"Shall we go?"

"May I wash my hands first?"

He followed her into the kitchen and stood at the doorway as she soaped and washed her hands.

Mickey did not utter a single word during the drive to the station. She turned as far away from him as she could, her body leaning towards the passenger window.

In his office she remained silent as her fingerprints were taken.

Jansen pushed a piece of paper across the desk.

"Please fill in your details," he said. "Name, address, identity number, telephone number."

Mickey took the pen from him. She stared at the blank page.

"Miss Graham? Your details, please."

She looked up. He thought he glimpsed a flicker of fear.

"I don't understand. You have that information. You know all my details."

"It's for our records," he explained.

The pen shook in her hand, inches above the page.

"Is there a problem?"

She began to write in large, round, looping, carefully-shaped letters.

The questions followed. Where had she been on the night in question? Did she have an alibi – anyone who could confirm that she had been in bed, asleep at that time? Why had she visited the site of the murder next morning?

Who specifically had told her of the occurrence of the fire? Had she set fire to the warehouse? Had she plotted to kill Black as a revenge for his alleged crimes against her?

Miss Graham kept her hands folded in front of her, as though she were praying.

Her voice was so low he had to strain to hear her answers. She gave nothing away.

Finally, he let her go. He told one of his staff to take her home.

Jansen opened her file and pulled out the rape docket. He examined Graham's written statement. The handwriting had a flowing style. *'Cursive'*, he thought, was the word used to describe such writing. It was distinctive though perhaps slightly illegible with all the exaggerated tails, the elevated capitals. He placed the page she'd completed that morning beside the statement.

He saw, with a thrill of disbelief, that the handwriting on the statement bore no relationship whatsoever to the writing on the page of details she'd just completed.

He'd noticed something that hadn't gelled in the way she'd first hesitated before self-consciously forming the rounded shapes of the letters as though writing for the first time.

For whatever reason, Mickey Graham felt the need to conceal the nature of her real handwriting from him. Either the woman was psychotic or she'd written something which, if found, might prove incriminating.

Mickey phoned Chris.

"I'm running out of time," she whispered. "He knows. He has the black book. He has a sample of my handwriting. He'll call in experts. I'll be arrested!"

"We're ready," he reassured her. "Tomorrow, then?"

"Tomorrow."

Inga froze with dread. "So soon. I hoped, perhaps, a few more days?"

"Lie here with me."

They lay like lovers entwined together, her head upon his chest, his arms clasped about her, breathing as one. Bo folded himself into the narrow space between her legs and his. They fell asleep to the vibrato of the cat's rapturous singing.

A schoolboy had found Mickey's black book. He'd walked with friends to Otter's Lane on the day after the fire to check out the place where two men had burned to toast. By chance he'd discovered a black notebook half buried in dry shrubbery.

There were a few pages of writing but otherwise the book was new. The boy ripped out the used pages, screwed them up and tossed them to the ground where the wind blew them in the dust. As he walked away, he could see paper balls lifting merrily into the air.

He slipped the notebook into his blazer pocket – *finder's keepers!*

Chapter 21

Ginny

We didn't know it at the time, but it would be the last warm day in St Jude before the weather turned. From my deck that morning I saw a rubber dingy heading out to sea. I recall there were three passengers in the boat: two slight figures, hair blowing in the wind, and a third leaning back in the hull. I couldn't see who they were: from where I sat, with the sun behind, the images were in silhouette. I watched the dingy cut through the water until it became a lurching dot on the horizon and vanished from view.

Late that afternoon I spotted two red, white and yellow National Sea Rescue boats setting out to sea from the beach and wondered if they were on another exercise or whether one of the fishing boats might be in trouble.

The dingy and its occupants didn't enter my mind. Next morning I woke to the thrumming of NSR helicopter blades above the waves and knew instantly that something was horribly wrong.

Fynn Harding, from the National Sea Rescue Institute in Saint Jude, received the call at approximately four in the afternoon. The caller sounded scared to death, voice breathless and shaky. He had to ask her to repeat herself twice before he understood that a small inflatable dingy with three passengers had set out at ten that morning and not yet returned. Six hours at sea in a dingy was pushing it – particularly as the woman reported one of the passengers was ill.

This begged the question why the three had set off in the first place but Fynn knew better to waste time with pointless enquiries and asked the caller instead to describe the craft in detail and say where they were headed.

"It's blue," said the woman, whose name he couldn't catch. "Blue and silver with a small outboard motor. I don't know where they were going. Out to sea for a couple of hours they said. Oh please, please send someone to find them!"

"Do they have flares on board?"

"Flares? No, nothing like that. They have no way of sending out a distress signal." The woman's voice sounded all choked up.

"Look," he said kindly, "no need to push the panic button yet! I'll send out a couple of boats. There's a pretty good chance we'll find them. Name's Fynn, got that? Keep in close contact. OK?"

The woman, whoever she was, sounded incoherent. Fynn put the phone down and summoned the team.

In the next half hour, he had dispatched the eight metre inflatable *'Lily II'* and the thirteen-metre all-weather rescue craft *'Good Hope'* but, by that time, strong offshore winds were gusting thirty-five knots and the sea was rough.

Ginny had had a sense of dark foreboding all day. It felt like indigestion, sitting high in her chest. That morning, packing a lunch for the journey, she'd been so nervy she'd cut her thumb slicing the bread.

"But are you well enough to go out in the boat, darling? You look so weak!"

"I'm feeling good, Ma. And it's the most beautiful day!"

Inga had touched her arm briefly. "I'll take care of him," she'd said, quietly.

"Oh, I trust you, dear. I do. It's just that it doesn't feel right with his being so sick. What if the wind comes up? What if there's a storm? How will you manage alone? If you have to go, let me come with you, please. I'd feel so much..."

"Inga is an experienced sailor, she's been sailing for years. Don't fuss, Ma. Please?" It seemed an effort for him to speak.

"You won't be long, will you? A couple of hours, you said, no more! Don't get over-tired, darling."

"It's what I want, Ma. I've been dreaming about this, about going out in the boat on a day like today. This is probably our last chance with winter coming. You do understand, don't you?"

Their eyes locked. His words sounded heavy with meaning. She tried to grasp what he was saying, beyond the obvious. She gazed apprehensively at their faces.

Inga seemed distracted and Mickey downcast and silent. Only Chris smiled with grateful pleasure, as, between them, they helped him across the grass, to the jetty where the boat was moored.

"Will you be warm enough?" Ginny ran back indoors to retrieve a heavy waterproof and a woollen cap.

"A flask of tea," she'd said, handing it to Inga. "Sandwiches and fruit. Will that be enough, do you think?"

Inga had hugged her. "More than enough," she'd whispered, turning her face away.

"What's the matter? You seem upset?"

"I might be getting a cold." Inga's voice was husky as though she were fighting tears.

"Come here, Ma!" Chris had held her, pulling her close, kissing her on both cheeks, on her mouth. "I love you," he'd said. "You know that, don't you?"

"Of course. And I love you!"

"Goodbye, Ma." He kissed her on the mouth once more and held her tightly, pinned against his bony frame.

"What time will you be back?"

Her question had been drowned by the raucous shrieks of seagulls. She'd called again: "Darling! When can I expect you back?"

Inga had started the engine. There was a gush of foaming white water, the smell of oil and smoke. His eyes were on her until the boat turned into the Serpentine Canal. He gave a frantic wave before they disappeared around the bend.

"Not so fast! Non-wake speed!" she'd shouted, cupping her mouth so that her words would carry.

Long after the boat had disappeared from view Ginny had stood motionless on the jetty having an argument with herself. Why was she feeling this way? They were going out in the dingy for a few hours on a perfect day. The sky was cloudless with hardly a breath of wind. It would do them all good. Burn some colour into their cheeks. Chris had always adored sailing and this might be the last time he'd be strong enough. Inga *was* a good sailor; she had sailed as a young girl. She'd take care of Chris, as she always did. He was in good hands.

Silent, Mickey with her strained white face was an odd choice but perhaps Chris thought she needed an outing, the company of sympathetic friends? It all made sense… and yet?

And yet, deep down, she knew something was wrong but couldn't put her finger on exactly why she felt so troubled.

Later that morning, she thought about the way he'd held her. Clinging as though he'd never let go. The way he'd said he loved her.

The searching look he'd given, saying goodbye. That frenzied wave before the boat turned.

The stone she carried in her chest grew heavier. *Something was wrong.*

Ginny paced the deck from two in the afternoon, feeling the sun on her back, staring at the bend in the canal, waiting for their return.

As the minutes slipped past, her sense of dread heightened. She dialled Chris's mobile and heard it ringing upstairs in his bedroom. Why hadn't he taken it?

Inga's phone had been switched to voice mail. She left a message, not caring how desperate she sounded. "You've been gone so long! I'm beside myself! Call me please. Please call!"

By three o'clock, when they'd been gone five hours, she knew with certainty that the sense of foreboding she'd had all day had been an omen. This morning, helping them get ready for the outing, slicing bread, cutting her thumb, she'd had a premonition of some kind. She'd known the unspeakable was about to happen. Known that life as she knew it would soon end.

She should have stopped them! What kind of mother allowed her desperately ill son to go out in an old boat with only two frail women on board? She should have done something and now it was too late!

She phoned the National Sea Rescue station and spoke to someone called Flynn and when he asked whether they had flares in the boat had been overcome with fear. No flares! No way of sending out a signal for help! They might have been swept out to sea, unable to turn back...

Wild weeping had followed, her voice sounding more animal than human.

Finally, when she could speak, she'd called Ben. "They're lost at sea!" she'd cried, without explanation. "I need you!" Please come!" As she opened the door, her knees had given way and she'd collapsed in his arms.

Fynn Harding arrived just after nine that evening. Ginny led him to the kitchen. "Tea? Coffee?" she asked mechanically. She registered his face, warm, brown eyes; ruddy cheeks; generous smile. "A whiskey would go down well!"

Ben followed her to the drinks cabinet. He felt clumsy and

inadequate in the face of her anguish. What to do? What to say? He had no idea.

"Let me," he offered. "Sit, Ginny. Relax. I'll pour the drinks."

"Relax? How can I relax? I am wound like a spring. I must keep myself busy to stay sane. Please, Ben." She gave him a gentle push. "Go and talk to Fynn."

She fumbled in the drinks cabinet. Poured a whiskey. The glass shook in her hands as he took it.

Fynn lowered his bulk into a chair, gulping the drink.

"No sight of the dingy yet," he apologised. "They've suspended the search until tomorrow. Never fear – we'll send the teams out again at dawn"

He asked the names of those on the boat and scribbled on the back of a cigarette pack.

"Your boy is sick? That right? That's what you said?"

"Yes."

"Well, how sick? Strong enough to go out in a boat?"

"I didn't think so. I should have stopped him. But he wanted to go. It was such a lovely day. I thought they'd be gone for a couple of hours, no more, and the fresh air would…"

"They take weather-proof gear with them? Life jackets? Food?"

"Chris had a waterproof jacket. I'm not sure about Inga and Mickey. Not much food."

Fynn heaved a sigh and then, aware of the frightened expression on Mrs Lourens' face, collected himself.

"Here's the plan," he said. He explained the station crew were working out a rescue mission modelled on ocean current, wind and weather patterns.

Ginny listened, trying to understand what the man was saying, but heard nothing that made any sense.

Rescue mission. Modelled on… A wall of words, all meaningless. Ben asked questions, Fynn answered. She couldn't concentrate.

She got up and left the room. She climbed the stairs, dead weights on her feet.

She knew exactly what had happened: the dingy had sunk and all three had drowned.

Ben found her on Chris' bed, hugging his pillow. The cat lay quietly at her feet, head on his paws.

"They're dead!" she cried. "I know it! All of them drowned!"

"You don't know that, Ginny," Ben said, soothingly. "Give it time. They may still be found. Don't give up hope yet." There was the creak of the mattress as he sat beside her. He pulled her towards him. She held herself stiffly in his awkward embrace.

Hope? She had no hope left now. They were dead. They were never coming back. Chris had left her. She'd be alone forever. She had not said goodbye, not properly, not knowing this would be the last time.

The cat had stopped purring. Was utterly silent. Another sign. How many omens had she missed? Why had she let them go? Why had she not known: mothers should always know. Instinct should have told her.

"Why?" she asked Ben. "*Why, why, why?*"

As soon as light broke, Fynn Harding despatched volunteer crews on the *'Lily II'* and *'The Good Hope'* and sent out the NSR surf rescue helicopter.

There was a better chance today of locating the dingy; the wind had dropped to fifteen knots and the sea was calmer. As soon as the boats were out, he called Ginny Lourens.

"Weather conditions are expected to remain favourable," he said in what he hoped was an optimistic tone. "Today we'll extend the search beyond the coast, towards Port Victoria. They may have tied up in one of the coves with a dead cell-phone. Kind of thing that happens all the time."

Harding didn't feel as confident as he sounded though. A sick man and two women out in a small inflatable all night with the off shore South Westerly blowing like hell, waves battering the boat: it didn't look good. There was a chance the dingy would have flipped. They'd never have survived in seas that cold, that rough.

After lunch, Harding despatched two additional search units: a patrol boat and a utility craft.

By nightfall, by the time the boats returned, the NSR team had covered sixteen hundred nautical miles of ocean between Saint Jude, Betty's Bay and Port Victoria, stretching as far as the Penguin Islands; a wildlife refuge to the west of the coast. There was no sign of the dingy or any of its passengers.

Early next morning, Edwina went down to the harbour to wait.

The sea was calm with small waves breaking gently on the shore.

She saw Fynn in discussion with a group of volunteers. She walked up to him. He tugged respectfully at his cap.

"Any news?"

"No, 'fraid not. Blessed if I know what's happened to that dingy. No sign of it anywhere. With four search units and a helicopter, we should have located boat and crew by now. Damned frustrating!"

"Have they drowned?"

"Can't say for sure."

"How long will you continue to search?"

"Resources are limited. We can stretch to one more day before we call it off. But that's it!"

"I can help if you need additional funds."

"Good of you!" He nodded. "Thing is, Mrs Hurley, if we've searched thousands of square miles of ocean and haven't seen a blessed thing, well, frankly there's not much point in going on."

"I see."

"Something strange about all this though. Something not quite right."

"What do you mean?"

"One of the passengers, Chris Lourens, was desperately sick. Went out to sea with two women on what appears to be a pleasure trip. No safety equipment on board to speak of, no food. Taking a risk, they were. A helluva risk!"

Edwina gazed out to the grey and sullen sea. In the distance she could see the lighthouse: a virginal white tower reaching into the sky. Waves broke upon the sand. The sound was hypnotic. She tasted sea-salt in the wind.

Everything was the same. Nothing was the same.

"A tragic accident," she said, at last. "It must have been a tragic accident."

The next day, newspaper reports carried the story of the missing dingy.

"The National Sea Rescue Institute have called off an intensive search for an inflatable boat, carrying three passengers, presumed lost at sea since disappearing three days ago. The crew included the renowned artist and sculptor, Chris Lourens and two female friends: Inga Johansson and Mickey

Graham. Four search vessels and a rescue helicopter, despatched by the NSRI, have been scouring the ocean since late Thursday afternoon, when the boat was first reported missing.

Despite unusually good weather conditions, searchers have exhausted the area from the coastline of Saint Jude to Betty's Bay, Port Victoria and beyond to Penguin Islands. A tip to the Coast Guard that a dingy had been sighted off the coast north of Port Victoria failed to reveal any sign of the missing boat.

Fynn Harding, head of the St Jude NSRI station, reported that searchers had taken wind speed and ocean currents into consideration when determining where the boat might have drifted. "We've saturated the area with rescue units and found nothing," he said. "It's a mystery! We can only conclude that the dingy met with an accident and the crew drowned."

Grace arrived with tranquillisers and sleeping tablets.

Ginny refused them. "I have to keep my head. There's a chance they might still be found alive…"

"They'll help you through the next few days, Ginny."

"I'm not ready, Grace! I thought I was. I knew he was dying. But not like this! It's such a shock!"

Grace considered her words carefully. "It's what he wanted, Ginny."

"What do you mean?"

"To die with dignity. Without prolonging his pain and your suffering."

"You think he killed himself? Drowned on purpose?"

"Don't you?"

"Yes!" the word was a howl. "Yes! I have been thinking that he may have tried to end it all. He had these dreams. He spoke of them often. He was always going on about floating in the waves, sinking to the bottom of the ocean. I thought he was feverish. Didn't listen properly. But the signs were there. Even this morning, I had this splinter in my heart, this sharp pain. 'Something's wrong', I said to myself. And then the way he said goodbye!" Tears streamed down Ginny's cheeks, dripping from her chin. She didn't try to wipe them away. "But the girls, Grace? Inga and Mickey! Where are they? What's happened to them? How are they involved in this?"

"I can't speak for Inga but I know Mickey was in some kind of trouble with the police."

"Inga was in love with Chris. She'd have done anything for him."

"Could it have been a suicide pact?"

"Oh God!" Stricken, Ginny clapped her hand over her mouth.

"We're guessing, Ginny. They might have met with an accident. We've no idea what really happened."

"I wanted Chris to die in his own bed with me at his side, loving him to the end. And now he's gone. I'll never see him again …"

"Did he leave a note?"

"I don't know. I can't bring myself to search his room, his things."

"Do you want me to look?"

"No! Suppose you do find a note? I'd have to read it. Then I'd know for certain that he had planned to kill himself."

"At least you would know…"

"But why didn't he tell me? Why not talk to me? His own mother! Leaving a note…" She buried her head in her hands. "I didn't say goodbye! Not the way I would have, if I'd known. There's so much I wanted to say, when the time came."

Grace went to the kitchen for water and handed Ginny a glass and two tablets.

"Take these and try to sleep. I'll stay until you nod off."

Sickly white, Ginny leaned back against the sofa and allowed Grace to cover her with a quilt. "It makes no sense," she whispered. "Chris was dying, we know that. But Inga and Mickey? They must have been *desperate* to go along with such a plan."

"Perhaps they were."

"Oh Chris!" Ginny whimpered. "What have you done, darling? What have you done?"

Detective Inspector Hector Jansen met Fynn Harding at the NSRI station.

"You say you've had no sight of the inflatable? How does a dingy carrying three people disappear like that?"

"Beats me."

"Is it a trick of some kind?"

"What are you getting at?"

"Mickey Graham, one of the crew, was a suspect in a murder enquiry."

"Ah!"

Jansen waited. Finn appeared lost in thought.

"What?"

Fynn pulled a face. "Well," he said, slowly, "that changes things."

"How?"

"Chris Lourens was sick. Some say he had a terminal disease. Now, if Mickey Graham was wanted by the police, maybe their drowning was intentional? Some kind of joint suicide?"

"That's one scenario. Here's another – maybe they haven't drowned. Maybe they've escaped? Set sail for the coast beyond Port Victoria? Landed at one of the small fishing villages?"

"Less likely."

"Why do you say that?"

"We'd have spotted them in our search. Don't forget, Inspector, we had four rescue craft and a helicopter looking for that dingy for three days."

"Fair enough. But let's take your suicide pact hunch. What happened to the boat? Why hasn't it washed up? Where are the bodies?"

"Can't say, for sure. The ocean holds its own. The weather was bad that first night. Thirty-five knot gales and high seas. Chances are the boat capsized. Thrown in the water, the crew would never have survived the rough, icy conditions without life jackets."

"What do you know about the second woman? Inga Johansson?"

"Nothing much. Some say she was Chris Lourens' lover. I suppose we'll find out, in time."

Fynn Harding gave the Inspector a quick glance. "Looks like you lost your suspect."

"Maybe. Maybe not."

"Still think they've made a run for it?"

"There's a chance…"

"I can think of easier ways."

"That's the problem. So can I."

Jansen found the door to Mickey's house had been left unlocked. The place was dusty but tidy. Her clothes hung neatly in the cupboard and he located an empty suitcase at the back of the linen closet. There was milk in the fridge, two eggs, a small pat of butter, half a loaf in the bread bin.

Nothing to indicate that Miss Graham would not be returning home that evening or that she'd taken anything from the house in preparation for a new life outside Betty's Bay. There was no suicide note.

Stumped, he sat on the small wooden chair in the kitchen and felt the slender legs splay beneath his weight. He got up quickly. No sense in breaking one of the few pieces of furniture in the house.

A yellowish light filled the room picking up silvery dust motes.

So, she'd gone. He snapped his fingers and the sound reverberated in the empty room. Just like that. She'd climbed aboard a small inflatable boat with two others and they had wound their way across the canal to the river mouth and from there out to sea. After six hours the NSRI had been summoned and two rescue craft dispatched. There'd been no sighting of the dingy that afternoon or during the next three days. The boat along with its three passengers, had disappeared like magic.

Or sank like a stone. Either way, Mickey Graham had vanished.

Without the prime suspect in the Black and Miller murders, he had no case.

He could alert the police in Port Victoria and beyond to keep an eye out for Graham. Send a photograph of the suspect. But the case against her was thin with no evidence to speak of, other than his excellent intuition, which, of course, didn't really signify.

Tomorrow he'd arrange a meeting with the Chief Inspector. "The suspect is presumed drowned," he'd say, feeling foolish for letting her slip through his fingers. The Chief would be unimpressed. What with arson experts and forensics, considerable resources had been spent on the investigation. The story would die a natural death. The file would be closed. The case would go cold.

The papers were full of the missing dingy now and for days, perhaps a week or two, the press would speculate on the mysterious disappearance of the three.

Only he knew the truth. Only he knew for sure that Mickey Graham had murdered two men in cold blood and got away with it.

"You win," he said, aloud. "You win!"

That night, after closing the gallery, Sarah wandered through empty corridors, Lucky at her side.

The news that Chris, Inga and Mickey had gone missing in a dingy had shocked her rigid. She'd been unable to visit Ginny or even to pick up the telephone and call.

Not so long ago, Chris had stood right here at this easel, giving art lessons, teaching perspective, light, shade, depth.

His students had loved him. Post-menopausal housewives and grandmothers became girlish in his classes, archly tossing greying curls, competing for his attention. They'd blushed as he leaned over their sketch blocks, taking their pencils, redefining lines, adding dimension, transforming flat and lifeless drawings into something like art.

Sarah examined his paintings: The Seascape; the portrait of Ginny; the angel.

They were all magnificent. The work of a gifted artist who, a few days ago, had set out to sea with two friends and mysteriously disappeared.

This morning's newspapers had salaciously speculated at a suicide pact. The press had got wind of the fact that Chris had suffered from a 'life-threatening illness' and Mickey Graham had been seriously depressed. Inga Johansson was said to be Chris' mistress and there were rumours, laughable really, that all three might have been lovers!

So far, none of the papers had tumbled to the fact that Chris had been gay and dying of AIDS, but for how much longer could that remain a secret?

Surely Chris, amongst the three, was the only one with reason enough to contemplate suicide? Mickey didn't strike Sarah as someone who would intentionally harm herself, and Inga had everything to live for. And yet, what did she really know of any of them? What did anyone know?

Sarah touched the thickly raised paint on the angel's wings, running her fingers delicately across the stiff ridges and depressions on the canvas.

An accident! It *must* have been an accident. They'd have drifted off course. Been swept out to sea. Perhaps the outboard engine had cut out? The National Sea Rescue Institute had reported fierce winds and five metre waves. How could anyone have survived such conditions?

Lucky brushed against her legs, gazing up with loving brown eyes.

"I must call Ginny," she said to the dog. "Call and say how deeply sorry I am."

She rubbed the place between his pricked ears. "I'm such a coward!" she admitted miserably. "I'm Ginny's friend, she needs me and yet I have no idea what to say to her." Lucky's tail swished against the floor.

Sarah felt the pressure of tears behind her eyes.

"I'll call tomorrow," she whispered to the dog. "First thing. I Promise."

Edwina was in a dreadful state. Once the NSRI station called off the search she withdrew to her bedroom and drew the curtains. She refused to eat or drink.

Sleep evaded her. Questions and doubts crowded her mind. How had this happened? What had she done? And what in God's name had Chris been thinking of?

She tried to recall his exact words.

"I've had an idea. Tell Mickey to come and talk to me."

Trustingly, she'd sent Mickey to talk to Chris. Somehow an horrific plan had been hatched between the three of them.

Some of the guilt was hers. She'd pulled the strings and engineered the meeting. The angel had sent a message... Had she misunderstood? Imagined a message when there'd been none? Is this what happened when you were dying? You clung to hope with the adhesive, stickiness of a tenacious limpet on a rock? Your mind unhinged itself so completely that you saw a simple wooden statue as a divine messenger?

She'd poked her nose in where it wasn't wanted. Played the Good Samaritan and ended up giving Chris the means to end his life and despatching Mickey and Inga to their deaths as well. Her intentions had been good, nobody would doubt that, but it had all gone so terribly wrong. She wondered at the motivation of her actions. Had the desire to help them all been a determination to transcend her life, hardly one of cheeseparing selflessness, so that at the end, she might not be remembered as a wealthy bitch who'd lived a life of indulgence – but more fondly, as a kind-hearted and generous benefactor? *My legacy*, she thought. *Perhaps it all has to do with wanting to be remembered well?*

Between midnight and three in the morning Edwina's imagination ran riot.

She saw pale bodies dragged from the sea: skin luminous as mother-of-pearl. She saw the three of them, lying prone, dripping into the sand, sightless eyes wide and accusing.

What have you done, Edwina? What have you done?

"I have something to tell you," she confessed to Thomas at daybreak, when, leaning heavily upon his cane, he brought her a cup of milky tea, most of it spilled into the ivory pile of the carpet.

"Yes, my dear. What is it?"

"I am partly responsible! It's my fault!"

"Eh?"

"For their deaths. Chris, Mickey, Inga: the drowning at sea."

"Eh?"

"Can you hear me, Thomas? Is your hearing aid tuned? It's not easy for me to talk about this and I certainly don't want to repeat myself."

"I can hear very well," he bristled. "It's just that I don't understand a word you're saying."

"Chris asked for sleeping tablets. I sent a large quantity. I knew he wanted them to end his life. I felt pity. I've often thought of doing something similar to spare myself pain and suffering, when the time comes. I asked him to help Mickey. I sent her to him..."

"You've thought of taking your own life?"

"Stay with me, Thomas! This is important! Somehow they concocted this plan: the three of them, or perhaps only two of them with Mickey an unwilling participant. An escape of a kind, I suppose, though nothing like what I had in mind. Oh, Thomas, if only I hadn't listened to the angel..."

"The angel?"

"There was a message. She told me to send Mickey to Chris. I did as she asked, Thomas!"

Thomas was silent. Had Edwina lost her mind? She was ranting, talking utter nonsense. Her cheeks burned. Her hair was wild. Her expression harrowed.

"I am *wracked* with guilt, Thomas. I can't forgive myself. I am such an interfering old busybody."

"Well, that's true..."

She wept on his shoulder. her tears soaking his navy blue silk dressing gown.

Thomas gave a shudder. Edwina weeping? Edwina hardly ever cried.

He dabbed inexpertly at her wet face with his pocket-handkerchief.

"We have blood on our hands."

He gasped in horror. "Blood?"

"Not you! The angel and I."

They sat together holding hands.

From the very beginning, from the first moment she'd clapped eyes on it, she'd been bewitched by the angel. He'd tried to warn her, talk sense into her.

“Touch it,” he’d said. “Tell me what you feel? Wood. All wood. No brain, no heart, and certainly no soul!”

Nothing he’d said had made any difference. She was convinced that the angel had cured her; that it had dissolved away the tumour.

She’d believed the angel had the power to help others, had asked for help for Mickey and now Mickey was dead.

He could feel Edwina’s painful guilt spilling into the room. He patted her hand. He gave a heartfelt sigh. He tried to think of something comforting to say to her. “My dear,” he murmured. The words would not come. There was nothing to be said. Silence fell.

Chapter 22

James and Ginny

It was not the first time a boat had been lost in the icy waters of the Eastern Cape. Years ago, travelling out to sea to scatter his beloved wife's ashes, a world-renowned scientist had vanished somewhere between Port Victoria and Jake's Cove. An exhaustive search had been called off after four days and sailboat and sailor were never seen again.

The missing dingy, with its motley crew of three, was the talk of St Jude. Everyone had a theory about what might have happened.

Most were convinced the small boat had capsized in treacherous waters and the passengers drowned. A few, who knew that Mickey had been questioned by the police in the Black/Miller case, suggested the disappearance had been orchestrated so that she could flee the village and assume a new identity elsewhere. They had no convincing explanation, however, as to why Chris and Inga might have thrown in their lot with such a plan. The suicide pact theory was a favourite, although few could guess at why the lovely Inga had seen fit to end her life.

The mystery surrounding the tragedy deepened as days turned to weeks and neither boat nor bodies washed up on the shore.

Caron found herself in a no-man's-land of suppressed emotion. She felt as though she'd vaporised, leaving only a fragile husk to carry on with the day-to-day task of caring for James and maintaining a polite and distant relationship with Alec.

In just three weeks she'd pack her clothes, books and the very few personal possessions she'd brought to the Grant household and leave them both for a life in Port Victoria.

'Trial separation' was the term they were using which was easier to say than 'divorce' but probably misleading. Once she'd left there'd be no turning back and that would be that. The divorce would follow in time and from that point their only contact would be infrequent phone calls, e-mails and cards with birthday and Christmas wishes until even they would cease.

For some reason, perhaps because she felt as breakable as glass, the disappearance of the dingy affected her deeply. She fretted for days, waiting for news of the recovery of the boat and its passengers, appalled when the NSRI admitted defeat and reluctantly cancelled the search.

The idea of them left alone and abandoned, written off as dead and yet perhaps still alive, still floating in an endless expanse of water, filled her with outrage.

Why should they be assumed dead after only three days when people had survived at sea for much longer? Three days was nothing! Why not continue to search for the missing crew?

Why did she care so much? She knew very little about the three. Chris was an artist who'd been kind to James. She'd seen Mickey once or twice – a landscape gardener who'd sold a brand of herbal products in the gallery. Caron had bought a few bunches of dried lavender and camomile tea. She'd never met Inga, who was foreign, and said to be a yoga instructor.

They meant nothing to her and yet she felt fiercely protective of all of them.

In no time at all they'd become the subject of gossip; their names mentioned everywhere.

Only yesterday the rodent-faced pharmacy assistant announced to all in sundry that Chris had been taking anti-retroviral medication for AIDS.

"Makes you think, doesn't it?" she'd smirked.

"Surely that's confidential information?" Caron had snapped, slapping a handful of coins on the counter and snatching her package from the woman's hands.

She'd felt James' eyes upon her but he'd looked away when she returned his gaze. Had he heard? How shameful people were! How cruel! She could imagine what they would have to say about her once she had left St Jude. With no one to defend her, she'd be torn to shreds.

James wondered if he should introduce the mystery of the boat lost at sea in his book: '*The Human Alien*'. He'd been with Caron, walking on the beach that first afternoon and seen the red, white and yellow NSRI boats racing to sea, zigzagging through the crested waves. He wished he'd been on board the '*The Good Hope*', hurtling fast towards a thrilling adventure.

"A practice mission, I should think," Caron had remarked, although he hadn't spoken. They'd been collecting seashells and rare pieces of sea-glass to make a wind chime. Caron's suggestion and a totally cool idea, though he hadn't admitted that to her. He'd made a pact with himself to pretend she wasn't there because, very soon, she wouldn't be. It was easier that way. When she left, it wouldn't hurt so much. He'd said hardly anything to her for days. Sometimes, when he thought about her going, he felt scared and so he filled his brain with other stuff like smart chess moves he could use to beat Mr Paton the next time they played. The thing was, he'd got used to Caron and though he didn't love her the same way he'd loved his mother, he knew that, in a funny way, he'd miss her.

When James wondered what it was that he liked about Caron he thought it was probably that she made him feel safe. Though nobody ever said anything about it, he'd discovered he and Caron were quite similar in many ways. They both liked everything to be clean and neat and put back in it's proper place. They liked things to happen at the same time: breakfast at seven exactly, not before or after. They liked reading and finding out stuff about, well, about anything. They both had good memories and could recall dates and spellings and place names and odd facts very easily. They liked to be quiet sometimes, quite a lot actually, and not to talk and talk the way some people did. Caron also hated sports and thought that games like chess and Scrabble were more fun than kicking a ball around. Come to think of it, she didn't have any friends either.

They weren't *exactly* the same though. She like touching: liked kissing and hugging and holding hands. He didn't like being touched; it was like something you had to do for other people, not for yourself. When people got too close James wanted to push them away. She liked gardening, which was boring and listening to music and cooking but, when he thought about it, he knew that he and Caron were more the same than they were different.

His not talking was making her unhappy, he could see it in the pleading way she looked at him. He was glad. He wanted her to be miserable considering what she was going to do. Sometimes, though, he wondered if the plan was such a good idea. There was a good chance he was making Caron so wretched she'd be glad to leave and wouldn't miss them at all.

Caron had been interviewing for a housekeeper. The person who got the job also had to help supervise his homework after school. He'd seen lots of different people coming and going: old and young, fat and thin, shy and talkative.

Some interviews were short, some longer, but last night he'd heard Caron tell his dad that she hadn't found anyone suitable yet. "You're cutting it pretty fine," his dad had said. "What's the problem?"

"It's James," she'd said. "I can't find anyone I trust to take care of James."

"Perhaps you're too fussy?"

"Too fussy?" her voice had been incredulous. "How can you be too fussy when it comes to James? It needs a special person to understand him…"

His father had groaned. "Oh, Caron!" he'd said. "What are we doing? Why are we going through with this?"

Caron's reply had been faint. He'd heard a subdued, "Don't Alec!" and then her voice had dropped and James hadn't been able to hear what came next.

When Caron first came into his life he'd wished with all his heart for a magic spell to make her disappear. He'd heard dad say, during one of their fights, that he wished they'd never got married. In a way, their wishes had come true and yet it was funny, not funny ha-ha but funny peculiar: now that Caron was going away, he and his dad both wanted her to stay.

The day after seeing the rescue boats, James had been awakened by the noise of a helicopter so loud it seemed to hovering just above his bed.

Half asleep, he'd run to the window, craning his neck to see powerful rotor blades whirling high above the roof, leaves swirling in the updraft. In seconds the chopper had darted away like a silver dragonfly, zooming above a smooth, unruffled ocean.

Caron had made scrambled eggs for breakfast.

"A boat has gone missing," she'd said.

James pushed the eggs around on his plate. Finally, curiosity got the better of him. "Whose boat?"

Caron had explained that Chris Lourens and two friends had set sail in a dingy yesterday and had not yet returned.

His heart had started hammering. *Chris Lourens!* Chris was his favourite artist! Chris had helped him paint the clay animals that he and Ginny made together. James loved them! Striped and spotted and splashed with brilliant colour, they stood in a precise row on his bookcase.

James forgot about not talking. "Those search boats yesterday, the ones we saw! They must have been looking for Chris and his friends! What's happened to them? Where are they?"

"Nobody knows yet, James. I heard on the radio that the National Sea Rescue Institute has sent out four search boats and a helicopter this morning. Don't worry. I'm sure they'll be found."

After hearing the news, James couldn't concentrate, couldn't think of anything but Chris and his friends out at sea in a small dingy. He'd seen the boat once, a blue rubber duck: small and, he thought, quite old. It had patches on the sides and an engine that smoked.

"Can we help look for them?" he'd asked.

Caron had taken him to the NSRI station where Fynn Harding and some of the other volunteers waited for news.

"Will you find them?" James had blurted.

"I hope so, lad. Hope so!"

"But, what if you don't? What will happen to them? Will they die?"

Raising bushy brows, Fynn had given Caron a helpless glance.

"You will find them, they can't have drifted off too far?" She'd kept her voice neutral.

"We'll do our best," he'd replied. "Can't do more than that."

Fynn stopped them as they were turning to go. "Since you're so interested," he'd said, leading James to a computer screen.

James had peered closely at a multi-coloured map divided into a complex grid pattern. "They're out there somewhere!" Fynn had declared, knocking on the glass with a hairy knuckle.

"How do you know?"

"Unique software programme," he'd explained. "You feed in drift data and most probable location based on wind speed. Then you surround the location with a forty kilometre radius of uncertainty and, hey presto!"

James had listened intently.

"The rescue craft have each been assigned a grid cell. The helicopter has the grid with the highest probability. Now all we do is wait. That's the tough part."

"Thank you for showing me this," James had breathed. "It's brilliant! Bet you find the missing boat today!"

Fynn had seemed less confident. "This programme has saved many lives," he'd said. "But it's not infallible. No guarantees."

"Is it top secret?"

"Nah! We've been using computer aided search solutions for years now."

"Well, the reason I'm asking, is I'd like to write about it in my book. That is, if it's not secret and you don't mind?"

Fynn had laughed. "Writing a book, eh? Why am I not surprised? Go ahead, feel free!"

James had held out a hand for a formal handshake.

"You've got a great kid there," Fynn had whispered to Caron.

Ginny found the letter from Chris concealed in a book of pencil sketches on his bedside table. She didn't open it for fear of falling apart. The creamy envelope, her name scrawled in black ink bleeding into textured paper, confirmed her worst fears.

It was true. Chris had chosen to end his life and, presumably, had persuaded Mickey and Inga to do the same thing. There was nothing he could say in the letter that would make her feel anything but betrayed.

Holding herself together so far had been the hardest thing she'd ever had to do. This morning, lifting her toothbrush to her mouth, she'd had found it impossible to brush her teeth and simply stood there, brush in her mouth, toothpaste fizzing on her tongue, wishing she too were dead.

She slipped the letter, unread, beneath her pillow and got into bed. The sheets were crumpled from a restless night, the flattened pillow felt like a stone, but she fell asleep immediately. Waking, hours later, she was conscious of noises from the kitchen. Water draining into the sink, the clatter of cutlery. Muted voices.

Listening to footsteps on the stairs, Ginny was reminded of how she had felt as a child, lying sick in a darkened room, waiting with longing for the special treats accorded to a girl with measles or a painfully swollen throat: bowls of jelly or glasses of lemonade tinkling with ice cubes. Perhaps she slept again. When she awoke, dazed, the lamp was burning and someone had softened the glow by draping the shade with a pink scarf.

There was a bottle of mineral water and a glass on the table but she had no strength to reach for them.

"Ginny?" Sarah's voice. "Can you sit up and drink a little water?"

Her head felt like a cannon ball. "No!"

Her eyes leaked tears.

"Are you ill?"

Her voice was a croak. "I think so."

"Shall I call the doctor?"

Ginny closed her eyes against the pink light. Hot and feverish, all she wanted to do was sleep.

Darkness and light separated the days, flowing one into the other.

Sarah or Ben, taking turns, fed her with aspirin and fluids at regular intervals, punched pillows and straightened bedclothes. Perhaps Grace had been to see her, she couldn't remember, but she gathered she had a virus of some kind that had felled her as surely as if she had run full-tilt into a speeding train. She lost herself in dreamless, fathomless sleep. Waking was terrifying. Emerging through layers of cottony blackness, she'd become conscious that something was dreadfully wrong and then it would all come back: Chris was dead, the girls were dead and she had nothing to live for.

How ironic, Sarah thought, that she and Ben should be taking care of Ginny together.

She'd seen another side to Ben these past few days as he carried trays up and down stairs, patted Ginny's blisteringly hot forehead with a facecloth and sat at her bedside for hours on end, watching her sleep.

"You're good at this," she'd said, admiringly.

"Out of my depth," he'd confessed, honestly. "I feel pretty useless. How do you comfort someone who's lost a son? What do you say?"

"Well, just being there helps. She's not alone. She knows how much you care and that must be very comforting, I should think."

Privately, Ben wondered how much of a comfort he really was. Knocked for six by the virus, Ginny slept as though drugged and during her brief waking moments an awkward silence had descended between them. It was obvious that the relationship, still new, was being severely tested and he was unsure of how to deal with her raw pain and grief.

This evening he discovered her awake when he arrived and though obviously still sick and feverish, she was, thank God, dry-eyed.

"How are you feeling?"

"A little better, I think."

He'd taken her hot hand, stroking the back of it with his thumb.

"Poor you," she had whispered.

"Why me? What about you?"

"We were so happy – and then all this! You don't deserve it. It's not fair."

Her eyes were huge. Her wiry hair, escaping from her plait, framed her face with springy curls. She gripped his hand. "What I'm trying to say, Ben, is that I'll understand if you feel you want to run from all this."

He wasn't sure how to reply.

"I have no expectations," she continued. "It might be for the best."

She smiled then. A brave smile through dry, cracked lips. It touched his heart.

"I think I'll hang around for a while," he said. "If that's alright with you?"

Thomas called Caron and asked if James might be available for a game of chess that afternoon.

They played in the library and Thomas won again.

"A few tips that might help elevate you, in time, to champion status," Thomas said and proceeded to demonstrate a variety of clever opening moves. "You seem distracted, my boy? Anything wrong?"

"I'm thinking about stuff."

"Ah! *Stuff.* Anything in particular?"

"That boat. The one that got lost. What do you think happened?"

"I have drawn the unhappy conclusion that the crew met with an accident. I fear they're drowned at sea. What ideas do you have?"

"Maybe they were eaten by sharks?"

"I hope they met with a more peaceful end."

"Remember Steve Irwin? He was snorkelling and got killed by a stingray!"

"An unlucky and highly unusual accident. I doubt that..."

"The stingray moves its tail like this..." James made a weaving motion with his hand. "And then it throws out a sharp spike like a javelin. This one landed up in Steve Irwin's heart."

"Highly improbable that our three have been killed by stingrays, wouldn't you agree?"

"Dunno." James sat pondering for a while. "Chris was my friend," he said sadly. "He showed me how to paint clay animals and now he's dead!"

"Hard to believe, I know."

"Don't say anything about heaven!" James cautioned Thomas. "People always talk about heaven when somebody dies."

"Very well," Thomas said. He drummed his fingers on the table. "How are things at home? Everything alright?"

James shrugged. "That's another thing I don't want to talk about."

"I see. What would you like to talk about?"

James told Thomas about the brilliant NSRI computer programme that, supplied with drift and weather information, drew a detailed grid map giving the approximate locality of those lost at sea.

"Except," he added sadly, "in this case, it didn't work."

When Caron came to collect James after the game, Thomas beckoned her closer.

"A word," he said, quietly. "I wonder if I might have a word with you?"

"Yes, of course. Now?"

Thomas glanced at James who, staring with forced concentration at the chessboard, was clearly listening to their conversation.

"No, later if you don't mind. May I call you?"

Caron gave a nod. "Ready, James?"

Thomas watched them walking away. James ignored Caron's outstretched hand and marched ahead stiffly, his expression downcast.

Just before dinner, Edwina received a phone call. Thomas heard the phone ringing in her room, heard her answer and then deliberately lower her voice to a whisper.

The conversation, so hushed that he heard none of it (although he was positioned directly outside her bedroom door) was lengthy. At last he heard Edwina saying goodbye. He knocked hesitantly.

She opened the door and helped manoeuvre his chair through the arched doorframe.

"Who called?"

Edwina switched on the lamps and in the yellow light he saw that her expression looked surprised, relieved, almost happy. She sat on the edge of a chair, facing him.

She gave a smile. A bright, glittering smile.

"Shall we go out to dinner?"

The question astonished him. "But, you're not well!"

"I'm feeling better. And I'm rather hungry. The French restaurant I think. Do you agree?"

"I'm confused, darling. You've been so depressed. Are you up to it?"

"I've been wallowing in guilt and self-recrimination. I'm tired of beating myself about the head. Putting it all behind me. Life must go on!"

He drew an astonished breath.

Edwina flung open her wardrobe and began to sift through the contents; lifting the plastic covers of apparel returned from the dry-cleaners.

She pulled out a stylish grey silk with a feathered trim and held it to herself.

"Will it do?"

Thomas frowned. To go from darkest depression and weeping to this vain, frivolous pirouetting at the mirror?

He heard her humming. Disbelieving, he leaned slightly forward, cocking an ear in her direction. He wasn't mistaken. She hummed a cheerful tune he couldn't quite place, the kind of piece you tapped a toe to, upbeat and positive.

He recalled the ringing of the phone followed by whispering. She was concealing something from him? What was she hiding and why?

"Who called?" he repeated. "Who was on the telephone?"

"Oh, no one."

Edwina tossed the grey gown on the bed and opened her jewellery box, rifling through the contents. She lifted hoops of dull silver to her ears.

"The telephone! I heard it ring. Heard you talking. You *whispered!* Why? What's going on, Edwina? Tell me!"

Edwina widened her eyes, her nostrils flared. "Don't shout, Thomas. I won't have it. Don't *dare* shout like that!"

He glared, angry, puzzled and hurt. "But I don't understand? Why won't you tell me?"

"The call was private! It had nothing whatsoever to do with you. I owe you no explanations. If you are going to be difficult, Thomas…"

"What?" He scowled. "That sounded like a threat? What will you do if I am difficult?"

Edwina deflated suddenly. He saw the energy drain from her. She collapsed upon a chair and rubbed her eyes.

"I've changed my mind," she said. "I think I'll have an early night. Please organise your own dinner."

He was overcome with remorse. "Shall I have a tray sent up?"

"Good night, Thomas!"

Dismissed, he drooped, wheeling the chair towards the door. He'd made an unholy mess of things. Her face looked pinched, cold and distant. It would take ages for her to come around. Why had he made such an issue about the blasted telephone call? Of course Edwina was entitled to a little privacy.

Appetite lost, Thomas nibbled upon a solitary supper of cold chicken. He was halfway through the meal when the thought struck that privacy was one thing but secrets quite another. He'd never seen the need for secrets. Had nothing to hide. But Edwina clearly did. Women were complex creatures, Edwina especially so. He thought hard. He went back over the sequence of events… The missing boat. Edwina's overwhelming guilt and sorrow after the shocking disappearance of the crew. Her withdrawal, in grief, to her room. And then the mysterious telephone call that had immediately lightened her spirits and made her feel, as she said, that life goes on.

He felt like a scientist on the brink of a discovery. He mulled. He cogitated. At last he nodded off. When he awoke, the table had been cleared and a cup of filter coffee set before him. Thomas stared into its cold, murky depths. He yawned. He could live, he thought, to be one hundred or more and would never discover what made Edwina tick and why she behaved as she did.

Unfathomable, mysterious, baffling, Edwina had the power to lift him up or cast him down: he was entirely at her mercy. They were partners, had once been lovers, but had never been equals. An apology would be required and a degree of grovelling in order to be forgiven and welcomed back into her good graces.

Edwina ruled like a Queen and he was foredoomed to always play the courtier or, worse, the jester. It wasn't fair: a man could grow weary of such capriciousness and yet, did he have a choice?

Edwina tossed the grey silk onto a chair and sat before the dressing table applying face cream. Thomas had spoilt the evening with his petulant behaviour. That ridiculous outburst! The way he rolled his eyes and swung his arms with that silly, disgruntled expression on his hot, cross face!

He will never know, she thought, *wild horses wouldn't drag it from me. Thomas will never discover the truth.*

She hugged the secret to herself. No one will ever know!

Ginny opened the envelope and withdrew the letter. She flattened it carefully.

His hands had touched these pages. Writing this might have been one of the last things he'd done. She felt him everywhere. She lifted her eyes to the first line.

She heard his voice. Saw his sweet smile. Felt his loving eyes upon her.

"Your happiness means more to me than anything in the world."

When she'd finished reading the letter, she read it again searching for meaning: an explanation of why he had done this, why he'd left her in this way without a proper goodbye. Why now, when they might yet have had months together? Why had he taken Inga and Mickey with him?

"You have given me life and love and all that matters most!"

She felt his love in the room: encircling her with warmth. She pressed the pages to her lips. "I miss you!" she cried.

The letter held no explanation for his actions but she knew something of what must have happened. He'd taken his life to spare them all: his mother, Inga and even himself. He'd swallowed tablets and sleep had taken him. He'd chosen to be buried at sea. It was a choice she'd have to make peace with. What else could she do? Ginny remembered the sketchpad. Opened it and flipped, slowly, through the pages. The book was filled with pencil drawings. Here she was, feeding ducks. Standing barefoot, pegging washing upon the line; eyes closed against the sun. Kneeling in the garden, pulling weeds. Asleep in a chair, Bojangles lolling at her feet. Sitting on the jetty a daisy threaded into her coronet of hair. Page after page of drawings of her; each line executed with loving tenderness.

Sarah brought a bottle of iced mineral water, a glass of apple juice and two aspirins.

"I'm off," she said. "Need anything else?"

Ginny swallowed painfully. Her throat, still thick and sore, felt as though it had been lined with hooked barbs. "I found a letter."

"Oh?"

"From Chris."

She could see at once that Sarah was not surprised, and had probably been expecting a suicide note. "I'm sorry, Ginny."

"Don't be. It's what he wanted. I see that now. In a way, it's a relief, knowing the truth."

Sarah straightened the quilt.

"He left this for me, too."

Sarah took the book and opened it, turning the pages.

"Oh Ginny!" She gazed at the pencil drawings, page after page of them.

"His parting gift," Ginny said and, behind the tears, there was such pride in her voice.

"It's going to be so hard for you," Sarah said, knowing that this was a mild version of the truth. Hard? Dealing with loss and grief and despair was much more than *hard!* It was like taking a nosedive into hell! Ginny was at the beginning of the cycle, while she was emerging at the end. Now she knew that what they'd all said about 'time as the only healer' was true. But she wouldn't tell Ginny that. Wouldn't dish out all those dismal, worn out platitudes.

What she would say to Ginny, when the right time came, was that she'd be there for her: to prop her up, provide a shoulder to lean or cry on and help her stand upright in the dark days ahead. That's what real friends were for.

Chapter 23

Edwina and Caron

The weather changed. The sky darkened, rain threatened and there was creeping chill in the air. The sand on St Jude's beach blew in swirling eddies and the sea wall appeared to be sinking; the newly placed giant boulders sucked deeply into the sand as though they were no more substantial than a row of hen's eggs.

Edwina, who was widely known to be funding much of the beach restoration programme with her own capital, called a halt to the activity until erosion experts had been consulted. No expert myself, I could see with my own eyes that, bit by bit, St Jude's once glorious beach was vanishing – only a narrow strip of soft white sand remained and soon, even that would disappear as, heaving and groaning, the sea inched closer.

The problem, Edwina thought, was that they'd taken the beach for granted for years. Waves had come and gone at the whim of the tide but the beach had always been there: high tide or low tide, you'd always been able to walk across miles of sand along a shoreline scattered with seashells and strewn with red and green seaweed. Now the beach had vanished and, from where she was sitting, was simply not coming back. No matter what one did or how much money one threw at it, St Jude's beach was, frankly, fated. She'd listened to what the so-called experts, the consultants, had to say. Acting by rote she'd taken detailed notes, posed probing questions and made suitable and intelligent observations, all the while pondering why she was doing this and, more to the point, why she'd taken back the torch that, not so long ago, she'd entrusted to her successor, Ian Frey?

Her mind spun with all the so-called erosion solutions presented by experts: artificial reefs, groynes, revetments and beach nourishment; each proposal requiring an infusion of more funds than the village would ever be able to raise.

At Edwina's behest, Ian attended the meetings and appeared, at the end of it all, mightily confused. "Beats me!" he admitted, sheepishly. "Whatever we do seems a lost cause." Reluctantly, Edwina was inclined to agree. There were many lost causes. The village was changing: St Jude simply wasn't the place it used to be.

Only yesterday, in the name of progress, one of the developers had started digging up one of the last few remaining green fields; laying water pipes, building drains and, in the process, scattering mongoose, mole rats, honey badgers, storks and cranes. She'd winced with shame watching the gentle creatures scuttle in terror from their once-safe natural habitat. There was a strong temptation to throw in the towel. No one could blame her. She was too old for this kind of thing and as she hurtled down the slippery slopes towards decrepitude she longed for a life less committed to the welfare of St Jude. Responsibility hung heavily, dedication weighed her down.

"I'm tired of all this!" she complained, pushing aside her untouched breakfast – an organic soft-boiled egg and a slice of four-grain bread. "What do I care if the beach is lost to the ocean? What's it to me if they build upon every square inch of good green space in St Jude?"

Mildly, Thomas looked up from a bowl of wrinkled prunes, eyes glazed behind dusty spectacles. He smiled vaguely and removed a prune stone from his mouth.

"Did you hear me, Thomas?"

"Yes, dear. I heard you clearly."

She looked nonplussed. "Well? What do you have to say?"

Thomas glanced furtively at the wall clock and patted his lips with a napkin.

"Good gracious! Is that the time? I am late!"

"Late for what?"

"An appointment." He lifted a delicately flowered Royal Dolton cup swiftly to his lips and gulped a mouthful of cold tea. "Do excuse me, m' dear."

Head bobbing with concentration, Thomas wheeled himself smoothly from the room.

"Where are you going?" she called, but there was no reply.

Edwina flung her teaspoon upon the plate so that it bounced and clattered. How infuriating the man was! How very rude! An appointment? Ha! He was being deliberately secretive in order to punish her for not revealing the name of the mystery telephone caller. He'd been sulking for days. Such behaviour could not be tolerated. She would have to have it out with him!

Caron Grant was shown into the library. Thomas offered tea and invited her to sit down. She perched nervously on the edge of a leather-buttoned armchair.

"Mrs Grant," he said, drawing closer. "Thank you for joining me. It's about James."

"Yes?" She clasped her hands in her lap. One foot tapped the floor.

How to begin? He uttered a dry cough. Her face, lifted towards him, was filled with dread.

"James reminds me of myself at that age," he started. "I was rather solitary. Had more books than friends. Spent a great deal of time alone. Preferred chess to outdoor games. Grew up with a tutor…"

"Oh," her face tensed. "I see where you're going with this. James is going to school next term. He'll have the opportunity to mix with other students and make friends. His life will be less *solitary* …"

"Ahem!" Thomas stopped her by holding up a hand: fingers splayed in the air.

"That's not it at all, Mrs Grant. Not what I'm getting at. If you'll indulge me for a few moments, please?"

A frown. A nod. Her foot continued to tap the floor.

"Forgive me, Mrs Grant. I hope I'm not speaking out of turn, but I have a sense that James is scared and dejected. His life is in turmoil. He's had to handle the devastating loss of a beloved mother and now, the stepmother he has grown so fond of, is leaving him too!"

She looked up from her shoes. "He told you this?"

"Not in so many words. I lost a mother at a young age, I know how he feels. Lonely and scared. Abandoned. Guilty even! James has a fear that he may be the reason for your leaving, that he may have done something unforgivable?"

Thomas saw a flicker of surprise cross her face. "That's not true! His father and I have had problems. Our marriage hasn't been easy. Alec married too soon, before he'd was over the death of his first wife…" She stopped, embarrassed.

She gave a shrug. He noticed she was not wearing a wedding ring though there was a pale strip of flesh where the ring had been.

She continued. "And, to be perfectly honest, my relationship with James has been difficult from the start. I've tried to win his approval and lately I felt we'd grown closer but, well, there've been some problems and now I can't reach him at all."

Suddenly reckless, Thomas inched closer. "I believe James is preparing himself for your departure, Mrs Grant. Punishing you the only way he knows how. Sulking, moodiness, behaving badly: it's all a cry for attention! How else can the boy demonstrate the sorrow he feels about at your leaving?"

She gave a pensive nod. "Yes, I know that's why James has sealed himself off from me. I know that's the only way he can protect himself. I see that. But let me ask you this, Mr Paton – is it fair to James if his father and I remain locked in an unhappy marriage? There's so much bitterness between us and James feels it. He's caught in the middle of it all: all the rows and recrimination. Torn apart by it, just as we are. I can't see any other way. My leaving seems the only solution."

"I see." Thomas felt the fight leaving him like water swirling down a plughole. No easy answers here. Perhaps, if the marriage was this broken, James was better off…

"If James loved me," she cried, "if I felt we had a bond! That it wouldn't always be such a struggle to get close to him…"

Thomas was astonished. "But, James does love you! He is not a demonstrative child. I'm sure you know how hard it is for him to express affection. He does this in unconventional ways. You might have missed the signs!"

Signs? She remembered the card he'd given her after she had lost the baby. The naïve crayon drawing of a stick woman holding a boy's hand: a tiny baby cradled in the crook of the boy's arm. She thought about the way he'd flung himself into her arms that day and how he'd cried: *'I missed you!'*

There'd been many moments when he'd let his guard down. On a few occasions he'd impulsively taken her hand in his, not for long, but long enough to express trust. There'd been that day when he'd proudly read his story of an African Hoopoe, eyes gleaming. She'd seen the signs and they had stirred her with hopefulness.

But then all expression of affection had ended after she'd arranged for him to return to Betty's Bay Primary School in the new term. He'd pulled up the drawbridge again. Stopped talking. Ceased eye contact. If she got too close, if she touched him, he flinched as though scalded.

How much more punishment could she take? And why was it always her? Why did James never feel the need to punish Alec?

"Mrs Grant?"

"Sorry. I was thinking about James. You're right. There have been signs that he feels some affection for me..."

"There! What did I say?"

"But, it's not enough, Mr Paton!" She twisted her skirt into rigid pleats. "I must get away. From Alec, James, the house, this life in St Jude. From all these people: so cold and judgemental, always comparing me to Deborah, with me coming off worst. It's so hard, trying to fit into their lives, trying to adjust, doing my best and yet never succeeding, love so *grudgingly* given..."

Thomas drew back from her impassioned gaze.

"I had no idea," he mumbled. "I'm sorry, my dear. Forgive my meddling. A case of fools rushing in."

"You meant well."

How attractive she looked, he thought, with her trembling mouth; once she relaxed her face, lost that tension in her expression, she was almost pretty.

"I wished only to tell you that James does care for you. And is desperately sad at the idea of losing you. But, I see that there's more to it than you and James. Marriage is a tricky business and, after all, what do I know?"

She seemed to have run out of steam, her head wilting upon her neck. She reached for her handbag. "If there's nothing else?"

"No, nothing. Thank you, Mrs Grant. I wish you well."

She gave a bleak smile and walked awkwardly to the door, shutting it soundlessly behind her.

Thomas sat quite still for several minutes. He'd made rather a mess of everything, and achieved nothing other than to come across as an interfering old geezer with too much time on his hands. Poor James. Poor Mrs Grant, come to that.

The woman looked exhausted: at end of her tether. There was no doubt she'd flee St Jude, leaving behind husband and stepson. Who could blame her, given the circumstances?

"Love so grudgingly given," she'd said and his heart had gone out to her in pity and understanding. He knew what *that* was like; love meted out in mean spoonfuls when one wanted generous shovel loads given unstintingly, unceasingly.

Edwina rapped on the door. "So, your mystery visitor was Caron Grant!" she announced, triumphantly.

"No mystery. Organising chess lessons," he lied.

His shifty swivelling eyes were a dead giveaway. His expression was self-conscious: that wide rictus of a grin. For some reason, Thomas was fibbing. How very curious.

Edwina removed her shoes and curled up on the sofa. Silence fell.

A blackbird warbled in the garden hedge. The fountain splashed. There was the sound of a garden rake, tines hitting upon pebbles. One of the gardeners was trimming the hawthorn hedge with a pair of loppers: the noise was rhythmic and soothing.

Thomas bowed his head, his eyes drooped, his fingers ceased their St Vitas dance. She heard a snore.

"Thomas?" No reply. He'd lied about the chess lessons but what did it matter? Everyone needed a quiet corner in which to be alone. A few, harmless secrets. Being joined at the hip was all very well but occasionally one wanted to break free from potentially suffocating proximity to a loved-one.

She lay back against the cool leather, closing her eyes.

He woke with a start. "You do love me, Edwina?" His voice sounded woeful.

"You know I do."

"How much?" Oh, that childish question again. She suppressed a fluttering of annoyance. "With all my heart," she answered patiently.

He mumbled something under his breath. She did not catch what he said and then there was a guttural snore as, chins shuddering, his mouth dropped open.

She smiled. He looked, at that moment, like a newborn baby: albeit a hairy, wrinkled one.

Silence pressed upon her. So many blessings to count. The love of a kind and dear man. Cherished health. A beautiful home and garden. The wise and caring counsel of the angel. She sent out a quick prayer.

"Thank you," she whispered fervently. "Forgive me for ever doubting you."

Ginny ached. Confined to bed for almost three weeks, her skin hurt as though a web of irritated nerve endings pulsed at every touch. The prickly cactus still bloomed in her throat so that swallowing became an action to be carefully considered and only when absolutely necessary. She wasn't sure if the virus were to blame or if mourning Chris had made her this ill.

A memorial for the missing three had been arranged at the gallery. Sarah and Ben had sent out invitations: over two hundred, although Ginny would have preferred something more intimate.

The day arrived, grey and damp. Sarah had helped her dress that morning and pinned the black velvet skirt to fit her shrinking waist but the jacket made her look like a scarecrow. "Black is not my colour," she had joked, standing at the mirror as Sarah held out the grey cashmere sweater with the tiny seed-pearl collar at the neck which seemed appropriately sober.

It was while she was plaiting her hair that Ginny noticed a wide streak of pure white like a snowy pathway through her parting. His death had done this. Changed her. "I'm glad," she said to Sarah, showing her. "It seems only right that I should look different. I *feel* different! I'm not myself. My whole world has been turned topsy-turvy. Nothing will be the same again."

The long hall of the The Two Potters was decked with saintly white lilies.

The memorial was to be held in the gallery: the only room that could easily accommodate so many guests. Chairs had been arranged in a semi-circle and a table set with large silver-framed photographs of Chris, Mickey and Inga. There were church candles on the table and a large spray of ivory roses.

I wonder if I can stand this? Ginny thought. *I wonder if I can endure it all without collapsing or screaming my head off?*

Most people wore black or charcoal and looked stern, as though it might be a sin to smile on such a day. Everyone insisted upon grasping one of her hands enfolding her in a hug or pecking at both cheeks with their wet lips so that, after a while, she felt pulled and pummelled with their collective sympathy.

Nobody mentioned the word suicide. Instead they used words like 'tragedy' and 'loss' and said they would all be greatly missed.

Ginny was shocked to see Caron with James. "Should he be here?" she whispered to Caron. "It doesn't seem right, somehow."

"He wanted to come," Caron answered. "He insisted."

James saw their heads together. "Chris was my friend," he explained to Ginny. "I'm sad he's dead."

"Yes, I am too." Ginny took his hand.

James stared at the framed photographs. The light from the windows fell in shafts, bathing them with a white glow. Mrs Lourens' hand, icy cold, gripped his fiercely.

People stood murmuring, staring blankly at one another, waiting.

James wondered what Chris would have thought if he'd been here to see his own memorial. The gallery looked the same. People looked the same, except their clothes were mostly black and some of the women wore funny hats. There was a smell of flowers in the air. Nothing had changed except that Chris and his friends were not here and would never be here again.

The rain spattered at the window. There was a low echoing rumble of thunder. Poor Chris. Never to see rain again! James hugged himself. Thinking of it was hardly bearable.

Three musicians arrived carrying violin cases. They started tuning their instruments. There were caterers with silver trays, hot snacks and tiny pastries.

"No, thank you," said James, though Ginny took a prune wrapped in bacon on a stick and held it politely for a few minutes before depositing it in an ashtray.

Finally, the minister arrived – a young woman from Port Victoria wearing a clerical collar and a plain grey suit. Sarah had discovered her after Ginny had confessed that neither she nor Chris had ever been fond of the Reverend Watson.

"Too sanctimonious," Ginny had said. "Too holier than thou."

"Call me Pastor Jane," the young woman said, introducing herself to Ginny.

James thought she looked very clean as though she'd just had a shower. Her face and hair were shiny, her teeth were white and she had short, pink fingernails.

He could see his reflection in her serious black shoes.

"Let us pray," she said, closing her eyes so that long black lashes fanned her cheeks.

Ginny felt numb, muffled in dense swaddling, the words coming from somewhere far away. Concentrate, she said to herself. Listen carefully so that you can remember something of this …

"*Grant them peace from their inner turmoil,*" intoned Pastor Jane.

Her voice rang like a clear bell through the gallery. "*Grant them the compassion of your love.*"

Ben put his arm around her waist. She leaned into his warm bulkiness.

"Comfort those who mourn the loss of their loved ones. Help them to reach out in love..."

"She knows," Ginny whispered, heavily.

"What?"

"She knows how they died."

He tightened his arm around her middle. "She knows they were lost at sea," he mouthed. "That's all."

But Ginny knew that Pastor Jane knew. She'd been told. Or read about it in the newspapers. The prayer was most specific. *'Inner turmoil'* was one clue. *'The compassion of your love'* another. Did everyone know, then?

She closed her eyes and stopped listening.

Caron, watching James, saw his face crumple as the woman began to pray.

She navigated the room unobtrusively until she reached his side and grabbed his hand, leading him away from Ginny. They stood in the gallery entrance, watching a silver shower of falling rain.

"Perhaps it wasn't a good idea to come," she said quietly.

He sniffed loudly. "Chris was my friend. I wanted to be here. Anyway, I'm not crying. I never cry!" He chewed his lip and stared at the rain.

"It's OK to cry, James."

He squeezed his eyes shut. Large tears dripped and fell.

"Come here!" She pulled James towards her and wrapped her arms around him.

He stiffened. She waited for him to break away but, with a shudder, he sank, weeping into her woollen skirt. She touched his back, the vulnerable ridge of his spine. She rubbed the crown of his spiky head. She felt a flooding of unbearable love. "Oh, James!"

He pulled away, glaring up in fury through misted glasses. "Why are you going?" he demanded. "Why are you leaving us?"

She dropped to her knees. She gazed intently. "Tell me honestly, do you want me to stay? Would you be happy if I stayed?"

Her words shocked. Startled, he blinked away hot tears. Sniffing loudly, he pulled a tissue from his pocket and blew hard.

"Yes," he mumbled. "Yes, please."

They regarded one another awkwardly. Caron gave a quick nod, a fleeting smile.

The sound of violins soared from the gallery. The notes rose higher and higher.

"Shall we go home, then?"

He wiped his face with the balled tissue.

Music flowed like silk, filling the room.

"How long will you stay?" he asked deliberately. He stared with taut attention.

Caron took a deep breath. "For as long as you want," she answered.

The music seemed to swell in his chest.

He deliberated. "OK." He gave an emphatic nod.

She opened the umbrella and held it out in the rain. "Ready?"

They ran together towards the car.

The caterers served white wine with an endless supply of snacks. Voices grew louder: erupting now and then into laughter. The three dark-suited violinists swayed together, eyes half-closed, lost in the ecstasy of surging chamber music.

Ginny found herself searching for his face amongst the crowd of mourners.

He would have stood taller than anyone else, moving with an easy grace, that lazy smile, his eyes meeting hers with affection.

"I miss him," she said to anyone who asked how she was coping.

They left early: Ginny, Sarah and Ben, trusting the caterers to clean up and lock the gallery afterwards. Sarah went home to pick up Lucky and joined them in the kitchen. Rain pattered on the roof and slid down the windows. Ben set out mugs and brewed a pot of strong tea. "I'm glad that's over!" he said, fervently.

Ginny reached out her arms to both of them. "You've been so wonderfully, selflessly kind! I would never have managed without the two of you!"

They stared at one another, wordlessly, each lost in their private thoughts.

Ben marvelled at how much they'd endured and survived since that day when Chris and the two women had gone out in the boat. How every day their love seemed stronger. *This is it*, he thought, *this is what I've been waiting for.*

Sarah felt grateful that she could now look upon Ben and Ginny and feel happy for them. She'd had her chance with Ben and thrown it away. Now it was Ginny's turn and nobody deserved the love of a good, kind man more than Ginny, especially now she'd lost her beloved son.

Ginny fretted over whether Ben would eventually grow weary of all her messy tearfulness, grieving and sadness and turn away from her. How would she stand it? *He's all that keeps me together*, she thought. *All I have left.*

Lucky slept soundly beneath the table soothed by the endless tapping of the rain.

Grace lifted her glass to Edwina.

"You're looking well," she commented, against the crescendo of violins.

"Thank you." Edwina bowed her head in acknowledgement. "I feel it!"

Dressed from head to toe in blood red, Edwina's concession to the seriousness of the occasion was a miniscule cap of black feathers.

"Red becomes you!"

"Chris would have approved, I think. As for this ..." She waved her wine glass in the general direction of the gathered assemblage. "Too mournful by far! He would have preferred a rousing, drunken party to celebrate the end of his life."

Grace deliberated. "I disagree," she said, finally. "I think Chris wanted to leave quietly, fading from sight without a fuss. No final farewells of any kind."

"Not my scene! Bells and whistles for me when the end comes!"

"Speaking of that, I'd like to do some tests. Are you open to the idea?"

"Tests? What kind of tests?"

"Blood tests. Scans. I'd like to check the progress of your cancer."

"No. Absolutely not! I've told you before! No tests. No chemo. No radiation treatment."

"Hear me out, Edwina. I'm curious. You appear to have cured yourself with vitamins, an organic diet and yoga, or whatever it is that you do. All this goes against my experience, my instincts! I'd like to do some tests to satisfy myself that your cancer is in remission. No charge, this is for my own account!"

"Good grief, Grace! I'm not a guinea pig. My cancer has been cured. I don't need to prove it to you or anyone else. Just look at me!"

"But…"

"There will come a time when I will need your help, in which case I shall ask for it. You may trust me on that. Until then, I suggest that, as an up-and-coming doctor, you keep an open mind regarding alternate cancer therapies."

"Fair enough. What do you put it down to, then? What *specifically* do you believe has cured your cancer?"

"Faith, I think." Edwina sipped thoughtfully from her glass. "That and divine intervention. Do you believe in angels, Grace?"

"What were you and Edwina talking about?" Ian asked his wife as they gave their farewells and prepared to leave.

"Mumbo jumbo," said Grace crossly. "A whole lot of silly mumbo jumbo!"

When Alec returned home that evening, the kitchen smelled of burnt sugar. Caron and James were making fudge. His heart lifted at the sound of James laughing, it had been a long time, forever really, since he'd heard his son hooting with mirth. He stood dripping in the gloom of the darkening hallway, fearful of breaking the spell.

"Knock, Knock, who's there?" Caron's voice.

"Lettuce!"

"Lettuce who?"

"Lettuce in, it's cold out here!" A burst of manic giggling from James.

Alec pushed open the kitchen door.

James, cheeks flushed, wore one of Caron's baking aprons. He was lifting squares of hardened fudge from a baking tray, placing them in a plastic container.

"Hey Dad! Fudge! We've chocolate and vanilla! Want a piece?"

With a curious glance at Caron, Alec crammed a square into his mouth.

"Good news, Dad!"

"Yes?"

"Caron's not going away! She's staying here with us. Forever!"

Disbelieving, Alec searched her eyes. She stared back, steadfastly.

"Is that true?"

"I'd like to talk to you about it ..."

"You are staying!" James dropped a piece of fudge on the floor. "You said so! You promised!"

"Yes, I am, James. But I must talk to your Dad. There are things we need to discuss."

"I'm glad!" Alec burst out. "I'm glad you've decided to stay. It's what I always wanted!"

"We'll talk about it, later." Her voice was quietly firm.

Alec took James upstairs and ran the bath for him. James was excited, silly, laughing at nothing.

"Say 'knock, knock' Dad! Go on, say..."

"Knock, knock, who's there!'"

"Police!"

"Police who?"

"Police let me in!" James shrieked with laughter.

Alec felt a wave of sympathy. Poor kid. His heart throbbed perilously with love and sorrow in equal measure. "I'm sorry, James," he said. "You've had a rough time. Things will get better, I promise."

"Knock, knock!" James shouted. "Your turn! Knock, knock, who's there?"

They waited until he had fallen asleep, exhausted from over-excitement.

"What changed your mind?"

"Thomas Paton."

"Who?"

"The man James plays chess with. He told me James loves me and doesn't want me to leave."

"I could have told you that."

"I might not have believed you, but I believed Thomas. He knows James. He had nothing to gain by telling me."

"Where do we go from here?"

"We start again. Try harder. Make this work, if we can. If only for James."

He leaned towards her. "But it's not only for James. He's important, I admit. But we've got to make this work for us too. We were happy once, in the beginning, before we..."

"I want to make some changes. I want us to do things differently."

He murmured consent. He could tell from her expression that there was no room for negotiation here: he was going to have to take a back seat, play it her way.

"No more home-schooling. You were right. James needs the company and stimulation of other children."

"Does he know?"

"Not yet. No sports, Alec! He prefers other things: chess, astronomy, debating. He's hopeless at sports."

He heard himself sigh. "Whatever you say," he replied, obediently.

"There's to be no more quarrelling between us. James has heard and seen too much. We've got to make more of an effort. You'll have to learn to control your temper. We'll try to talk through our problems: he doesn't have to know what's going on, what's happening between us. It's not fair to subject him to…" Her voice was filled with righteous anger.

"I get it, Caron! I do. I know where we've gone wrong and I want to make things right between us. I want us to be a proper family."

She quietened.

"What about you? What are you going to do?"

"Go back to teaching, as we planned. There might be a post for me at Betty's Bay Primary, I'm waiting to hear from Helen Morris. I'd like some help at home. I've found someone who can come three days a week."

Alec reached out and took her hand. She resisted the impulse to pull away.

"Whatever you want," he said humbly, gratefully. "I'll go along with whatever you want." He took her hand. "You're not wearing your wedding ring!"

She gave a wry smile. "That's the bad news," she said. "I've lost it. You'll have to buy me another."

The next morning, Caron phoned Thomas.

"You were right about James," she said. "He needs me. I think we might be able to make this work. I've decided to stay."

She heard a rattling intake of breath. Thomas cleared his throat. "Good!" He tried to muster enthusiasm. "Very good! James must be so pleased?"

"Yes, he is. I wanted to thank you for being so candid and honest. For caring enough to tell me about James…"

There was a pregnant pause during which Thomas wondered what else he should say and came up with nothing more than, "Well, thank you for calling, Mrs Grant. I hope that all goes well."

Replacing the receiver, he was assailed by misgivings, doubt and dread.

He'd meddled in Caron Grant's life. Changed the flow of it. The outcome. She'd been soon to flee. The marriage, she'd said, had been difficult. Complicated. He'd heard rumours; Alec Grant was said to be something of a selfish bastard. There were suspicions that she'd lost a child, had a miscarriage.

Now she'd decided to stay and all because he'd told her how wretched James was at the prospect of her leaving. What had he done? More to the point, what had it to do with him?

Single-handedly he'd transformed the lives of three people through a mistaken idea that by imparting information, he might be helping in some way.

Remorse pricked. He'd spent too long with Edwina. Had picked up her habit of prying and snooping and intruding in the private lives of others. Had he done the right thing or should he have left well enough alone? Would he ever know?

Only time would tell.

Chapter 24

Edwina, Grace and Alec

'So, they have gone
All of them
Silenced forever.
And in the wake of their going
Lies become truth
As surely as the present
Becomes the past.
You can hear gates
Clanging
As they fade
Into darkness.
Memories become myths
Colours fade to monochrome.
Now that solitude is upon us
Tell me, did they ever exist?'

Dawood Hill. Poet Laureate.

Six months lapsed and the village returned to 'normal'.

St Jude emerged from the grip of a hard winter and waited expectantly for the healing warmth of summer.

I had spent the season confined to my study, writing this account of what happened that year. There were a few loose strands yet to be tied but, at this point, the story seemed complete. Except...

Except the disappearance of the three remained an unexplained enigma. Two months ago the remains of a deflated, damaged blue dingy washed ashore near Hamilton Cove, thousands of nautical miles beyond St Jude. Ginny identified the dingy as the Lourens' boat. The three bodies were never found. The mystery gnawed at me.

Soon after the memorial, Inga's father; Professor Erik Johansson, arrived unannounced in Betty's Bay where he was seen to be discretely and systematically arranging Inga's affairs: packing her possessions and organising the sale of her loft studio. Those who offered condolences said the Professor appeared civil but emotionless. Inga's good friend, Nina, who'd been weeping in fits and starts since Inga's disappearance, threw herself sobbing at the Professor and was mortified beyond words as he winced his way out of her tight embrace and, straightening his jacket, asked in a stilted voice for her name and her relationship to his daughter.

"That frozen stare!" she exclaimed. "Erik Johansson is as 'cold as ice'."

Mickey had left a sealed will in one of her desk drawers nominating Edwina as her executor. Mickey's estranged father, the famous horticulturist Michael Graham, politely declined to attend the memorial or participate in the dispersal of her possessions and so the task fell to Edwina to ensure that The St Jude Animal Shelter received all proceeds accruing from the sale of the Northwind Nursery and its contents.

Interestingly, it was Sarah, seeking a new challenge now that the gallery ran like clockwork, who purchased the house and nursery and, together with Ginny, turned the entire area over to the planting of a massive herb garden.

The two women, along with a couple of paid helpers, set out rows of pink, white and French lavender, lemon verbena, rosemary, sage, fennel, dill, chives, basil, chamomile and coriander and transformed the house into an airy, open-plan room where herbs could be dried and packaged fresh, ready to be marketed.

Groves of fruit trees: apricot, peach, cherry and lemon interspersed with olive and almond trees were planted so that, later, when the trees bore fruit, there would be an opportunity to diversify into producing jars of preserves, thick lemon marmalade and cherries in brandy. The almonds would be sold plain or toasted; the olives bottled or crushed for oil and paste; the lavender flowers dried or used to make lavender oil and water. It was Sarah who insisted on retaining the 'Folly's Garden' brand name, together with the original labels designed by Chris as a way of keeping the cherished memories of Mickey and Chris alive.

For Ginny, grieving and sorrowful, the routine and hard work needed to plant the herb garden came as a blessing, providing a reason to get out of bed and a way to keep sane during that long, cold, desperately sad winter.

People got on with their lives.

James Grant went back to school and made a friend.

Abigail Lake was tall for her age, freckled and plain with a mane of wild, curly hair that, as she grew older, would become her best feature but was for now simply untidy. She felt her heart lurch with love the moment she saw James shuffling into Mrs Morris' classroom.

"I also wear braces!" she announced at break, leaning close and offering a wide and gleaming grimace. James fastidiously averted his eyes and nibbled at a cream cheese and cucumber sandwich cut in a perfect triangle. Abigail delved into her own plastic lunch box and, extracting a leaking jam roll, gobbled it down in three greedy bites.

"Yuck!" said James, pulling a face and brushing a stray crumb from his chin.

He sternly ignored Abigail for three days during which time he discovered that, next to him, she was the brightest in the class. Abigail Lake's hand was raised so often in response to 'who knows?' questions that she generally kept her right arm lazily folded over her unruly head, ready to fling it aloft whenever the occasion demanded.

Clearly fond of Abigail, Mrs Morris permitted her the 'teacher's pet' blackboard cleaning and classroom monitor privileges denied less ambitious students and allowed her to confidently read aloud the morning prayer every Monday morning in her husky, rasping voice.

It was when James discovered Abigail was not only a fellow Harry Potter fan but also a member of the Chess Club and said to be keen on astronomy, that he finally relented.

"Do you want to be my friend?" he demanded.

"Yes, please!"

"OK, well, stop following me about then."

When Caron came to collect him that day, James introduced the tall, ungainly girl towering above him: "This is my new best friend, Abigail!"

Abigail grabbed Caron around her waist with her long, strong arms and gave an exuberant grin. Caron laughed: with her dress rucked up in the back, shoes unlaced and straggly hair falling over her eyes, Abigail seemed an unlikely companion for finicky James.

Inserting a rough, inky paw into Caron's hand, Abigail prodded James. "Your mum's very pretty!" she whispered hoarsely.

Face solemnly lifted, James looked at Caron. "Yeah!" he agreed. "She is."

Alec put the house on the market and discovered another near the beach that he hoped Caron and James would like.

Selling the house was probably one of the hardest things he'd ever had to do, akin, he thought, to brutally lopping off an arm or a leg, but it was his way of demonstrating readiness for a new beginning and a life no longer coloured by the memories and possessions his first wife had left behind.

The house was a square, unpretentious structure of rough unplastered brick, painted white and hidden behind a row of tall pines and cypresses. It had a steep thatch roof and ample fireplaces in both sitting rooms and all four upstairs bedrooms. From the upstairs balcony there was an undisturbed view of the ocean, the garden and a winding path that led from the rusty wrought iron gate directly to the beach.

Caron loved the house. She loved its simplicity: the lofty ceilings, chaste white painted pine floors, the pristine sweep of an oak staircase and complete absence of anything linked to Deborah. "Our house," she said to Alec. "It feels like *our* house!"

James, who'd been horrified at the idea of selling the family home and told them both sternly that he wouldn't move a single centimetre unless he could find a bedroom *exactly* like the one he had, confused himself by also approving of the new house although the bedroom singled out for him couldn't have been more different.

He thought there was something magical about the way the house turned its back upon the village and hid behind a rustling screen of fragrant Christmas trees. The upstairs bedroom, the one he chose as his room, was the smallest of the four, with a dormer window through which he could clearly see the endless blue of the sea. There were white shutters at the windows and a curved window seat. He could hear waves breaking on the shore and smell salt in the air. "This is a good place to look at the moon," he said thoughtfully, standing before the window, gazing above the tops of the trees at the space where he imagined a blanched moon. "I like it here."

Agreeing to sell the house was only one of the concessions Alec willingly made. There were many others. The basketball hoop had been stored in the garage along with various soccer balls, tennis racquet, baseball bat and cricket bat he'd bought as gifts for James.

There was a housekeeper now: a sunny, energetic woman who cleaned the house and supervised James' homework on days when Caron had to stay late at the school. Caron taught six-and-seven-year-olds at a feeder school for Betty's Bay and earned a modest salary that gave the taste of the freedom and independence she craved.

The most important change in all their lives, was the closeness that had grown between Caron and James. Alec wondered that he'd never observed the similarities between them before. With their shared quirkiness, private obsessions and desire for perfection, they could easily have been mother and son. Sometimes he jealously resented their newfound intimacy and felt Caron had taken James from him but then he remembered the way it had been with Deborah and James and was glad for his son.

"Are you happy?" Caron had asked the other night.

He'd kissed her in answer, filled with an indescribable yearning for something he couldn't put his finger on.

He wasn't happy in a reckless, jaunty, frisky high-spirited way. Not the treading on air, mad with love happy you'd give your back teeth for, nothing like that. He supposed *contented* might describe his condition better.

Things were better than before. They'd got past the endless, senseless arguing and cold, empty silences.

They made love regularly but sex had become more ordinary. The way it did, he supposed, amongst most married couples once the mystery had worn off.

James, however, was truly happy. You could see it in his face, his eyes, the way he sang under his breath in that tuneless way; the skips of excitement he gave when walking; the way he slipped his hand into yours and left it there. James was happy and, when all was said and done, that was all that mattered.

"Are you happy?" Caron had asked Alec. He'd pressed his lips on hers, taken her into his arms, rested his chin on the top of her head, but hadn't answered, which had been answer enough. He felt the way she did then.

She was considerably wiser now, not as happy as once she'd hoped either. Many of the things she'd once adored about her husband had begun to seem annoying. The way he dressed. His expensive shirts, ties and designer suits, the polished leather shoes and Rolex watch no longer filled her with swooning pride but made him appear conceited and smug. His dashing looks no longer melted her heart. There were times when she saw right through to the insincere heart of his urbane and charming manner. His persuasiveness now seemed like bullying, his sensitivity like weakness and his authoritative strength like control.

She loved him still though, in spite of his many flaws and insincerities. She'd discovered that knowing your partner could be profoundly liberating and no longer in his thrall, under the spell of him, she had the strength to reclaim some of the power in the relationship so that he no longer had things all his own way.

She'd made peace with the fact that James would be her only child. "My son," she always said, introducing him and seeing James' quick, shy, rapturous glance at her in response.

In a way, she was relieved that her internal clock had stopped its infernal tick-tocking and things had worked out as they had. The responsibility for two children in a world gone mad, a world filled with unspeakable terrors would have been too much. James was enough: more than enough: he was all she wanted and needed.

Edwina and Ian quarrelled.

She instructed him to resume joint responsibility for the Environ and Save the Beach projects. "I've changed my mind which, as you well know, is a woman's prerogative," she announced peremptorily. "My work here is done! Now it's your turn!"

"I've told you," he said irritably. "Not my thing. Find someone more capable."

There ensued a frosty silence, unbroken for five weeks during which Edwina reluctantly resumed funding of building operations and the seawall grew higher.

Ian was the first to come around. "I've had an idea," he said. "Can we talk?"

He brought a sheaf of drawings and laid them on the table. Edwina gave them her full attention. They were rather well rendered pencil illustrations of what appeared to be a stone jetty, running parallel to the stonewall on the beach. Odd macaroni shapes, in various sizes, protruded from the stone.

She looked up, perplexed. "I don't understand. Do tell!"

He jabbed at the drawing of the jetty. "Granite slabs," he explained. "There's an old house being demolished. I can salvage some of the stone. We'll have to buy the rest."

"But what are these?" Edwina pointed to the curious tubes emerging from the stone.

"Ah!" he grinned. "That's the sorcery! PVC pipes and cement tubes used to create a musical masterpiece."

Instantly intrigued, Edwina's brows ascended as she peered at the drawings. He told her the story in a rush. He'd read about an acoustic sculpture in San Francisco, created on a spit of land, jutting into the bay. Crafted by an artist and a stonemason, the sculpture was a complex, stepped platform made from PVC pipes, cement tubes, stones and blocks.

"Pipes are located at different elevations within the jetty. Waves hit against the pipes and seawater floods in and out as tides rise and fall. The rushing movement of the water creates music."

"What kind of music?"

"Rumbling, wheezing, thundering. Sharps and flats. Noises like drums, harps, woodwind, cymbals, percussion – you name it!"

Edwina imagined waves slapping against vibrating metal. She heard the gurgling, hissing, boiling and whistling of salty water pouring through open pipes. The music resonated in her head. *It might sound something like the whale song*, she thought. High trills and delicate chirps caught between long, deep moans and dull, echoing roars.

"Environmental music!" she said. "How inventive!"

They smiled at one another.

She came to her senses first. "But what does any of this have to do with erosion? How will your musical pipes help save our diminishing beach?"

Ian gave a careless shrug. "Oh, it won't. But, think of the publicity! People will flock to listen to the music. It'll call attention to our plight. Perhaps we can start some kind of erosion fund? Encourage donations?"

Edwina tapped her front teeth with a scarlet fingernail.

"You can do this? Build the stone jetty? Install the pipes? Get them to make music? You're absolutely sure?"

"I think so. Not my original idea – it's been done before so it's obviously possible. It'll be a case of trial and error. I'll start with a model and take it from there."

Edwina leaned back in her chair, eyes half-closed. She could see it all!

A glorious summer's day: a lapis lazuli sky with seagulls circling. A catered picnic on the pier, perhaps.

A formal unveiling: the bright flash of scissors shearing a length of wide blue ribbon. She would give a short, poetic speech. Something about a hypnotic symphony created by the union of land and sea. Sacred music. Someone – who was it? – had a line: '*wild sounds civilised into time and tune*'. That would do rather well.

Journalists on the guest list, loads of publicity.

"*Today, St Jude's Edwina Hurley, Chairperson of Environ, unveiled a new musical masterpiece...*"

"I have the perfect name for it!"

"Yes?"

"St Jude's Pan Pipes!"

"Good." A nod. "I take it you approve?"

"Approve? My dear Ian it's a stroke of genius! This is inspired. I take it all back. All the insults and brickbats. You really are a very clever boy!"

Grace found herself becoming more spiritual.

That thing with Edwina, the metastasised tumour healing itself, confused her. It went against scientific training. She spoke to several highly reputable oncologists who agreed that it simply wasn't possible – and yet, it had happened and she'd witnessed the 'miracle' herself. With Edwina's reluctant permission, she'd even taken photographs of the shrinking tumour, once the size of a grapefruit, now reduced to a small egg, a pigeon's egg. Exactly *how* had the tumour healed itself? The patient had religiously followed an organic, meat-free, fat-free, sugar-free nutritious diet supplemented with vitamins and antioxidants, had regular massage sessions and used yoga as a method of relaxation.

"Faith", she said, finally, to her colleagues. "Faith cured this patient."

Their expressions betrayed either lightly veiled amusement or outright cynicism and scorn. They thought she had lost it and 'gone over to the other side' and, for the shortest while, she had. She signed on for 'Alternative Cancer Therapy' workshops and discovered a great deal about Enzymatic therapy, Electrotherapy, Bio-resonance, diet and food therapies and oxygen and ozone treatments.

"What have you learned?" The question had been asked in mocking tones at a Breast Cancer Symposium by Port Victoria's leading oncologist, Iris Bloom.

Doctor Bloom; sixty-something with a man's haircut, was a traditionalist, known to pooh-pooh all alternative cancer therapies.

Grace considered the question. "I've learned to keep an open mind," she replied diplomatically.

"Indeed?" There it was again, that withering expression.

"Yes!" Grace held her ground. "I plan to use some of the more successful alternative treatments as an adjunct to traditional cancer therapy."

At that point, Dr Bloom snorted: "Quackery!" and pointedly engaged one of the other medical practitioners in conversation.

Grace cleared her throat and sang out bravely: "They say that doctors integrating traditional and non-traditional therapies are making the greatest progress in the fight against cancer…"

Her words fell upon deaf ears.

Always one to count her blessings, Grace took to regularly visiting a small church in Betty's Bay. The church was ordinary, with little to commend it other than a pretty stained glass window depicting twin panels of birds and flowers in opalescent glass.

The church had become her refuge, a place where she could rest and think and give thanks. Grace told no one of her visits, not even Ian, in case he'd think she'd suddenly become 'born-again' for this was not the case.

It was truer that she'd become more superstitious: her visits to the church a form of ritual, like touching wood to prevent harm falling upon the family.

They'd survived dark moments: Ian's crippling depression and the fire that had almost destroyed their home. There'd been tragedy: the three suicides and the untimely death of more patients than she cared to remember.

She lit candles: for Ian, steadfast and loving; for Josh and Rosie, the joy they gave. Flames flickered for Chris, Mickey and Inga, for young lives wasted. Candles glowed for the sick and the dying. Frail shadows loomed on walls, light spilled.

Grace thawed in the soft, white radiance and murmured grateful thanks for abundance bestowed. For life, love, health and happiness.

Thomas looked forward to James' visits.

Caron brought him to play chess after school every Thursday afternoon from three until four thirty and every second Friday afternoon they spent an hour or two bird watching and pouring over Thomas' rare, out-of-print books on ornithology.

Because he was so interested in the subject, Thomas presented James with a gift of '*The Mute Swan*' and a book about golden eagles.

Thomas discovered that he longed for these chess afternoons like an impatient child, watching the hands of the clock until they reached three when James would arrived in his hardly-creased school uniform and, after depositing his satchel, settle comfortably in the chair opposite and politely enquire whether Thomas was ready 'to be checkmated'.

James kept him on his toes; made him think and provided a rare opportunity to hone what he imagined might be rapidly disintegrating grey matter, falling to dust, gone to pieces, his memory shot to hell.

More and more he saw himself in James at the same age. His unloving and aloof parents had paid him scant attention. Books had saved him. Music had saved him. Chess had given him something of a reputation.

"You could be my alter ego."

With a quizzical look, James had shaken his head doubtfully. "I don't think so. Caron says I need to develop my self-confidence."

"No, no!" Thomas had given a wheeze of amusement. "An alter ego is a second self. A very dear friend."

"Oh!" James had beamed. "Brilliant!"

Last week he'd taught the boy '*The King's Indian Attack*', a system used by White in reply to almost any Black opening moves and this week he planned to demonstrate the very useful '*Queen's Gambit*'.

Edwina found Thomas in the library, preparing for James' visit. He was bent almost double over the board, muttering to himself.

"What's that?" she enquired. "What did you say? I didn't catch it."

"White starts by moving the Queen's pawn to 'd4'..."

"Oh, Thomas! Surely you can beat a child at chess?"

"Can *you?*"

She was discomforted, but only for a moment. "Not my game!" she retorted. "Besides which, I don't promote myself as a former 'grandmaster'."

"Do shut the door," he replied rudely, "on your way out!"

She laughed in spite of herself. "You've suddenly become shamelessly brazen! I wonder why?"

"Libido?" he suggested, with a goblin gleam.

"Ha! You've as much libido as a feather duster!"

His face fell.

She took pity. "Hubris, perhaps?" she volunteered.

He brightened. "Isn't that the same thing?"

"Almost!" she offered, kindly.

He smiled tenderly. "I do love you, Edwina."

She looked down at the top of his head: the tender pink freckled scalp, the few white wisps of elderly hair, so carefully combed. His milky blue eyes sought her approval.

I love you too, she thought. *More than you could ever imagine.*

"Silly old thing!" she said, slamming the door behind her.

Ben learned to take life one day at a time. Ginny's period of mourning, he knew, would be long – with no easy way to shorten it. He was reconciled to the idea of simply doing his best to be there for her. His practice grew alarmingly so that it seemed that he worked all the daylight hours and sometimes, since sheep were lambing, late into the night. With breakfast of an apple and lunch a snatched sandwich; he was ravenous, pulling up outside Ginny's house after a long, hard day.

She was always there to greet him, her lovely face glowing; a casserole in the oven, wine opened, music playing.

Agreeing to keep their separate homes, they'd made a promise to enjoy dinner together as often as possible, mostly at home, sometimes in a restaurant.

When he was not on call, Ben spent free weekends at the Lourens' house.

He kept a change of clothes in Ginny's cupboards: his dull brown trousers hanging between exotic skirts, formal white shirts amongst vibrantly hued blouses, scarves and shawls. His toothbrush, cologne, deodorant and razor made their way into her bathroom and he showered using Ginny's fragranced soaps and special shampoos to tame curly hair.

Ben loved Ginny's house: the warmth and comfort of thick quilts, soft pillows, clean sheets.

He was charmed beyond words by the feminine clutter of her

jewellery on the dressing table along with glass bottles of perfume, pots of creams and lotions and the heavy silver-backed mirror that had once belonged to her mother.

He loved the incongruity of her small, embroidered slippers placed neatly besides his enormous mud-caked boots in the hallway, his fleece-lined jacket nestling intimately against her fine, purple wool cloak. It had been years since he'd lived with a woman: with flowers arranged in vases, knitting or sewing half-forgotten on a chair, a cake cooling on a rack.

"I don't know if I can ever return to bachelor life," he'd admitted.

She'd been pleased, he could see. There was that telltale flush, the lowering of her eyes, a shy smile, her head tilted. "Good! I'm happy too! I'd like everything to stay like this. Just as it is, forever and ever."

Ben wasn't sure about that. For his part, he'd have preferred a greater commitment, life together under one roof. He was ready to sell his place and use part of the proceeds to make improvements to Ginny's home. Some of the windows needed replacing. The kitchen could be modernised. The thatch roof needed repairing.

He'd brought up the idea once or twice but Ginny had seemed uncomfortable and quickly changed the subject. It was the age thing, he suspected, that stopped her from making that final move. He didn't care that Ginny was older than he but she frequently drew reference to the number of years between them.

He'd tried to reassure her. "I love only you, Ginny. I don't want anyone else. As for age, well, it's only a number."

It was Sarah who'd given him a nudge. "Don't rush her," she'd warned. "It's too soon. There'll come a time when Ginny will be ready to settle down. Until then, take it slowly."

She was right. In the last few months he'd witnessed a subtle change in Ginny: she seemed to laugh more readily, to sigh less. The tension and sorrow in her face began gradually to fade. He didn't comment. To say anything or call attention to her new happiness would be to remind her of the pain of losing Chris and the duty of a mother to grieve for her son. But his heart felt buoyant and boyish with the anticipation of a long life together with a woman he'd come to love.

Sarah was interviewed by a journalist from the high-circulation, glossy feminist publication: 'Ms.' and though, on first sight she took an instant dislike to Jayne Horne, Sarah had to hand it to her; she'd researched Sarah's background meticulously and knew all the details: Sarah's previous career in marketing, David Kennedy's life and death, the acquisition of shares in The Two Potters and the recent purchase of Folly's Garden Nursery.

"You've been a busy girl!" Jayne announced approvingly, lighting a cigarette and exhaling blue smoke.

"Yes, I suppose I have." Sarah tried not to stare.

The woman's beige, powdery face appeared to have been softened by too many glasses of wine and her lipstick bled into fine puckers above her mouth. Matte black hair scraped back in a too-tight chignon lifted her eyebrows several centimetres.

Jayne Horne placed a small, black recorder on the table and switched it on. "Do you mind?"

"Not at all." Sarah coughed. Smoke circled lazily above the journalist's head.

The interview lasted over an hour.

"You're the kind of woman our readers admire," Jayne Horne remarked appreciatively at the end, unplugging the recorder. "Strong, gutsy, entrepreneurial. Fiercely independent, visionary even! I take my hat off, I really do!"

Sarah had squirmed with discomfort. "That's not how I see myself…"

"It's how our readers will see you. You're *inspirational!*"

Jayne towered above Sarah, thin as a stick insect, gathering her things.

Her leopard print pumps marched aggressively to the door. "It's been a rare privilege!" she concluded, with a firm handshake.

"God, David!" said Sarah in the silence. "I've been interviewed. People will read about me. It seems unreal. What's happening?"

She picked up David's photograph. His image gazed serenely back at her with an untroubled expression. What would he have said? She tried to imagine his response. *"I'm so proud of you, darling."* Was that it? He might have laughed at her hard-won: 'five minutes of fame!' On the other hand, there was a good chance he'd have been annoyed at her being interviewed by, of all things, a stridently feminist publication.

She had no idea what David would have thought or said about the interview. No idea whatsoever. She replaced the photograph on the table.

Lucky sat waiting, tail beating rhythmically on the floor, mouth open in a wide, sloppy grin. He gave a yip. Sarah clipped on the leash and led the excited dog outdoors. The sky was with clouds that looked like white doves in flight. The wind whipped a swirling veil of sand from the rippled dunes: the tide was rushing in, covering the stretch of hard, flat sand. Sarah let Lucky off his leash and watched him bound ahead.

She felt a catch in her throat. *Inspirational!* she thought. *Me?*

Chapter 25

Chris, Inga and Mickey

I had reached the end of my manuscript and concluded my tale with life in St Jude returning to some kind of normality, with many lives transformed and restored and more than one happy ending.

But what in God's name had happened to the three in the boat? I couldn't get them out of my mind. When I began writing this book I imagined that, by the end, the mystery would have been resolved, I'd know exactly what had transpired on that fateful day and yet, here I was, no wiser. The truth had been lost amidst a welter of rumour, suspicion, mistrust and conjecture. No one uttered their names any more other than in hushed whispers as though speaking of a guilty secret.

I considered inventing an explanation since this was, after all, a novel and I was entitled to throw imaginary light upon the disappearance and present my own fabricated conclusion. I considered the suicide pact: the three of them swallowing a lethal handful of pills, saying their tragic goodbyes…

I considered the tiny craft accidentally capsizing and hurling them into icy waves, saw them hanging on, growing numb and frozen…

But what had really happened?

It was almost unbearable not knowing the truth.

On an impulse I made a call to Stockholm to speak to Professor Erik Johansson. There was a very good chance he'd refuse any conversation with a resident from St Jude, the village he'd lost his daughter to, but I thought perhaps he might have softened during the past months? Perhaps he had some ideas about his daughter's death that he might be persuaded to share with me? Perhaps she'd written to him telling him something of her plans. His behaviour when he came to sort through her things, his deliberately chilly manner and taciturn silence indicated something of the kind.

I rehearsed my introduction. I planned to tell the professor that I was a respected author with a number of moderately successful books to my credit.

I had been writing an account of...

A woman answered. "The professor is not at home," she replied softly. "May I give him a message?"

I couldn't believe it! "Is that you, Inga?"

There was a pause before the receiver was quietly replaced and I heard only the distant, protracted hum of dialling tone.

My first emotion was one of overwhelming triumph and elation. She's not dead!

Inga Johansson had not drowned on that foredoomed day. Unless I was much mistaken, she was alive and well and living with her father in Stockholm.

I called again immediately and heard a man's recorded voice: deep and guttural, speaking in Swedish.

My next call was to my travel agent to book a return trip to Stockholm.

"Are you sure you want to travel now?" she asked. "The Swedish winter can be grim. Why not wait for summer, or at least, for spring?"

"I must fly at once!" I announced. "When do I depart?"

I packed a small suitcase with warm clothing and left for Stockholm late the next afternoon.

The capital of Scandinavia was new to me but I'd done a brief crash course, skimming through a selection of tour guides during the flight.

By the time we landed, I knew Stockholm had been built on rock, sculpted and polished by glacial ice and was considered one of the cleanest capital cities in the world. It was certainly one of the coldest. So cold, I could feel the hairs in my nostrils freeze like icicles.

After the lassitude of St Jude, the pace of pulsing Stockholm overwhelmed me so that I stood rooted to the spot, all agog, gazing about and trembling with a combination of cold and amazement. I had to withdraw shakily to a street corner coffee shop where I ordered an expensive espresso and studied a map before plucking up the courage to navigate my way to my city-centre hotel.

Next morning, it was simple enough to discover exactly where the Professor lived.

I called the University of Stockholm and informed his secretary that

I had an appointment with Dr Johansson at his home and had mislaid the address.

"I do apologise," I said, humbly. "Would you mind giving it to me again?"

The professor lives in a modern apartment in the old harbour area: a convergence of city and archipelago. There were gulls drifting lazily between steep rooftops and tall buildings decorated with ornate Art Nouveau windows and overweight stone cherubs blowing trumpets.

Inga opened the door at my knock. Slight and pale, she was dressed in a black cable sweater, jeans and leather boots. Her hair had been cut like a boy's: short and feathery. It suited her.

"I have been expecting you," she said, stepping back to let me in. She looked tired and strained.

"Me?"

"Someone called. I have been waiting for the caller. I expect it was you?"

"Yes."

She showed me into a vast sitting room with breathtaking views of the harbour.

There was a dramatic painting of wild herons sweeping low over a watery reed bed. The work looked familiar. She caught me staring and pointed to the name on the canvas: *Chris Lourens.*

"His parting gift to me," she said shortly. "I mailed it home, long before…"

We sat opposite one another.

"You must be wondering why I'm here. Let me explain," I said. "I'm writing a book about St Jude and the people who live in the village. The story culminates with the disappearance of three people in a boat. I need to know what happened."

She gave a determined shake of her head that set the crystal drops on her earrings swaying. "I'm sorry. I can tell you nothing. Surely you know that?"

I hastened to reassure her. "The book will be viewed as a work of fiction. Names of the characters have been changed. Events have been altered. The truth can't harm you."

"If the work is fiction, why not make up your own ending?"

"Good question." I shrugged. "I can't. It makes no sense. There are several theories. Suicide pact. Accident. Some people think the three of you made a bolt to assume new identities elsewhere. I need to know the *truth*."

"Why does it matter so much?"

I wondered about that for a moment. Why did it matter? I answered as honestly as I could. "I've become involved with all the characters in my book. Too involved, perhaps. The disappearance of the three in the boat haunts me still. Try as I might, I can't stop thinking about it. For my own satisfaction, my peace of mind – I have to know what happened!"

Inga contemplated me with searching eyes. Her expression remained impassive: remote, even.

I tried again. "I thought you were dead!" I said. "Everyone thinks so. And yet here you are, alive! I can't tell you how happy that makes me!" I smiled broadly to demonstrate something of the relief I felt at seeing her in the flesh.

There was not even the slightest glimmer of a return smile on her melancholy face, not even an upturning of her lips. She raked her hands through her short hair.

"Nothing is what it seems."

Silence enclosed us. I waited for her to speak. After several minutes she politely offered tea and left the room to make it.

Outside, in the twilight, rain began to fall. Reflected streetlights glowed in the slippery concrete pavements. The sky above, a gloomy grey canopy grew surly with dark clouds. I felt a sense of rising desperation. *I've come all this way*, I thought, *for nothing. She's like a stone. She has a splinter of ice in her heart. I'll return to St Jude, no wiser than before, except I'll know she did not die.*

Inga returned, carrying a tray of tea in thin red china cups and a plate of almond biscuits. She poured slowly, her face pensive.

"You will have to promise," she said, handing me a cup, "that Mickey will be protected. She is wanted by the police but, of course, you know that. I need your word that you will not betray my confidence."

"You have it. I give you my word." I could hardly breathe.

"If what I am about to tell you endangers Mickey in any way, I would *never* forgive either you or myself."

"I won't reveal anything that might put Mickey at risk. You can trust me."

She sat quite still, hands in her lap; long legs planted on the carpet, leaning slightly forward, her eyes on mine.

"I've never told anyone," she said. "Not even my father knows all the details though he's guessed at some and has an idea of what happened. We never speak of it. Never!"

Inga turned her gaze toward the painting of the herons. She spoke as though she were reading a story or recounting an episode from a life not remotely connected to hers. Her voice with its foreign accent was pitched low, just above a whisper.

"For the longest time," she said, "Chris wanted to end his life. He was weak and in pain. He had dreams. He dreamed of being embraced and cleansed by the sea. He wanted his body to be taken by waves. He saw himself sinking to a grave in the ocean floor. In his dreams death became a cleansing, forgiving ritual."

She looked straight at me. "This is not so strange," she said. "Chris's astrological sign is water. Pisces. The fishes. Water was his true element. I always said that Chris was like water: like a river running deep and strong. Do you believe in such things? In signs?"

I gave a quick nod, not wishing to halt her flow with a debate about astrological signs.

She sensed my impatience. "Well, anyway, he devised a plan and asked for my help. I agreed because I loved Chris and would have done anything for him! At first, the plan was simple. We were to go out in the boat together. He would take an overdose of sleeping pills and I would bury him at sea. I would say there'd been an accident: he'd fallen overboard and drowned. There would be no shame of suicide. No one would know about his AIDS. Ginny would be protected."

Inga faltered, a knot of tears in her voice.

"Mickey was a complication. Edwina sent her to Chris. She needed to escape from the police. Questions were being asked. Mickey believed she would be arrested. Chris changed the plan for Mickey."

Inga fell silent, motionless.

I waited. Minutes ticked by. I hardly dared move. The tea grew cold in the cup.

She took a breath. "I was deeply afraid when Chris told me of his new plan. There were so many things that could go wrong. When she heard of it, Mickey was also afraid. No, Mickey was *petrified!* When we went out in the dinghy that day, only Chris was at peace. It was what he wanted more than anything..."

She covered her face with her hands. I heard a strangled sob.

I rose from my chair. "I'm sorry! I didn't think! I can see this is painful for you!"

Inga walked to the window and stood with her back to me.

"The day before, I took two backpacks to Curlew Creek. I buried them in the sand and placed a marker, a stick in the shape of a cross, on the top."

She traced falling raindrops on the pane.

"When we set off, the day was beautiful. The sea was navy, there was no wind, not a breath, and the sun was hot. It was perfect, the way Chris had dreamed it would be. Not long into our journey Chris began to take the tablets. He swallowed a handful at a time with tea from a flask. At that point, Mickey took over control of the boat and I stayed with Chris."

She pressed her forehead against the window. The rain began to fall more strongly. There were three birds on the windowsill, their backs to us, a sad cluster of drenched, grey feathers, clinging together for warmth and comfort.

"When he'd taken the pills, Chris became quiet and sleepy. He tried to talk but his speech grew so distorted I could hardly understand a word. I had to ask him to repeat himself many times. He became confused, rambling. He shouted my name. He called for his mother many times. At last he grew still. I had his head in my lap, stroking him, talking to him. I held him in my arms until I could no longer feel his chest move. No breath from his mouth or nostrils. His eyes looked dark and sunken. For a short while I felt a pulse against my thumb, weak and fluttering. Then there was nothing. His face, at the end, was peaceful, beautiful…"

She stopped. She waited for control.

"When the last light went from his eyes, I closed his lids. I held him to me: I could not let him go. But then the wind came up…"

Her voice was indistinct, I could hardly hear.

"We lifted his body between us. I held his arms, Mickey his legs. He'd been sick for so long. He was as light as a child."

Her eyes shimmered, tears fell.

"Oh, Inga!" I waited until she recovered composure.

"We let him go. The waves carried him for moments. He disappeared beneath the surface. I watched for a while, but never saw him again."

She looked up, face contorted.

"I had brought flowers from Ginny's garden. I threw them on the water but the waves were choppy and they sank in seconds. Mickey was hysterical. She shook violently and became ill. She lay down and I took over the boat. In two hours we reached Curlew Creek. The weather worsened, the wind came up. I turned the boat before we landed at the cove so that the wind could take it. We swam to shore. By the time we set our feet on the beach, I saw the boat skimming towards the horizon."

Inga stood and paced the room. She walked up and down, hands thrust deeply in her pockets, head bowed.

"We were frozen, in shock. We hardly spoke. We dug up the backpacks, changed our clothes and spent the night walking. Next day we took a bus to the airport. I feared the police would be looking for Mickey but nobody gave us even a second glance. We flew to Stockholm. Mickey sheltered in my father's apartment for a time. Almost immediately she called Edwina and explained what had happened. She asked Edwina for a loan and told her to repay herself from the sale of the nursery. Edwina deposited money into an account for Mickey. She was most generous."

She sank into a chair. She looked exhausted.

"What happened to Mickey?"

"I can tell you that she spent some months taking refuge in a convent. Not in Sweden. After that, she got a job in a nursery garden. I cannot say where."

"And now?"

"Mickey is safe. She's changed her name. She has a dog, a stray she found wandering in the streets. She is making a life for herself. The last time she called she sounded almost cheerful. She has nothing to fear any more. I pray she will, one day, be happy again."

"And you?"

Inga looked small and frail, her cheeks streaked with drying tears. She raked her hands through her hair again. I saw this had become a habit.

She turned to the painting.

"I miss him," she said simply. "My life is empty. Inga, the person I once was, has gone. I am a shell of myself. Without him, life has less meaning. There will never be anyone else."

"What will you do now?"

"I am studying art at Stockholm University. I have no skill, no talent, but it passes the time. Chris taught me a love of art, before him, I knew nothing..."

Silence fell between us. I drained the last drop of icy tea in the cup and inched towards the edge of the chair. There was one more thing I needed to know...

"Was it worth it, Inga? You gave up an entire *life!* Your thriving Yoga Centre, clients, reputation, success. You left it all behind."

Inga eyes were luminous. "What kind of life is that? The Yoga Centre, my clients, this success you speak of? What do they mean?"

She answered herself. "They mean nothing! Chris was my life. When I lost him, I lost everything."

I set the cup on the table. "I'm grateful to you for telling me this, for your honesty. know how deeply painful this has been..."

She leaned forward, her expression intense. "When he first met me, Chris saw me as an angel. A guardian angel, he said. I was a divorced woman, trying to make a life in another country. I was selfish and self-seeking, rather vain and very proud, certainly no angel. But Chris painted and carved me as an angel. He gave me gigantic wings and made me strong, powerful even. He made me what I am."

Her voice shook slightly with emotion. I saw a pulse beating at her throat. She looked bloodless, pale as snow.

"People have said things of the statue Chris made for Edwina. Some say it has the power to heal the dying or save those in need. Do you believe that? Do you believe those wicked *lies?*"

I was mildly alarmed at her fervour. "No, of course not."

"That carving is *nothing!* It was once a tree in a forest. I am the true angel! *Me!*"

She gestured, motioning to herself, her fingers touching her breastbone.

"I was entrusted to love and care for Chris until he drew his final breath. Mine was the last face he looked upon as he lay dying. Before he lost his speech, before he began calling my name, calling for Ginny, he took my hand and pressed it to his mouth. 'You are my angel!' he said. Those were the last meaningful words he ever spoke. '*You* are my angel!'"

Rain peppered the windows. The light dimmed. The birds on the sill flapped their wings. The room was utterly still.

A single gleam of sunlight struck Inga's beautiful face.

She was incandescent.

"Now you have your truth," she said.